VOIDFARER

Sean McMullen

A TOM DOHERTY ASSOCIATES BOOK
NEW YORK

This is a work of fiction. All the characters, organizations, and events portrayed in this novel are either products of the author's imagination or are used fictitiously.

VOIDFARER

Copyright © 2006 by Sean McMullen

Map by Zoya Krawczenko

A Tor Book
Published by Tom Doherty Associates, LLC
175 Fifth Avenue
New York, NY 10010

www.tor.com

Tor® is a registered trademark of Tom Doherty Associates, LLC.

ISBN-13: 978-0-765-35292-7
ISBN-10: 0-765-35292-3

First Edition: February 2006
First Mass Market Edition: April 2007

Printed in the United States of America

0 9 8 7 6 5 4 3 2 1

For Zoya

ACKNOWLEDGMENTS

My thanks to Catherine Smyth-McMullen, Zoya Krawczenko, Paul Collins, Faye Ringel, and Jack Dann for their input and advice, and especially to June Young for the most thorough consistency check I have ever seen.

My most particular thanks go to H. G. Wells for writing *The War of the Worlds*.

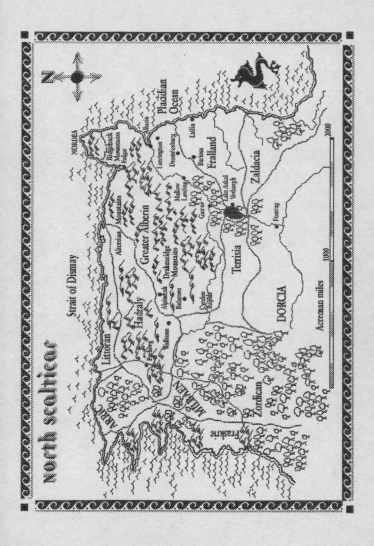

CONTENTS

VOIDFARER

Chapter One

EVE OF THE WAR

No one in Scalticar would have believed that in the last months of the year 3143 they were being watched keenly by intelligences from another world. "If they are so very intelligent, why are they bothering to look at *us*?" would have been the reaction of Empress Wensomer. "Would have been" were the three critical words, however. Empress Wensomer had gone missing, and Scalticar was experiencing what historians annoyingly refer to as interesting times. Times were about to become considerably more interesting, however, because in the first month of 3144, the Lupanians were ready to do a lot more than merely study us from a distance.

My name is Inspector Danolarian Scryverin of the Wayfarer Constables, West Quadrant. Danolarian Scryverin is not the name that I was given at birth, but my birthname has the very angry survivors of a rather unfortunate accident in search of anyone bearing it. Thus I go by Danol Scryverin's name, and although he is dead, nobody needs to know that. The truly annoying irony is that I had never done anything other than be born to the wrong parents. Even though I am eighteen, I give my age as twenty-three, and I carry the papers of a sailor named Danol Scryverin who would be about twenty-three were he not dead. The date of my actual birth is the seventeenth day of the first month. I celebrate it every year, but that is the only link I keep with my past.

On the day that the Lupanian invasion was launched, I was leading my command through the Drakenridge Mountains. The upper trails of the highlands have the most enchanting vistas that you could ever hope to see. At fourteen thousand feet there were alternating layers of dusky sandstone, creamy marble, green granite, and speckled schist, all capped by snow and embroidered by racing meltwater streams and spectacular waterfalls. At that time of year the skies tended to be clear, and even the great Torean Storms had abated somewhat. The air was as clear as a crystal lens, and very, very cold. Little more than tough, dry lichen was growing at this altitude, and there were certainly no villages or inns to be found. Thus we slept in the open, and staying warm was always a problem. Even when we boiled water, it remained tepid even though it bubbled furiously.

All these discomforts were as nothing compared with what I had to endure from the trio who comprised the little squad that I commanded, however. As commands go, it left a lot to be desired, consisting of Constable Riellen, a former radical student of sorcery, Constable Roval, who had a serious drinking problem, and Constable Wallas. Wallas had once been a courtier of great consequence, until he had assassinated an emperor, then managed to offend some important magical personage. I have never heard the full details of what happened, but Wallas had been transformed into a rather overweight black cat.

We had stopped for lunch at a quite breathtaking vista looking north across the mountain peaks, but while I gazed at the achingly beautiful view, Riellen read a book of political theory, Roval muttered curses at a char-stick sketch of a woman in a locket, and Wallas scoffed down a handful of dried fish pieces. I unfolded a sketch of a beautiful albino girl. Very gently, I caressed the cheeks of Lavenci's image, as I had each day for the ten weeks since I had left Alberin. Presently I took out my almanac to memorize a few matters that someone pretending to be an amateur astronomer would be expected to know. I noticed that it was the seventeenth day of the first month, and after a few moments' thought I decided to have a little celebration for my birthday.

"Why have you put a candle on that gingernut biscuit?" asked Wallas as he sat up and began to wash his whiskers.

"I felt like being a little formal today," I replied stiffly. "It's an improvised cake."

"Oh. So when you shook up two dried grapes, some melted

snow, and a half gill of rum in that beer bottle, was that meant to be improvised wine?"

"If you don't want any—"

"No, no, I didn't say that! It's probably your birthday, is it not?"

"It might be. Riellen, wine for you too?"

"Wine is a poison sapping the strength of the downtrodden commoners, and I drink only ale because it is the drink of the oppressed," she declared automatically; then she looked up and added "Sir!"

"Even as a gesture of solidarity between downtrodden Wayfarer Constables?" I asked.

The words "gesture," "solidarity," and "downtrodden" did their usual work in her mind.

"Er, oh, in that case, yes."

"Afraid I can't offer any to you," I said to Roval. "Orders, and all that."

"Brought low by a woman," muttered Roval, whom I had forced to confine his drinking to the occasional tavern as we traveled.

Thus it was that I toasted my birthday with two of my companions, Wallas lapping from his tin bowl, Riellen pretending to sip daintily from the beer bottle with a reedpaper straw—but actually drinking nothing, out of solidarity with the downtrodden, ale-drinking masses—and myself drinking from my half-gill measure. I lit the candle from a tinderbox with some difficulty, then hurriedly blew it out before the wind beat me to it. Finally I broke up the gingernut biscuit and shared it around before starting to pack up.

"Not as good as Fralland-Style Kitty Krunchies," muttered Wallas as I picked him up and put him on the rump of my horse.

"Next time I'll have your share," I said as I set off, leading the way.

By now we had been leading our horses for nine days, for they were not coping well with the altitude, and had to carry their own fodder as well as our packs. The trail was wide, well made, and in good repair, but even on a good day we would be lucky to cover a dozen miles. Generally it was less.

"I was once great, I was once a courtier," Wallas's voice droned from behind me.

"Brought low by a woman," mumbled Roval, his thoughts far away.

"Actually it was not a woman, it was two women who brought me low," said Wallas. "Low, as in reduced to a cat situation, that is. One was a glass dragon, the other was a sorceress. I was used as a pawn. Can you imagine that? Me, a great courtier. Once I lived in a palace. Now look at me."

"Hard to miss you," I pointed out wearily.

"You should not be sad, Brother Wallas," said Riellen, who was leading her own horse behind mine. "Fate has saved you from becoming an establishment exploiter of the downtrodden people."

"I never asked to be saved."

"But you *were* saved, when you were transformed into your present, er, circumstances. Now you can go on to a great destiny."

"How can a cat have a great destiny? I don't even like cats! I'm a dog person."

"But as a cat you are liberated, Brother Wallas. You were freed from your aristocratic chains when you were transformed."

"I paid a lot of money for those chains! Once I was rich. Now I get a mere ten florins a week from the Wayfarers because I'm just a cat. Blatant discrimination."

And so it continued for the next hour. *I too was rich,* I thought as I walked, but I did not miss any of that. My parents had educated me well, and had me taught fencing, archery, and riding by the finest masters. I had never wanted for anything until, at the age of fourteen, I was left with just the clothes I stood in. My education and skills had proved to be worth more than a wagonload of gold, however, and now I was eighteen, wise beyond my years, and feigning to be twenty-three.

We reached a milestone with thirty-seven chiseled into it, and it was at this point that my patience with those whom I commanded finally ran out.

"Constables Riellen, Roval, and Wallas, stay here with the horses while I go on ahead," I said as I handed the reins of my horse to Riellen. "I'll make sure the way is clear."

"Yes sir!" said the thin, intense girl as she saluted.

"Is there danger?" called Wallas anxiously from atop a saddlebag.

"If I thought there might be, I would send you," I responded.

"Brother Wallas, have I ever told you my theory of inner liberation?" asked Riellen.

"Aye, and I've told you what you can do with it!" snarled Wallas.

Roval took out his locket, flicked it open, and began to abuse the image therein.

I left them to their bickering and curses, because the milestone we had just passed meant that we were nearly at the end of our journey. The narrow road was wrapped hard against the slope of a mountain, but to the right was clear air, straight down, for a very, very long way. The voices of Riellen, Wallas, and Roval faded as the bend hid them, then Alpindrak was before me.

It was as if colossal white crystals capped with silver domes encrusted the summit of the mountain, which was the highest on the continent of Scalticar. The building had once been the summer palace of a very rich king, Senderial IX, who had the rather unusual vice of merely loving to gaze up at the night sky. That was simple and harmless enough, but it turned out to be the most expensive individual vice in the history of the continent. There was no place in Scalticar where the air was more clear than on Alpindrak, so he had had a palace built there at a cost that half emptied his treasury. After he died, the place was stripped bare by his son. The buildings could not be moved, however, and none of the king's comfort-loving descendants wanted to live in a cold, remote place which was so high that even breathing was difficult and water boiled when it was only lukewarm. The place was assigned a small garrison of soldiers who were sent there as punishment, but otherwise abandoned.

Alpindrak Palace had experienced sixty years of neglect when some scholar had realized that the newly invented farsights could be used a lot more effectively in the study of other worlds if they were sited very high, where the air was more clear. The monarch of the time bequeathed the otherwise unusable palace to the Skeptical Academy, and ten years later it had become one of the greatest research centers for the cold sciences in the known world.

The place was truly beautiful. I had seen glorious paintings done from the place where I now stood, I had read exquisite poetry inspired by this view, and I even knew hauntingly evocative songs that tried to encompass it. I had indeed been expecting beauty that no art could possibly describe, and the idea of my first glimpse of Alpindrak taking place while Riellen and Wallas bickered about politics and class distinction beside me had been too depressing to contemplate. Thus I was alone when I first caught sight of the palace. I was not disappointed; in fact I was quite overwhelmed. For many minutes I just stood there, letting the mountain, the palace, the deep blue sky, the sound of the wind, and even the chill on the air etch themselves into my memories. After unfolding Lavenci's sketch and showing the scene to my girl's image, I walked back and signaled Riellen and Roval to bring the horses on.

"Obscene excesses of the ruling establishment," declared Riellen as she caught sight of Alpindrak Palace.

"And now a fantastic observatory and cathedral of scholarship for the cold sciences," I responded.

This put Riellen on the moral back foot. Although she had once been a student of sorcery, she felt solidarity with all scholars—except those who wrote histories and chronicles glorifying monarchies, of course.

"Not a patch on the emperor's palace in Palion," said Wallas, poking his head out of a saddlebag. "Did I ever tell you I was once the seneschal there, before I was transformed?"

"As I heard it, the appointment lasted only ten minutes," I replied, hoping to silence him as well.

"Er, well, were it not for the unfortunate death of the emperor it would have been longer."

"Brother Danol told me that you assassinated him," said Riellen in a very approving tone.

"That is not true!" cried Wallas. "I was an unsuspecting pawn in some royal intrigue."

"Oh yes, you were *exploited* by the *ruling establishment*," said Riellen, admiration dripping from her words.

"Stop it, both of you!" I snapped irritably. "We are about to enter Alpindrak Palace, and I want no mention of magic, dead emperors, or liberating the riffraff from the yoke of imperial rule. Riellen, you and I are to be Wayfarer Constables."

"But we *are* Wayfarer Constables, sir. My badge number is two-oh-three, and my guild number is—"

"I mean I want us to be three unremarkable, ordinary, *male* Wayfarer Constables, who will not cause comment. Tie back your hair, and pull your cloak over your breasts."

"It is a sad statement on the state of society that I must take the guise of a youth in order to experience enough freedom to—"

"Assume the guise of a youth, Riellen, and that is an order."

"Yes sir."

"And Wallas, remember that you are a cat."

"I would have thought that depressingly obvious—sir."

"I mean you are to act like a real cat, because the person we are stalking knows about you. While we are within the walls of Alpindrak you are to say nothing but 'meow' to anyone else but me, or I shall perform a simple but highly distressing operation upon you."

"No need to be crude, sir. I may look like a cat, but I *can and do* follow orders."

"Roval, there is a final climb of five thousand stone steps to the palace," I said, pointing ahead and upward. "Get drunk in the palace tonight, and you will wake up with the shakes tomorrow. Five thousand steps with the shakes, Constable Roval, think about it. If you can't walk down, you will have to roll."

"If she could have explained that I would be just one of many, I would have understood," sighed Roval. "But she said there was no other but me. I gave her my hearts."

We trudged on. The road ended about three thousand feet below the summit, but there was a gate station there. Separating the road from the gate station was a chasm about two hundred feet wide and roughly a mile deep. At the bottom of this was a raging meltwater river. We stopped at a small stone landing, directly opposite the gate station. Beside the landing was a stone arch of green and red granite, and within this was suspended a large brass bell. I untied the clapper and rang it five times, paused, rang twice more, then waited. After a short time there were three peals from a bell on the other side. I replied by ringing twice more.

The doors of the gate station opened outward, and then a large dragon's head emerged. It was a red, square-sided head, about eight feet high. The jaws were open as it slid out over the chasm. It belched a streamer of burning hellfire oil. Riellen gasped and skipped back, and Wallas gave a yowl of fright before ducking back into the saddlebag.

"An enclosed bridge," I said to reassure Riellen, who was so astonished that she had not even made a sneering remark about establishment extravagance. "It's in my brief. The covering is lacquered hides over a wicker frame. Only the flooring is wood."

"But it breathed fire," said Riellen.

"A simple flamethrower," I explained. "It's designed to frighten superstitious peasant outlaws looking for easy plunder."

"Well I'm no superstitious peasant, and I got such a fright that I wet the blanket in my saddlebag," said Wallas. "What's here to plunder? Who would want to steal giant farsights?"

"They make Senderialvin here."

"That's not right, it comes from vineyards on the Cyrelon Plateau, fifty miles southeast."

"Sorry, I meant Senderialvin Royal."

There was a gasp from the saddlebag; then Wallas lapsed into awed silence. Senderialvin Royal was the rarest, most costly, and delicious wine in the known world.

The fantastic bridge reached the landing, and the lower jaw locked into a slot in the stone lip. Peering in, I saw a grille-work door just inside the throat. In the gloom farther down the throat there was a guard approaching. He unlocked the door, then walked out onto the landing.

"Name, rank, fealty, and business," he said, holding his hand out for our papers.

"Inspector Danol Scryverin, Wayfarer Constables, delivery of dispatches from the Alberin Academy of Cold Sciences," I replied, saluting.

"Constable Riellen Tallier, Wayfarer Constables, support for Inspector Scryverin," declared Riellen smartly.

"Constable Roval Gravalios, Wayfarer Constables, support for Inspector Scryverin," said Roval in a flat voice.

The guard began to search our packs and saddlebags, and before long he discovered Wallas.

"What the— Blow me away! A cat?"

"Special delivery for Stormegarde Garrison," I explained casually. "They've got a rat situation, like."

"What's this tag on the collar? *Ratsbane Pouncer Blackpaw the Seventh*?"

"That's his name. The Blackpaw family is highly regarded in ratting circles. He got the title Ratsbane after three hundred confirmed kills."

"Looks a bit fat to be much of a ratter."

"Oh it's all muscle," I assured him.

The guard grunted as he lifted Wallas out to check the bottom of the saddlebag.

"Well, mostly muscle," I added.

"Aye, suppose he'll need some padding, 'cause it gets mighty cold over at Stormegarde," said the guard as he replaced Wallas. "Know the rules for crossing? One at a time, leading your horse. One false move, and a special mechanism releases the lip and hinges the neck to point straight into the chasm—"

"—and dumps me one mile down into the Glacienne River. Should I grab on to something, large rocks will be dropped down the throat of the bridge as an incentive to let go."

"Aye, that's it. I see you've been briefed. I stays here with your weapons until you're all across, and under escort. Then I follows with the weapons, which will be impounded for the duration of your stay."

Crossing the bridge was an anticlimax, because it was steady underfoot, and totally enclosed. Riellen followed me, then Roval. We had a short rest, during which Wallas dragged the sodden blanket out of his saddlebag, and Riellen, Roval, and I massaged, oiled, and rebandaged each other's feet. Then we shouldered our packs and began the climb to the palace at the summit. There were five thousand steps cut into the rock, zigzagging up the slope. Near the end of the climb my pack seemed to have tripled in weight, and we swapped the saddle-bag containing Wallas nearly every minute.

The sun was nearly on the horizon as we reached the landing in front of the palace gates, and we stopped to catch our breath as the guard went inside to present our papers. I gazed at the glorious splashes of color all across the western sky. Miral's immense green face and ring system had the classic shape of a giant crescent bow with an arrow, aimed to fire at the descending sun. The moonworld Dalsh was a bright mote a few degrees from the lordworld's rings, while Belvia was a tiny half disk near the Zenith, shining like a glowing sapphire. Between them was Lupan, a minute, bright crescent. Lupan was the trickster in sky lore, because it could be brilliant white or blood red. Tonight it shone red.

"How are you doing, Ratsbane Pouncer Blackpaw the Seventh?" I asked.

"Veteran of three hundred kills," sounded from the saddlebag.

"Did he really . . . kill three hundred rats . . . sir?" wheezed Riellen between labored breaths.

"No, sometimes one has to lie when duty to the service requires it."

"I once killed a mouse," protested Wallas.

"Aye, when you fell off a barrel while drunk and squashed it."

"That took real skill, I'm famous around the Alberin taverns for it. You know that song, 'The Cat on the Barrel'?"

"I think you are getting fame mixed up with infamy, Wallas. Now then, we're about to enter the palace, so do you need to step out for a kitty crappy?"

"No, I'm busy licking my arse. It's the worst part of being a cat."

I had actually meant for him to share the beautiful view of sunset, with Miral, Dalsh, Lupan, and Belvia strung out above it, but after that comment I decided not to risk further damage to my memories of the glorious vista of lights and colors. For a moment I wished so intensely that Lavenci were there that the feeling was a real ache; then I glanced over at Riellen, who was hugging her knees and breathing through her mouth.

"Will you hear me play the sun down?" I asked.

"Lower-middle-class male exclusionist ritual . . ." she managed, then lapsed into labored panting.

Although she was wiry, tough, and determined, the thin air at seventeen thousand feet had Riellen close to her limits of endurance. I noticed that she was actually looking at the sky over her spectacles, however. This really did surprise me, until I realized that by now it was too dark for her to read her political book. She was looking up at Lupan.

"When Lupan shines so deeply red there will be deaths," said Roval as he sat rubbing the cramps from his legs.

"Mere superstition," Riellen panted, "from which common folk . . . should be liberated."

"It's nearing inferior conjunction, its closest approach to us," I said. "Sometimes I wonder if there are folk on Lupan, looking up at the night sky and wondering about our world."

"Well *I* was wondering if there are downtrodden peasants there living under the yoke of an oppressive royal establishment," said Riellen, who then fainted with the effort of speaking such a long sentence in the rarefied air. The guard called out from the palace gate that our papers had been cleared.

Thus it was that I entered Alpindrak Observatory, gasping like a landed fish, feeling so giddy that I could hardly walk in a straight line, my lungs burning like a smithy's forge, generally feeling as if I were eighty instead of eighteen and not wearing my years well . . . and carrying two backpacks, Wallas, and Riellen. The badly cramped Roval was also holding on to me for support. In spite of all that, there was one thing more that I had to do, one of those life's ambitions that has no foundation in common sense.

Leaving my squad in an untidy pile just inside the gates, I took my pack and climbed the steps of the palace wall. There, working with great haste, I assembled my bagpipes. The three extended drones and their special reeds went into the stock within a couple of dozen heartbeats, and the custom-built chanter was already in place. The mountains were jagged on the sun's face as I propped Lavenci's sketch up with my ax, stood, and puffed into the bag. Now I pressed down hard with my left arm, spoke the drones, and began to play "Evening's All for Courting." Even customized, the pipes were not at their best in the thin air, but I did manage to play the sun down from the highest peak in all of Scalticar. With the sun down but the horizon still glowing, I played "Truelove's Fancy," then finished with "Stars in My Lassie's Eyes." As I ended, there was a pattering of applause, and a few cheers came from some guards down on the battlements. Down in the courtyard I saw Roval saluting me.

"Lass, if only you could have been here," I whispered to Lavenci's portrait.

Chapter Two

IN ALPINDRAK PALACE

Half an hour after we arrived I was summoned to meet with Nortan, astronomer general of the Skepticals and head of Alpindrak Observatory. Announcements of great discoveries at Alpindrak were sent to the outside world via carrier pigeon, but most sketches, data tables, and suchlike were carried down annually by horse, in a large satchel. Observation requests were handled the same way. I presented a satchel of observation requests from the Skeptical Academy of Cold Sciences, and Nortan told me that a satchel of observations for the year past would be ready for me to collect the following morning. We Wayfarers were then invited to join him for what was for us dinner, but was breakfast for Nortan.

"Your first time up here at the palace?" he asked as we sat down to bowls of leek, cabbage, and chicken soup, washed down with a light red wine.

"Yes sir, I volunteered for the trip" was my reply. "I wanted to play the sun down with my bagpipes."

"Oh I heard, I heard. You played 'Evening's All for Courting.' What's your set?"

"Alberinese parade pipes, by Carrasen, modified by Duntrovey."

"Wonderful. I'll add all that to the register."

"You have a register?"

"Oh yes, we keep a register of all who make the journey here, and of anything special that they do. Brilliant idea, playing the sun down on the summit of Alpindrak, well done!"

"Thank you."

"Was that the only reason you volunteered to journey here?"

"Not entirely. I am something of an amateur astronomer."

"Oh, very good!" he replied, clapping his hands with delight. "I am unused to meeting couriers who have not been given the trip up here as punishment. What do you think of breakfast?"

"Delicious. You eat well."

"The staff grow most of what we need in the palace greenhouses."

"You do? But hardly anything grows outside," I pointed out. "Why is it different in the palace?"

"I concede that the air is thin, but cold and lack of rich soil is most of the problem outside. Our greenhouses are warm and, er, well manured, if you catch my meaning. There are only two dozen of us here, so they produce more than we need. We also grow grapes and make Senderialvin Royal, our famous heaven wine."

"I once met a man whose commander had tasted it," I said suavely.

"Try some?"

I very nearly fell from my chair. Senderialvin Royal sold for eleven gold crowns a jar in Alberin, and the jars were very small. I nodded my head, my mouth hanging open. Roval shook his head, but to my surprise, Riellen nodded also. *Must have decided that this is a case of the delights of rich oppressors being shared among common people*, I thought as the astronomer general left the table. He returned with three tiny crystal goblets and a jar about as long and thick as my thumb. There was a splash of golden stars across the label, which bore the year 3140. The wine had a distinctly golden color, and although I am no wine fancier, I sniffed the bouquet and examined the color in the lamplight before taking my first sip.

"What do you think?" asked Nortan.

"It's liquid enchantment," I said softly, although the words did not even come close to defining the experience of drinking Senderialvin Royal.

"You have just drunk the value of at least half a year of your wages," he laughed. "A reward for coming all the way up here."

"But surely it will be missed," I replied.

"No, we are allowed a jar or two in return for helping with the cultivation. I am not much of a drinker, so I share my ration with the few fellow lovers of celestial beauty who manage the long and difficult trip up here. Constable Riellen, what do you think?"

"Riellen?" I prompted, but she was asleep, still sitting up. I now realized that her earlier nod was actually her nodding off to sleep. "I'll carry him to bed once we've eaten."

I reached out and shook Rovel, but he too was asleep.

"Your men have had a hard day of it," observed the astronomer general.

"Rovel takes a few drops of sleeping draught when the opportunity to drink is upon him. He was sent with me to reform his drinking habits, and it is his last chance with the Wayfarers. As for Riellen, don't ask."

"Well then, best not waste any."

With steady hands and great care, Nortan poured Riellen's share back into the jar, then corked it and handed it to me.

"Surprise him with this later," he said genially.

"It will be greatly appreciated," I replied, but thought, *Mind you, I'm not going to say just who will do the appreciating.*

"Is not Riellen a girl's name?" he now asked.

"He is from Alberin. Stress the second syllable and it is a girl's name. Emphasize the first, and it names a boy."

"But she—er, he has a Sargolan accent."

"He was a student there."

"I see, I see. Well, you two have come a very long way, so I should not keep you from your beds," he said, ringing a small bell for the table maid. "I, on the other hand, must get to work."

"With Your Lordship's permission, I would like to take my own little farsight out onto the battlements. It's only a Cassentron Brothers foldaway with a two-inch objective, but I have had a brass stand made for viewing the heavens."

"Of course, why not?" he said expansively. "King Senderial would have been proud of you—but what am I thinking? Come to the main dome once you have put your men to bed. I shall give you an entire hour; I'll show you the lordworld and moonworlds through our giant fourteen-inch reflector."

My cunning plan had fallen flat on its face. Rather than have an excuse to go prowling the palace grounds and battlements for the whole night, I would now have to spend at least an hour with the astronomer general. I dumped Riellen onto her bed and flung a quilt over her without even bothering to remove her trail boots, then fetched Roval to his own bedchamber. Back in my own room at last, I dragged Wallas out of the saddlebag by the scruff of the neck and held him up.

"It's night," he mumbled peevishly.

"Cats are nocturnal," I pointed out. "I brought you a chicken wing."

"Probably cooked with no great skill, but leave it in my dish, I shall consider it presently."

"I also brought half a jar of Senderialvin Royal."

Wallas suddenly became a large, furry ball of thrashing, frantic limbs and tail. I dropped him on the bed, but he immediately bounded off and sat beside his bowl looking expectantly up at me.

"Well don't just stand there, pour it out!" he demanded. "Have you tried any yet?"

"Only after you have searched the palace for the empress," I said sternly.

"What? That will take all night! We don't even know she's here, and, and . . . what heartless, cruel torturer could make me wait all night for a taste of Senderialvin Royal? Er, what year did you say it was?"

"I didn't, but it's 3140."

"Oh yes! Yes! Yes! Yes! A classic, from before the Torean Storms."

"But as the great Captain Gilvray once said, *Victory first, victory feast second.*"

"I don't believe you really have a jar of Senderialvin Royal at all!" Wallas suddenly exclaimed.

I took the jar from my pocket and held it out for him to see.

"Bastard," he muttered, with a very feline scowl.

"I saw the duty-roster board when I called in at the kitchen to collect your chicken wing. There are twenty-eight people in the palace: Riellen, Roval, me, the two dozen who live here, and one other guest."

"A visiting astronomer, no doubt," he grumbled.

"I wonder. For the past three nights Riellen has noticed magical activity in the area when she goes into her darkwalking trances. There is a powerful sorcery initiate nearby, and there is one extra person in the palace. Find that person, Wallas, and a generous measure of what is left in the jar is yours."

I shook the jar, to show that some was left.

"Don't, you'll bruise the wine!" he yowled.

"Rendezvous with me every hour at the north tower," I said as I put the jar away. "There's a little courtyard at its base. I shall be with the astronomer general for the first hour, and when I have escaped his tour of the skies, I shall want a full report on likely places to hide in the palace."

✳ ✳ ✳

Although the buildings of the original palace were fashioned from thick, finely wrought blocks of granite faced with marble, the domes housing the farsights were merely of lacquered wood painted white on the outside. The brass and crystal instruments and their clockwork drive engines had been far more costly to build than the domes, yet they crowned the palace beautifully, and gave it the aspect of a temple.

It was two hours past sunset when the astronomer general finally sent for me. He was in the main observation dome, which was lit dimly by a single lamp with a red shade.

"Come in, Danol, come in," he said without looking up from the farsight's eyepiece as I entered. "You are just in time. Miral is on the horizon, but you can still see a lot."

Through the eyepiece I saw on the lordworld's surface great swirls of green in many different shades. The simple bands that the naked eye can make out on our lordworld are actually made up of an intricate embroidery of whorls, eddies, swirls, and spirals. The rings were nearly edge-on at this time of the month, and when the astronomer general trained the farsight on them and put a more powerful eyepiece at the focus hole in the main mirror, I could see tiny twinkles. There was perhaps one flash every two or three seconds.

"They sparkle and glitter," I breathed in heartfelt wonder.

"We think the rings are made of tumbling blocks of ice, some the size of this palace. Every so often one catches the sun, and you see a little flash."

We continued our celestial tour. Dalsh, the closest moon-world to the lordworld, was no more than a mottled crescent of gray, white, orange, green, and blue.

"We think Dalsh is more similar to our own moonworld than any other," said the astronomer general. "You are seeing forests, seas, and clouds. Now let us swing right up past Lupan to Belvia."

Belvia was mostly covered in oceans; in fact, its entire land area was less than that of our continent of Scalticar. I saw a half disk of dark blue, with white caps of ice at the poles, greenish splashes that were its islands, and vast, ragged cloud systems.

"Last of all, I give you Lupan," said my host as he moved the farsight again.

At this time Lupan presented itself as a thick crescent. Most of the sunlit part was reddish orange, with smears of white at the poles. Its seas were no bigger than Belvia's islands, and there were the famous canals, of course. Some meandered like rivers, but others were quite straight, and there were thickenings where they intersected.

"I see the canals," I said slowly.

"Ah no, that is vegetation spreading out in their vicinity—and they are not really canals, they are channels. Scribe's error in the original pronouncement of discovery, you see."

"How could such straight, regular features not be artificial?" I asked.

"They might be great earthquake cracks filled with water, perhaps. One must keep an open mind, else we would return to magic and all be mere sorcerers."

"I defer to your scholarship, my lord," I said, reminding myself of my place.

"Danol, you too speak with the tone and authority of a scholar," he observed. "How came you to be a Wayfarer?"

"An unfortunate incident in my past," I volunteered without looking away from the eyepiece.

"Would you consider a vocation to the Order of Skepticals?"

"Such a vocation would not suit me, sir. It shames me to admit it, but I am too fond of drink, song, and alluring women."

"Ah, pity. So, do you like the farsight? It is called Gigoptica, and it is the largest in the known world. The brass tube is twenty feet long, with a silvered concave mirror at the base and a secondary at the top. The main mirror is the real treasure. It is fourteen inches in diameter, two inches greater than the next largest anywhere."

"And where is that, sir?"

"Why in the north dome, of course. We have here the four largest farsights ever made. This one, the twelve-inch, and two eleven-inch reflectors. There is also a very-short-focus ten-inch reflector. That one is for wide-field viewing, we use it to hunt comets and other moonworlds."

"Others, sir?" I asked innocently. "There are only four."

"Oh no, there are nine now. The five new ones are quite tiny, in fact the two smallest are in orbit around Lupan. Moons of a moonworld, can you imagine that? We discovered them all. What sorcerer could ever do that with magic? Let me check my tables, I'll try to find a comet for you."

He went off to a side room, leaving me to observe Lupan alone. The farsight was of the type that had a second, smaller mirror at the top end, and a hole for an eyepiece in the main mirror at the base. As I gazed into the eyepiece, I saw what was familiar to me from drawings, except that it was now so real that it seemed almost artificial. Lupan was strangely sharp in the field, too bright, too well defined, too stark, too intensely colored. The clockwork drive clacked steadily, keeping the moonworld in the field of view. Its two tiny moons gleamed like luminescent diamonds beside it.

"I see very few clouds in Lupan's atmosphere," I said as Nortan returned.

"That's why it shines so red tonight," he replied.

Through the largest farsight that existed, I was gazing at another world's orange deserts, little blue seas, and dark green vegetation. *Forests or cultivated fields?* I wondered. The lines looked so deliberate, they had to be artificial canals across the deserts. Where they intersected there was always a dark dot. Were these cities? Several canals ran to the gleaming white polar cap.

"Lupan is always good value for a viewing," Nortan remarked.

"It's quite beautiful," said I, enraptured.

"Your interest gratifies me. I have had dukes, counts, princes, even kings in here, but they merely squint, grunt, then ask what else they might look at."

"Those canals simply have to be artificial," I speculated again.

"Why? Is there evidence?"

"Some sorcerers say that they are aware of castings done on Lupan. They say that they could make contact with the minds of Lupanian sorcerers if—"

"If they had a sufficiently large research bequest," interjected the astronomer. "Sorcerers just talk, but what we have here is a direct view, not some dream journey that nonsorcerers are cut off from forever. I am a Skeptical, all of us here in the palace are Skepticals. We believe only what is before us, and what is before us is the face of Lupan, with seas, rivers, forests, deserts, and polar wastelands. That is fact, and fact is all that there is."

As he was speaking there was a faint flash, no more than a twinkle, on the darkened area of Lupan's disk. I gasped, and the astronomer general asked what was the matter.

"I saw a small flash on the dark side of Lupan."

"A flash?"

"And now there's a sort of faint glowing dot against the darkness."

"A dot?"

"It's very, very faint."

"Twenty-one minutes past the ninth hour of noon by our escarpment clock," mumbled the astronomer general, and I heard the frantic scratching of chalk on slate. "Quickly now, let me see!"

He was at the eyepiece for a long time, all the while writing and sketching on his slateboard.

"I estimate that it is squarely on the equator, where the Lontassimar Canal crosses the Florastia Desert. There are known to be isolated mountains in that area . . . and there is a definite glow that is spreading in a circle, but it is fading as it spreads. A volcanic eruption, I would say."

"Might it have been artificial?" I suggested.

"Oh no. That cloud is by now larger than a small kingdom. No civilization could stage such a massive blast."

"Four years ago our own civilization set off an ancient weapon that destroyed a continent," I pointed out. "That triggered the Torean Storms, and after nearly four years they have only just started to decline."

"Yes, but that was an accident."

"Indeed, lordship, but Lupanians might also have accidents."

"They would not be so silly."

"Well, three years ago our sorcerers girdled our entire world with that ether machine Dragonwall, lordship. It melted several cities when some very vindictive people got control of it."

"And several of *our* temples! That was a typical sorcerer's endeavor. All lights and spectacle, no theory or principles. No wonder it self-destructed and killed them all."

"But perhaps there are sorcerers on Lupan, making the same mistakes as did ours."

"The Lupanian would be far too sensible to build a thing like Dragonwall."

"What basis in fact do you have for saying that, lordship?" I asked innocently.

That remark struck at his honor as a Skeptical. He looked up from the eyepiece, glared at me for a moment, seemed to privately concede that I might have a point, then looked back at Lupan about as eagerly as a drunkard taking a swig from a jar of good wine.

"There's a bell rope to the left of the door," he said urgently. "Kindly give five rings to summon the other astronomers here."

Five rings was clearly the code for a summons of the very greatest possible urgency. The four other astronomer Skepticals arrived within a half minute, followed by the four artisan technicians, a serving maid who wanted to know if anyone wanted a cup of tea, the cook with a tray of shortbreads, and nine guards who looked as if they were rather bored and were hoping for a good show.

The astronomer general hurriedly explained what I had seen, what he could see, and what it might mean. The other four astronomers scattered to the other four farsights, followed by various members of the palace staff. I considered the situation. There were by now only two guards actually on duty, and they were three thousand feet below in the gate station. Everyone else was in the five farsight domes.

I slipped away, met with Wallas, and listened to his report on the palace. He had done a fairly thorough general search, but being unable to open doors meant that virtually every small room and bedchamber would have to be checked by me.

"The thin air makes exertion all the more unpleasant," Wallas complained.

"So, you finally exerted yourself enough to notice."

"Can I have my Senderialvin Royal 3140 now?"

"No! While I check the small rooms, you must keep watch for anyone slinking about, trying to change their hiding place."

"What about Riellen and Roval?"

"Riellen has been walking all day, and is liable to faint again unless she gets a few hours of sleep. Roval has taken his sleeping drug, but you spent the day in a saddlebag and are ready for anything. Get moving, exert yourself again."

I left him, and began to search the palace complex. No doors were padlocked, except for the Senderialvin Royal stores, but the racks of grotesquely expensive wine were visible through a grillework door, and I could see that nobody was hiding in there. The large halls were empty, cold, and still bare, but the greenhouses were planted to capacity and still warm from the day's sunshine. There were literally hundreds of bedchambers, parlors, and sunrooms to check.

I prowled the corridors, battlements, and cloisters for hour after hour, but found nothing. It was tiring work, for I had been walking all day and the air was very thin. All the while I was unaware that a thing was now hurtling through the void, on course for our moonworld. Even had I known, I could scarcely have believed it. The night was clear, tranquil, and exceedingly cold, and Lupan seemed so very far away as I caught sight of it through a sunroom window.

By nearly two hours past midnight I had found nothing, yet I had explored less than a quarter of the palace. I needed help. Roval had drugged himself asleep, so Riellen would have to be roused after all. Returning to her room, I rapped at the door. There was no sound. No sound from my knuckles, that is. *Some sort of muffle spell,* I guessed. I reached down for the latch, but traceries of blue fire lashed out and stung my hand. *Magic,* I thought, rubbing my fingers. I knew just enough about sorcery to be wary of guard spells and castings. Some of them could remove a finger. Riellen was probably sleeping safely inside the chamber, unaware that she was trapped. I was still free, of course . . . but it was now obvious that my quarry knew we were in Alpindrak to find her.

The bell of the clock in the north tower clanged out the second hour past midnight, so I hurried away to my rendezvous with Wallas. He was not there when I arrived, and at fifteen minutes past the hour I decided that he would not be meeting with me. We hunters had become the hunted, and our ranks were already down by three-quarters.

I abandoned my lamp and hurried away into the shadows. If the empress knew we were after her, she would certainly not be asleep. She might also have been watching me search the palace. There was no way for her to know that we had not left more constables to form a roadblock on the track down the neighboring mountain, so she would not try to escape that way. She *could* escape, however. She was a sorceress as well as a monarch.

My eye was caught by a bright flash of light on the western battlements. *Magic, she's there*, I thought at once; then I reconsidered. Timed castings were possible; in fact, those on Riellen's door would probably dissolve at dawn. Empress Wensomer's dazzle casting would annoy the astronomers, but was probably meant to catch my attention. Another flash blazed out at the same place, tempting me to go there. The wind was coming from the west, meaning that the eastern battlements were relatively sheltered. *That* was where she would be.

I was probably more hasty than I should have been as I hurried along to the east of the palace. There was a long, wide balcony built into the main wall, about halfway down. Once courtiers and ambassadors had milled about there, wearing furs against the cold, breathing heavily in the thin air, and sipping warm drinks as they attended the eccentric king who liked to hold court beneath the glory of the stars. Now, for the first time in seven decades, another monarch was present.

My expectation was that Wensomer would use huge etheric wings to escape. I had never seen such a thing done, but I knew it was possible. Wings of ether could be cast by a really skilled initiate. The wings weighed nothing, and could be used to ride the air currents and glide dozens or even hundreds of miles if the winds were favorable. I had expected that she would have been busy casting the giant wings, putting all of her power and concentration into the task. I was wrong. I have since realized that I had been dealing with one of the most intelligent and cunning people on the continent.

A dazzle casting burst before my face as I hurried out of the archway leading onto the balcony. I flung myself down at once, but my momentum carried me across to the smooth tiles to the railing at the edge. I clung to a stone pillar, aware that there was an immense amount of nothingness mere inches away, terrified of what I knew was there, and blind. Something lashed at my upper body, something that wrapped itself about me very tightly and bound me to the pillar. Empress Wensomer had not been busy casting wings for an escape, she had been waiting in ambush for me.

"Your Majesty, I am your servant," I wheezed hopefully. "Inspector Danolarian Scryverin, at your service."

The reply was some time in coming, but I could hear someone pacing about, and the jingling of buckles.

"The Wayfarer inspector," she said at last. "I saw you climbing the steps this afternoon, then I watched you searching the palace. You were sent to find me, let us have no stories to the contrary."

"Yes, Your Majesty."

"You are the same Wayfarer who nearly caught me at Malvar, Dekkeridge, and Green Castle?"

"Indeed, but—"

"Your dedication, resourcefulness, and intelligence leaves me astounded. It also annoys me a great deal."

"I apologize, Your Majesty, but—"

"You are not trying to kill me. You had the chance at Dekkeridge but did not take it. Just why are you chasing me?"

"Your empire needs you—"

"My empire needs me like a fish needs a towel. I am *not* going back, and there's an end to it."

"But a usurper—"

"There's a usurper already? Wonderful."

"It's Regent Corozan."

"Even better. My rather decadent rule will seem a golden age when compared to his."

"You cannot mean that."

"Oh yes I can. What was all that fuss earlier tonight? I heard talk of a mighty explosion."

"There was a huge explosion on Lupan, Your Majesty."

"Lupan the moonworld, or that place in south Alberin— Lupan's Discreet Entertainments for Discerning Ladies?"

"The moonworld, Your Majesty."

"So, that is why everyone is in the domes. The astronomers must be as happy as pigs in a cesspit. So, you are Inspector Danolarian Scryverin of the Wayfarer Constables. You saved my sister's life just before I abdicated."

"Ah, that is not so, Your Majesty," I said after thinking carefully. "The only princess I ever served was Senterri, daughter of the Sargolan emperor. I was but a humble reccon in her escort."

"But my sister is also a sorceress—albino girl, your height, and her eyes are black from being treated with squid ink."

Every muscle in my body clenched for a moment; then everything collapsed from beneath me. My stomach became a chasm deeper and darker than that whose edge I was lying on.

"Lavenci?" I gasped. "Er, that is, Lady Lavenci? She is your *sister*?"

"My half sister, we have a mother in common, with whom

she runs a secret academy of sorcery. I made her a noble before I abdicated, she's now a kavelen. Anything more elevated and she might get ideas."

That had been a bad moment. Wensomer as my sweetheart's sister would have meant that my sweetheart was *my* half sister. The world suddenly became a warm, bright, and wonderful place again—even though I was still blinded, and bound to a pillar at the edge of a shadowy chasm that was about a thousand times deeper than was necessary to kill me.

"So, where did she have you?" asked Wensomer. "The pantry, or the towel cupboard?"

"I—er, your pardon?"

"You know, skirts up, drawers down. Don't tell me it was in bed! She's such a biter, Laron still had the marks on his neck twenty days after their first night together."

"Laron, as in the presiding advisor to the regent of Alberin?" I asked as the solid flagstones beneath me suddenly became a mixture of chilly quicksand and acid.

"Didn't you know? Oops, what a gossip I am."

"Your Majesty, I'm but a lowly inspector with the Wayfarers," I said, reeling from her candor. "I'd not have dreamed of courting a great and powerful noblewoman, had I known."

"I'd not let that worry you, Danolarian. Lavenci has laid amorous ambushes for more than her share of spotty students in Mother's academy—she likes them intelligent, you know. She raised her skirts for . . . Ulderver, Decrullin, and Laron, to name but a few. Then there was the prefect, Lees, oh, and that chinless tutor, Haravigel. Actually, she managed an encounter with Laron on the roof, I chanced upon them during the very act."

"Never!" I cried involuntarily. "Never! Never! Stop it, damn you! Stop it!"

"Whatever is the matter?" asked Wensomer, her tone suddenly one of puzzlement, and sounding almost concerned. "Just what did she do with you?"

By now I was beyond humiliation. The world had ended; what did I care what people knew of me, or thought?

"We held hands, danced, kissed goodnight five times, shared groundnut rolls at the market, and watched two sunsets."

For a moment or two Wensomer actually had to stop and think.

"And that's all?"

"Once . . . once I made so bold as to caress her breast. She slapped my hand away."

"What? She's had more hands on her breasts than I've had hangovers. Dear me, why were you so low in her esteem, Danolarian?"

"You must have another sister," I said desperately.

"Only one is still alive. I know she likes a bit of adventure to spice her lust, she's the grope and fumble type. I, on the other hand, like huge beds, silk sheets, a feather-down mattress deep enough to suffocate in, sweet pastries and fine wine to hand, and the privacy that locked doors provide. So you and she never, you know, did it?"

I was lying on cold flagstones, blinded, and bound to the base of a pillar by etheric tendrils with the strength of steel, yet the distress caused by what I had just been told was far worse. In an instant I had learned for myself what had made Roval curse the image in his locket for three years. My only attempt at love, flung down, shattered, and trampled. I resolved to preserve a little of my pride, if that was at all possible.

"No," I said with as much dignity as I could muster.

"Really? I wonder why. She had two broken ribs the night she met you, care of the Inquisition Constables. Perhaps she was waiting for them to heal before supporting your weight . . . yet there was nothing to stop *you* supporting *hers*. I know that she researched your background in the government archives."

"She did?"

"Yes. She said you were once a rather thick-witted sailor, and that you vanished on a voyage to Diomeda. Two years later you were back in Alberin, speaking nine languages, able to read, write, and quote from the classics, and proficient with half a dozen weapons. You had been in the escort of a Sargolan princess, a hero at the Battle of Racewater Bridge, and a member of the Regency Guard of Capefang."

"I believe in self-improvement."

"And eleven inches taller."

"Nutritious food and healthy exercise."

"You seem to have grown back an eye lost in a tavern brawl."

"I, er, met a skilled sorcerer."

"Presumably he also restored the ear you lost to a broken bottle in yet another tavern brawl?"

"Er, yes."

"Inspector Danolarian Scryverin of the Wayfarer Constables, you know that you are not Danolarian Scryverin, I know that you are not Danolarian Scryverin, and you know that I know that you are not Danolarian Scryverin. I also know that you know that I could be very indiscreet about what I know about you, and that you would prefer that nobody else should know what I know about you."

"Very knowledgeable of you, Your Majesty."

"Did you kill Danolarian Scryverin?"

"No."

"Then what?"

"It was in Diomeda, when the Toreans invaded. They turned on free beer and wine in the city for an entire night, to get the locals sympathetic to them. The next morning I found Danol's body on the banks of the Leir River. More people died of the drink that night than died in the fighting for Diomeda. I looted his papers. It was easy to change identities in the confusion."

"Who were you before that?"

"A humble Torean refugee," I said as respectfully as I could, and I heard her laugh softly.

"The only Toreans in Diomeda were sailors and marines who were with the invasion fleet. Four years ago. That would make you rather young then."

"Nineteen."

"Really? Sailor or marine?"

"Deckhand."

"Interesting. An educated youth would have been made a cabin boy, a shipmaster's clerk, or a navigator's apprentice. To enlist as a deckhand implies that you wished to conceal your excellent education. Perhaps a pregnant girl somewhere back on Torea? Or perhaps a pregnant sister, and her dead lover's blood on your knife?"

"It was a matter of honor," I said vaguely.

"I thought as much."

My eyes were beginning to clear, and I could see the blue

tracery of a tether casting wrapped tightly around me. I could also see a darkly dressed figure kneeling nearby, wearing a pack and snowmask. Two spires of pale light were growing out of the palms of her hands, and they were already about ten feet in height. As they grew, they faded. From my general reading, I knew this to be the etherwings casting. An experienced sorcerer can cast a spike of energies, split it, and mold it into two mighty wings that weigh nothing at all. A sorcerer so powerful that even the minor gods are nervous about offending can grow a double spike. I knew that the empress was not to be trifled with, but had not suspected her powers to be in this sort of league. The casting did seem to be a strain on her, however, because she was breathing heavily.

"Your eyes must be recovering by now, Danolarian. Can you see that I have . . . lost a great deal of weight?"

"I'll be sure not to tell anyone, Your Majesty," I replied at once.

"You had damn well *better* tell them! I worked hard to lose those one hundred and thirty pounds, and I want *everyone* to know it. Three years as empress! My word was law. Orgies . . . almost daily. My pick of the most delightful . . . expensive and exotic foods. Several dozen lovers . . . or was it several hundred? When I fled . . . had to be shipped out . . . in a firewood wagon. Quite humiliating."

It seemed to me that the spikes of faint, shimmering light were about a hundred feet high when she spoke some words of power that caused them to separate. As the two spikes folded outward they grew broader, flattening into intricately patterned, delicate structures, like dragonfly wings. Occasional gusts of wind pummeled them about.

"That is the hardest part of the casting done," Empress Wensomer panted with relief. "I shall soon be gone. Your tether casting will collapse around dawn."

"But why flee, Your Majesty? Your rule was wise, there was peace and prosperity. Nobody else could have so cunningly conducted the Inquisition against sorcerers while sending the Secret Inquisition Constables out to rescue them. What shall I say to my master?"

"What indeed?" she panted, now fashioning harness castings and control tendrils for the enormous wings. They glowed very faintly, like a tapestry of spiderwebs, and they probably weighed even less. "Excess began to make me . . . very sick. I was confined to my bed . . . without company. Had time to think. Dangerous pastime, thinking. Do you know . . . why magic is like too many really wild orgies?"

"Why— What? I, er, no," I confessed. "I have no magical talent, and I've not ever been to an orgy."

"Both are bad for you in the long run," she explained, her breathing now becoming easier. "Vices should be enjoyed sparingly, and with a guilty conscience. Magic is like that, too. Before the Inquisition we had magical academies churning out an entire sorcerer class! There were whole industries based on magic. Then our sorcerers were stupid enough to link together, and create vast ether machines. They wiped out entire cities and temples with Dragonwall."

"But it was destroyed."

"Hah. Pure luck. The monarchs are right to ban all magic and sorcery. Giant ether machines have destroyed one continent, two islands, and several dozen cities, temples, towns, and castles in just under five years. At that rate the entire world will be merely a thick layer of char and melted rock within a century. When I became empress I banned sorcery in public while supporting in secret. Soon it was thriving as never before, and I discovered that I had organized a mighty and effective secret government. I had also begun to resemble my father. He was not a nice man. I imagined him as the emperor of all Scalticar. I compared him to myself. The resemblance was disturbing in the extreme. I had become empress by accident, but I was about the most dangerous person who could have blundered her way onto the throne."

I lay thinking for some moments, shocked beyond bearing. Far from sorcery being a dying and persecuted art, it was a conspiracy to rule the continent.

"This is like a nobleman ordering the slaughter of some village of his own people, so that he can have an atrocity to blame on an enemy," I said forlornly.

"Bright lad. I disbanded the Secret Inquisition Constables, I put several thoroughly nasty little bastards in places where they had access to dangerous amounts of power and secret information, I destroyed the sorceric government by a series of carefully staged betrayals, and then I vanished."

I had been a founding member of the first squad of Secret Inquisition Constables, so I well remembered the incomprehension in our ranks when we were disbanded. Some of us had become very sympathetic to the sorcerers, so we had voluntarily continued with the secret rescues.

The empress began to insert her arms into the harness built into the fantastic wings. The wings trembled and wobbled slightly with every puff of turbulence, even though we were in the lee of the palace and sheltered from the western wind. She stood up, very slowly and carefully. In spite of her heavy clothing, I could see that she was now fit, lean, and strong. My master had warned me that she had the willpower to transform herself from being helplessly overweight to fit enough to join the Special Warrior Service. With three months of manic exercise and dieting, she had done it.

"I am no longer a monarch, Inspector Danol, so tell your master that I've abdicated. And do not cause trouble for these kind Alpindrak folk by telling people that they sheltered me. Last of all, do not try to follow me, or I shall get very, very angry. A pleasure to do blackmail with you, but it is time to go—and don't think about letting the pure and virtuous Constable Riellen, the heartbroken and alcoholic Roval, or the fat and furry Wallas betray me in your stead. I shall hurt *anyone* who corners me."

"Ladyship, I will be ordered to go after you again."

"Then you will have to face me when I am very, very angry. Pity, you strike me as rather cute. I tell you what, as my last act as empress I order you to stop following me. Oh, and one more thing."

"Yes?"

"I loved it when you played the sun down with 'Evening's All for Courting.' It set me shivering with delight. I might . . . I might even wish to meet you again, Inspector, under nicer circumstances. Half sister Lavenci might be stupid enough to spurn you, but I am not. Take that as a compliment, but for now, goodbye. It's been a real challenge eluding you."

Without another word Wensomer took a short run at the railing, jumped up, pushed off over the chasm with one foot, and went sailing out into the darkness. After only a moment I could see her no more, for Miral and the three moonworlds were all down, and the stars gave very little light by comparison.

Wensomer's tether casting bound me tightly for the rest of the night, so I had a lot of time to think. I thought mainly about Kavelen Lavenci, half sister of the empress. After my colleagues and I had rescued her from the Inquisition Constables, we had gone to a tavern, and there we had danced for a time before I had walked her home. We had kissed at the door, and agreed to meet again. I remember four afternoons spent at Riverfront Market, wandering among the stalls and holding hands. On our last evening together we had shared a groundnut roll for dinner, watching the sun set behind the Ridgeback Mountains; then we had kissed, pressing greasy lips together in the deepening shadows. I had fondled her left breast, and had had my hand slapped for my trouble. I had felt rather foolish and chastened as we walked slowly to the doorway behind which was her home. She had not kissed me goodnight.

The next day had seen Constable Riellen released from three weeks in the public stocks for incitement to riot, Constable Roval released from two weeks in the stocks for being drunk on duty, and myself promoted from lieutenant inspector to inspector first class and awarded a field magistrate commission. A three-month tour of duty, with secret orders to seek out the empress, was assigned to me, along with instructions to leave Alberin that day, before Riellen found another crowd to address, or Roval got anywhere near a tavern. I had sent many letters to Lavenci since then, but no replies had arrived at the regional Wayfarer offices that I nominated in my letters.

The annual climb of Alpindrak for the collection of observation sketches had also been assigned to me as a means to search out Wensomer. *Lavenci, sister of the empress.* The thought conjured a feeling like acid in the pit of my stomach. *Lavenci, a kavelen and an academician, as well as a sorceress.* She had told me none of that, nor had she discussed allowing the most extreme of intimacies with students and tutors. Then she had slapped my hand when it had merely wandered to her breast. Why was I so very repulsive? I gazed over the edge of the wall, contemplating the long, long drop to jagged rocks and realizing why suicide can hold such an allure for some lovers.

I was watching the sun rise over the Drakenridge Mountains when the casting finally collapsed and released me. I was numb, stiff and cold, and dismayed to see that clouds were gathering, foreshadowing bad weather. Worst of all, I was wretched to the very core of my soul about what Wensomer had told me. In addition to all that, I was also slightly depressed for failing my master. I had been ordered to find the empress and bring her back. The idea that she had fled deliberately had never entered anyone's thoughts. The concept of sorcerers persecuting sorcerers in the cause of wiping out sorcery so that sorcerers could rule all Scalticar was so confusing that I was still not entirely sure if I had the story right.

The castings on Riellen's door had collapsed while she was still asleep. I entered and woke her.

"Apologies for being so tired, sir, my lungs are not adequate for the thin air," she said sleepily.

"No problem, Constable, in fact you are authorized to sleep in this morning."

I took out a silver florin, put half a dozen scratches across the likeness of Empress Wensomer with my knife, then dropped it into her hand.

"Sir, you have defaced a coin of the realm," she said uncertainly.

"I found the empress and spoke with her. She is no longer empress. That is a one-florin bonus for you, because I feel like doing something to celebrate. Now go back to sleep, we'll be going home later today."

Wallas had been hidden in the one place I would never have thought to search: my own room. He was on my bed, tied in a sack.

"Cunning bitch was too fast for me!" snapped Wallas as I released him.

No creature other than a cat can put quite so much venom into the word "bitch." He sat on my bed and began to groom himself.

"Brilliant woman," I sighed as I sat on the bed beside him. "Well, she's gone now."

"As in flown away?"

"Yes, and—hold a moment! How did you know she could fly?"

"I am a cat with a past. She fancied me when I was a man."

"Just shows, one does not have to be stupid to be tasteless."

"Hah! Pure jealously—and where's my jar of Senderialvin Royal 3140?"

"Well, I suppose you've earned it," I began as I reached into the pocket of my leather trail coat.

I drew out the corked neck of the shattered jar, which must have broken when I threw myself down on the balcony after being blinded by the empress. Wallas stared in wide-eyed horror for a moment, then fell sideways on the bed in a dead faint.

Now I went next door and woke Roval, who swung his legs over the edge of the bed and rubbed his face. I sat down on the bed beside him, handed him my half-gill measure, and produced my little jar of rum.

"I am violating my orders concerning you, Constable Roval, but I am in need of someone to drink with just now," I said as I removed the cork. "Will you swallow a half gill with me?"

"Mission failed, sir?" he asked, looking genuinely concerned.

"The mission failed, it is true, but at least I managed to speak with the empress this time."

"Then you are celebrating?" he asked, brightening slightly.

"No. She let slip some words about another woman . . . my truelove."

"Lavenci?"

"Aye. The wench has a grubby past and a grubbier present," I concluded miserably.

"I wager she has shared her charms with another since you have been gone," said Roval, shaking his head knowingly.

"Worse, much worse."

"May your revenge be sweet and artful, sir."

"I'd not hurt her," I sighed. "A cat cannot help being a cat after all. No, I shall merely tell her what I have discovered about her. Then I'll say I promised Mother on her deathbed that I'd never consort with naughty girls."

"Did you, young sir?"

"Actually Mother is probably still alive."

"Probably, sir? Do you not care?"

"Of course I care. If she is indeed alive, I shall have to keep avoiding her."

We chatted of this and that for the next two hours, until called to the astronomers' 6:30 A.M. dinner—which I chose to call breakfast. After that, I was given a tour of the palace by one of the technical artisans, but he spent more time talking excitedly about the enormous explosion on Lupan than relating the history of the palace. We had what I called lunch with the astronomer general, who was about to go to bed, and after this were formally presented with a satchel of notes and observations for the academy in Alberin. We spent most of the afternoon descending the five thousand stone steps to the gate station. This was made particularly depressing by Wallas complaining about the broken jar of Senderialvin Royal at nearly every step.

At the base of the steps I got out my bagpipes and played the sun down again, this time for the guards at the observatory's gate station. The sun had been behind an overcast at the time, but they appreciated the gesture. They then invited us to share whatever the meal is that observatory guards have when the sun goes down, and we spent the night in their bunkroom. Riellen managed to get the guards into a conversation about liberation economics, but within ten minutes both had fallen asleep. Wallas made the mistake of reminding me that I had broken a jar of Senderialvin Royal 3140, which caused me to seize him firmly by the scruff of the neck, stuff him into a sack, and leave him hanging up for the night in the pantry. Roval stole a large jar of cheap wine from the guards and drank himself into oblivion. I dropped the empty jar into the chasm. By then I had been awake for two days and one night, so I slept like a dead man.

At dawn the following morning we had saddled and loaded our horses, and the dragon bridge was being wound out over the chasm when the exhausted astronomer general himself arrived at the gate station. He had descended the five thousand steps from the palace in the darkness to present us with one final dispatch.

"There was another flash on Lupan last night," he panted as he broke his seal on the satchel and inserted the latest observation folder. "It was at precisely the same place as the night before, but fifteen minutes later by the clock. This is very, very significant."

"Why is that, sir?" I asked.

"The Lupanian day is precisely fifteen minutes longer than ours. Both flashes happened at precisely the same local time on Lupan. That could *only* be due to intelligent beings doing something timed by an accurate clock."

We crossed the bridge and set off down the trail, and I contemplated the fact that I was carrying proof of intelligence on Lupan! I had history in my saddlebags! Inevitably, my thoughts strayed back to Lavenci. I dropped back a little to walk with Roval.

"Constable, could I speak with you for a moment?" I ventured.

"I apologize about the wine, sir," he replied listlessly.

"I mean privately, as a friend."

"A friend?" he asked, as if surprised to learn that he had one. "Aye."

"Were a girl to sport with scabby knaves in the most supremely indelicate way, yet give an honorable admirer nothing but chaste kisses and elevated conversation about poetry, what might that very confused youth draw by way of conclusion?"

"He must know she is playing games of power," he said sadly, looking me in the eyes for a rare and fleeting moment before shaking his head and returning his gaze to the trail. "She means to elevate him to within a step of the summit of all hopes, then cast him down by showing how even some muck-shoveling churl is higher in her esteem. It happened to me once. Such a woman brought me low."

"But why?" I asked, aghast.

"For the pleasure of seeing a strong man crushed. For the feeling of power."

His words left me with much to think about, and none of

my thoughts were happy. That evening I lit a fire with the reedpaper pages of a letter that I had been writing to Lavenci, then stared up at Lupan for a long, long time, wondering if lovers on that world also did such cruel things to each other.

Chapter Three

THE FALLING STAR

We managed the fourteen-day journey to the pigeon roost at Bolanton in ten days. There I sent the special news ahead to Alberin by carrier bird, as the astronomer general had instructed me to. After that we were low enough for the horses to carry us again, and five days later we reached the bottom of the Cyrelon Rapids. From here the Alber River was navigable all the way to the sea, so we boarded a barge for the two hundred mile voyage to Alberin.

For five days I did very little, other than rub medicinal oil into my feet, sew up damage to my uniform, polish my axe, read a book of Sargolan erotic poetry from the twenty-eighth century, talk with Wallas about royal scandals—to distract him from talking about Senderialvin Royal 3140—and sleep. On what turned out to be the last day of our voyage, Roval somehow managed to get his hands on a jar of fortified wine belonging to one of the crew, liberated the contents, and retreated from his memories into drunken oblivion. Riellen practiced her public speaking almost continually, which was mildly annoying, but inevitable.

Riellen was nineteen, very thin, and wore thick spectacles with wire frames. She had studied sorcery, but I wondered if she had studied only so that she could be a student agitator. What I did not realize was that two years in the Wayfarer Constables had taught her a lot about leadership skills and tactics. Even I knew that good leaders give clear, simple orders, repeat them often, and get their followers to repeat them back.

Riellen wrote her speeches with these principles in mind, learned them word for word, then rehearsed them. While aboard the barge, she practiced on a cargo of sheep being taken to the Alberin markets.

"The nobles, kings, and emperors are meant to attend the welfare of the people that they rule, yet does anyone attend *your* welfare?" she demanded of the bland stares before her.

"Baaa!" one of her audience replied.

"No, they don't!" Riellen assured it. "They rule for their own pleasure and convenience! Oh yes, but although despotic rulers are often overthrown eventually, what are they replaced with?"

"Baaa!"

"Other kings! And then the new king, once crowned, makes it his highest priority to execute those who led the uprising. This makes sense for a king, but as a system is it fair?"

"Baaa!"

"You are right, brother, it is quite unjust. You should not just shout *down with the king,* you should shout *down with the establishment.*"

"No being fleeced without representation!" called Wallas.

"Brother Wallas is correct. If you pay taxes you must have a say in how they are spent. You must decide . . . er . . . I'd better change that."

Riellen knelt down, dipped her goose quill in a jar of ink, scratched out some words, then scribbled a few more. She stood up again.

"Think of government as a battle between two armies. Kings make decisions about strategies and tactics, but an army of peasants could also make such decisions. They could vote on everything."

"Too slow," I called. "Most decisions in battles have to be made quickly. By the time you have had a vote about tactics you could be defeated or even dead."

"They . . . must vote for . . . a ruler with their confidence!" cried Riellen, while kneeling down and scribbling something new into her speech. "Someone to rule . . . for them."

"Ah, so instead of an autocracy, why not a voteaucracy?" I suggested. "Rule of the vote?"

"Voteaucracy . . . it does not have an inspiring ring to it," said Wallas.

"What is a vote but a demonstration of the people's will?" said Riellen.

"Demonaucracy, then?" I suggested.

"No, that sounds religious," responded Wallas.

"Electocracy?" said Riellen. "Rule by election?"

"Electocracy," said Wallas thoughtfully. "Electocracy . . ."

"The word has a good edge to it," I said, feeling a little sorry for Riellen for some reason, and trying to be positive for a change.

"Yes, yes sir, electocracy is what it must be!" she cried; then she stood up again and faced the sheep. "Electocracy is what you must be ruled by, brothers and sisters. The elected choice of the voting majority must rule. Those who pay taxes, vote. Those who labor, paid or unpaid, vote. Each of us must have one vote! Each of us must want electocracy! Each of us must want it now! *What do we want?*" shouted Riellen.

"Cat food!" called Wallas.

"When do we want it?"

"Meow!"

Some speakers deal with annoying hecklers by witty, cutting responses that deflate them completely. Riellen dealt with hecklers by treating them as if they were enthusiastic supporters. Wallas was very effective as an annoying heckler, however, so she was getting a lot of practice at fielding sarcastic comments.

"One vote per person will unite the people against the royal establishment. United, the people are bigger, stronger, more clever, and more powerful than any establishment ruler.

"United,

"The people,

"Can never be defeated!"

"Baaa!" replied one of the more vocal and politically conscious sheep.

"United,

"The tomcats,

"Can never be castrated!" suggested Wallas.

Faced with a female Wayfarer Constable preaching revolution to a cargo of sheep, and a talking tomcat heckler, the steersman on duty took a jar from his pocket, stared at it for a moment, then tossed it overboard. A sickeningly sharp pang reminded me of something that I also needed to do. I took a small camphorwood box from my pack, wrapped it in Lavenci's portrait, then dropped the package over the side. The silver chain and black opal within the box had cost my wages for two months.

Riellen sat down beside me to write some refinements into her speech, and Wallas sauntered off to sleep on a pile of sacks at the bow. Now a thought crossed my mind. Wensomer had said that Riellen could be hurt. It did not seem likely that Riellen had anything shameful in her past, or was even capable of doing anything shameful, but the matter had been nagging away in the recesses of my mind.

"Riellen, may I ask a personal question?" I began awkwardly. "About your background, that is."

"Certainly, sir!" she declared brightly, sitting up straight and giving me her entire attention.

"Look, I only ask as your superior. Please bear in mind that we conduct some very secret and sensitive business for our master, under the guise of being Wayfarers."

"Yes sir."

"Do you have anything shameful in your past that, well, enemies of the master might use to blackmail you?"

"I have done no shameful things, sir," she said readily and calmly. "Although there are things in my past that have caused me distress, and on one occasion shame, there is nothing I would not admit to."

"Ah, yes, I understand," I said quickly, suspecting the worst. "Most girls have some tale of unwanted amorous attention foisted upon them that—"

"Oh no, sir, nothing like that."

"Oh? Indeed!"

"It was when I was sixteen. I was asked to be Queen of Alberin Agricultural Market, at the midsummer fair. One had to be sixteen, and the most comely virgin of all the stallholders' and merchants' daughters."

"Ah, a great honor," I commented.

"I too thought that, sir, then some girls . . . confronted me. They revealed that I was the *only* girl of sixteen who was a virgin, and they said most pointedly that my thin figure and spectacles rendered me ugly. My virtue became a thing of shame. I had to endure a day of wearing a beautiful robe, leading the dancing about the ribbon pole, and parading before the revelers in the fair, all the while knowing that I was despised for being too plain to allure any youth. I smiled and acted graciously all day, but thereafter I locked myself in my room and wept for an entire week. My father was prosperous, and he loved me dearly, so he promised to send me far away, to escape my humiliation. I went to the Sargolan Empire, and studied at a provincial academy. There I met students who had ideals, and who valued me for my opinions and ideas, rather than mere feminine allure."

"Ah yes, that was in Clovesser," I recalled. "You and your friends, the Clovesser Sorceric Conspiracies and Occult Plots Exposure Collective, managed to set part of the city on fire with some dangerous etheric experiment."

"It was nothing shameful, sir."

"And touched off a riot bigger than most battles."

"We raised the consciousness of the oppressed people."

I smiled and shook my head, trying not to laugh.

"Well, you certainly have ba—er, guts, Riellen. You have risen above what those silly, jealous girls could ever become, and I admire you for your unbendable spirit."

"Sir, do you really?" she gasped. "That means a lot to me. While I do not agree with your conservative political outlook, I have found your honesty, integrity, compassion, and sense of honor to be a great inspiration. I am honored to serve under your command."

"Really?" I exclaimed, staggered that she thought about me at all, let alone esteemed me—and suddenly worried that she might propose that we go belowdecks and relieve her of that bothersome virginity, which I suspected was still intact. "But I'm just a lad in the Wayfarers," I protested.

"You could easily be more than that, sir, but you choose to be a good and honest Wayfarer inspector, striking down the unjust, and serving those in the establishment who secretly work against it."

"Riellen the master is—"

"I understand, sir, I shall be discreet, even though I have deduced what the master is doing. I choose to serve him, because I choose to be what I am as well. I could have been the wife of some merchant, writing his letters, totaling his ledgers, and bearing his children, but I chose to be with the Wayfarers so that I can travel, observing the plight of the downtrodden commoners, and teaching them the means to raise themselves up."

When I did not reply to that, she dipped her quill in the ink again, then stared at the paper for some moments, as if her mind were elsewhere. To my astonishment, she began to sing in a soft, but clear and steady voice.

> *"I was the most pretty*
> *In Alberin City,*
> *The bride of midsummer*
> *And queen of the fair."*

That fragment from the last verse of "Bride of Midsummer" was the only music I have ever heard Riellen sing that was not some rousing political song at one of her rallies. I could think of nothing else to do but take out my bagpipes, detach the high-altitude reeds and extender pipes, then play. I started with "The Half-Copper Reel." After listening to me practice the trills and runs somewhat unsteadily for a few minutes, Riellen declared that the reel was a fine demonstration of the creative genius of the common people, then went back to refining her latest speech. I played on.

It seems strange to say it, but even though the sun was warm, the sky was clear, there was no wind, and the river was almost dead flat, I suddenly had the feeling that a storm was not far off. It was my fancy that the cheery little tunes that I was playing might hold the unseen blackness away a little longer, and so I played long into that tranquil afternoon.

⁕ ⁕ ⁕

We were some days upriver from Alberin when the barge docked at the river port of Gatrov that evening. A boy came running along the docks with a sealed note for me as we tied up. It was an instruction to leave the barge and go to a tavern that was visible from where we were moored. The Jolly Bollard was a crowded, smoky place, and popular with travelers.

Because so many diverse people gathered there, it was also a place to see unusual sights. Nobody gave a second glance to a large black cat on the serving board, lapping wine from a dish. Even Riellen trying to raise the revolutionary consciousness of the serving maids drew curious stares but no particular interest from the patrons. Interestingly, the place was about evenly divided between male and female patrons, because this was the week of the World Mother Festival, when women entered the generally male preserve of taverns. Social restraints and conventions were more relaxed, and people were expected either to court each other or to keep closer company than usual with their partners—all in the name of general fertility.

"Inspector Danol, shame on you for letting the enemy catch you from behind," said a soft voice behind me.

"Marshal Essen, the day you become my enemy is the day I change sides," I said as he came around to stand beside me.

"Should I just take your report and satchel, or will you let me buy you a drink?"

Now I stood and grasped wrists with Essen, my old marshal from when I was in the Sargolan Empire's service. We called a serving maid over, ordered a jar of wine to share, and sat down. She quickly returned with our jar.

"How much?" I asked her.

"You're the lad who played the sun down on Alpindrak with bagpipes, aren't you?" she asked.

"Aye," I replied, surprised that she knew of it.

"Then for you, sir, it's free. Can't wait to tell my Donny that I met you."

The serving maid skipped off, leaving us with our free jar. Essen and I filled our mugs and clanked them together.

"Where is Gilvray?" I asked. "I thought you were to be here with him."

"Dead, murdered," he whispered, his face blank.

"Murdered?" I gasped.

"Here, a week ago, in a room upstairs. I was asleep next door, but I heard nothing. His body looked like it had been chopped open with a white-hot ax blade. The militia is investigating, but they would have trouble finding a beer barrel in a brewery. There was a similar murder in Alberin a month ago.

The court minstrel was the victim. Of course the regent blames sorcerers, but sorcerers don't kill like that."

"What, then? Did Gilvray and the minstrel have anything in common?"

"Nothing that I know of. I doubt they ever even met. The militia's Commander Halland thinks some daemon has escaped an illegal experiment involving sorcery."

"Captain Gilvray, a brave and honorable man," I said, oddly surprised to suddenly feel sorrow for anyone other than myself. "His lady will be desolate with grief."

"As all of us are. Do you have any cheerier news?"

"Sir, I found the empress," I declared softly. "I spoke with her."

Essen twitched, even though he was trying not to display any reaction. I had achieved what every other official, constable, warrior, and noble in the empire had not been able to.

"What is her situation?" he asked urgently.

It did not take long to tell him of the abdication of Empress Wensomer, and that the disbanded High Circle of Scalticarian Initiates was intact, and probably plotting the greatest coup in the continent's history. He betrayed little emotion, merely sitting quietly and sipping his drink from time to time.

"So, there was no coup, assassination, or abduction?" he concluded when I was done.

"That is correct, sir, she merely ran."

"'Ran' is a passable strong word, lad. She weighed two hundred and sixty pounds when she vanished."

"Actually, she said she had herself shipped out in a crate."

"Ah, that explains much. She has halved her weight, you say?"

"Yes sir. She has a very strong will, when she chooses to use it. Manic dieting and ruthless exercise were probably her path back to a more conventional size. She looked to be in excellent trim. Quite alluring if the truth be known."

"Ah."

He did not elaborate on that single, and rather brief, word. The silence lengthened. I drained my drink.

"Sir, how have things been in Alberin for the three months I've been gone?"

"Poorly, lad. Six more of the sorcery folk were caught and killed last month alone, now that Regent Corozan is running the empire."

"I heard that two client kings have died in mysterious circumstances, and that some of the former Secret Inquisition Constables had been seized and executed."

"Not so. The empress kept us so secret that there was no paperwork to betray us."

"Who would have thought our cover jobs in the Wayfarer Constables would become our real jobs?"

He looked across to where Wallas was now sitting on a serving maid's lap, and being fed scraps of marinated fish by another serving maid.

"About that rather overweight black cat," began Essen.

"Yes, it's Wallas."

"Hah, what a life. Surrounded by women, who stroke, cuddle, and feed him."

"But he can do no more about it than purr," I pointed out. "How would you feel?"

"Well at my age I'd also be happy enough to just stretch out and purr. Some of the time, anyway. What of Roval?"

"I managed to dry him out, but he still broods about what the sorceress Terikel did to him. Tonight he is off duty, and probably drunk."

It was about now that Riellen was ejected by the taverner's wife for saying disloyal things about the regent, preaching electocracy, and trying to get the serving maids to agitate for better pay and conditions.

"Some things never change," commented Essen. "So, can I have the satchel of observations and drawings from Alpindrak?"

"Aye, here you go," I said as I handed over what had taken so long to secure.

"Big revel outside the Bargeman's Barrel after dusk," said Essen as he checked the seals.

"Indeed? I asked Riellen to get us rooms there."

"Bring your pipes, you'll be welcome, especially after Alpindrak."

"Will you be there?"

"Afraid not, I'll be on a barge for Alberin in a half hour, with your report on the empress, and the Alpindrak sketches.

Oh, and one more thing. There's a lad name of Pelmore Haft-brace lives here. He's wharfmaster of Middle Wharf, so he gets to see a lot of what comes and goes. About twenty-five, blond curls, tall, well built, and a champion dancer."

"Were I a lass I'd ask where he drinks."

"Many lasses do. He's also the barony's agent of the Inquisition Constables."

"Really?" I exclaimed softly. "I thought it was Halland, the commander of the town militia."

"Apparently not. The list with Halland's name on it was a deliberate leak, to have folk like us wary of the wrong man. Now then, here's the master's orders. You're to contact a woman, name of Norellie Witchway. Tell her that Pelmore's of a mind to denounce her when the district inspector of the Inquisition visits here next week. Here are border papers for her. Escort her through Waingram Forest and into Fralland."

"Norellie Witchway. Where's she to be found?"

"Walk out the door, turn right onto Wharfway Plaza, take the fifth laneway, and she's in the ninth cottage, just behind the militia headquarters. Her sign says 'Norellie Herbs and Healing,' and she's expecting you."

"Sorceress?"

"Not exactly, but she deals in enough magic to get herself a brushwood footwarmer. You must flee with her in three days, when the barony's country-dancing championships are held. Pelmore's something of a dancer, he'll be competing dawn till dusk, and will not notice she's gone until it's too late."

"Norellie Witchway, five lanes to the right, nine doors down, flee in three days, I'm expected, and mind out for a dancing wharfer named Pelmore Haftbrace."

"Sharp lad. Well then, I'll be off, must catch my barge. Watch your tongue and back."

"But I'm just a loyal Wayfarer inspector," I said innocently.

"Well, just make sure folk keep thinking that."

"Convey my condolences to Lady Dolvienne for Captain Gilvray, sir."

"That I shall."

I stayed behind after he left, relieved to be alone again. For the first time in uncounted weeks I was not being whined at by Wallas, moaned at by Roval, or lectured to by Riellen. The prospect of not having to travel on the following day was also rather pleasant. A serving maid interrupted my reverie.

"Yer pardon, sir, but some important lady what speaks proper wants to talk with ye."

"Er, have you got the right man?" I asked. "I'm just a Wayfarer inspector."

"Aye sir, she said ye were that. She asked if ye'd like to sit at her table. She's the one with long white hair."

I looked around, and caught sight of a tallish, elegant young woman with pure white hair, a proud, angular face, and wide lips painted the color of arterial blood. She did not look like a typical albino, even though her hair was so white that it almost seemed to glow. Her eyes were as black as anthracite coal, due to some treatment with squid ink to improve her eyesight. She was dressed in fashionable riding gear—boots, calf-length skirt, and ruffle blouse—and at each shoulder she had a coat of arms that featured an eagle, sable, on an azure field.

Kavelen Lavenci Si-Chella, half sister of the empress, I thought with resignation; then I gave the serving maid a copper and stood up. After walking across to Lavenci, I bowed, then brought the edge of my hand to my forehead and swept it down to my side in the Wayfarers' salute.

"Danolarian, it seems we have both had a change in fortune since our last meeting," she said with a suave smile, leaning back against the wall on her stool.

"Ladyship, I am honored to be in your presence," I said slowly, and with meticulous formality.

"Oh that! *Kavelen Lavenci,* what a joke. The empress elevated me for unimportant services to important people. Sit down, Danolarian, sit down. Wine? You must be off duty if you are drinking already."

"That I am, ladyship."

"Please, it is Lavenci to you." She laughed. "I notice you have the olive-brown tan that comes from traveling in high mountains. How was it on Alpindrak?"

"A severe test of endurance, but the most beautiful place in the world."

"So I have heard. I also heard you played the sun down on Alpindrak with 'Evening's All for Courting.' That must have been wonderful."

"It seemed like a fine thing to do, so I did it."

"It made you famous, everyone's talking about it. I also heard there were flashes on the face of Lupan, and that glowing clouds the size of a kingdom were observed. Have you heard of it? The news caused a sensation among the cold-science astronomers. They think it signifies intelligent life."

"Aye, I saw the very first of them, then there was another."

"Two, you say? Ah, but you were on the road and could not have known. Carrier pigeons have brought word of ten such flashes and clouds while you were traveling. One every night for ten days, then no more."

We lapsed into silence for some moments. A very unpleasant subject needed to be raised, and I was avoiding it. I decided that first she needed to be warned about the Inquisition's spy, just in case she still practiced the forbidden magics.

"Ladyship, I have word of an Inquisition spy, Pelmore Haftbrace," I began.

"The young dancing wharfmaster, is he not?" she responded at once. "I know of him already. Pelmore has won three medals for his dancing in former years."

"Oh. Ah, well . . . good."

"I do still dance, in fact I have danced a lot since arriving here. I have even danced with Pelmore."

"Champions can be fine tutors, ladyship."

"Have you forgotten that I once danced with you?"

"I remember our dances together with great pleasure, ladyship. I just wanted to warn you against possible danger from the wharfmaster Pelmore. As you already know of him, I shall bother you no further."

At this point I gave in to a fit of blatant cowardice. I stood up to go instead of saying what I knew I had to say, but Lavenci just blinked with mild surprise before waving me down again.

"Stay, I would hear of the flashes on Lupan from you. You say you saw the very first?"

I described what I had seen, quite proud of the fact that I had chanced to see the first flash of all, yet anxious to be out of Lavenci's presence. She listened carefully as I spoke, but had an odd, haughty air about her, as if she were having to strain to tolerate me.

"I suspect that Lupanian sorcerers are experimenting with huge ether machines, just as ours once did," she explained once I had finished.

"Perhaps they follow our example," I said. "After all, the destruction of Torea would have been visible from Lupan, if they have farsights such as ours. Assuming that there really is intelligent life there."

"I would call it stupid sentient life, rather than intelligent," replied Lavenci. "Large ether machines are a very bad idea."

"True, we proved that."

Again there was a silence. Again Lavenci chose to break it.

"You seem to have a very good education for a mere inspector, Danolarian. Three years in the Wayfarers! You should be a marshal by now, you could even rise to quadrant inspector if you put your mind to it."

"I'm not a good leader, ladyship," I replied, trying to bring the conversation to a close. "I'd rather just be out and on the roads."

"Out on the roads and not writing to me?" she said pointedly, her voice hardening a trifle.

"I wrote you eleven letters, ladyship."

"You did? None reached me. I thought something had happened to you. All I got was the note you left under the door, saying that you had to leave for three months, and apologizing for taking such bold liberties with me."

"Nevertheless, I wrote eleven letters and submitted them for carriage to Alberin," I said, my tone and manner suddenly sharpening, and probably bordering on rudeness.

"Well then, did you bring me a present from all your travels?"

"My apologies, ladyship. I bought you a black opal on a silver chain. Black for your eyes, silver for your hair. It cost four hundred florins, nearly all the money I had."

"Oh, a sophisticated gift!" she exclaimed, her eyes widening. "Well, where is it?"

"It was lost overboard during the voyage here on the barge."

"Lost overboard?" she laughed. "Surely you can do better than that?"

By way of reply I emptied my purse onto the table. Three coppers were all that fell out.

"My past month's pay is due tonight," I added.

I was finding Lavenci's company something of a strain by now. It reminded me of being a very small boy, trying to be nice to some elderly, bad-tempered aunt who was looking for an excuse to give him a damn good thrashing. The silence between us lengthened. Yet again Lavenci broke it.

"Danolarian, why do you not respond to my advances?" she suddenly asked, looking me in the eyes and running a fingertip along the back of my hand.

"With respect, ladyship, you slapped my hand away when last we were together, and bid me goodnight in a very chilly manner."

"Well, quite properly, too," she said haughtily. "You must learn that a *lady* does not tolerate such unwanted familiarities."

Something inside me snapped, and I drew my hand back off the table and folded my arms. *Well, time to destroy my career in the Wayfarers,* I decided. *On the other hand, where do I go? I have the death sentence for desertion in the Sargolan Empire, I'm liable to be recognized by some Torean refugees in Diomeda, and now I'm about to become unemployable in the Scalticarian Empire for being rude to someone with Kavelen in front of her name. I know a bit of Vindician, perhaps I could pick up some mercenary work there. Time to be rude to a very important lady, and for no better reason than self-respect,* I concluded.

"I most humbly beg your pardon," I said coldly.

"A ready apology, perhaps there is hope for you," she laughed, with a flick of her hand. "A lady cannot take up arms to defend her honor, so she must deter unwanted familiarities before they begin. Now then, I must bid you do something to earn my forgiveness."

"Begging your pardon, ladyship, but your sister, Her Majesty Empress Wensomer, told me that you were indeed delighted to accept the most intimate familiarities possible from Student Ulderver, Student Decrullin, Student Laron, Prefect Lees, and Tutor Haravigel when you raised your skirts for them in the academy's pantry and the academy's bathchamber towel cabinet. Except for Laron, of course, who was given access to much more of your esteem than I could ever hope for on the academy's roof. If you wish to tell me why I am so much more despicable, loathsome, repulsive, and revolting than those young men, then I shall consider whether or not I *want* your forgiveness."

I had spoken in a level, soft voice, so that nobody else in the taproom would hear. Lavenci's suave smile had vanished as I spoke, and all traces of color drained from her face. Her eyes left mine, and she stared at her mug for quite a while. Finally she picked it up and drained the contents in a single swallow, then ran her tongue over her lips.

"Danolarian . . . I come from a very odd family," she began slowly, then seemed to lose track of what she was thinking to say.

Nobody knows that better than me, I thought. "Ladyship, I must assure you that I shall never again mention these matters," I declared. "I should now like to be off to collect my pay, I have been eating poorly since I spent two months of my pay on the black opal that I later tossed into the river. Are you done with me?"

"Me done with you?" she said in a whisper that I barely heard above the background babble of the tavern. "Inspector Danolarian, *you* are done with *me.*"

"May I go, ladyship?"

"Go where?" she asked listlessly. "Am I permitted to know?"

"The Bargeman's Barrel, there is a big dance outside it tonight. I'll ask if they need a spare bagpiper, I might earn a couple of florins."

Again she sat in silence, this time scratching at the tabletop with a fingernail.

"Danolarian . . . you are like nobody I have ever met," she declared in a voice scarcely above a whisper.

"Judging from your treatment of me, ladyship, this is painfully obvious."

She gave a loud sniff, and a pearly tear trailed down her cheek. Suddenly she stood up and walked around the table, unfastening her ruffle blouse. Sitting on my lap and snatching up my hand, she pressed it firmly against a bare breast. The other patrons of the taproom gasped, then whistled, clapped, and cheered.

"Well, Inspector, this time I am not slapping your hand away," she declared firmly, oblivious of the fact that we were the focus of attention of the entire taproom, and with forced frivolity in her tone. "Come, let us find a pantry, and I can lean on a cheese barrel while you raise my skirts and do what you will. If your taste is for a bed, I must warn you that I bite."

"Ladyship, I think that we have both experienced sufficient humiliation for one night. May I go?"

After seeming to think on my words for a moment, she raised my hand to her lips, gave it a little squeeze, then released it. She looked rather crushed as she stood up before me, refastening her blouse.

"Is there nothing that I can do for you?" she asked forlornly.

My position was by now more than clear, and I decided that a concession was in order. I wanted to leave her, not hurt her. Even in circumstances such as these, I could not bring myself to dislike her. She was like that pleasant but expensive drink, caffin, to which I am allergic: I liked her, but I knew she was bad for me.

"May I have a dance or two with you, tonight?" I asked, trying to sound friendly without sounding too friendly. She brightened at once.

"Yes, yes, on my word, yes. We danced on the night we met, and I would love to dance out our farewell. I'll be away, and change," she said with a flourish. "Silk skirts, lips waxed red, cascades of snowy hair, and a hint of perfume, just so that you can be seen with the most beautiful woman at the dance, and be the envy of every man watching."

"You are too kind."

"Shall I meet you there?"

"I shall be waiting."

I waited until Lavenci had gone; then I went across to the maids who were stroking and feeding Wallas. I told them that I was away to the dance, and asked them to look after my cat. They said that Wallas was welcome to stay in the tavern for the night, and sleep in the kitchen.

"We sleeps there too, luv," said the one who was feeding scraps to Wallas. "Yer pussy will come to no 'arm, why 'e might even like to share my bed."

If only they knew, I thought.

"Cross words with your lady, then, luv?" asked the other maid.

"She was never my lady," I said as I turned to go.

Riellen had been waiting outside; in fact, she had been watching through the window. She bailed me up as I stepped outside, reporting that rooms had been secured for sleeping, the laundry had been left with laundresses, Roval was blind drunk and asleep in his room, and that she had collected our back pay. She presented me with a purse.

"Very good, Constable Riellen, now take the rest of the night off," I said grandly, pleased to be able to at least make someone happy.

"Sir, you were touching that woman's breast," she observed.

"It was a very nice breast," I replied, suddenly as annoyed with her prudery as with Lavenci's excesses.

"Women who let you do that usually want you to do a lot more, sir."

"Indeed, Constable? And here was I thinking the night had no promise."

"Oh sir!" she cried, stamping her foot.

"I must be on my way, Riellen. Will you be at the dance?"

"Sir, country dances are an ideologically correct manifestation of toiler-class solidarity against—"

"In Alberinese we say 'yes' or 'no.'"

"Yes sir."

I set off to the right, and wandered along the plaza. Skirting the dance crowd outside the Bargeman's Barrel, I turned in to the second lane beyond it. Nine hovels down, there was Norellie's sign. Now I turned back, deciding that Riellen could arrange the meeting between Norellie and I while I danced with Lavenci. If Riellen saw nothing, I would not get lectured about consorting with immoral lower-upper-class exploiters of upper-lower-class toilers.

I returned to Wharfway Plaza, which was an open, cobbled space between the wharfside buildings and the river. The clear evening sky was already studded with the brighter stars and two moonworlds. Music spilled out from the crowd near the Bargeman's Barrel, and I recognized several morris dance tunes. Nearby, standing on a beer barrel, was Riellen, exhorting half a dozen drunks to go on a drinking strike to bring down the price of ale.

"Champion of lost causes, and a third of my command," I sighed to myself. She had managed to coax her listeners into a rousing chant, having failed to get them to hold the tune of a revolutionary song.

"What do we want?"

"Cheap ale!"

"When do we want it?"

"Now!"

It was then that I saw it out of the corner of my eye, a thin, green streak of brightness coming out of the western sky, a brilliant point of light that left a glowing trail behind it. I had seen many shooting stars in my life, but none flew so slowly as this one.

It passed almost directly overhead, and I saw that it was roughly cylindrical, with the suggestion of shimmering wings extending to either side of it to about four times its length, in a V shape. A moment later it was lost to view behind the buildings of the river port. I glanced around, noting that every other person on the waterfront was looking in the direction that the vanished shooting star had traveled. I remember distinctly that the music had stopped, and that there was absolute silence all around me. Suddenly there were two mighty thunderclaps. Now people began shouting and shrieking, gesturing to the sky, and pointing. The greenish trail above began to disperse, and then there was a rolling rumble in the distance. For some time people ran about, pointing east and talking about a shooting star falling.

"Shootin' star," said a man who was standing nearby, a straw hanging out of his mouth.

"Seemed the size of a carriage," I replied. "Lucky it didn't land on us."

"Reckon it come down in Waingram Forest," he said, staring up at the dispersing trail of green smoke with his hands on his hips.

"Is that far?" I asked.

"'Bout five miles from the town walls. Will ye be goin' there, bein' a Wayfarer inspector an' all?"

"Aye, I'd reckon," I said, without really thinking about it.

"When?"

"Think I might wait till morning," I decided, in no mood to be floundering about in a forest during the night. "Besides, I'll need to hire a horse."

"Oh I'll loan one ter ye, and be yer guide. Name's Grem, I'm an ostler by trade. Been unloadin' hay from the *River Princess*." He gestured to a grubby barge. "I'd like ter see a real star up close. Fancies a bit o' the cold sciences, I does."

"That's good of you, Grem. I'm Inspector Scryverin, of the Wayfarers."

"Done, then. Meet me in stablers' row at the market, about the ninth hour?"

"The ninth it is."

I had the impression that the cylinder had been a relatively small thing flying low, rather than something immense at a great height, so at that stage it was not a great wonder to me. Thus I was not particularly excited as I set off again, to fulfill my last obligation to Lavenci.

Chapter Four

ON WHARFWAY PLAZA

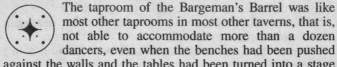 The taproom of the Bargeman's Barrel was like most other taprooms in most other taverns, that is, not able to accommodate more than a dozen dancers, even when the benches had been pushed against the walls and the tables had been turned into a stage for the musicians. Thus it was that the dance was being held in Wharfway Plaza, between the tavern and the wharf's edge. A bagpiper was playing a bracket of reels, totally drowning out half a dozen pipers and rebec players who were going through the motions of playing along. About three dozen couples were dancing in a double line while a substantial crowd of drinkers watched, clapped, cheered, waved tankards, and spilled ale.

The taverner had set up a serving board beside the front door, and it was before this that Riellen suddenly appeared, at the head of her delegation of drunks. She presented the taverner with a petition demanding cheaper ale. She was told to go away. Actually the taverner expressed it a little less discreetly than that, and it was quickly established that negotiations would not be entered into. The taverner then set Riellen's petition afire, and his wife appeared, brandishing a cleaver. The drunks hastily abandoned Riellen; then Riellen finally abandoned the cause. After allowing a minute or so to pass I sauntered over to her. She was watching the dancers, her arms tightly folded, and her expression sullen.

"Another victory for the establishment, Constable?"

"I was not able to instill sufficient unity in my followers, sir," she muttered. "How do you feel?"

"Very well, so far. I have even been asked for a dance by a bawdy wench."

"How bawdy, sir?"

"Well, she did let me feel her breast."

"Oh sir! Not the white-haired tart from the ruling establishment."

"Yes indeed."

Although I was feeling quite desolate, I was not about to let Riellen know that, mainly out of sheer pride. *Strange how I feign to court Lavenci to annoy Riellen, yet have just spurned Lavenci,* I thought.

"So, the curse-headache has not hit you yet?" she asked, looking around as if expecting someone.

"No. For a change, it's the end of a mission, yet I feel wonderful."

"Could I get you a celebratory ale, sir? It is the drink of the toiling classes."

"Why thank you, Constable."

Riellen made straight for a serving maid with a tray of full mugs, rather than face the taverner at the serving board. They seemed to talk for a long time. With our ales secured, we toasted the end of another successful mission, then watched as a team of morris dancers did a stick dance. Once the morris men had finished, the musicians began a bracket of jigs. I recognized the ostler, Grem, dancing between crossed axes with a pot of ale balanced on his head.

"Hie, but it's nice to be in uncomplicated company," I said as Riellen and I stood together.

"Was your company in that other tavern complicated, sir?"

"More than you could ever imagine," I said truthfully.

I was unwilling to say anything bad about Lavenci after hurting her so much. I hated myself, but although I wanted to hate Lavenci, I could not. I also wanted more sympathetic company than Riellen. A familiar twinge of pain lanced into existence behind one eye.

"Kavelen Lavenci is an upper-class exploiter of the honest, simple, toiling masses—" began Riellen quite suddenly, but I nudged her before she got any further.

"There she is!" I exclaimed as I caught sight of Lavenci across the dance square. She was now wearing a calf-length red dress that looked to be of real silk. "Right on cue. Beautiful woman arrives just as my migraine does."

"She is startling of features, sir."

"But strikingly attractive," I replied at once.

"Sir, casual and fleeting indulgence in the pleasures of the flesh is a manifestation of decadent—"

"Oh nonsense," I laughed. "The whole of life in the Way-farers is casual and fleeting."

"Well *I* choose to forgo the pleasures of the flesh and dedicate myself to using my travels in the Wayfarer Constables to spread the revolutionary ideology of equality."

"Lost cause."

"Why so, sir? The empress *may* have abdicated because she grew tired of oppressing the downtrodden toilers."

"Strange one, the empress. She despised rulers before she was crowned. There were some of us who doubted she could endure being one for long, but she lasted for three years. Now she really is gone. Pity. Things were peaceful in Alberin's domains under her rule."

"Oh but sir, what about skirmishes between warlords, raids by brigands, riots over tournaments and cockfights, and border disputes?"

"Aye, but they're not serious altercations."

"Sir, those altercations were serious for those caught up in them," insisted Riellen doggedly.

"Pah! The casualty lists never rose above a few dozen. Besides, Empress Wensomer also provided a string of royal scandals to fuel the production of scandal sheets for the public bulletin boards. That's a royal duty, and she performed it well."

"Sir!" Riellen exclaimed, outraged.

"Joke, Riellen, joke," I sighed, then took another swallow of my ale to distract myself from the growing pain in my head. "Look, the albino lady is not dancing with anyone else—oh, and she just declined that carter's invitation to take to the square."

"Her hair is still down, that means she is waiting for her beau," said Riellen.

"She's obviously waiting for me," I declared, wiping my lips with the back of my hand.

"But sir, your head—"

"Is hurting already, but I still have a chance to make a good impression tonight, then meet her tomorrow when I am feeling better. Some women like a man who is not too forward."

"Sir, will you *really* meet this upper-class, exploitative oppressor of the honest toilers tomorrow morning?"

"No, I've a mind to ride over to the forest and see the shooting star that fell there this evening, then report back by lunchtime."

"Oh very good, sir, duty and all that. I knew you were teasing me."

"On second thought, perhaps I could meet Kavelen Lavenci for lunch."

"Oh sir!" Riellen exclaimed. "She's even *dressed* as a class enemy."

"But I'm definitely going to the forest."

"Am I coming too, sir?"

"Yes! I get nervous about leaving you anywhere where there is a crowd of people, a barrel to stand on, and somewhere to run when the militia is sent to arrest you."

"Sir, you're just saying that to be nice," giggled Riellen, giving me a coy push.

Somewhere in the distance a crier rang the bell for an hour past dusk. I rubbed at my temples as the pain intensified.

"Sir, you should lie down. I have rooms upstairs booked for us."

"Actually I did notice the sign of a healer in a nearby lane, Riellen," I said, remembering Norellie. "Perhaps you could go there and see whether she has a spell or charm to counter the pain in my head. Second lane on the right, and go to the ninth house on the right. There should be a sign that says 'Norellie Herbs and Healing.' Tell the healer my problem, then fetch her here."

* * *

With Riellen gone, I set off to fulfill my obligation. I was soon close enough to Lavenci to touch her. She was drinking from a wine cup, and watching the locals doing slip jigs as I approached.

"Ladyship, why do you not dance?" I asked, stepping up beside her and giving a sort of sideways bow.

"I have not noticed you dancing either, Inspector," she replied smoothly.

"Ah, but I am waiting to have a dance with you."

She gave me a curious little frown, then began to tie up her hair. My headache was getting worse with each passing heartbeat. I saw Riellen hurry back with a woman dressed in dark robes, then lead her into the tavern. *Well, perhaps the pain will not be too bad tonight,* I thought hopefully.

"Are you ready for our dance?" Lavenci asked.

Waves of molten glass started to slosh about in my head. I was beyond caring about anything other than oblivion.

"A dance?" I echoed stupidly.

"Yes, a dance. People hold hands and jump about in time to music. We danced together three months ago in Alberin, you may remember."

"My pardon," I said, offering her my arm.

I led Lavenci into the dance square just as the opening bars of a reel were being played, more or less in shock to even feel her hand in mine. We danced through quite a long bracket of reels, and I had to concentrate hard on remembering some of the steps. I noticed Riellen near the band, presumably waiting to whisk me away to the healer. The bracket finished with a leisurely triplestep, which is danced in a light embrace. The music stopped, and we all clapped.

"My lady, I may have to retire early," I announced.

"*Sir,* that is uncommonly forward of you!" my albino partner laughed. "Were I a nice girl I would slap your face, but I am a hoyden, so may I retire with you?"

"Ah, sorry, no, no," I babbled. "I meant that I've had a long journey today, and I am very tired."

Suddenly Lavenci put a hand to her head and staggered slightly. I caught hold of her, thinking she might fall.

"Ladyship, what is the matter?" I asked.

"A sudden strangeness, like a wave of tiny, hot needles sweeping over me," she said as she opened her eyes again. "I have an odd, metallic taste in my mouth, an odd dizziness, yet a feeling of great well-being."

"As a field medicar, I think it might be delayed shock. A reaction to our hard words of an hour ago catching up with you at last."

"The feeling is familiar, but . . . can't think clearly."

"Breathe deeply, and clear your mind."

A couple of minutes had Lavenci out of distress, in fact she rebounded into very high spirits. The opening bars of "All the King's Lancers" blared out. "All the King's Lancers" was a tournament dance, and a muscular young man with a wharfmaster's plate at each shoulder and curly blond hair danced a challenge jig, then bowed to a girl. A bearded youth with a red shawl in his right hand now danced another challenge set. The two raised their right arms and charged each other. The wharfmaster caught the scarf as they passed, and they spun in a half circle before the bearded youth lost his grip on the scarf and went stumbling away into the crowd to the sound of a mighty cheer. A girl now skipped onto the floor and the blond youth danced a set with her, but tucked her scarf into his belt. The rest of us stood clapping as another youth took up the wharfmaster's challenge.

"Tha's young Pelmore, 'e canna be beat," cried a grizzled timberjack beside me, indicating the blond wharfer with his pipe.

Six more youths had been sent stumbling away and six girls had shared a dance with Pelmore before the young, blond wharfmaster approached Lavenci and gestured to her. She offered me a scarf.

"Take my favor, joust for me!" she shouted above the music. "I rather fancy that blond wharfer."

"He's an Inquisition spy, remember?" I hissed in her ear.

"Spies make the best lovers!" she giggled.

Against my better judgment, and with my head filled with hot needles, I accepted her scarf, entered the space, and danced a challenge. My estimate was that Pelmore had a thirty-pound advantage over me, for I weigh a mere hundred and eighty pounds. We charged, closed, and he seized the scarf. I whirled around, and we began to spin. Nobody else had lasted more than two turns with Pelmore, but I spun five times before my feet left the floor. I then hung on for two more flying rotations before the scarf actually ripped and I went flying off into the crowd.

By the time a serving maid was helping me back to my feet, Lavenci was dancing with Pelmore. Riellen appeared by my side.

"Are you hurt, sir?" she asked briskly, staring down the serving maid. "It's all right, miss, I am qualified to look after him."

"Ooh, so am I. Not a night goes past when I don't help at least half a dozen fallen drinkers back to their feet."

"I do regret your loss, sir!" barked Riellen.

"It's just a dance, Constable, but I hope she doesn't expect me to pay for the scarf. What is the situation with the healer woman?"

"I'll let you know when she is ready for you," said Riellen, now looking a lot more relaxed.

"Do you think she might fancy me?" I asked teasingly.

"Oh sir! Can you not appreciate merely subliminal esteem?"

By the time the set ended, Pelmore had the scarves of a dozen girls tucked into his belt. As everyone clapped, he held Lavenci's scarf high, signifying that she was his choice to be queen of the tourney. They grasped both hands together while the dancing master tied the remains of Lavenci's trophy scarf around their hands. They were now expected to untie the knot with their teeth, and this was meant to be the opportunity to exchange a kiss. Sorrow clutched at my intestines, even though my mind kept telling me that she was no longer any business of mine.

"It seems that you were the excuse for her to meet the dance champion, sir," declared Riellen.

"I'm from the government, and I'm here to help," I replied with a sneer. "Speaking of service, when will that healer be ready to provide some? If she can blunt my migraine, I may have a chance with that serving maid with the big, um . . ."

"Smile?"

"Ha ha, very funny, yes, the one who helped me up. She did smile at me rather encouragingly, come to think of it. Perhaps if I fell down in her vicinity again?"

"It probably happens a lot, sir."

"What do you have planned for the night, Constable?"

"I shall be reading *How to Win Crowds and Influence Rioters*. It is an excellent—"

"Good, good, you must tell me about it once you have finished," I said hurriedly, rubbing my bruised backside again. I put my hand to my head. "Actually, could you go inside and hurry your healer woman along—oh, and which room am I booked into?"

"Sir, I have you booked into the room with the green door," barked Riellen, then she vanished into the crowd.

Now I sought out Lavenci, who was, predictably, still in the company of Pelmore.

"My apologies, ladyship, but your favor was not up to the strain," I said as I handed the scrap of scarf back to her.

"Oh, do you hear that, mighty Pelmore, he blames my favor for his loss!" she replied very theatrically.

"Had I not already beaten him, I would issue a challenge," laughed Pelmore.

"Oh apologies, mighty lord, beautiful ladyship, I meant no offense," I said as I spread my hands and dropped to one knee. "I am a mere inspector, too rough of manner to know when I cause offense."

"In that case, I forgive you!" said Pelmore grandly.

Technically, he was now in breach of manners. The champion should be strong and fight bravely. His lady's role was to be wise, pass judgment, and bestow forgiveness. On the other hand this was not the royal court in Alberin, so who cared?

"And what do you do to keep shelter over your head, my lord Pelmore?" Lavenci asked her champion.

"I am but a simple wharfmaster, ma'am."

And part-time Inquisition spy, I thought as I sipped at my drink.

"You dance so well, and look so comely," replied Lavenci in a tone that she had certainly never used with me. "Surely you could be some prince in the guise of a wharfmaster."

"No more than you could be a princess in the guise of a merchant's daughter," he said, doing a courtly flourish.

"Why would I take the guise of a commoner were I a princess?"

"For the same reason that I might. To seek sincere and true love, a love that is not clouded by awe for one's position."

There is nothing quite so uninteresting as someone else's courtship banter, so it was at this point that I took my leave of them and sought out the friendly serving maid. I secured a drink from her, and she very pointedly put my copper into her cleavage. She also said that she hoped I would be doing a lot more drinking that night. I assured her that I would, then turned away—and nearly collided with Riellen. She saluted.

"Pleased to report that the woman will await your pleasure in the room with the green door, should you give her a further ten minutes, sir! The fee will be four florins hourly."

I winced, swallowed, and sucked a breath between my teeth.

"Four florins?" I managed, unable to think of any words capable of saving my reputation with the serving maid.

"She is reputed to be very good, sir!" declared Riellen, again saluting smartly. "One of the serving maids told me as much. Will that be all?"

"Yes, yes. Dismissed."

Riellen departed at once. The serving maid took a drink from her tray and flung it in my face, then stormed off. Lavenci and Pelmore now approached me again.

"I see you have charmed a free drink from the serving maid," observed Lavenci, both of them looking mildly amused.

"One might put it that way," I said as I wiped my face, almost nauseous with the pain in my head.

"But that's not the type of charm a lad needs to win a secret princess," said Pelmore, giving all his attention to Lavenci.

"Noble Pelmore, what secret princess could I possibly be?" laughed Lavenci. "As an albino princess I would be recognized at once, no matter what guise I assumed."

"Then a prince in disguise would love you for your beauty alone. Your hair gleams like the ice of the Drakenridge glaciers."

"I have read of those glaciers, you flatter me greatly." She winked conspiratorially. "But this ice-white hue may not even be my hair's natural shade."

"Oh indeed?" he replied. "But there are ways and ways to know such things."

About as subtle as a pig in a pastry shop, I thought. Lavenci put a hand on her waist and tilted her hip slightly in Pelmore's direction.

"Ah, so you wish to know if *all* of my hair is of this color?"

The surprise on my face was probably as bright as a beacon pyre, and Pelmore's eyes certainly widened too. Why should she take words like that from him but not me? Sorrow stabbed through my intestines at least as sharply as the pain in my head. I made a silent resolution to register a complaint with Love next time I was near one of her temples, and to send a cover copy to Romance as well.

"That sight must be one that even gods would die for," sighed Pelmore in reply.

"You are comely enough to be a god," said Lavenci in a silky voice, "but you do not have to die."

Pelmore blushed, and his lips parted slightly, but for once words failed him.

"I'd better leave you to it," I said, raising my mug. "Time for me to crawl off and die somewhere."

Tilting her nose upward and giving a slight sneer, Lavenci dropped the tatty scrap of her scarf into my unfinished mug of wine and minced off on Pelmore's arm. *Oh well, mission accomplished,* I thought as I watched them go with a mixture of desolation and relief.

※ ※ ※

So, that was how some spies got girls to sport with them, I pondered through a haze of pain. I had in fact done a lot of espionage work, but my contacts had all been men. I was fairly sure that a complaint to either my master or the directant of Wayfarers would not improve matters, however. I walked around the corner of the tavern to a quiet spot, sat down on the cobbles, and wiped my face with wine using the scrap of scarf from my mug. Presently I felt well enough to attempt walking, so I stood up very slowly and entered the tavern. Ten minutes, Riellen had said. Had ten minutes passed? I neither knew nor cared.

I took a rack lamp from the hospitality counter, climbed the stairs, and found the green door straightaway. I pressed the latch and strode in—and was confronted with Lavenci sitting on the edge of her bed and removing a boot, and Pelmore in the process of lowering his trews and presenting a view of his hairy backside that caused severe damage to my aesthetic sensibilities. Lavenci screamed and pulled her skirts down over her knees. Pelmore pulled his trews back up and shouted at me to travel to the nethermost circle of all hells and there engage in reproductive activities with one of the more repulsive locals. I backed out hurriedly, and after pulling the door closed behind me, I checked the other doors. I discovered the basis of my mistake.

"Constable Riellen, where are you?" I shouted as I stood in the passageway, passably close to vomiting from raw distress.

"The green door, sir!" she called.

"Riellen, *all* the damn doors are green!"

"Oh, sorry sir, this one," she said, opening the door to the room next to the one I had entered. "Madame Norellie is ready for you."

I entered. A woman of about thirty was sitting on the bed. She had dark, wavy hair that reached down past her breasts, and wore a dress in the style of the windrel women of Acrema. A cord belt emphasised the fact that she had a pleasantly narrow waist, but I was well past appreciating that sort of thing. Riellen knelt down on the floor. She appeared to be writing out a receipt.

"Sir, this is Norellie, and we have negotiated an agreement on a rate of four florins per hour," Riellen said without looking up. "Revolutionary sister, I shall be in Room Eight with the inspector's purse, so knock on my door as you leave and I shall make payment."

"Aye, a constable, is it?" said the woman on the bed with an appraising glance in my direction.

"Inspector, actually," I responded hoarsely.

"Ever do anything brave?"

Norellie had an unusually deep and mellow voice. She also had astonishingly large breasts and an odd, almost rakish demeanor about her bearing. I opened my mouth to reply, but Riellen was quicker.

"Oh Inspector Danol is very brave, he has worked hard with me in the service of the downtrodden and exploited people for three years."

"Aye? Inspector, are you then? I was once a lamplight girl. Ever arrest someone like me?"

"I'm not that sort of inspector," I said, tossing my purse to Riellen for safekeeping.

I took the scrap of scarf from my mug and wiped my forehead again, then put the mug down beside the hearth. It was now that I noticed a regular *creak-gasp* sound coming through the wall.

"Inspector Danol is a servant of the hard-pressed and downtrodden minorities!" continued Riellen.

"Sounds like someone next door is getting pressed down pretty hard," commented Norellie.

"Have you ever thought of forming a healers' collective?" asked Riellen, looking up from her receipt. "You could then organize a healer women's liberation lobby to press for reforms in the laws that oppress you."

"Er, what's a collective?"

"It's like a guild, but all may join as long as they work together. United, you could have a say in the running of Gatrov."

"Us?" she laughed. "A few raggy healer women?"

Through the wall I could hear that Lavenci and Pelmore were making their *creak-gasp* sound in 2/4 time.

"Riellen, can this wait until later?" I asked. "My head feels like—"

"How many like you are there in the district?" asked Riellen, totally focused on her potential revolutionary audience of one.

"A dozen or so healers," replied Norellie, "and maybe a dozen more from the farms and villages who know the arts but work at other things. Busy port, is Gatrov."

"That is a substantial number, sister. Together, you are an important economic force in the town economy."

"Riellen, this woman charges by the hour!" I croaked hopelessly.

"Think of it, sister. Two dozen women who buy food, clothes, and all the other things that towns provide. Taken together you are not to be trifled with. You pay taxes and dues, like everyone else."

"Aye, true," said Norellie, sitting up on my bed and putting her arms around her knees. "I suppose there's even more of us than cobblers, tinkers, or tailors hereabouts."

"I can write out a charter for you."

"Really? Will you?"

"I shall need some details from you first, and you will have to form an electocracy."

"What's an electocracy?"

"It's from the Diomedan word *electrel,* meaning many things acting together."

Realizing that I was being ignored completely, and rather distressed by what felt like a very large, white-hot coal behind my left eye, I backed out of the room. Besides, I was convinced that no charm or spell by even the greatest sorcerer in the world could ease the pain in less time than it would take for the dance outside to end. The *creak-gasp* from Room Ten was lancing through my head like a volley of hot needles, and nausea was getting a pretty good grip on me as well. It was not until I was back in the taproom and returning my lamp that I remembered tossing my purse to Riellen. Rather than bother to go back to fetch it, I just continued on out to the stables.

I collapsed in some hay after dousing my head in the horse trough. The windows from the upstairs rooms looked out over the stables, and they were all open because of the night being very warm. The *grrrok-snurf* of snores came from Roval's room at the end, someone was playing "The Balasra Hayricks" on a whistle in the next, *creak-gasp* was announc-

ing what was going on in Room Ten, while "... the principles of electocratic liberation from the monarchistic oli-
garchy that oppresses the freedom-loving..." was
emanating from the window of what was supposed to be my
room. One the positive side, nobody was in Riellen's room,
and the remaining five upstairs windows were on the other
side of the building, looking out over the street and the
dance.

A horse began to nibble at the hay that I was lying on. I got
to my knees, shuffled over to the muck-out trough, and threw
up copiously. This induced brilliantly flashing lights behind
my eyes, and waves of pain like storm surges of white-hot
needles. I felt a serious need to die rather than face any more
of the headache. For a time I hit my head against the side of
the muck-out trough to the beat of *creak-gasp*, then lay exhausted on the ground while Riellen explained to the woman
who was supposed to be healing me that "... authoritarian re-
pression of women of independent means can be overcome by
means of solidarity!" The pain intensified further, and was
soon so bad that I felt as if my mind were detaching itself
from my body to escape. Somewhere nearby, a horse voided
its bowels. One of my boots was closer to the site of impact
than I would have preferred, but somehow that was no longer
a serious issue for me.

"Mee-ow! Mee-ow!" echoed out nearby in Wallas's characteristic tone, in time with *creak-gasp*, and *grrrok-snurf* of the
snores. After a minute someone from the adjoining building
instructed Wallas to "Gerroutavereyabassardt!" and this was
followed by the crash of breaking glass.

"2042 Halsborn, you're drinking cheap!" shouted Wallas,
before reverting to cat language. More bottles, jars, and abuse
followed.

At around this time some couple arrived and sought the discretion of the hayloft to do something rather indiscreet. They
were panting heavily, and had presumably arrived from the
dance, but they too turned out to be noisy lovemakers.
Through waves of pain I suddenly realized that all of the
sounds had somehow locked into the 2/4 time of the "The Balasra Hayricks," in a fantastical concerto of *grunt-gasp, creak-
gasp,* "Mee-ow!," "Gerrovaere!," *crash-tinkle,* and *grrrok-snurf.*

I felt myself drifting off toward either unconsciousness or death, and was not really concerned about which of the two it might be.

I awoke on a darkened riverbank, lying on black grass. As I sat up I noted that the pain behind my eye was gone. That was good. Nearby was a stone pier, flanked by a small black tower topped by a burning torch, and beyond that was absolute darkness. That was bad. Tied up at the pier was a snowy white punt garlanded with primroses, and with a small toy bear dressed as a sailor tied to the bow. That was unexpected, but I was nevertheless fairly sure that I was dead.

"Oh shyte, I thought that last migraine felt like a real killer," I muttered aloud.

A figure materialized out of the darkness, a woman wearing a red gown that was slit all the way up to her waist, and whose breasts were not so much covered as vaguely supported by some skimpy red lacing. She reminded me of a woman who had run an establishment in Palion, and whose girls charged a hundred florins an hour—and where I had once conducted a business transaction because I was rather lonely and it seemed like a good idea at the time. The figure before me carried a picnic basket on one arm, and had a white ferry pole over her other shoulder. I got to my feet hurriedly and bowed.

"Danolarian, you once served with my Andry in the Wayfarer Constables," she declared as I stood before her, apprehensive yet dumbfounded. "Sit down, young man, sit down. Creamcake? I mix honey in with the cream."

"I—er, thank you. I know Andry's had a lass or two, but he's never mentioned you, Madame Death—or is it Lady Death?"

"Ferrygirl, actually. I was once Madame Jilli of Palion."

"*That's* where I know you from!"

"Oh very good! You were the young reccon who had just survived some awful battle and was celebrating still being alive. You paid for Rosita's bliss and serenity services, then just took her out to dinner, walked her back to my front door, and kissed her goodnight."

"Er, I—"

"I felt really terrible about that, but by the time Rosita had explained and I ran outside to persuade you to stay, you were gone."

"I just wanted company, not an orgy—"

"But I'll make it up to you, now that I have died and become the ferrygirl. Wine?"

"Yes please—no, I mean . . . Look, how long before you ferry me to . . . wherever I'm going?"

"About sixty years."

"What? You mean I'm not dead?"

"No."

"Then what am I doing here?"

"I told you, I want to make up for that night with Rosita, three years ago. When you return to your body, your migraine will be past."

"And will everyone be quiet?"

"Certainly."

"Even the albino lady and her blond bedmate?"

"Oh yes. Poor girl, growing up in the shadow of her mother and sister like that. You would not believe what a burden presses down upon her."

"It was Pelmore by the sound of it."

"Pah, in another time, and in your reality, Pelmore is already leaving Lavenci's bed in shame and disgrace."

"Really? It sounded to me like he gave her the ride of her life."

"The girl's plight is worse than Pelmore's. You can help her."

"What? Me? Er, what is her plight?"

"Were you dead, I might be tempted to tell you . . . but you are alive, so I cannot."

With that Madame Jilli rolled about on the black grass, giggling hysterically and exposing vast amounts of shapely, bone-white leg. Then she rested her chin on her hand and smiled at me in a very sly and inscrutable fashion.

"Dalliance is as easy as rolling on top of me, young man. You may do so if you want proof of my words."

"Look, given the circumstances, I'd not be at my best. I mean, nothing personal, but I like a bit of fun and seduction first, not just mechanical jiggery."

"What do you think?" asked the ferrygirl, now looking past me.

"*You may go now,*" declared a soft but terrifyingly strong voice behind me.

The ferrygirl faded from sight, and I turned to see . . . well, I cannot relate what I saw. It was like making love: I felt, saw, heard, and even savored the presence that confronted me.

"*You know who I am, Danolarian.*"

"You are Love?" I ventured.

"*Close, I am Romance. Love and Seduction wanted to be here too, but together we would have overwhelmed you.*"

"Er, ah, honored to meet you."

"*Danolarian, be at ease. I am very pleased with you. I am just here to tell you that making love is easy, but making friends is much harder.*"

"With respect, ladyship, I've been finding invitations to make love few and far between, of late," I managed, then immediately regretted my coarse words.

"*Danolarian, you worry about how people feel, and that is very rare. You are a good friend to those close to you . . . but even you need more than a friend sometimes. You need this.*"

Her face loomed before my eyes, I felt lips against mine, all warm, live softness, tingling and silky smooth.

"*Your body is past the worst of your migraine,*" she announced after some indeterminate length of time, "*and your life is past the worst of its nightmares. I shall send you back, but first I have a question.*"

"Er, is this one of those riddles that gets me rowed over to the afterlife if I get it wrong?" I asked nervously.

"*Oh no, it is just something I want to know. Even a goddess cannot know everything.*"

"Ask, then."

"*Why did you choose 'Evening's All for Courting' when you played the sun down on Alpindrak? We divinities all thought you would play 'Farewell the Day.'*"

"Is there *anyone, anywhere,* alive or dead, god or mortal,

who does not know that I played the sun down on Alpindrak?"
I exclaimed.

"I believe it was my turn to ask a question," Romance
replied huffily.

"Oh yes, sorry. Well, I suppose I just don't like farewells, I
prefer to look forward to meetings and assignations."

*"I see, how very romantic. You are definitely in my favor.
For answering my question, I shall give you some advice in return. Act with honor, even when the entire world screams at
you to act with common sense."*

"But I have lived my life by common sense, ladyship."

*"Indeed, but now it is time to stop. I am Romance, remem-
ber? Common sense and I have little in common. Remember,
too, what I said earlier: the worst of your nightmares are over.
Go now, return, I am watching over you. . . ."*

I was awakened by Pelmore falling over me in the shadows of
the stable floor. In the weak light I saw him aim a barefoot
kick at what he thought he had tripped over. This turned out to
be a wooden pail of horse droppings, and he spent some moments gasping, cursing, and hopping about holding his foot. I
noticed that he was dressed only in his trews, and speculated
that he might have been ejected from Lavenci's room in something of a hurry, hopefully for some matter of failed perfor-
mance. He snatched up his scattered possessions, then put on
his tunic, coat, and boots. Finally he hoisted his pack and
limped away to climb the wall of the stable yard. Dawn was
definitely in progress; there was no mistaking the soft glow
from the sky and general stillness.

I heard a giggle from the hayloft—then realized that my
headache was gone! The nicest thing about migraine
headaches is how good everything feels when they stop. They
are a bit like the reverse of a hangover: pain first, then bliss.
For a time I lay there, contemplating a vivid, even lurid,
dream involving an encounter with the Ferrygirl on the banks
of the river between life and death, then a kiss from Romance,
the very goddess herself. Romance. I struggled to recall her

form, but could visualize only wavy black hair cascading down past the waist of an hourglass figure, and lips that filled the entire world.

It was, of course, a dream, yet it had been curiously real as dreams go. There was the taste of honey and pastries on my lips as I licked them. Kissed by Romance. Why me? Oddly enough, I had dreamed that Pelmore would slink away from Lavenci's bed . . . but was that so surprising? Falling in love is easy, the tricky bit is crawling out again.

It was now that another vision approached me. It was that of a woman I had once escorted, Terikel, and she was dressed as a Metrologan priestess. Faint blue light spilled from her eyes and mouth, and the glare shadowed her face almost beyond recognition. I could feel considerable heat as a clawed hand stretched out to hover above my face.

"The young and gallant reccon," declared a voice like dry leaves thrown onto glowing coals. "You are not the one."

I squeezed my eyes shut in an extended blink, and when I opened them again she was gone. Heat. Claws. *Could she have been something to do with Gilvray's murder?* I wondered. Had she even been real?

Feeling somewhat disoriented, I entered the darkened tavern, climbed the stairs, made my way along the corridor—and fell straight over Riellen, who had apparently been waiting for me beside my door but had fallen asleep.

"Sir, sir, Norellie is ready for you," she whispered as we both got to our feet.

"Are you sure?" I muttered. "No more political theory, consciousness raising, representative-election principles, or organizational solidarity for working women against male-dominated societal infrastructures?"

"Oh! So you were close enough to hear?"

"Yes! I was down in the stables, having a migraine headache that bordered on a near-death experience, and you had the window open. I also heard more than I really wanted to from two copulating couples, Roval snoring, a drunk whistle player trying to learn 'The Balasra Hayricks,' a serenading tomcat named Wallas, and someone throwing bottles at him. Oh, and a horse shat on my boot."

"Sir, I am *so* sorry. In my zeal I forgot that you were in ex-

treme distress—but Madame Norellie did say she had a powerful herbal infusion bag that you might use next time. She's still
in your room with the lamp burning, reading my copy of—"

"She is?"

"Hurry in, sir, she is waiting to treat you."

"Riellen, why bother? My migraine's peak has passed. I
am currently feeling a little wrung out, but otherwise well."

I pushed open the door. Madame Norellie was curled up on
my bed, and Riellen's book was beside her, open at page one.
I stared at her with my hands on my hips for a moment, then
shook my head.

"Is there a problem, sir?" whispered Riellen.

"Riellen, she's asleep."

Riellen returned my purse. I counted out four silver florins,
placed them on the pillow beside the healer's head, then
turned away for the door.

"Sir, four florins is very high payment for, well, nothing at
all," Riellen whispered. "I'll just wake her—"

"No! She looks rather sweet asleep, I'd prefer not to disturb
her—and *you* wasted several hours of her time with your collective electocracy rubbish."

"Sir, I . . . oh. Again, my apologies."

"Well next time, think!"

I picked up my change of clothing, then took Riellen by the
back of her collar and marched her out of the room.

"It's past dawn," I said as we reached the stairs. "We are going down to the stables, where *I* am stripping off these clothes
and *you* are going to pour a couple of pails of water over me
as I wash. You are then taking my clothes down to the market
and having a laundress wash them, to make up for what you
made me endure a few hours ago."

"Sir, I shall pay for it out of—"

"Riellen, shut up."

"Sir!"

"I'll then be riding out to investigate that falling star from
yesterday evening. You are coming with me."

I checked Roval's room before I left for the market. There
were seven empty wine jars on the floor. Roval was on the
floor too. I decided that if he had not been in a fit state to find
his own bed, he would not be of much use finding a fallen star.

Chapter Five

THE CYLINDER OPENS

 I met with the ostler Grem at the stablers row in the market. There I bought breakfast for both of us, and he provided a jar of wine for the journey. I hired an extra horse for Riellen, and as it happened, the stablers row was beside a speakers wall. There were walls like this in every market in the empire, and they were meant to be where prophets, lunatics, and deranged agitators could blow off steam and rhetoric harmlessly while being ridiculed by idlers. They were also where disguised agents of the local magistrates sometimes lurked in search of those preaching treason. Riellen was there as I arrived, and as usual, incitement to affray was her strong point.

Riellen viewed any crowd with an almost erotic longing. If people were gathered, she had to tell them something. It did not seem to matter what the message was, it was the act of telling that appealed to her. Handing out pamphlets was also rather high on her list of favored vices.

The ostler and I were actually with our horses and about to mount up when Riellen climbed onto the speakers wall and waved a sheaf of pamphlets. She had her constable's coat inside out, and thus resembled an artisan, but her hair was unbound and it was obvious to the onlookers that she was female. She wore her spectacles halfway down her nose, as a sort of declaration that she could read—and thus that she spoke with added authority. With one hand on her hip and the other raised above her head and waving the pamphlets, she began to speak.

"Brothers! Sisters! You all know me! You all know why I'm here!"

Nobody in fact knew her, and certainly nobody knew why she was there. A dozen or so idlers began to move in her direction to try to find out who she might be, and why she was actually there. Besides, female speakers were very rare, so she also had novelty value.

"For too long you have been taxed without any say in how your taxes are spent," she continued. "What does the regent know about your needs? What does *any* king know about *any* commoner's needs? Does the regent care about the pothole in Featherheap Lane? Does he know that the north end of this wall is crumbling?"

There were the inevitable jeers and catcalls, but they were peppered with cries of "She's right!"

"Who knows best where the taxes and levies should be spent?" demanded Riellen of the crowd, which had by now been swelled to about a hundred by the relative novelty of a woman skirting the borders of treason. "*You* do! *You,* the vendors, marketeers, and honest folk of the town who come here to buy and trade. *You* know how to spend taxes where they need to be spent. *Not* the regent! *You,* the *citizens*! *You* must have a say in spending your taxes. Each of you must have a *vote.* If you had to vote on whether to spend taxes on a new crown for the regent or repairing this wall, what would you vote for?"

A general groundswell of "The wall! The wall!" now competed with the jeers.

"Should it be a new gold ring for the regent or filling the pothole in Featherheap Lane?"

"The pothole! The pothole!" overwhelmed the jeers; in fact, several of those jeering were now being shoved and cuffed by those around them.

"So, are you going to just stand there, and take it lying down?" demanded Riellen. "What must be done? Ask yourselves! *What must be done?*"

Riellen intended her audience to pause for thought. The pause was meant to be just long enough for them to realize that they did not have the answer.

"This is what you must do!" she declared, brandishing her sheaf of handwritten pamphlets. "Form a neighborhood issues group. *Vote* for a *delegate. Vote* on what must be repaired. *Vote* on *every injustice* that must be addressed. *Scribe* it onto a notice. *Post* it on the market bulletin board. But here is a warning. *Never, never* accept an invitation to meet with great lords.

That is their way of *finding* your leaders, *seizing* your leaders, and *killing* your leaders."

Riellen began to fling her ten handwritten pamphlets into the by now eager crowd.

"But what if our notice is ignored?" bawled a costermonger from the back.

"Yeah, we got no army ter back up our words," shouted a fishwife near the front.

"But the regent has one, Miss, er—" began the costermonger.

"Riellen!" called someone who was holding a pamphlet, and could apparently read.

"Then, brothers and sisters, you must form *voters' militias* to defend yourselves!" shouted Riellen, waving both fists in the air.

"But who would tell us what to do after that?" called the costermonger.

"You must *vote* for a *presiding officer,* a leader to put your decisions into action. A *presidian*! But that is in the future. For now you must elect a market delegate, and a market delegate committee."

"Well I votes fer Miss Riellen as delegate!" bellowed the costermonger passionately. "Who votes aye, Miss Riellen fer delegate?"

"Aye, Miss Riellen for delegate!" roared most of the crowd, which was by now in the vicinity of a thousand souls.

"No, no, brothers and sisters, you don't understand," called the suddenly alarmed Riellen. "I am not one of you, I am only spreading the message of electocracy. You must vote for one of your own people, one whom you know and trust, and who understands the issues here."

"The town militia!" cried someone above the tumult. "The town militia is coming!"

"Stop them, don't let them take Miss Riellen!" called the costermonger.

✳ ✳ ✳

No single person had a complete picture of what happened next. The militia had probably been told that a riot was in progress, and once they arrived at the outskirts of Riellen's crowd, a riot most certainly did erupt. Canes, swagger sticks, staffs, knives, and stones met the militiamen's reversed street axes, spears, and shields, yet there were a mere score of militiamen against the hundreds in Riellen's audience. What was certain was that the audience carried the day, then dispersed before a hundred lancers rode in from Castle Gatrov wearing full armor and brandishing field axes.

By now I had managed to get hold of Riellen, bind up her hair, get her constable's coat reversed again and back onto her, rub dirt onto her face, and heave her onto her horse. We rode out past the cultivated fields for the forest with the ostler, but were not pursued.

"Do you really believe all that rubbish?" asked the ostler as we traveled.

"Yes, I do!" muttered Riellen. "It makes a lot of sense."

"It's a wonder nobody was killed back there," I grumbled. "If the town magistrate ever catches up with you, it will be on-the-spot execution for incitement to affray."

"Affray is only what you define it to be," began Riellen.

"As long as you happen to be the magistrate," I countered.

"Please, no more politics!" pleaded the ostler.

"I shall begin a new speech tonight," declared Riellen. "It will contain a plea for the people to support the sorcerers and initiates against persecution from the ignorant and greedy monarchs who fund the Sorceric Inquisition."

"Sounding like borderline incitement to affray," I sighed. "Words like you used today are liable to get a lot of important people upset."

"Oh I can do better than that," said Riellen proudly. "Listen to this: *Voters must understand that sorcerers are not their enemies. The sorcerers who built the terrible ether weapon, Dragonwall, are all dead. The sorcerers and initiates who the Inquisition now persecutes are the very sorcerers who opposed Dragonwall! They are good sorcerers, and friends of voters. Allow the Inquisition to kill all sorcerers, and we shall be at the mercy of rogue sorcerers from beyond Alberin and Scalticar. Hide the brave, loyal sorcerers of Scalticar, oppose the oppressive killers who sit on thrones and squander the taxes and levies bled from the hardworking voters who are the lifeblood of the continent.*"

"I rest my case," I commented. "Now then, Constable Riellen, I am your commander, and I command you to *stop talking politics*. Is that understood?"

"Yes sir," she replied reluctantly.

"Is she really a Wayfarer Constable?" hissed the ostler as Riellen dropped a little behind.

"Mind your own business," I muttered.

"Oh sir, I spoke to Madame Norellie this morning," called Riellen. "You should have stayed and spoken with her last night."

"Riellen, how was I supposed to get a word in edgeways while you were sitting there explaining voting procedures for the Electocratic Collective of, er—"

"Entertainment and Therapeutic Artisans, sir. I completed a charter for them before I went to sleep."

"Does the constitution include a clause for talking politics all night on the client's time?"

"No, but—"

"Did you, at any stage, ask her if she was willing to stay and listen to your radical political theories without payment?"

"Er . . . no. But sir, she did seem sincere, and genuinely interested. I shall restore the four florins from my own purse, that is, when I have saved enough to—"

"Never mind."

For all the infuriating peculiarity of Riellen's ideas and beliefs, I kept talking to her for the rest of the ride to the fallen star. Silence meant that thoughts of Lavenci would come flooding back. Lavenci sitting on the edge of her bed and undressing for her lover of the night, Lavenci's gasp for every creak of her bed, all in 2/4 time, and as always, my hand being slapped away from her breast.

The cylinder had fallen to earth about seven miles west of the town, and near the edge of Waingram Forest. It had come down at a shallow angle, smashing a path through farmland fences, hedgerows, and isolated trees for fully three hundred yards, before splashing into the rich, dark earth of the ploughed fields. It had come to rest half buried at the end of a long ditch of its own making.

There were two hundred or so people gathered about the ditch, mostly peasants from nearby estates, but there were also several nobles and merchants on well-groomed horses. I appeared to be the most senior member of any civil enforcement service present.

Riellen and I declared ourselves to a couple of members of the local farmland watch as we pushed our way through the crowd. People not only made way for us, they even muttered words along the lines of "Took yer bloody time gettin' te scene!" A Skeptical preacher was standing at the north edge of the ditch, performing a superstition exorcism, while on the south side a priest of the Brotherhood of the Great White Ram was chanting a healing prayer for the wound in the soil. Beside him was a rather stern-looking man wearing a sign declaring THE END IS NYE, and beside him was an equally stern woman whose sign merely read REPONT.

The cylinder was fifteen feet in diameter, from what I could see. Recalling its shape from when it had flown overhead, I estimated the length to be at least fifty feet. The shape suggested an egg that had been stretched to several times its former length. A river barge would be about the same size, yet the idea that it might be a vessel did not occur to me at once. It was still warm, for the loam around it was steaming. Its bright orange color gave the impression that it was glowing like a live coal.

"What I wants to know is who pays for fence and sheep's shade trees?" said a peasant in a lamb-docking smock as we stood there taking in the scene.

"Well yes, and these are *my* lands that have been gouged," said a rather elaborately dressed peasant beside him. "What I want to know is, who should be prosecuted?"

"An act of the gods, Viscount," suggested the ostler.

"That's all very well, my man, but gods are notoriously hard to serve with a writ," replied the better-dressed peasant. From his collar crest I now deduced that he really was a ludicrously dressed viscount.

I had the impression that the man did not get away from his

estates and tenant farmers very much. He wore a burgundy work tunic of fine wool, over which was a half smock of red silk, and his grubby gloves were kid leather. His work clogs were of the same Acreman mahogany as was used for expensive bagpipes. Obviously all this impressed the peasants who surrounded him, but I suspected that he was not the laughingstock of his peers only because he had little to do with them.

"What do you think, Constable?" I asked Riellen.

One glance at the cylinder told anyone without serious eyesight problems that it was not a meteorite. Meteorites are irregular and pitted, but this one was smoothly rounded and symmetrical.

"Looks to be an immense egg" was all that she could suggest.

"What manner of bird has a bum big enough to lay that?" asked the ostler.

"A dragon, perhaps," I suggested.

"A dragon? But it looks to be five yards across. For a dragon to lay an egg of that size, it would have to be, er . . ."

"A hen twelve inches high can lay an egg two inches long," I said. "From what I remember of this egg flying over last night, I would say it is three or four times longer than its diameter . . . so six times fifty feet is a reasonable estimate for the creature that laid it."

"Six times fifty is . . . er . . . um . . ."

"That is a three-hundred-foot dragon, sir," said Riellen diplomatically.

We all glanced fearfully to the sky for a moment, but no three-hundred-foot dragon with wings half a mile across was diving upon us. Those who had been standing close enough to hear now hurried away to spread our theory to anyone who would listen.

"A dragon, you say?" the viscount asked in a tremulous voice.

"I can't be certain," I replied hastily. "We need a sorcerer to look at it."

"Allus knew it were a bad idea te kill all our sorcerers," said the peasant in the smock, waving in the direction of the thing from the sky.

"What I want to know is what is the empress doing about it?" demanded the ostler.

"She's vanished, Regent Corozan is running the country," I explained.

"Well, what's the regent doing about it?"

"I'm the regent's representative," I said reluctantly.

"Well, what are *you* doing about it?"

I put my hands on my hips and glanced over the scene with the professional skill of someone whose life often depends on assessing a dangerous situation quickly and accurately.

"Riellen, go to those boys who are throwing stones at the egg," I said, pointing along the ditch. "Send them on their way—and stop that clown splashing exorcism oil on it."

The viscount, ostler, and peasant fell in with me as I descended into the pit. Somehow having someone—anyone—take charge seems to always allay people's fears. Confront a leaderless crowd of two hundred with three or four well-led militiamen waving riot sticks, and they will scatter. Give that same crowd a leader, then confront it with a three-hundred-foot-long dragon breathing white-hot hellfire, and it will attack. In the latter case the crowd will get itself collectively reduced to a puff of smoke, but it will do so heroically. Thus I found myself in charge, and obliged to examine what nobody else was quite willing to approach. For some perverse reason I suddenly wanted to be the first to touch the cylinder.

"With respect, sir, best I go first," I said to the viscount. "No sense losing a nobleman should the worst happen."

He was all in favor of that, and thus I was the first to step out onto the cylinder. Squatting down, I lowered my hand to the surface very slowly. It was about as hot as a slate roof at noon on a summer's day, and was covered in oxidation that had the texture of waterworn granite. It was a uniform deep orange in color, and for some reason this now made me think of the moonworld Lupan. *The very same color as its deserts,* I thought. *Could there be a connection? Perhaps a dragon from Lupan flew across the gulf between our two moonworlds.*

"Seems safe enough," I called.

"What do you make of it?" the viscount asked.

"This might well be from Lupan," I suggested. "Scholars of the cold sciences think there might be creatures living there."

"A dragon from Lupan? Why come all this way to lay an egg?"

"Storm cranes spend the winter in northern Acrema, yet fly here to nest in spring," I pointed out. "Perhaps dragons fly here from Lupan to lay their eggs."

"We'd have noticed if this happened before. I mean a three-hundred-foot dragon is bound to draw attention to itself."

"They may only do it every ten thousand years."

"Well, where is the dragon?"

"They might be like turtles. They lay their eggs and then abandon them."

"I say, do you mean to say that a dragon from Lupan will hatch on *my* estate?" exclaimed the viscount in a voice that had suddenly lost all trace of fear.

"Could be. Make friends with the chick, and you could ride it all the way to Lupan when it grows up."

My words were meant as a joke, but the nobleman took them seriously. He jumped from the torn soil onto the cylinder, and his peasant tenant was close behind him.

"I say, this egg from Lupan did come down on my land," he pointed out to us, "and thus it is my egg."

"My leasehold!" cried the peasant, pointing at the soil. "*My* egg."

"I hereby claim this bounty as my property under the Marine Salvage Act of 2877," the viscount declared, even though the object had fallen from the sky and we were several days' journey from the sea, even a couple of hours by horse from the river. "All of you, get away from it!"

"Smashed me bleedin' wall," declared the peasant. "I demands compreysation."

"I could fashion a saddle for you to ride the young dragon," suggested the ostler to the viscount. "Of course it would involve more work and materials than a common saddle."

"Ah, really? Would it be safe?"

"Lordship, my work's guaranteed."

"I 'ad seeds planted in this 'ere field, and now it's rooned!" interjected the peasant.

"I would want gold studs in the leather," said the viscount.

"And there's the damage to me wall, trees, an' hedgerows," insisted the peasant.

It was about now that I felt the first tremor through the soles of my boots. The viscount, ostler, and peasant felt it too, for they fell silent at once. There was another tremor, or rather more of a heavy thud. The thuds became regular, at about the rhythm of someone chopping wood.

"It's a-hatchin'!" shouted the peasant, jumping from the cylinder and scrambling up the side of the ditch. "Run fer yer lives! Dragon hatchin'!"

Many of the crowd had overheard our earlier conversation about this being a dragon's egg, and our words had been spread to the others very quickly. Thus the peasant's cry of "Dragon hatchin'!" conveyed a pretty strong sense of alarm in an instant. The crowd shrank back—but it did not flee. The threat of danger was finely balanced by the chance to see something interesting happen in a place where the highlight of the social calendar was the beer-barrel race at the Gatrov Annual Fair.

It was now that I noticed that oxidation was falling away from the end of the cylinder. I stepped onto the soil beside it and looked more closely. The thing was actually a stretched teardrop, and a circular endpiece was gradually being screwed out of the structure. There was a hissing sound, and putting out my hand, I could feel air escaping. I could also smell the familiar reek of tar, and of something else. Tar was used to caulk the seams of ships, to make them watertight. *Bodies,* I thought suddenly. *That's the other smell: stale sweat.* Very unusual sweat, but definitely sweat. It had once smelled like that on the ship, when I had been bunked belowdecks with the other crewmen on the long voyage over from the doomed continent of Torea.

Suddenly I knew what the cylinder was. The thing contained air and was sealed tight with tar. It had flown between moonworlds, where there was little or no air, and the air that was now escaping smelled as if folk had been living in it for a score of days. It was just then that Riellen scrambled down to stand beside me.

"Sir, may I respectfully advise you to climb up to the edge of the ditch, then instruct everyone to run away very fast?" she said softly, while tugging at my arm.

"A voidship, carrying voidfarers," I whispered to her, coining the two words and speaking them for the very first time on our world. "This is an entrance hatch. There are voidfarers from Lupan inside, trying to get out."

I reached out and picked up some flakes of oxidation that had fallen to the soil. Around the section that was unscrewing I could see what seemed to be gleaming white porcelain, and more was being exposed with every thud from within.

"First creature the chick sees, that's the one it will take for its mother," the ostler was saying to the viscount.

"Is that so?" the nobleman cried. "I say, you there! Wayfarer Constables! Get away from there, get out of the ditch! This dragon is mine, you hear? All mine!"

I climbed out with Riellen, keeping the hatchway in sight all the while.

"The Lupanians seem to be having trouble opening the hatch, sir," she commented.

"I've seen that with hatch seals aboard ships in the tropics. The tar seal softens in the heat of the day, then sticks tight in the night's chill. Some voidfarer is battering it open from inside with a hammer."

My theory was confirmed when a dark band of tar became visible, then another, and then a third. Roughly half a foot of banded porcelain was by now visible. It was a voidship of porcelain, whose hull was a foot thick.

I took out my farsight and focused on the hatch. At that very moment the hatch cover popped loose and tumbled onto the soil. On its underside I could see three pairs of heavy lugs, which had obviously been attached to levers inside during the voyage. The viscount peered into the opening.

"Cheepy, cheepy, cheepy, hullo!" he cried. "I'm your daddy. Don't be afraid."

For some reason I had expected it to be dark inside the voidship, but it was internally lit and I could see a hint of mechanisms inside. For an instant I saw something moving; then a sort of tube on an articulated arm emerged. A flat mirror in the tube surveyed the scene around the opening. Even at this early stage I concluded that this was some sort of viewer device like a farsight or a children's periscope toy. Suddenly a tentacle lashed out of the opening, wrapped itself around the viscount's chest, then lifted him into the air. With a deft flick it then dashed his brains out against the side of the voidship.

It took a moment for the event to register with the onlookers, myself included; then a bedlam of screams, shouts, and shrieks erupted all around me. Several hunters from the forest hurriedly strung their bows as the ostler leaped for the side of the ditch and began scrambling up. The crowd shrank away from the edge, but did not break and run. Unfortunately for the ostler, he was visible from the hatchway. Some thirty or forty feet of tentacle poured out to snare his leg, and he had time for a single, terrified shriek before he was dispatched in the same manner as the viscount.

Arrows shot by the hunters began to clatter against the hull, and at least two flew true to enter the hatch. More tentacles emerged, and two of them held a globe. This was perhaps eighteen inches in diameter. For some reason I had thought that the Lupanians would know nothing of magic and merely be vastly superior in the cold sciences, but this globe was definitely a magical casting. It seemed to be a tangle of glowing orange and red worms, but unlike the bright blue castings of our own sorcerers, it gave off bright green smoke, along with a low, heavy rumble that hinted at titanic, pent-up energies.

There was a sizzling crackle, like a drop of fat falling onto hot coals; then the hunters on the edge of the ditch began to flash into flame and collapse. My soldiering instincts took over, and I turned to run. I saw Riellen some yards away, decided that the half second available before the weapon swung around to roast us was not enough for explanations, then leaped and brought her down. In deciding to save Riellen's life, it turned out that I saved my own life as well.

My tackle not only brought her down, it knocked the wind from her lungs. We lay still as those fleeing past us were burned down, and I felt something disturbingly hot passing just above me. Because my head had come down on its side, I could see the magical globe held high over the lip of the ditch, directed by the farsight as it turned in a full circle. The left side of my forehead had been cut open on Riellen's ax, which was still in her belt. Abruptly the crackling sound stopped, leaving only the deep throbbing. The viewing-tube thing did another complete sweep of the field, and then both devices were lowered back into the ditch.

All was quite silent at first; then I heard thudding and clanging from down in the ditch.

"Riellen, nod if you are all right," I whispered.

She nodded. Very slowly, I turned my head. A year as a mercenary in Acrema and three more as a Wayfarer in Scalticar had taught me to always note the nearest cover wherever I happened to be, no matter where it was. At the Wayfarer's annual picnic I looked for trees to dodge behind if necessary, and in taverns I noted the closest table to dive beneath. Thus I was aware that there was a stream running through the field, and that it was about thirty yards away. The water was a foot below the level of the field, so it could be cover.

"Riellen, I want you to crawl for that stream ahead of us, directly north," I whispered. "Do not raise yourself up, and only move one limb at a time. I'll try to keep myself between you and that heat-weapon thing. Is all that clear?"

She nodded again, and we began to crawl. It must have taken twenty minutes to reach cover, but finally we eased ourselves down into the chilly water.

"What happened, sir?" asked Riellen as we waded away, doubled over. "I saw tentacles come out of the egg—er, voidship."

"The beings from Lupan may be intelligent beings, but they also seem to be particularly dangerous intelligent beings."

After about half a mile of wading along in the stream, we reached a stone arch bridge. From the shelter of this we straightened and looked back across the field. A large part of the forest nearby was burning, as was every hedgerow, haystack, bush, tree, and cottage roof in a circle as far as we could discern. Nothing moved. Every person, horse, sheep, and cow had been cut down. Greenish smoke was rising from the ditch.

Suddenly I became aware of a third presence beside us.

"What sorts of friggin' magic were that?" rumbled a voice almost too deep for me to understand.

I turned, to be confronted by a bridge troll. It was about my height, but was far more powerfully built, and was covered in coarse hair. About its loins was a scrap of something that looked a bit like tatters of decayed waterweed, but was probably leather. It carried . . . well, there is no word for a weapon that consists of a length of wood with a large rock tied to one end by whiskery rope.

"Those are sorcerers from the moonworld Lupan," I replied.

"Oooh. Don't they know sorcery's banned 'ere in Scalticar?"

"Feel free to pop over and tell them," I replied, turning back in the direction of the cylinder.

"Rather not. Melted a line in the stones of me bridge, they did."

"I doubt they will be paying compensation," I suggested.

"They are imperialist Lupanian sorcerers, come to oppress the freedom-loving people—and trolls—of our moonworld," declared Riellen.

"And kill them," I added. "That thing in the field is a void-faring ship."

"Oi Hrrglrrp, what's about up there?" called a voice from the reeds.

"Imperialist oppressors from Lupan," the troll called back.

"They look like ordinary folk to me."

"Nah, they's those in the voidfarin' ship what ploughed inter Mucktailer's field last night."

We were joined by another six trolls, all of whom looked much the same—apart from the varying amounts of slime and mud adhering to them.

"What I want to know is what's the govvyment doin' abaht it?" asked a newcomer.

Riellen took a deep breath.

"The oppressive regime of the regent in Alberin has no interest in alleviating the sufferings of the freedom-loving people of—mmph!"

"The regent does not know about this yet," I explained, keeping a hand firmly clamped over Riellen's mouth.

"Who's she then?" asked the one whose name sounded rather like a drunk being sick.

"We're Wayfarer Constables," I explained, then added, "Inspector Danolarian and Constable Riellen of the Wayfarer Constables."

"Are ye then? We're civil servants too. Customs, excise, and toll collectors, we are."

"So you're toll trolls?" I asked.

"Aye. Collection's been contracted out. Why pay for a customs man who needs a cottage, firewood, holidays, an' all, when us bridge trolls is happy ter do the job fer five percent of takin's and live-in muck? Everyone gotta use bridges, and we already lives beneath 'em."

"Well take my advice and don't try to charge those characters from Lupan anything should they want to use the bridge," I said as I removed my hand from Riellen's mouth. "Come along, Constable, time to be leaving."

" 'Ere, Inspector, sir," Hrrglrrp called after me. "Ain't you the one who played the sun down on Alpindrak?"

✳ ✳ ✳

We followed the stream until a low hill cut us off from the line of sight of the ditch and its cylinder from Lupan. Soaked, covered with reeking silt, and shivering with cold, we cut across a newly ploughed field to a road, then ran as hard as our lungs and legs would allow for the shelter of Bald Pate Hill. Here we requisitioned an elderly plough horse that had been hobbled and set out to graze. The horse was not happy about carrying the two of us, but for Riellen and I it was vastly superior to running.

There was an abandoned castle with a ruined tower a mile from the cylinder, and it was here that we stopped. Climbing the stone stairs that wound around the outside of the tower, I pointed out a line about an inch wide where the heat weapon had glazed the surface of the stone and reduced the moss growing on it to ash. With my farsight I was able to see the ditch, and I could just make out that the arm holding the viewing tube was now fully extended and keeping watch above the cylinder.

"Lucky we crawled away when we did," I told Riellen. "They've posted a sentry now."

I have since learned that the tentacles' control mechanism had still been inside the voidship and blocking the hatchway during the initial massacre. The heat-casting and viewing tube had been withdrawn so that the Lupanians could partly disassemble the thing to get it through the hatch. Had the tube remained on watch, Riellen and I could never have escaped. I chipped off some samples of melted stone from the tower with the back of my fencing ax while Riellen had a turn at the farsight. I made some sketches and notes in my field journal; then Riellen added her own amendments and observations.

"From Lupan, you say?" she asked.

"Yes, and I think I saw it launched, weeks ago, at the observatory on Alpindrak. Ten of them were sent."

"Ten, sir? One seems enough."

"The rest should arrive one day apart, every evening. When the others arrive, we must have flamethrowers ready to pump hellfire oil into the cylinders the moment that the hatches open. They caught us by surprise this morning, but they will never do it again."

We abandoned the horse and hired a ponycart for somewhat more than its worth at a nearby hamlet. We tried to warn the peasants to hide from the Lupanian invaders until we returned with the militia, but their reaction was along the lines of "Pull the other leg, it jingles."

"Why did our brothers from Lupan start killing people?" Riellen asked, glancing behind us nervously as I urged the pony to greater speed.

"Those are probably their rulers," I speculated. "Knights, kavelars, whatever. They are here for conquest, and judging from the strength of their magic, they will have an easy time of it."

"The Lupanian *establishment*? Here?"

"Yes, and don't even think about trying to go back and organize a protest rally with the bridge trolls."

Riellen tore a strip from a relatively mud-free area of her tunic and bandaged my forehead to keep the flies off the wound. For the rest of the trip she was strangely silent. On the positive side, however, I realized that I had been free of morose thoughts about Lavenci for the first time in weeks.

Chapter Six

HOW I REACHED MY ROOM

There was something surreal about Gatrov as we drove the cart through the west gate and into the busy streets. Women were hanging washing out to dry, artisans were at work in their open-fronted shops, peddlers trudged about with their wares on their backs, and children played in the roadside dust. Within a few minutes we were at the docks, and I sent Riellen to stable the cart and pony while I hurried on to the militia headquarters. I made my report, but I had the sense to put it in terms of some sort of local invasion with fantastic weapons. Predictably, the marshal on duty still thought that I might be exaggerating.

That done, there was no further role for me to play. Unless pressed into service, the Wayfarers have a civil rather than military role, and this was clearly a military matter. The authorities would send a few hundred men out with crossbows and hellfire-oil projectors, and it would all be over within an hour—or so I was assured. I made my way to the Bargeman's Barrel, and the town's single-handed escarpment clock was striking the hour past noon as I entered the taproom. It took some time for me to secure a sorely needed mug of beer because of the lunchtime crowd. During that wait, I heard snatches of conversation that concerned a silver-haired girl and a local wharfmaster with golden curls. What a strange thing it is that a girl who shares her favors is considered to be a slut, while the youth who mounts her is spoken of as a dashing young lad, even a hero. I had drained about half of my beer when I caught part of a nearby conversation that was rather more specific on the events of the night before.

". . . white-haired slut wipin' the tables."

"He rolled her and ran, ye say?"

"Knocked the breath out of her, did it all night, then left her wi'out threads and asleep at dawnlight. Got out with her purse, pack and threads, everything. Canny lad, our Pelmore. Heard he was in the market this morning. He's bought a new gown for his lass."

"Oh aye? Well, the lad put in a couple of hours of hard work for it."

They chortled together, and I began to scan the taproom discreetly. I quickly caught sight of Lavenci. She was collecting mugs on a tray and wiping tables, and was wearing a dress that looked as if it had been borrowed from someone with a much fuller figure. Her manner was somewhat hunted and miserable, yet also defiant.

I considered my options. Here was a woman in humiliating circumstances. That alone made me seriously angry. While I am rather too shy to be a great seducer, I do not condemn such behavior by others. To me, sex is the ultimate act of trust, and to betray such trust is occasion for serious punishment. I recalled a dream of meeting the goddess Romance. Was this the time to abandon common sense? Here was a cat who had clawed me, and now she was surrounded by terriers.

Gathering back Lavenci's possessions would be difficult, and restoring her good name would be traumatic for all concerned, I decided. At the end of it all, she would despise me for showing mercy. Yes, common sense was definitely not involved here, not even personal honor. Only compassion seemed to be guiding me—but then I am a compassionate lad, even though I try to hide it. I decided what I would do based on honor as pure as the windblown snow . . . yet as an added bonus, here was also an opportunity to be seriously horrible to a member of the Inquisition Constables.

Riellen entered, marched straight over to me, and asked if I had any orders for her.

"Remember a youth from last night, name of Pelmore?" I asked. "The wharfmaster?"

"What was his likeness, sir?"

"Perhaps twenty five, straw-blond curly hair, broad chest, blue eyes. He won the tournament dance."

"Did he dance with that upper-class member of the conspiracy to impose oligarchical oppression—mmmpf!"

"Yes, that one," I said, clamping my hand over her mouth, then releasing her again.

"And spend the night with her in Room Ten, where they—mmrff."

"Yes, yes, yes, that one! It has come to my attention that he robbed and dishonored Revolutionary Sister Lavenci—oh damn you Riellen, now I'm saying it! He robbed and dishonored *Her Ladyship, Kavelen Lavenci Si-Chella.* Find him, arrest him, and bring him to me. Start with the market."

I released Riellen's mouth again.

"But sir, honor is merely an upper-class and upper-middle-class code, while robbery is a provincial rather than an imperial offense, and thus not within our charter unless we chance upon the actual act. The town militia—mmmmrng."

"Riellen, every time *you* stand on a barrel and give one of your speeches, you preach enough incitement to affray to get yourself hanged, so don't argue fine points of law with me. Besides, any offense against nobility is classed as an imperial, not a provincial offense. What Pelmore did *is* within our charter."

"But sir, only if the local authorities are not capable of—mmrff."

"Riellen, I've just had a very, very bad morning and I want to take it out on someone who is not armed with a weapon that can melt stone at a range of one mile! Pelmore will do splendidly. Find him, arrest him, bring him here!"

"Sir, why did you not say it was for recreational gratification?" she suddenly asked brightly, and with a smart salute. "I'll be back."

Having sent my eighty-seven-pound weapon on her way, I went over to the landlord and discussed several matters with him to clarify Lavenci's current circumstances, then half emptied my purse into his hand. Finally I walked across to where she was working and dropped to one knee before her, still encrusted with mud and smelling like a troll's privy.

"Inspector Danol Scryverin, Wayfarer Constables, Western Quadrant, at your service, ladyship!" I said briskly.

Lavenci glared at me, automatically assuming that I was mocking her, but with no fight left in her to retaliate.

"Have you not heard?" she muttered, balling up the wet towel cloth in her hands.

"Yes," I replied simply, hoping that a single word had little scope for misinterpretation. For once, I had said the right thing. Her features softened a fraction.

"He took my shoulder crests, my purse, my knife, my medicines, my seal, my writing kit, border papers, clothes, everything! I had to leave my room wrapped in a sheet, I had to borrow this serving maid's dress, and now I have to work out the week washing tankards and mugs *as* a serving maid to pay for the cost of my room, then more to buy passage on a barge back to Alberin."

"I have—"

"And worst of all, I cannot afford the cost of a bath and, and—oh, would that I had a florin for the number of times I have heard 'Nine Times Astride Her' sung today. Some damn drinker composed it this morning."

"From what I heard through the wall, Pelmore was very, er, enduring."

"Inspector, a thick book is enduring, but if you are forced to lie in bed and read it from cover to cover after a very bad day, it becomes an intolerable bore. He gave no caresses, he did no little endearments, all he gave was rough, slobbery kisses and—Inspector, you men have no idea what a chore a surfeit of endurance can be."

"I shall take your word for it, ladyship. Famine has been stalking my love life for some time past."

"But he never saw me naked, that is one tatter of self-respect I can cling to. I have never let anyone see *all* of my unblemished skin."

"Ladyship, we have business to conduct."

"Of course, what can I do for you, Inspector? A pint of ale? A mince pie? If you tip me a copper I'll not scream if you pinch my bottom."

"I'm on duty, ladyship, but my thanks anyway. Steps are being taken to recover your property, and I have paid your debt to the landlord. You are free to go."

"Inspector!" she gasped, too shocked to even smile. "You did all that?"

"Best to leave Gatrov today, however. Reputation, and all that."

"Inspector Danolarian, you despise me, yet you do this for me?"

"I do not despise you, ladyship. A cat cannot help acting like a cat, and cats can sometimes be cruel to mice. Squeak squeak, and all that. If it is your pleasure to slap my hand away from your breast, then take Pelmore to your bed—"

My reflexes are very fast, but even I did not anticipate the slap that lashed across my cheek. Immediately she had hit me, Lavenci convulsed, clutched at her head as if it were about to explode, then seemed to regain control of herself. Amid the ripples of laughter from the nearby drinkers, she straightened and looked me in the face.

"Never, *never* forget that I offered you my body on a *silver platter* last night, Inspector, and that *you* spurned that offer," she shouted for all to hear. "I pressed your hand against my breast, and I twice invited you to spend the night sharing my bed. Pelmore was a lump of rancid meat who ran a very poor second to yourself in my esteem."

"My humble apologies, ladyship," I said, genuinely mortified as I rubbed my cheek. "I forgot the evidence. Not something that an inspector should do, forgetting evidence."

Lavenci now slumped to a bench, picked up an empty wine jar, wiped the table, then put the jar down again. Awareness of my own role in all this, along with the guilt associated therewith, was rapidly shredding my nerves. I sought to change the subject, being the coward that I am.

"I have assigned Constable Riellen to track down and apprehend Pelmore."

"Riellen, your skinny little constable? Against *Pelmore*?"

"Oh yes, and may the gods of Miral have mercy upon his soul when she catches him."

"Riellen's a *girl*?" exclaimed Lavenci.

"Yes, the Wayfarers are actively recruiting women as constables. The empress was responsible for that initiative."

The drinkers were still casting sidelong glances at us, and there was a hush of anticipation laced with giggles. I did not mind. I had plans for everyone in the taproom. I had to keep Lavenci in that hateful place for a little longer, however, so I kept talking.

"Ladyship, would you take a little advice?" I asked in what I hoped was a gentle tone.

"Advice?"

"Next time some boy that you genuinely esteem caresses your breast, do not slap his hand. Just take his hand away with an affectionate squeeze and a caress. He will understand."

"That slap," she whispered, holding up her left hand and frowning at it.

"He might become frightened and ashamed, baffled that you would be revolted by his touch while giving others your body's ultimate intimacy."

"One little slap," said Lavenci. "So much pain from one little slap."

Being an officer of the Wayfarer Constables, I see many people in the extremes of emotion. The light of insanity blazes up behind their eyes, and that light was bright behind Lavenci's black eyes as she turned to the table beside us and dropped her towel cloth.

"Ladyship, fifty florins should cover your passage on a barge back to Alberin," I now babbled, frantically trying to change the subject.

"Naughty left hand," she giggled, turning the hand back and forth before her face.

"You can take my purse, I'll keep my remaining florins in my boot."

"You slapped away my truelove, you took my clothes off for Pelmore, you even caressed Pelmore. Naughty hands must be punished, so that other hands act with more care."

Before I realized what was her intent, she placed her left hand on the table, seized the empty wine jar, and smashed it down across the back of her hand. The jar shattered. I saw blood and broken, jagged bones, but heard no cry of pain from Lavenci. The onlookers gasped and cried out; then a few sniggered. I picked up the towel cloth and tried to bandage her hand, but she convulsed and cried out as soon as I touched her.

"Some curse, malady," Lavenci gasped. "All morning, whenever a man even brushes against me. It's like a thunder-flash of hot needles through my head."

Just then there was a commotion at the door. To the sound of cheering interspersed with applause, Pelmore was pushed through the crowd to stand before us. Riellen was behind him, with her ax drawn.

"Watch and listen, ladyship," I said in a low, hard voice as I stood up. "I swear you will have both your good name and goods back within an hour's quarter."

I now advanced on Pelmore.

"Let 'im go!" called someone behind me.

"Aye, no shame doin' what lads do!" called another.

"Sir, I must explain that—" began Riellen.

"No harm's done, she's only a slut," bawled a drinker with a bushy black beard, one of Pelmore's wharfer colleagues.

"Excellent work, Constable Riellen, sometimes you truly amaze me," I declared for all to hear. "That is the fastest arrest that I have ever seen. Now guard the door and make sure nobody leaves or enters."

"Sir!"

I like to shun being the center of attention, but I was no longer quite myself. I had made a conscious decision to remove the leash from that part of myself that I had inherited from my father, and thus every other man in that taproom was in the most dire peril. I began to circle Pelmore, who was already looking submissive, and even frightened. For a moment I wondered what Riellen had done to him.

"Robbery of a noble, very severe penalties," I said softly but clearly.

I slammed my knee into Pelmore's groin, then smashed my elbow into his jaw as he doubled over. As he put his hands to his face I seized his right wrist in both hands; I bent my knees as I twisted his arm over my head; then, as his back rolled across mine, I straightened my legs with a rather considerable effort, and flipped him in a full circle—still holding on to his wrist. His feet struck the candle brace hanging from the rafters, and then his back smashed down across a table. The table shattered. Pelmore made a noise as if he were choking, then spat blood and a couple of teeth.

Two drinkers, who had not been warned off by what I thought to be a pretty impressive throw, advanced on me. Immediately I spun around and brought my foot up, expecting that someone was sure to be sneaking up on me from behind. My foot cleared a hand with a knife but struck the side of a head. Changing feet in a midair hop, I continued spinning and landed a boot heel on the temple of one of my forward attackers. His companion had a knife out by now, and I brought two spread hands down on his wrist while twist-dodging, spun around again while holding his knife hand over my head, then twisted his arm and slammed the side of my fist onto the back of his elbow. There was a snap, followed by a shriek.

Tavern fights are all about turning, so I spun yet again. A knife slashed my sleeve and forearm, but my boot caught the side of a knee and caused a gratifyingly loud snap. It was followed by a howl of anguish. At this point the landlord attempted to intervene by rushing at me with a cudgel. Although she could not have been any more than a third of his weight, Riellen stepped into his path, hook-locked his arm, tripped his leading leg while pulling him in an arc, then rolled him up over her hip, to spin in midair as he flew. He hit the wattle-and-daub wall feet-first. There was a crash that shook the tavern like an earthquake.

I estimate that nine seconds had elapsed since I had first struck Pelmore. Absolute silence had descended upon the tavern. The landlord was embedded in the wall, with only his head, chest, and arms protruding. It was time to assert authority, inspire blind terror, and create legends.

"Riellen, girl, how many times have I told you? *Never* throw people about like that during a fight. You might hit an innocent bystander."

She snapped to attention. "Sorry sir, I don't know what came over me."

"I appreciate your concern for my safety, but there's no real danger to be had here. These are only country folk."

The circle of drinkers shrank back. That was good; it meant I now had control of their minds. Pelmore was still lying on the floor amid the table's wreckage.

"Now then lads, I am sure that you are all stout, strong country folk who are bigger, healthier, and much stronger than we urban churls. You can probably outdo us in everything from dancing a double jig, to hog tossing. Bear in mind, however, that Riellen and I are professional killers, and we are *very* good at it."

For a moment the tavern was entirely still and quiet; then Roval wandered out of the crowd with a jar of wine in his hand. He looked down as he passed the landlord, muttered, "Brought low by a woman," then ascended the stairs to his room.

Nobody seemed interested in intervening on behalf of either the landlord or Pelmore. I snapped my finger for a pot of ale. A serving maid hurried over with one, curtsied fearfully, and offered it to me. She was the same girl who had flung a mug of wine in my face the night before, and she was goggle-eyed with terror. I fumbled for a copper, paid her, then took a sip.

"Sir, I do apologize fer last night—" she began, her face chalk white.

"Do you know Norellie, the healer woman?" I snapped. *"The one who Constable Riellen fetched to my room last night, to treat my HEADACHE?"*

"I, er, ah, aye—sir!" she managed, her terror now mixing with mortification.

"Go fetch her here. Several of the company are about to require her services. Constable Riellen, let her through."

The girl curtsied, apologized again, and hurried out past Riellen. Next I kicked Pelmore in the ribs, and exceedingly hard, too.

"Get to your knees," I ordered.

"Mighty lordship—"

"Shut up!" I barked. "Now I would like to point out that although I am just an inspector earning a mere fifty florins per week, plus expenses, I do know all about the manners, conventions, and protocols of the nobility. My job includes the escorting and protection of nobles sometimes, so I am expected to display gracious and seemly behavior."

I was turning slowly as I spoke, keeping everyone staring deferentially down.

"Nobles treat dalliance very differently to peasants, artisans, and other worker folk," I continued, making up a code of morality for Alberinese nobility as I went—although it was not far from the truth in some households. "As a rare sign of extreme trust and great esteem, a member of the nobility will sometimes share a dance with one they esteem. The young lady with the black eyes and milk-white hair chose to extend such an honor to this pail of pigswill at the tourney dance last night. He chose to piss on her esteem, dishonor her, rob her, and leave her in humiliating circumstances."

With no warning at all I delivered a very heavy kick to Pelmore's groin, to emphasize the point and to remind them that

I was just a tiny bit vindictive, as well as very dangerous. He doubled over on his side, his legs moving as if he were trying to run.

"You will return *everything* that you stole from Ladyship. *Now.*"

With some difficulty Pelmore unclenched his body, then he fumbled with the pack's drawstrings. He drew out a purse and offered it to me.

"I—spent, er, spent five gold ones. On these. Take them. Take them all."

There was quite an expensive gown of violet and gold, two gold rings, a belt of green leather, dancing slippers, also of green leather, two combs carved from bone, and a lace tablecloth. At this point the serving maid entered with Norellie.

"All my own work," I said with a gesture to those on the floor. "However Lady Lavenci has suffered an accident and is in more urgent need of your attention. I shall pay for her." I turned my attention back to Pelmore.

"Only three crowns, one noble, and six florins left," I observed as I emptied the purse onto the palm of my hand.

"I'll sell all this again. I'll sell my pack, sell my knife, everything."

"And where are Ladyship's clothes, papers, pin of office, purse, knife, writing kit, border papers, medicines, and pack?"

"Sold, at the market, but I'll get them back. But first please, please, have her lift the—"

"Shut up!" I shouted again, then shook out his pack. "What have we here? More combs, a jar of expensive wine, and, er, ah . . ." I held up some type of undergarment that appeared to be mainly thin strips of frills and lace. "Doesn't seem to be your size, whatever it is."

"It's for my truelove."

"Ah, you have a truelove?"

"Yes, great lord, the marketeer general's daughter."

"So, you rob a great lady, then leave her in the most dire and humiliating circumstances. Next you go out to the market to buy presents for your truelove?"

In truth he had probably sought to humiliate Lavenci so badly that she would be too ashamed to report the crime. I had presided over two cases of that happening to noblemen at the hands of peasant women. Although the roles were reversed here, it seemed to be much to same thing.

"Ah, I see," I said as I circled him, then I looked up at the circle of faces. "You two: bald head and eyepatch. I heard you discussing Ladyship earlier, and I did not like what I heard. Empty your purses onto the floor before Constable Riellen, now! And you, and you, and you three, I remember hearing you talking while I waited to buy a drink. You four on the floor, who attacked me, I think you are obviously accomplices, so you must also forfeit your tunics, coats, and boots. Let's see now, who else?"

I walked past the bearded wharfer, seeming not to notice him—then whirled suddenly and slammed the back of my fist into his mouth. Several of his teeth cut the back of my hand rather severely as they broke off. He fell backward to the floor, his beard flecked with red blood and yellow teeth.

"That is but one part in a thousand of what will happen to anyone in this town, should I hear that they have spoken the word 'slut.' You are fined *everything* that is on your person, including your clothes."

Before long five hundred and seventy-two silver florins were in a little pile at Riellen's feet. I turned back to Pelmore. I had managed to excuse Lavenci's indiscretion with him and restore a fragment of her honor, but now it was time to demolish Pelmore's honor entirely.

"Master Pelmore, bearing in mind that my job includes killing people, and bearing in mind that I am very, very angry with you—and that I am not far from handing you over to Riellen, who will do something so pointlessly hideous to you that nobody in this room will ever again be able to walk past a butcher's stall without being violently ill—answer me one more question. Ladyship told me that she has a mole in the shape of a crescent, halfway up her left thigh. What moonworld's color does it have?"

"Lupan, it is red like Lupan!" exclaimed Pelmore at once, looking relieved.

This was a very reasonable answer. Moles all tend to be brownish, orange, or even red.

"Ladyship, would you—?" I began, but Lavenci was already drawing up her skirts to expose her left thigh's entirety.

The skin was completely without flaw. She let her skirts fall again.

"So, you *say* you spent the night with Ladyship, you *say* you left her naked at dawnlight, yet you don't know what she looks like without her clothes on? Who ever heard of a lover not being allowed to see his lass naked?"

Pelmore's face reddencd, but he did not reply.

"I put it to you that you escorted Ladyship to her room's door, where the most you might have been granted was a goodnight kiss before that door was locked in your face. You then found a ladder in the stables, waited until she was asleep, then climbed in through her window, which was open due to the night being hot. You boasted about bestriding Ladyship nine times, but I would wager a month's pay that the only dalliance you got last night was a wank in the stables. What do you say to that?"

The taproom was in absolute silence while Pelmore thought through possible answers, and the probable consequences if he got anything else wrong.

"I do admit it, I robbed Ladyship but I did not lie with her," he said, staring at the floor. "And I boasted of sharing her bed so that folk would think better of me."

"Good, good, I am glad to have that matter set right. Now then, there was a song being sung about your lies all morning, one beginning with the word 'nine.' I want the composer of the song to step forward."

A ginger-haired man with a scraggy beard was pushed forward by those around him. Without any prompting he dropped to his knees and emptied his purse.

"Very good," I said softly. "Now get out of here and start running—and do not ever stop running, except to sleep. Ever. If you do stop, and I come to hear of it, you will not live to see another evening. Neither will anyone else who ever sings your song."

He hurried out, and I never set eyes on him again. I turned back to Pelmore.

"How many times have you ever managed to get it up with the local girls in one night?" I asked, pausing slightly after each word for added emphasis.

"I, er, that is . . . twice?"

"Goodness! As little as that? I cannot imagine how you added one plus one to get nine. Numeracy standards must be slipping, I blame the regent's cuts to temple-school subsidies. Constable Riellen?"

"Sir!"

"Gather up Ladyship's money, then escort Pelmore to the market to identify and buy back all that he stole and sold. Oh, and have Pelmore pull the landlord out of that wall, then take him along to carry Ladyship's things. I'll not have that filthy degenerate Pelmore touching anything of hers again. Lads, the rest of you are free to go. Pelmore, once the stolen items have been retrieved, you may consider yourself to have repaid your debt to society in general and Her Ladyship in particular."

Perhaps a dozen heartbeats passed between Riellen standing aside from the door and the uninjured drinkers vanishing from the taproom. I had expected the serving maid to dash away at the first opportunity, but she sidled up to me instead.

"Inspector, sir, about last night—" she began.

"Yes?"

"How can I ever make up for throwing that wine at you?"

"What is your name?" I asked, suddenly feeling very, very tired.

"Mervielle."

"Fetch me a towel cloth, if you please."

I walked over to Lavenci, who was being supported by Madame Norellie.

"Your name and honor, returned intact," I said as I gave her a bow.

"I—I can scarcely believe what you just did," she replied, sounding as if she were in a castings trance.

"Madame Norellie, what is your assessment of Ladyship?" I asked.

"She will have to come home with me. She has gashes and broken bones all through her hand."

"Bathhouse first," said Lavenci dreamily. "The stink of Pelmore's body is worse than the pain."

"I have a bathtub, Ladyship," said Madame Norellie. "Now come along."

With that they left, Lavenci trailing drops of blood from her hand across the taproom floor. I stood alone, leaning against the wall, my emotions and body utterly spent, and my father back on his leash again. Mervielle entered with a towel cloth.

"That dress that Ladyship wears, it looks to be your style," I observed.

"Aye sir, I felt sorry for her, like, and lent her a spare."

"You have a kind heart. Please accept a florin."

"From you sir? But the lady—"

"Can't easily untie a purse just now."

I went out to the stables and washed in the horse trough, then made my way up to my room wearing only the towel cloth and carrying my filthy clothes in a chaff sack. After changing, I made my way out into the streets and away to Madame Norellie's. Several injured drinkers from the Bargeman's Barrel were outside, awaiting her services, but at the sight of me they shrank back and gestured to the cottage door. I knocked, and called out my name. Madame Norellie called for me to enter. The front door opened into the kitchen. Lavenci was lying in a vat of steaming, soapy water, her bandaged hand over the edge and resting on a stool. She greeted me sleepily as I entered.

"I gave her a philtre to dull her senses," explained Norellie. "She is very drowsy."

Norellie had me sit at the table, with my chin resting on my hands. After examining my forehead and arm she began to collect bowls, jars, and cloths.

"Lucky I had some water on the boil," she said as she began to wipe my face with a scalding hot wet rag. "Even luckier I had some left after doing a bath for Ladyship. Bad humors abound in unboiled water. Never clean a wound with water that's unboiled."

"What about for all the lads outside?" I asked.

"They can wait. You have a very nasty gash in your forehead, Inspector, and a lesser one in your arm. Hold still, I'll have you sewn back together in less time than it takes to beat the stuffing out of a wharfmaster."

I sat with my elbows on the table and my chin resting on my hands. Norellie wiped my wounds with something that smelled sharp and stung exceedingly. She began to sew.

"I really should return your four florins," said Norellie as she worked. "I did not treat your curse-headache last night."

"No, but you did listen to Riellen for a couple of hours," I said, trying to hold myself steady. "Spare a thought for me, I've had to listen to her for three years."

"The whole town's talking about what you did for Her Ladyship."

"Well, you know what it's like with those noblewomen. They don't have a clue, always need a hero to look after them. No hero was to hand, so she had to make do with a Wayfarer."

I gave a little wave to Lavenci, and was rewarded by a smile in return.

"Sit still," chided Norellie as she finished with my arm and turned to my forehead. "This is quite a gash."

"I've had worse."

"How did it happen?"

"I fell on someone's ax."

"A lot of people seem to do that. Inspector. I must insist that you take back two of your four florins."

"Keep them for this work. You sew up wounds more gently than Riellen."

Footsteps hurried along the street outside. The feet stopped, and there was an exchange of urgent-sounding words with the men awaiting treatment. Someone banged on the door. Because I had neglected to push the latch home, the door swung open. Pelmore stood before us, his fist poised to continue knocking and his mouth hanging open. Norellie gave a sharp gasp of surprise, then continued to tie off her stitch.

"Come in, lad," Norellie said. "What brings you here, of all places?"

"Madame, I have a terrible affliction," he babbled, nervously glancing from Lavenci, to me, to Norellie.

"I didn't hit you all that hard, did I?" I called. "Oh, how rude of me. May I introduce Madame Norellie? This is Pelmore."

"Plough-bore, yes, we've met," said Norellie. "Cured him of the love pox last month. Hope you've been more careful where you've been shoving that thing, Pello."

Suddenly Pelmore fell to his knees beside the table, his hands raised and clasped as if he were praying to me.

"Mighty, wise, and merciful inspector, forgive me, forgive me!" he cried. "Lift this curse from my body."

"What do you mean?" I asked. "I'm a Wayfarer inspector, we're meant to arrest people doing magic, not do it ourselves."

"But my curse, my blight, my deformity!" he cried, terror in his tone.

"I have no idea what you mean," I replied.

"Great and mighty sorceress," Pelmore sobbed, shuffling over to Lavenci's tub on his knees. "Have mercy on me, lift your curse."

"Go 'way," mumbled Lavenci, splashing water at him with her right hand. "If you call me sorceress . . . sue you . . ."

"Madame healer, can *you* help me?" Pelmore pleaded, shuffling back to the table, still on his knees.

"Perhaps, but before taking your money I shall need to see the problem," replied Norellie as she tied off the fifth stitch in my forehead.

Pelmore stood up and pulled on the drawstring of his trousers. They fell to the floor. Pelmore's penis resembled nothing more closely than half a small, pink fig.

"I didn't do that!" I said once I had recovered my breath.

"Wish I had," said Lavenci, who then yawned widely.

"Pelmore, you need a drink," said Norellie. "There's mugs and a jar on the shelf under the window."

"There's ants in this mug."

"They're probably drunk and can't crawl out."

Pelmore shook the ants out and poured himself a measure of wine. He drained it in a single swallow.

"Constancy glamour," observed Norellie, tying a knot in my sixth stitch. "Only hedgerow sorcery can lift them, and I don't practice any sort of sorcery."

At this point Riellen entered, striding straight through the open door without even knocking. She had a large and bulging pack on her back.

"Sir, Revolutionary Sister Mervielle said you were here. I wish to report that most of Lady Lavenci's things have been retrieved and— Oh good heavens!"

"Riellen, you do, of course, know Pelmore," I said, my head

still featuring a needle and thread. "What do you make of his, well, condition?"

"Er, my mother told me to expect something a little bigger," Riellen managed.

"Consistency gammon?" asked Pelmore, staring at Norellie with suspicion.

"But sir, you, you, you . . ." stammered Riellen, pointing in my direction.

"Norellie is sewing up my wound."

"Ladyship!" shrieked Riellen, catching sight of Lavenci. "You're undressed."

"It is called a bath, young woman," said Lavenci. "Most people . . . do not have enough of them."

"But, but, people can see, er, lots of you!"

"Silly prude. . . ."

Riellen put a hand to her head, swayed, then steadied herself against the wall.

"Riellen, you need a drink," said Norellie. "Wine and mugs are under the window."

"But I am on duty."

"Consider it for medicinal purposes only," I suggested.

"In that case, sir, thank you, I accept."

Riellen picked up a mug, stared at the ants therein, drank several mouthfuls of wine straight from the jar, then sank to the floor, where she sat cross-legged. Lavenci's pack was still on her back.

"So, what have you to report, Riellen?" I asked.

"All Lady Lavenci's stolen things have been recovered, except for the medicinal oils in some of the phials. The oils had been discarded, and the phials were on sale for their own value."

"Doesn't matter," said Lavenci, struggling to stay awake under the onslaught of warm bathwater and Norellie's potion. "Can go a week . . . without."

"Oils?" Pelmore exclaimed. "Could they have been used to cause this, er, contingency hammer?"

"Respectable woman," slurred Lavenci. "Not sorceress."

"Well *someone* did this!" shouted Pelmore.

"Indeed," said Norellie, pushing her needle into my skin for the last stitch, and causing me to flinch. "And the term is constancy glamour."

"Was it you?" asked Lavenci and Pelmore together.

"Oh no," said Norellie. "I'm just a healer. I don't do glamours."

"You mean castings?" I asked.

"No, it's a constancy glamour," said Norellie.

"I've not heard of glamours," I said. "Are they a type of sorcery?"

"Yes and no. There were once some very skilled healers on Helion Island, far away in the Placidian Ocean. The Helionese men were fishers and merchant sailors, seamen who stayed away from home a lot. Some abused the trust of their wives while in distant ports, and this annoyed those wives. Then one of the healers developed a type of . . . well, it is hard to describe a glamour. Suffice it to say that the healer was able to link couples together by means of an act of intimacy."

"What do you mean, link together?" asked Pelmore, scratching his blond curls.

"Shut up," mumbled Lavenci.

"The woman would go to a healer, who would fashion a constancy glamour. That glamour ensured that the woman and her husband could not cheat upon each other. The woman would experience violent pains in her head at the touch of any man except for he who had been the last to arouse her in the most intimate fashion possible. That man was given a more . . . *physical* limitation."

There was silence for a moment. Norellie tied off the last stitch in my forehead, then began to bandage me.

"Inspector?" ventured Lavenci. "When . . . slapped you. Remember? Had head pains, like hot needles."

"My apologies" was all that I could think to say.

"How long . . . lasts?" asked Lavenci.

"Until someone knowledgeable lifts the glamour, or until seven years after one of you two dies," explained Norellie. "Of course if you and Pelmore got into bed together again, you could enjoy each other to the fullest possible—"

"Never!" rasped Lavenci, glaring up at Pelmore.

"Anyway, how *could* I do it?" demanded Pelmore, pointing at his groin.

"All done, Inspector," said Norellie, patting my cheek.

"What about me?" demanded Pelmore.

"Pelmore, while you and your constancy-glamour partner are in physical contact, your, ah, male talents are temporarily restored."

"Think I prefer the 'die' option," said Lavenci.

"There are checks against such easy solutions," said Norellie. "Lots of them. Remember, should one of you die, there will be a seven-year wait for the glamour to lift."

"So . . . Pelmore dies . . . I wait seven years?" asked Lavenci.

"Yes."

"Almost worth it."

"You will pardon me if I don't stand up," I said to nobody in particular. "All that sewing has me a little faint. So, a constancy glamour is not a magical casting?"

"Not real magic," said Norellie in a detached sort of way. "Not magic as we know it, anyway. Hedgerow enchantment. Nothing to do with etheric castings and forces. Glamours are magic that are . . . magical. No talent is required, just knowledge of incantations, herbs, and gestures, and belief that the glamours will work."

"Diomedan expression, *enthre d'han,*" said Lavenci. "Glow of strangeness. Thas . . . glamour."

"So you have heard of them?"

"Yes. Sorcerers hate 'em. Cannot be controlled. Anyone . . . can use 'em."

"As I said, fishwives on Helion Island had them inflicted on their husbands, but the practice died out for reasons that are probably obvious," said Norellie.

"Lads would soon be nervous about marrying a Helionese girl," I suggested.

"Indeed. Young men fled the island at every opportunity, never to return. It got to the point where there were five women for every man on Helion, then a vigilance committee of women was formed. They swept through the island one night and slew every healer, whether they knew the practice of glamours or not. First they tortured them, however, and extracted the names of those who had bought constancy glamours. These women were also killed. I believe that some twelve dozen women perished at the hands of their sisters in that carnage. Helion was then voiced about as an island overflowing with women, all desiring to entertain and enchant men in a strictly nonmagical sense. It was, however, a bad place to fall sick until new healers migrated there."

"Yet *you* know of the glamour's practice," I said, looking Norellie in the face.

"True. A lamplight woman, a harlot, had borrowed a book from one of the healers without that healer knowing of it. She thought to better herself through study, and eventually become a healer herself, but she was not on their guild's register. Thus she survived that terrible night, and so did the book. Apparently someone in Gatrov has read the book."

"But what am *I* to do?" demanded Pelmore.

"Oh do not despair," said Norellie. "You can still piss unhindered, and should this lady here touch you, your manhood will rise to the occasion."

"Rather bathe in pigshit," said Lavenci, settling deeper into her bathwater, then blowing a few bubbles. "Cold pigshit."

"*You* know so much about glamours," cried Pelmore, pointing at Norellie. "I'm betting *you* know how to conjure and lift them!"

"Anyone could," replied Norellie calmly. "Glamours are like knots. Pull on the right bit of string, and the whole thing pops apart. Pull on any other, and the knot becomes tighter. I suppose I could take a guess at the right bit of string."

"Well pull on it!" demanded Pelmore.

"Oh no, the practice of magic is a criminal act, even for the purposes of healing. Danol is a Wayfarer, so he is obliged to alert the Inquisition, which would have me arrested—"

"You can't do this!" shouted Pelmore angrily, reddening and balling his fists.

"Riellen, if he gets violent, kill him," I said calmly. "I'll write it up as resisting arrest or something."

Riellen shook off Lavenci's pack and stood up, drawing her ax. Pelmore's aggression dissolved.

"But it's not just," he whined.

"Neither is theft, and humiliating your lover of the night before," I pointed out.

"I served her tirelessly," mumbled Pelmore.

"So did . . . horses pulling the coach . . . that brought me here," Lavenci retorted, fighting to stay awake. "Doesn't mean they're . . . merry company . . . in bed."

"Might I make a suggestion?" I interjected. "A field magistrate can authorize a dispensation for the practice of magic under extreme circumstances. In this case, it is to destroy a glamour that has been cast maliciously, so I think a case could be made."

"Where can we find a field magistrate?" asked Pelmore.

"There are plenty in Alberin," I said.

"What?" shrieked Pelmore. "That's two or three days by barge, even at speed."

"And he may decide that he wants an investigation first, and that will involve the Inquisition. It could take months."

"But my wedding is tomorrow!"

"Well, your condition should be a source of surprise for your bride," said Norellie.

"I'll send word when we are leaving for Alberin," I said, gesturing to the door. "Now get out, Pelmore."

Pelmore took a step, but without remembering that his trews were still around his ankles. He fell headlong. A minute later he had his trews up again, and was through the door and gone.

"Of course some Wayfarer inspectors can also be field magistrates," said Norellie.

"Actually, I did pass a ratification test recently," I responded. "Dear, dear, how forgetful of me."

Norellie handed a thumb-sized bag of dried herbs to me.

"Inspector, Riellen explained that you get very severe migraine headaches at the conclusion of each mission with the Wayfarer Constables," she said. "I'm sorry that I did not treat your misery last night. Riellen was telling me some very interesting things and I confess that we forgot about you. You should have moaned and complained, like other patients. Next time the signs of a headache are upon you, drop that bag of herbs into a mug of boiling water, then drink it as hot as you can stand. It works for most people, but not all."

"Thank you indeed," I said. "And by the by, are *you* the woman from Helion?"

"No."

"Then who are you?"

"There is no name for what I am, and I do many things. Sometimes I heal, sometimes I cause distress, sometimes I strew joy in my wake. When I first came to Gatrov the folk asked what my trade was, and I always replied *which trade*? After a while I decided I liked the name, so I put it on my card. Would you pass my bag over, young Constable? There's a good girl. Here's my card, Danol."

I read the card, and it declared her to be NORELLIE WITCHWAY — HEALER TO DISCERNING FOLK IN NEED.

"Catchy," I commented, "except that you spelled 'which' wrongly."

"I know, but I think 'witch' gives it more bite."

It was at this very moment that Halland, the commander of the town militia, entered. He was about forty, with a neat, graying beard and the confident yet wary bearing of those who lead their men into real fighting. He glanced about. Three women and a lad in a room means either extreme guilt or extreme innocence. Apparently he decided that extreme innocence was easier to cope with than the alternative. He saluted. I returned the salute as best I could, given the state of my forehead and arm.

"Commander, how delightful to see you," said Norellie.

"Madame Norellie! You, ah, know the inspector?"

"Only professionally. He sent quite a lot of work my way today, and I sewed up his forehead and arm. Are you going to arrest me again?"

"Pardon?" I asked.

"My status in this town is akin to that of a lamplight girl," explained Norellie. "People want my services, but don't like me working in their neighborhood."

"My apologies, madame, but the Inquisition's agent has reported that your healing techniques border on sorcery, and I am meant to enforce laws against sorcery," said Halland, although he sounded embarrassed.

"Well, I have finished with the inspector, so shall we be going off to the stocks?" Norellie asked.

"Stay, stay," said Halland. "I am here for Inspector Danolarian."

"Me?" I exclaimed. "I've never practiced sorcery."

"You don't understand, Inspector, I've a message from the castle. The baron wants to see you. You're to go straightaway. Apparently he's planning an attack on the, er, Lupan folk from the shooting star, but he wants to hear all that is known about them first."

I had never met the baron, but his approach did seem sensible.

"Have you shown the samples I gave you to a scholar of the cold sciences?" I asked.

"Inspector, this is a river port. We have no academy, neither do we have their tools of trade or books." He held up a little pouch. "I had my armorer examine these, but he was of no help at all. That is another reason for me being here."

"Am I missing something?" asked Norellie.

"The Lupanians are very, very dangerous, and a detailed study of my samples could tell us much about them," I said, trying to sound neutral. "It does not really matter if the study is scientific or sorceric, as long as something can be learned."

Norellie looked to Halland. Halland hastily looked to me. I nodded.

"The materials, amulets, and devices confiscated from Madame Norellie's house last month had to be destroyed, and in the presence of a magistrate," mumbled Halland, then he went down on one knee before her. "Madame Norellie, good lady, might there be anything that we missed that you may use to examine these Lupanian objects?"

"You expect *me* to tell *you*?"

Halland thought about that for a moment. "Madame Norellie, I apologize for the raid from the bottom of my soul. I shall write out an order for the town militia to cease harassing you in perpetuity. It's the *absalver no trestipar.*"

"That means that from now on you shall be responsible for any breaches of the sorcery laws that I may commit!" exclaimed Norellie. "You are putting your life in my hands."

"Madame Norellie, I might have been forced to raid your house, but that does not mean I don't respect and trust you. With that in mind, will you help?"

There was an extended pause. I suspected that Norellie was making Halland squirm.

"Give me your samples, I'll do what I can," she declared, holding a hand out to Halland with just the trace of a smile.

"I'll deliver my pledge in writing within the hour," offered Halland, placing the pouch of stone chips and oxide in her hand. To me, his fingers seemed to linger slightly longer than was needed. Norellie selected a crumb of oxidation.

"From another world," Norellie said slowly, turning the orange chip over in her fingers "It has an odd feel about it."

"When will your work be done?" Halland asked. "The baron will want to know."

"The baron will have to wait. I'll need to buy a few things in the market, and Lady Lavenci's hand needs further treatment. Call past at dusk."

Chapter Seven

THE SORCERESS AND THE HEAT BEAM

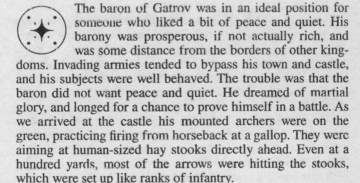

The baron of Gatrov was in an ideal position for someone who liked a bit of peace and quiet. His barony was prosperous, if not actually rich, and was some distance from the borders of other kingdoms. Invading armies tended to bypass his town and castle, and his subjects were well behaved. The trouble was that the baron did not want peace and quiet. He dreamed of martial glory, and longed for a chance to prove himself in a battle. As we arrived at the castle his mounted archers were on the green, practicing firing from horseback at a gallop. They were aiming at human-sized hay stooks directly ahead. Even at a hundred yards, most of the arrows were hitting the stooks, which were set up like ranks of infantry.

Halland, Riellen, and I were met by a steward at the gatehouse, and were taken straight into the throne hall. Here the baron had called a hasty war court of his kavelars and marshals, and once more I had to repeat my fantastic story and show my samples. Riellen stood listening at the back of the hall.

"Long tentacles, you say?" the baron asked as I stood before the throne, at the focus of a half circle of kavelars.

"At least forty feet in length, and very strong," I answered.

"And a sort of magical flamethrower?"

"A beam of pure heat," I explained.

"Well then, we attack!" he said happily, slapping the armrest of his throne.

"My lord, with respect . . ." I began tentatively.

"Yes, yes?" snapped the baron. "Come on, fellow, out with it! One mouth, two ears, so we should listen twice as much as talk. I'm listening, so you talk."

"Granted, an armored kavelar on horseback armed with a lance could have a chance against the tentacled monsters themselves, but what about their heat weapon? It melted rock at a distance of one mile, so I would rate it as quite formidable."

"Oh pish to that," the baron laughed. "Bald Pate Hill will provide cover to half a mile distance, then it's a charge over open, flat ground. We shall rally at the hill tonight, for a charge with kavelars, lancers, and mounted archers tomorrow morning. The sun will be at our backs and in the enemy's eyes, and we'll be upon them before they even know we're coming."

"But the heat—" I began again.

"We shall have the paint and heraldic devices stripped from our shields so that they reflect the heat away like a mirror, don't you see? Now then, I have twenty kavelars, fifty lancers, and fifty mounted bowmen. Should that be enough, Inspector Danol? How many of those tentacled bounders were there?"

"The cylinder would have been perhaps fifteen feet by about fifty."

"By Miral's rings, as little as that? Even packing their marines in like salted fish in a barrel, they could not have more than two or three dozen in their ranks. So, we outnumber them. Do they have horses?"

"I saw none," I answered listlessly.

"No cavalry? Capital! What about bowmen?"

"I saw none of those either," I reported.

"Maybe they are like an octopus, just a lump with tentacles. Not very fast on land."

"They don't need to be fast on land when they can do this at one mile," I said, holding a chip of melted blackstone out to the baron.

A marshal took it from me, walked up to the throne, and presented it to the baron. The nobleman turned it over in his fingers for some moments.

"Impressive, I'll grant you that," he said, tossing it over his shoulder, "but consider this: hold a polished shield with felt backing above your head while riding on a hot day, and you will remain as cool as if you were sipping wine in the shade of the castle's cloisters. Inspector Danol, you are to spend the afternoon briefing my kavelars on what you know of these Lupanians, then be ready to ride out with us at dusk tonight. I want to muster the attack force in the dark, then catch those damn Lupanians with their trews down at sunrise."

"Me, my lord?" I asked, hardly believing what I was hearing.

"Yes, yes, just you. Constable Riellen is much too small to look heroic alongside my men in the victory parade before the regent. Anyway, she's a girl, and we all know girls can't fight. Constable, you are dismissed. Inspector Danol, gentlemen of the court, come out onto the green and we shall work out some tactics on the horseflesh, so to speak. Oh, and did you really play the sun down at Alpindrak's summit?"

"Indeed I did, my lord."

"Splendid! Splendid! Look, I have a set of war pipes—by Barrington, cost me a fortune. Would you mind playing the sun down with them this evening, from my battlements? You know, just so I can tell people you've played the Barringtons."

"That bonehead is going to get ten dozen men killed tomorrow morning, and he wants *me* to be one of them," I muttered as Halland, Riellen, and I sat at a table outside the Bargeman's Barrel sometime after dusk.

We were sitting outside for privacy, and were staring with foreboding at the lingering colors on the western horizon.

"It's already later than when the other cylinder arrived," said Halland.

"It's probably a dangerous voyage through the void between the moonworlds," I responded hopefully. "Perhaps there was an accident."

"Let us hope that the odds against making a successful crossing are nine in ten, so we shall have only one cylinder to deal with," said Halland.

We contemplated that thought hopefully for a few moments.

"What did Norellie find out about that piece of orange stuff?" I asked Halland.

"Er, some sort of pottery, she thinks. I have the message here, that serving wench, Mervielle, brought it. The voidship is really a huge glazed jar. Is that not amazing? I just can't see how they'd prefer pottery to wood for a ship."

"A glazed jar sealed with wax and a cork can keep a reed-paper note dry while it drifts across an entire ocean," I pointed out. "Perhaps glazed pottery is a more sensible material for a ship than folk suspect."

"I tried to hold a rally to raise the uninformed and oppressed commoners' awareness of the threat, but Commander Halland had me arrested and locked in a cell for an hour," said Riellen sullenly.

Halland and I exchanged knowing glances.

"I've spread the word that a force of greenwood outlaws made camp at Bald Pate Hill, and massacred the viscount and some peasants," said Halland.

"Greenwood outlaws?" Riellen exclaimed in disbelief. "But—"

"Nobody would believe what is really out there!" Halland insisted defensively. "At least the pretense of a believable enemy lets me put the militia on alert for the night. The town's wall is being manned by militiamen with bows, and all men of able body are under orders to have arms within reach at all times."

"Immediate flight would be a more sensible course to follow," I suggested.

"Actually I have ordered the wives and children of some militiamen onto barges bound for Alberin, Inspector," said Halland.

"I could hold a rally in the market and alert the uninformed and neglected commoners to the nature of the real threat," suggested Riellen brightly.

"Riellen, I never thought I'd hear myself say this, but for once you may be right," I said slowly, hardly believing my own words. "What do you say, sir?" I asked Halland.

"In spite of my better judgment . . . I suppose I agree. But you would not be believed, Constable, and besides, the market is closed for the night."

"But a sizable number of the town's men will be in the taverns for the evening's pint," said Riellen. "I have studied rumor theory, and it is a fact that rumors are more readily believed than royal pronouncements. I can spread the word in the taverns, and the townsmen will take it to their homes."

Suddenly there was a green light in the sky, and we leaped to our feet to watch a second shooting star fly in low from the east. It passed to the north of us, no more than a few hundred feet above the fields, then it was lost to sight as it came down. Riellen and I followed Halland as he dashed for the port's watchtower. A minute later we were at the top, and looking to the northwest where a small fire was burning.

"Came down to the northwest, near the river," said Halland, gazing through my farsight. "Five miles distant, no more. That is perfect."

"Perfect for what?" I asked.

"Perfect for me to stand ready with a flamethrower and a cartload of hellfire oil, as you advised. As soon as the Lupanians have the hatch open, I'll char them black as toast in a smithy's forge."

"Wish I could be with you," I said sincerely.

"Rather than with the baron as he suicides? Just take a tumble as soon as the others begin galloping, lad, then play dead while they get themselves killed. Nobody will ever know."

"Will you take command of my constables, sir?" I asked, with my hand firmly over Riellen's mouth again.

Commander Halland cast an unenthusiastic glance at my constable as I released her. Riellen gave him a bright and enthusiastic smile.

"Aye, I suppose I will," he said wearily.

"Lass, I'm going to write a note assigning all three of you to Commander Halland's militia for the day to come," I said, turning away from the fire that marked the second cylinder's landing site. "If I do not survive, you are to follow his orders until someone of authority from the Wayfarers tells you to do otherwise. Tell Roval the same, when and if he ever sobers up, and don't forget Wallas."

"Aye sir," she said crisply, saluting.

Halland patted her skimpy shoulder and smiled.

"Well lass, looks like it's Halland and Riellen against the mighty magic of those sorcerers from Lupan. Now then, I suppose I'd better round up a dozen militiamen to go with us."

"A dozen militiamen, sir?" barked Riellen.

"Oh aye, but—"

"I'll do it, sir!" she said with another salute, then she hurried away down the tower's steps.

Halland and I also descended.

"You seem awkward about Madame Norellie," I ventured.

"I had her arrested several times over, ransacked her house, smashed her jars of substances, burned her books, and even put her in the public stocks for a week. Now, in my hour of greatest need, she agrees to help. What does that tell you?"

"She is very public-spirited?"

"Madame Norellie has honor, and I do not. Inspector— Danolarian, friend, tell me, why did she do it? To force me to be in debt to her?"

"It is not just you," I said as reassuringly as I could. "This afternoon Madame Norellie . . . let us just say she is genuinely honorable, as you are."

"How do you know I am honorable?"

"Because you also have a sense of shame. Now what of the flamethrower?"

"Easy, there's a dozen, mounted on wagons, to defend the river port against raiders. All that we need is . . ."

His voice trailed away. I followed his gaze to a rapidly gathering crowd. Just down the street, standing on the steps of the Gatrov Imperial Town Militia Offices, was Riellen, This time she was dressed as a Wayfarer, with her jacket rightways.

"Brothers! Friends! You all know why we're here!" floated out across the gaggle of heads to us. "Today the peace-loving people of the barony of Gatrovia lost two hundred of their brothers and sisters to the warmongering, imperialist, royal establishment sorcerers from Lupan. Now then, what are you going to do about it?"

The crowd of militiamen, some of whom had arrested her earlier, responded with cries along the lines of "Bastards!" and "Let's get 'em!"

"Inspector Danolarian Scryverin of the Wayfarer Constables of Alberin has been sent here to make a stand against the forces of warmongering, imperialist, royal establishment sorcerers from Lupan, and he has made an alliance with your brave and freedom-loving leader, Commander Halland. Your baron, however, has deprived Commander Halland of the services of Inspector Danolarian!"

There were cries of "Shame!," "Down with the baron," and "We're with Halland."

"How does she do it?" I asked softly. "Her speeches are so irritating when you hear them every day, yet people seem inspired when they get smaller doses of her."

"I wish she wouldn't use my name," muttered Halland, covering his face with his hand.

"Or mine," I added, hunching over with my arms folded tightly, and trying to shrink.

"Who will ride with Commander Halland tonight, as he does battle with the warmongering, imperialist, royal establishment sorcerers from Lupan in the second cylinder? Who will stand with him to defend your homes and loved ones against the deadly heat weapon of the Lupanians? Brothers! Who of you is with Commander Halland? He needs a dozen brave volunteers who have not been chosen to ride with the baron tomorrow! Who is with him?"

Seven dozen hands shot into the air, and there was a great deal of cheering. The militiamen swarmed up the steps, and Riellen was lost to view as they all tried to volunteer. Presently Halland was forced to expand his contingent of volunteers tenfold, owing to the threat of a riot if anyone was left out. It was a little more than my nerves could cope with.

"The baron might not approve of you raising such a large force," I pointed out later as I stood in Halland's office while he drew up lists and scribbled on maps. "He wants all the glory for himself."

"The baron could not find his arse with a tracker dog, Inspector!" muttered Halland. "Who do you think really keeps this town running and in good order?"

"Oh, the constables and militia," I replied tactfully.

"One hundred and twenty men. Perhaps we should take half a dozen flamethrowers. There's twelve on the wharves, so six could be left for the town's defense. Some cavalry would be useful if we need to move our forces quickly. I don't suppose you could assassinate the baron and take command of his riders?"

"The idea appeals, but no."

The baron's provosts arrived to escort me back to the castle, but there was one task left to me before I left the town. I made my way to the house of Norellie, the witch healer. I was hoping that Lavenci had by now examined the samples as well, as she was a sorceress from an academy, not just some hedgerow healer. To my surprise, Mervielle admitted me when I knocked at the door to the little cottage. She looked uneasy.

"Madame Norellie asked me to help, like," she said. "Fetchin' from the market, cleanin', carryin', all those things that serving maids are good at."

"Do you know if they've learned anything?" I asked.

"No, but that Norellie's been doing complicated stuff in the kitchen all afternoon," she explained. "And she's worried. I get nervous when clever folk are worried."

Norellie was transformed. Gone was her scrubbed, wholesome look, for her face was smeared with soot and her eyes were red-rimmed from the fumes that hung on the air. The floor, stools, and table were littered with bottles, jars, papers piled with powders of every color in the rainbow, and scrolls covered in symbols. Lavenci was sitting at a corner of the table, dressed in her riding gear again.

"She's burned her dancin' clothes of real silk," whispered Mervielle. "Burned everythin' that she wore while dancin' with young Pelmore. Don't seem sensible."

Lavenci was writing on a sheet of reedpaper. Three stones, an inkwell, and a goose quill were arranged neatly in front of her. Her left hand was heavily wrapped in bandages, with not even her fingers visible. She looked up and smiled as I entered.

"Welcome, Inspector," she said. Then she returned to her writing.

"That orange material, it's not of this world!" said Norellie in an urgent, awestruck tone.

"I'd worked that out for myself," I replied impatiently.

"Danolarian, this is no joke. Its feel and its aura are different to anything I've ever come upon, my spells and castings cannot touch it. I ground some of it into dust, added water, and had it fired in a neighbor's kiln. Once fired, it can scratch glass."

"It would have to be strong, to withstand the stresses of the flight from Lupan," I concluded. "What else?"

"Nothing. I am a healer, this is the sort of thing that even the greatest of sorcerers could not begin to guess at. I've been hard at work with all the alchemical skill that I can muster, but it's hopeless."

"How is Lady Lavenci's hand?" I asked.

"It took thirty-one stitches to close the wounds, and most of the bones behind the fingers have been crushed. She has maimed herself forever."

"My hand has learned its lesson, Inspector," said Lavenci, looking up from her writing again. "It will never slap you away again."

Her voice was cool and level, as if all emotion had been washed from within her.

"My lady, that was not necessary," I said, going down on one knee and bowing. "You esteemed the others more greatly, you need not explain the inclinations of your hearts."

Lavenci shook her head.

"There can be no excuse for what I did, Inspector. Words are so cheap, I shall not insult you by wasting them—but enough of that. I have the measure of the Lupanian weapon."

"You?" asked Norellie. "But you have only been writing for all this time."

"Look at these rock samples," said Lavenci, paying her no heed. "This is blackstone struck by lightning, and this is blackstone from coastal Torea —it was melted by the last of the fire-circles that destroyed the continent. Mervielle got them for me at the amulet stall in the town market. Compare them with the chip that the Lupanians melted on that tower."

"The lightning-struck piece is the least impressive, and the melt on the other two is about equal," I observed.

"Not so. The fire-circles that burned Torea each burned for perhaps a quarter minute, then the heat was many hours dispersing. How long did the Lupanians take to sweep the field with their heat weapon?"

"A quarter minute also, perhaps less."

"One mile, times twenty-two, divide by seven, double . . . over six miles. What width was the melted area?"

"Less than an inch."

"Assume a circle, one-inch diameter . . . a quarter minute is one part in two hundred and forty from one hour . . . the beam swept the tower at one and one half thousand miles per hour. One and one half thousand, five thousand two hundred and eighty, twelve inches . . ."

Norellie and Mervielle were huddled together by the door, not understanding much, but looking fearful.

"Roughly ninety-five million inches in a quarter minute, and that's fifteen seconds," said Lavenci slowly and deliberately.

"All those big figures, they're fair making my head spin," declared Norellie.

"I know, the figures are almost meaningless they're so large," said Lavenci. "Fifteen seconds for the outer fire-circle over Torea, and this happened." She held up the chip of half-melted blackstone.

"Lavenci, I can't stay!" I pleaded as she calculated. "The baron's provosts are outside, waiting to take me back to the castle. What have you discovered?"

"Danol, that heat beam swept over this blackstone with *six hundred thousand* times the intensity that the Torean fire-circles had."

I swallowed. "Six hundred thousand?"

"Approximately. Allowing for some rounding. Give or take ten thousand or so."

"Er, is that six hundred and a thousand?" asked Norellie.

"How much is a thousand?" asked Mervielle.

"Six hundred repeated a thousand times over," I explained as I struggled to link that figure to something closer to the reality that I was used to. "The baron seems to think that polished steel shields will reflect it away," I said weakly. "He

intends to charge the Lupanians with kavelars on horseback holding polished shields."

Lavenci gave me a cold, intense stare.

"The metal of the shields will explode like drops of water striking a white-hot horseshoe in a smithy's forge."

There was no reply I could make to that. We have since learned that the beam is much wider close up, but focuses to an inch at one mile, then widens again thereafter. Thus Lavenci's figures were for the worst possible case, but even the best case was not much better.

"The bodies in the field did look as if they had exploded," I recalled.

"I rest my case," said Lavenci. "Oh, and my feeling is that the orange ceramic material transforms very slowly under intense heat, and was probably used to protect their porcelain voidcraft as it streaked through our world's air."

I tried to think through what she was saying, but concluded that none of it could help us.

"Lavenci, the provosts are out there because the baron is taking me along for the charge against the cylinder," I explained. "How can we fight these things?"

She made a slight gesture, as if she wanted to take me in her arms but had remembered what the constancy glamour would do to her. She shook her head slowly.

"You cannot, Danolarian. Their power is beyond comprehension. You will die, and I shall mourn you."

A provost's whistle sounded in the street outside.

"Lavenci, ladies, I must go!" I cried.

"Danol, no!" Norellie cried. "The baron's cavalry charge will be suicide."

"The baron is insisting on having an advisor who knows the enemy. That man is I."

"You had better tell the baron that the enemy could take on the ether machine that destroyed the entire continent of Torea with a passably good chance of winning," said Lavenci.

A whistle sounded from the street outside, and a voice shouted, "Provost's first call for Inspector Danol Scryverin!"

"Ladies, at the third call I'll be considered under arrest!" I said urgently. "Look, forget about me, try to help Commander Halland. He is going to use flamethrowers when the second cylinder opens. If he's fast, he can roast the crew once the hatch unscrews, before they get a chance to use their heat weapon."

"Those in the first cylinder seem a little better prepared by now," said Lavenci. "*You* will be rendered into a rapidly dispersing puff of smoke."

"You need to carry a favor into battle," said Mervielle. "Do you have one?"

"Who from? Riellen? Talk sense."

"You need favors, from all of us!" cried Mervielle. "All the good wishes that you can carry. Here."

"This is a dishcloth," I said as she tied the cloth to my arm.

"Where's something that's mine, look at this mess," muttered Norellie. "A scarf, headband, handkerchief, *anything*!" She hitched up her skirts to display a plump but shapely pair of legs. "Here, take these!"

"A pair of drawers?"

Two blasts from the whistle outside heralded the cry "Provost's second call for Inspector Danol Scryverin!"

"I would like to tie my scarf to your arm, Inspector," said Lavenci, twirling her ragged scarf, "but I cannot touch you without being ill. Besides, I only have one good hand. A favor cannot be validly given unless tied by a lady's hands. Will you take my advice instead?"

"Please, speak."

I was seeing Lavenci as I had never seen her before: strong, sharp, and cool while everyone else was running about with their hands in the air.

"Fall from your horse as soon as the charge begins. Trust me, none of the others will live long enough to accuse you of cowardice."

A moment later I was dashing through Norellie's door as the whistle began to sound again.

"Provost's third and last call for Inspector Danol—"

"All right, all right, here I am."

"Two sweethearts?" asked a provost, eyeing the dishcloth and pair of drawers tied to my arm in the torchlight.

"Need all the good wishes and favor I can get," I muttered as I mounted my horse.

Chapter Eight

THE FIGHTING BEGINS

 The only good aspect of being among the baron's chosen warriors was that I was given a very good, if hasty, dinner. Next I was then fitted out with moderately expensive chainmail, helmet, shield, and greaves. I declined the offer of a lance.

"But it's a gentlemen's weapon, and the baron gave you leave to bear one," declared the armorer.

"Maybe so, but I am not a gentleman," I replied. "The fencing ax is my weapon."

Although technically I am of the nobility, I thought with a grim sort of satisfaction, *but a fat lot of good that will do for any of us.*

We set off in the dark, following a pair of lancers who were carrying torches. The baron had me ride beside him, and tell him every detail of the massacre that morning. No amount of detail about the Lupanian's overwhelmingly superior weapon could dissuade him from carrying the attack through, however. We reached Bald Pate Hill an hour or so after midnight. Here we dismounted, wrapped ourselves in blankets, and slept in our armor, under the stars, until dawn began to glow at the eastern horizon. I was roused by the baron himself, who wanted to check the disposition of the enemy before attacking.

Anyone who has ever slept in chainmail over a tunic of quilted felt padding half an inch thick will know how very wet and clammy the cloth can become. I was shivering, miserable, and smelly as we mounted up. The baron led the way up the shallow side of the hill. He surveyed the field using my farsight while I sat unhappily on a warhorse that I could not have bought with a year's wages. Even without the farsight, I could see that the Lupanians had thrown up earthworks around their cylinder. The baron reported that the arm with the farsight device was still on watch, but he did not seem very impressed with his first view of the Lupanian stronghold. Glancing behind us, I saw that his six score horsemen were by now mounted and waiting at the base of the hill. They were, of course, still hidden from the Lupanians. The edge of the sun finally rose above the eastern horizon.

"Good, good, the sunrise is right behind our line of charge," the baron declared as he concentrated on the pit area. "Not very savvy on defenses, are they? No pike walls or horse trap trenches, and no archers to break the charge. All they have is tentacles, you say?"

"And an invincible heat weapon," I reminded him.

"Oh that!"

"A heat weapon that makes a smithy's forge seem no warmer than a hot water bottle after a very long and frosty night."

"Well, I've campaigned in the Acrema deserts, I know all about heat. That thing on the arm, is that the sentry?"

"It seems to be an eye and farsight, all in one."

"It sweeps the field every half minute or so. Inspector, I have a cunning plan. We wait until it has just finished sweeping Bald Pate Hill, then charge. It will be another half minute before it is looking in our direction again, and by then we shall be upon them."

"The fight will be over quickly—" I began.

"Well, more is the pity."

For the Lupanians, passed through my mind, but I knew there was no point in saying it aloud.

"It will be too easy, no glory will be ours," continued the baron.

"The fight's history is told by the victor's chronicler," I said smoothly, snatching desperately at a chance to stay alive. "Tell your chronicler to embroider it a little."

"Chronicler, sir? I have no chronicler. The wife takes care of writing matters."

"Well then, where is the baroness?"

"Why back in Gatrov Castle, of course. War's no place for women!"

Obviously never met some of the women in my past, I

thought, but I held my tongue until I could dredge up more diplomatic words.

"Ah, such a pity," I said instead. "You see, my lord baron, if she were to stand on this hill she would see the entire spectacle. No warrior down there would have quite such a good view, so her opinion of events would be taken as the final truth. She could, of course, add whatever glory to that truth that you thought fit to include."

"I see . . . but the sun is rising now, and the castle is miles away! It would take hours to fetch her, and I have not two minutes."

"*I* could chronicle the fight."

"Oh Inspector Danol, I could not possibly deprive you of a part in this glorious victory!" exclaimed the brainless goat, and he meant every word of it.

"Very well then," I said brightly, getting ready to throw my last card down. "Who will use the farsight?"

"Farsight, sir? They're not for any but the nobility, who need an overview of battlefields—well, and for constables to spot miscreants at a distance, of course. Not a man of my company has ever touched one."

"Then who other than you and I is sufficiently familiar with a farsight's use to monitor the Lupanian's sentry, and signal when it's facing the other way?"

The baron's features froze, then twisted with anguish. I had him! He had not allowed for that in his plan of attack. He glanced to the rising sun, then to the Lupanians, then to me.

"You sir, do you have reedpaper and a char stick?"

"That I do, Baron, in my report kit."

"I see. Listen now, Inspector Danol, I hate to ask this of you, but Fate seems to be flinging obstacles onto your path to the battlefield. Could you see your way clear to signal us off, then chronicle this charge? Mind, you don't have to say yes, but I'm willing to perjure myself and swear that you rode with us to the field."

"That would satisfy honor—" I began.

"You're not just saying that to please me, are you?" he asked anxiously.

"Baron, I would be delighted to be your signaler and to help you write the chronicle of this day. I was in the charge at Racewater Bridge in 3141, after all. That was enough glory to last me a lifetime."

"Were you, by all the gods of Miral? Would have loved to have been there, we must speak on it sometime—but not now. Look, feel free to ride in and chop a few tentacles once the action is all but done, and here's a something to cover expenses—oh, and here's your farsight back, you'll be needing it, ha, ha."

He tossed me a purse and my farsight, and then he was gone, riding down the hill on his warhorse and shouting orders to his men. The horsemen moved off without any trumpet fanfare, to maintain the element of surprise. I watched the rising sun catch their polished shields, helmets and chainmail with near-horizontal rays, thinking how magnificent they looked and almost forgetting that they were riding to their doom. They began to skirt Bald Pate Hill, then stopped.

This was my moment. I took Norellie's drawers from my arm. They were of white cotton, and were embroidered with pink baby rabbits and dragons. There was a large heart encompassing a bull's-eye over the crotch. I brought the farsight up to my eye. The Lupanian farsight swept around, stopped, and examined me for a moment. My life began to flash before my eyes, starting with the time I had been sick all over the crown jewels during some ceremony on my fifth birthday . . . then the sentry seemed to assume that I was some local trying to arrange a truce, and thus worthy of being ignored. It returned to its scan of the field, and when it was a quarter turn away from Bald Pate Hill, I swept Norellie's drawers down.

Perhaps a fitting flag to signal brave men to go to their deaths, I thought as I tucked the drawers into my ax belt. The baron had his riders fan out into a crescent one deep, and he held his battle-ax high all the while. Finally he brought it down, pointing in the direction of the cylinder. On that cue, they charged.

Immediately I trained my farsight on the Lupanians. Their farsight arm was already whirling back.

"Of course the sound of several dozen charging horses is not going to be ignored, you clown!" I shouted after the baron.

The two tentacles with the heat weapon were rising as I

spoke, and I lowered the farsight to get a more panoramic view. The horsemen got to within about three hundred yards of the pit. The reason the Lupanians did not fire at them earlier was probably that they wanted them so close that none could escape back to the cover of Bald Pate Hill. The first I knew of the heat weapon striking out was the flashes of brilliance leaping from horseman to horseman. The polished shields protected the kavelars from the beam about as much as a reedpaper bag might protect a head from a battle-ax.

Horses and riders exploded in puffs of flesh, blood, and dingy smoke. The kavelars were the first to fall, being at the northern end of the crescent, but the archers were at the southern end, and thus they had a few extra seconds before the heat beam swept across to obliterate their bodies. Those seconds were enough for them to get within nearly two hundred yards of the cylinder, and in a truly magnificent display of futile, desperate bravery, the mounted archers let off a volley of arrows just before the beam cut them down.

Abruptly all became utterly silent and quite still, apart from dispersing smoke and a handful of descending arrows. Suddenly I saw a man clamber over the opposite lip of the pit and run for the stream. *Poor devil, he must have been hiding behind some rock in the pit ever since the first massacre,* I thought. Any moment now the Lupanian controlling the beam was going to turn away from the slaughtered horsemen and notice him . . . but then the arrows fell into the pit, and the Lupanian was again distracted.

At least one arrow must have struck something sensitive and caused considerable annoyance, as the tentacles holding the heat weapon casting suddenly writhed and twisted, as if in pain. Seemingly in a fit of temper, the Lupanian now swept the fallen mass of smoking cavalrymen and their mounts again and again with the beam, sending great clouds of dark smoke into the air. I turned my farsight back to the pit in time to see the arm with the farsight turn to Bald Pate Hill—presumably to check whether I was still there.

Without even thinking to spur my horse into flight, I leaped from the saddle. Behind me, I heard something between a wheeze and a whinny, and I glanced back to see the horse explode in a messy cloud of flesh, flames, and smoke. I lay still as smoking fragments of horse rained down around me, and I remember thinking that the smell was oddly appetizing. I lay very still for what seemed to be quite a long time.

"This does, of course, mean war!" declared a squeaky voice nearby.

The speaker was roughly nine inches high and was holding a spear about the size of a knitting needle. The top of his floppy red hat had been burned away, and smoke curled up from what was left. He wore a red coat over a green tunic and green trews. Taking off the remains of his hat, he frowned at it, then batted out the smoulders.

"Flame one grass gnome, you flame all grass gnomes," he continued.

"That can probably be arranged," I warned.

"It's them Lupanian imperialist oppressors of the freedom lovin' sentient entities," he said, oblivious to my warning.

He took off his coat and turned it inside out. The lining was a sort of streaky black and green, and blended in with the grass very effectively.

"Let me guess, you've been talking to the bridge trolls," I said, unsure about the wisdom of moving as yet.

"Nah, I knows a water sprite—no funny business, mind, we just exchanges fish for nuts every week. Anyway, she said that the bridge trolls told her that some constables got an eye on those Lupanians, and that they were going to sort 'em out. Didn't do a very good job, did they?"

"You mean that charge? They were nobles, not constables."

"Nobles?"

"They're the sort that have bags of gold and go around doing heroic things on battlefields. It's the World Mother's way of weeding out the stupid ones."

"Well I'd say it's time us grass gnomes entered into alliance with you big folk!" he declared, flinging down his spear, lowering his trews, and waving a small, pale bottom in the general direction of the Lupanians. "Burn that, ye bastards."

However good the Lupanian optics were, they were evidently not capable of picking up a target of that size, so no invisible beam of heat transformed him into ash and smoke.

"Look here, I don't suppose you gnomes are planning anything as foolish as saddling up a few rabbits and charging the Lupanians over open ground, are you?"

"Do I look stupid? We do candlestine warfare. We're sort of, well, built for it."

"I think you mean clandestine warfare, but . . . look here, if you want to make a real difference, you could spy on the Lupanians, then tell us what they are doing."

"Guv, that's just what I had in mind."

"I saw a man dash out of the pit and run for the stream, just as the nobles charged. He may be still alive, and if he is, he will have a day's observations of the Lupanians and their weapons. Could you tell the water sprites to tell the bridge trolls that I would like to speak with him?"

"Good as done!" he declared, saluting smartly. "Solonor's the name, by the by."

"Inspector Danol, Wayfarers," I croaked in response. "Did you see where my farsight landed?"

"Farsight?"

"A sort of tube thing with glass bits at either end."

"Oh, that. Came down on the east side of the hill, safe and sound."

"Oh good, it cost me a month's wages."

"Look, it's not as if it's my business or anything, but are you going to lie there all day?"

"Yes! Until after sunset, when it's dark."

"Why's that?"

"Because I am still within sight of the Lupanians, and I'm nine times taller than a gnome, you little twerp! The Lupanians can move their heat beam a lot faster than I can run!"

"All right, fair enough, no need to get personal."

The second massacre had taken place about five minutes after dawn, so I was faced with the prospect of lying there for the entire day. It began to get quite hot on the crest of Bald Pate Hill, and being covered in bits of half-charred, exploded horse did not make things any more pleasant. The flies seemed to have a good time of it, however. On the positive side, all that gunk protected my face from sunburn as I lay there, hour after hour. The gnome returned, and offered me a drink from a waterskin made from the hide of a field mouse. He reported that the escapee from the Lupanian pit was in the hands of the bridge trolls, and that he was being moved along the stream very slowly.

"You must be gettin' seriously hot, guv," the gnome commented at about noon.

"Whatever gave you that idea?" I mumbled.

"'Cause you've drunk thirty-seven waterskins in six hours. Think you can really last the hours until dark?"

"Better than I'd last the millionth of a second that the heat weapon would take to finish me."

"Oh, I see. Look, you just stay right there and I'll see what I can do."

I lost track of time after he left, and I definitely blacked out once or twice. I awoke to a trickle of water being squirted onto my face.

"Wakey, wakey, Lupanians about to be distracted!" squeaked Solonor as I opened my eyes.

"I'm awake," I moaned.

"Can you move?"

"I'd rather not perform a high-risk experiment to find out."

"Well when I says go, you just sort of spring up and leap down the hill, behind you, like," he said as he climbed onto a chunk of dead warhorse and peered out over the field.

"What are you going to do?"

"We're— Shyte! They're early! Move! Run! Jump! Go, that was it!"

Without pausing to ask what *that* might be, I lurched up, took a few steps doubled right over, then sprang down into the hill's cover just as the heat weapon returned to annihilate what was left of the warhorse. Solonor was standing nearby, pointing out my farsight.

"What did you do?" I asked as I reassured myself that I was still alive.

"Oh, we wove up a few men of straw; then the bridge trolls dragged them along the stream to near the pit, and held them up on sticks from the cover of the bank."

"Good to hear that nobody got hurt," I said as I scraped the congealed horse blood and muck from my face. "There's a lot of us men who could learn from you."

I was drinking from the stream when two muddy bridge trolls, six grass gnomes, and a stark-naked water sprite approached me along the bank. For a moment the thought crossed my mind that the mucky looking bridge trolls lived upstream, in the very water that I was drinking, but to dwell upon it would have been to throw up, and I was much too dehydrated to be able to afford that. A mud-encrusted youth in a tunic was walking between the trolls. On closer inspection I saw that he was not actually walking. Each troll had a hand around an upper arm, and his feet were some inches above the ground.

"This is my, ah, trading partner, Slivisselly," said Solonor uneasily, introducing the water sprite.

She was about three inches taller than he was, and I would have found her very alluring had I been about nine times shorter. A gnome with a blue rinse in his beard frowned at Solonor, but did not speak.

"Esteemed and handsome hero of the Wayfaring Constables, we bring you this refugee from the oppression of the Lupanian royal establishment," the sprite said with a gesture to the youth between the bridge trolls.

Her body moved in a quite alarmingly suggestive manner, and I shook my head and tried to focus on the trolls and their captive. One of the trolls holding the youth now cleared his throat.

"Yeah, we brung one of, er, your freedom-lovin' people what made a dash for freedom from the, er . . ."

A troll with massive, hairy shoulders whispered something to him.

"Thanks, sister. Yeah, er, from the oppressive Lupanian establishment sorcerers."

The escapee was set down. He was wide-eyed with terror, and did not try to move. The apparently female troll whispered something else.

"Can we have a receipt?" asked the spokestroll.

"I'll scribe one now," I said, fumbling for the report kit under my chain mail and dropping to one knee.

"And why have you got a pair of drawers in your belt and a dishcloth tied to your arm?"

"A display of cultural solidarity with my consultants in etheric scholarship," I explained wearily, with a reasonably straight face. Then I stood up and handed over the receipt.

The youth was pushed forward.

"Don't be afraid, lad, nobody's to hurt you now," I said cheerily. "What's your name?"

He took a soaked, grimy book from a pouch on his belt and opened it. Pointing at some lines of writing and a symbol, he bowed.

"Menni gil trekkit, pores," he declared, then added, "Azorian."

"Foreigner with a phrase book!" I sighed. "Give it here."

There was no Alberinese in the book, in fact there was no language that I spoke. Using signs, I established that he was uninjured, fed him some bread and cheese, then got him to follow me as I set off for Gatrov on foot. After about a hundred yards a voice squeaked out behind me.

"That's it lad, just follow the inspector."

I turned and stopped. Solonor was riding on the Azorianese youth's shoulder.

"Shouldn't you be back there, rallying gnomes or something?" I asked.

"Er, the wife's bein' a bit unreasonable, like, about my trading partner."

It was only now I noticed that he had suddenly developed a closed and swollen eye.

"Your wife? But I saw no women back there—well, not female gnomes, that is."

"'Course there were! They're the ones with their beards dyed Lavender Morning, or whatever the fashion is this month. Ain't no male gnomes that dye their beards . . . not that we likes to talk about, anyway."

"So . . . Slivisselly likes her lovers short and muscular?"

"Now don't *you* start! Looky here, Inspector, is there any chance of some, er, liaison work with the Wayfarers? Things is a little, er, awkward for me back at Bald Pate Hill, as of about three minutes ago."

"Are you saying that you fear your wife more than you fear the Lupanians?"

"Ain't married to the Lupanians. What do you say?"

"Oh very well, come along. The Wayfarer service is full of folk like you."

I paused, undid my belt, bent over, and shook off a mail shirt that would have required a decade-long mortgage to buy on an inspector's salary. Leaving the mail where it had fallen, I then snatched up the dishcloth and drawers, and stuffed them into my report kit before walking on.

"Won't you need that chain mail?" asked the gnome.

"For what?"

"Protection against the Lupanian heat . . . oh. I see."

About a hundred yards farther on I removed the greaves and discarded them as well.

It took us three hours to make the trek to Gatrov, crawling through open fields on all fours, dashing from tree to tree in woodland, and ever watchful for anything resembling a tentacle. It was early evening as I entered the town, and the sky was clouding over. I soon learned that Halland's flamethrower attack on the second cylinder had been successful. Burning hellfire oil had been poured into the hatch as soon as it had been opened, and whatever had been inside had been roasted within moments.

I chanced upon Riellen, who was addressing a crowd on some subject that involved freedom, oppression, electocracy, cheap ale for countryfolk, and oppressive royalist sorcerer lackeys of the tyrannical Lupanian establishment. Interrupting the rally, I gave the Azorianese youth and the adulterous gnome into her care, told her to report to the militia commander that I was on my way with a report, then hurried on to Norellie's house. On the door was a proclamation by Halland that any issues involving the practice of sorcery associated with Norellie were to be referred to him before any action whatsoever was taken. I knocked.

Norellie opened the door, and Mervielle and Lavenci were still with her. The serving maid cried out as she caught sight of me, swayed as if about to faint, then recovered her composure, flung her arms around me, and all but lifted me from the floor.

"You're meant to be dead!" Norellie cried, stamping her foot. "I performed the Soul's Release ceremony for you this morning."

"I lit a candle for your spirit in Lady Fortune's shrine before dawn," said Lavenci, looking vaguely annoyed. "Cost me five peons."

"I—er, thank, you. But how did you know about the battle?"

Norellie explained hurriedly. Some peasants from Bald Pate Hamlet had been lurking at a distance, watching the baron's charge in the hope of free entertainment. What they saw was the baron and one hundred and twenty of the empire's finest cavalry annihilated in somewhere between three and five seconds. Terrified witless, the peasants fled straight to Gatrov, bypassing their hamlet and running most of the way. They reported the fate of the baron and his men to the town militia headquarters.

"They said the squad was wiped out!" Norellie concluded.

I forced a smug smile onto my face. "I had myself appointed chronicler, and was forced to watch from a safe and distant vantage."

"I should have known you would not he stupid enough to get yourself reduced to overdone pork crackling," said Lavenci. "I—"

Away to the northeast a green star burst out of the gathering clouds and drew a line of fire with itself across the darkening sky.

"Another one," said Norellie.

"At least we now know that they can be roasted when the cylinders are first opened," I said, unhappy about the prospect of probably having to help the cook, but resigned to it nevertheless.

"The commander says Duke Lestor just arrived from the next province downstream with six river galleys loaded with the Riverway Militia," said Norellie. "He will probably lead the attack."

"So, no work for me, so I'll not need these," I said with some relief, returning the drawers and dishcloth. "I'm afraid I won no victories in your name."

"They're covered in blood!" exclaimed Norellie, holding her drawers up to the lamplight.

"Most of it's not mine. Now then, time to report to the militia."

"And time for me to give thanks for your safe return to many, many gods," said Mervielle.

"That probably didn't help," said Norellie.

"And probably don't exist," added Lavenci.

"Lady Lavenci, will you please come along and explain your mathematics of the heat weapon?" I said with a wave in the direction of the militia's headquarters.

"Nobody but you will understand, Inspector."

"You flatter me, ladyship."

Lavenci and I hurried across to the militia's headquarters, exchanging observations of Lupanian castings and science as we went. Riellen was waiting at the front door as we arrived. Although my report of the catastrophe at Bald Pate Hill had not been the first to be brought back to the militia commander, I had been closer to the action than anyone else. Upon entering the militia offices, I discovered that Duke Lestor was there. He had come from Siranta, the next large town downstream on the Alber. The baroness had fled for Alberin before noon, as soon as word of her husband's defeat had reached her. She had called in at Siranta long enough to tell the duke what had happened. He had immediately decided to throw a small force together and teach the Lupanians not to declare war without a proper exchange of diplomatic insults.

Having six river galleys and four times more fighting men than the Gatrov Militia, the duke felt that he should be in charge of whatever was being done about the Lupanians. Halland had thus put himself and his men at the duke's disposal. The duke had based himself in the militia offices, and was compiling the various reports of what had happened when I arrived. I was shown into his presence, and I gave my report as quickly and coherently as I could, leaving out such details as Norellie's drawers, Mervielle's dishcloth, and the offer of an alliance from the grass gnomes. Once I had finished I was told that I had done a good job, then taken outside and presented with a pint of ale and a slice of smoked ham in a bread roll. Halland then arrived with news from the watchtower. His estimate was that the third cylinder had come down about seven miles to the north, at a place where the River Alber runs close to Waingram Forest. The duke decided to convene a council of advisors.

"So, although these Lupanians are all but invincible, they are helpless for a few moments when their cylinders open," concluded the duke to his advisors, who numbered six river kavelars, the Gatrov mayor, Halland, Lavenci, and myself.

"Aye sir, for perhaps five heartbeats after the hatch opens," explained Halland.

"And they may be killed by a single warrior using a flamethrower and hellfire oil?"

"I used three flamethrowers, sir."

"Why three?"

"I could not fit any more around the hatchway."

"But one would do?"

"Probably."

"How quickly could a man learn to use a flamethrower?"

"Three or four hours of instruction and practice would suffice, but we have plenty of trained and experienced—"

"Enough!" barked the duke. "I shall take my flotilla of galleys up the river to where this cylinder has landed. On the way I shall take instruction in flamethrower operation. Commander, you will assign to me a man who participated in the attack on the second cylinder, purely as an advisor, of course."

Halland suddenly looked worried. It was nothing conspicuous, just a subtle twist in his facial features, but I knew worry when I saw it.

"Now, Commander Halland, I have a plan for the Lupanians from the first cylinder," the duke continued. "According to Inspector Danolarian, there is a stream running to within thirty yards of the pit. That will provide cover for you to take every archer and militiaman in the town to within bowshot of the thing. From that cover, the archers will lay down a barrage of arrows that will skewer everything made of flesh in the pit. The militiamen will then rush the pit with axes and spears and finish them off."

"A bold plan," said Halland, looking politely attentive. "If executed in the dead of night, it might work."

"Oh no, no, no, no, you *must* attack in daylight, I insist. Don't want any Lupanians to escape in the dark, do we? It will be magnificent, why I might even mention you by name in my report to the regent. Who knows, it could well be *Kavelar Halland* before a year or two have passed."

As soon as we had been dismissed and were clear of the militia building, Halland softly cursed the young noble to spend eternity in some very hot and unpleasant places, reincarnated as various items of reproductive anatomy—and then he remembered that Lavenci and Riellen were with us and began to apologize profusely.

"Life on the road has made me quite familiar with the colloquialisms of the oppressed and unrepresented people," declared Riellen.

"I've had a sheltered upbringing and I need to expand my vocabulary," added Lavenci.

"Is Duke Lestor really as stupid as he seems?" the grass gnome called from Riellen's coat pocket.

Lavenci shrieked, and Halland dodged away. I took Solonor from Riellen, introduced him to everyone, then swore him in as a Wayfarer auxiliary before we continued on our way. He had saved my life, after all, and I had a vague idea that he really might be of use in spying on the Lupanians. He was even smaller than Wallas, and seemed to be a lot braver.

"The duke's plan is as clear as a newly washed window," Halland suddenly ranted, really letting himself go after thinking through his orders. "*He* goes to the third cylinder, and roasts it. Meantime *we* get roasted by the Lupanians at the first cylinder as we attack in broad daylight. He then claims to have destroyed the Lupanians in both the second and third cylinders."

"Establishment lackey!" snapped Riellen enthusiastically.

"Aye, oppressor of honest lower-class warriors what don't have a voice in decision making," agreed Solonor, who was now riding on Riellen's shoulder.

"But the first cylinder does need to be destroyed," I pointed out.

"It's a definite danger," called the grass gnome, waving the charred remains of his hat.

"Yes, Brother Inspector, what to do about the first cylinder?" asked Riellen.

"I suppose the duke will order a night attack after you die, Commander Halland," I speculated. "He will say that he learned not to attack in daylight from your sacrifice."

" 'If' is the operative word, Inspector. I *shall* attack by day, as the duke has ordered, but first I shall set hay, tar, and hellfire oil alight upwind of the Lupanians, to lay down a smoke blind. Instead of bowmen, I'll take a squad of militiamen with flamethrowers along the stream to the first cylinder. If the wind is constant, the smoke will allow those with spears to get to the pit's edge alive, and the Lupanians will get a taste of what it feels like to be on the wrong side in a massacre."

"That should please the duke," said Solonor.

"The duke? Pah!" exclaimed Halland. "The duke *wants* us to die, dammit. Don't you see? He would oppose any plan that looks like leaving either Wayfarers or militiamen alive, yet use it himself once we are dead. Danol, Riellen, I am already disobeying the direct order of a nobleman, and so are you two if you choose to fall in with me. If I lose, we become a puff of smoke and a sprinkle of ash. If I win, we shall be courtmartialed and hanged. I am not a good man to side with."

"They have to catch us first," said Solonor.

"We could form a revolutionary committee and usurp his command," suggested Riellen.

"*No* we could *not!*" said Halland emphatically. "I will not attack my homeland's rulers and nobles, even if they are idiots. What I *will* do is disobey the orders of a noble for the good of my homeland."

"I'm with you," I said firmly.

Riellen scowled for a moment as she considered her options.

"I agree to ally myself with you as an act of social justice, rather than through an application of revolutionary ideology," she said with no less conviction than I had shown.

"I, er, accept that," said Halland slowly. "I think."

"Er, should I say yes, Inspector?" Solonor asked, and I nodded.

"If I can help I shall," said Lavenci.

"What's to be done, then?" I asked hurriedly, before another argument developed.

"You take your ponycart and a flamethrower to the third cylinder," said Halland. "I can secure a flamethrower that the duke does not know about. Go overland, go tonight, hide, and wait there."

"And do what?"

"If the duke fouls up, step in and do what you can."

"But the duke has six river galleys loaded with river marines," I replied. "Getting them to step aside could be a problem."

"I know, I know, but what can I do? I can't ask militiamen to go with you and fight imperial guardsmen. They're patriotic men, and it would be citizen fighting citizen."

"Perhaps I could help," said Lavenci.

"What? How?" asked Halland.

"Commander, I was once . . . engaged in sorcery. Before the enlightened prohibitions against magic and the glorious Inquisition, that is. I know little of combat, but I can do some powerful castings."

"Fireball castings to drop even two or three warriors would have you exhausted," said Halland.

"But one really strong brilliance casting would have all the duke's men floundering about sightless for a full minute or more," said Lavenci.

For the first time since our meeting with the duke, Commander Halland smiled.

"It might work, ladyship, it just might work," he said, nodding his head slowly, as if reluctant to accept good news.

"Now then, what else can be used to our advantage?" I asked. "Riellen, have you had any success speaking with that Azorian youth who spent a day in the first voidship's pit?"

"Azorian turned out to be his name, sir, not his country. I do believe he is a brother student, stranded here when Torea was destroyed."

I had lived in Torea until I was fourteen, spoke five Torean languages fluently and had a smattering of another nine, yet I did not recognize his speech. On the other hand, Torea had been a big place, with many kingdoms and tongues.

"There are refugee Metrologan priestesses from Torea in Alberin," I said. "When—if—we survive the hours to come, you must take him there."

"Why not straightaway, sir?" asked Riellen.

"Because if the attacks on the first and third cylinders fail, I also want you to report that to Wayfarer Headquarters. You will stay in Gatrov with Azorian. By noon tomorrow you should know how the attacks turned out, and after that you will take the first barge or boat for Alberin. Take Mervielle and Norellie with you—oh, and sober up Roval to travel with you as a guard."

"What about Constable Wallas, sir?"

"I have other duties awaiting Constable Wallas."

Riellen saluted, then strode off with Solonor. Halland, Lavenci and I gazed after her, all shaking our heads.

"Remarkable girl," said Halland. "Can she be trusted to do all that?"

"Oh yes, but she is also liable to do considerably more. *That* is what worries me."

"The hours ahead look bad," said Lavenci.

"We still have hope," I replied.

"I would be happier if we were not fighting our own idiot nobles as well as the invaders," Halland said quietly. "You know, Inspector, it suddenly strikes me that Riellen could be right about needing to overthrow them."

"It's been tried, time and again," I replied. "Those who overthrow nobles end up becoming nobles themselves."

"Must it always be thus?"

"Give me a viable alternative system, sir, and I'd be the first to run over and sign up."

"Only if you can run and sign faster than me, Inspector," said Halland. "Follow me to the armory. The blacksmith there can be trusted, and he has enough spare parts to toss a flamethrower together in an hour or so. After that, it is all up to you two."

Chapter Nine

IN THE STORM

Thunder rumbled in the distance as Lavenci, Halland, and I walked to the militia armory, then on to Norellie's house. As we walked we speculated on whether Lupan had thunderstorms, because if not this could give us yet another advantage. Arriving at Norellie's house, I told the healer that I was about to lead an attack on the third cylinder. She collapsed onto a stool, took a small jar of fortified wine from a nearby shelf, flung the cork into the fire, and drained the contents.

"Ladyship, I am willing to give you too a declaration of *absalver ne trestipar* to accompany the inspector tonight and throw a brilliance casting," Halland offered as Lavenci handed him her roll of notes

"So you will take the penalty for any crime I may commit?"

"If you are caught, yes," said Halland. "It will be in the service of the regent."

"Sort of," I added.

"That is gracious of you, Commander," said Lavenci.

"I shall write one out now, if Madame Norellie thinks you seem trustworthy," said Halland as he sat down at the table.

"If *I* think as much?" exclaimed Norellie.

"I hold you in high regard, madame. It may not seem so, but—"

"Yes, yes, very well. From what I know of Her Ladyship, she abuses no trust."

Thunder rumbled ever more loudly outside as he wrote. I witnessed Halland's signature, then gave the declaration to Lavenci to read.

"Effective until noon tomorrow," she noted.

"What the inspector and you must do will be later tonight—" began Halland.

"Tonight?" exclaimed Norellie. "In the rain? How many hours will it take?"

"If all goes well then perchance, oh, twelve hours away from Gatrov."

"*Twelve* hours?"

"Work must be done that requires the combined skills of a warrior and sorceress."

"But look at him!" Norellie barked, waving a hand in my direction. "Have you any idea how much he has been through in the fifty hours just past? Two battles with the Lupanians, a very rough tavern fight, a severe migraine—"

"Half a dozen of Riellen's speeches," I added.

"Nevertheless it *must* be Danol who leads this venture," said Halland. "The Inspector has survived two encounters with the Lupanians. There is nobody else in all the world better suited to lead the attack than he."

The storm was almost upon us as we walked to the Bargeman's Barrel for our packs, then to where my hired pony and cart were stabled. The storm clouds had cut off all light from Miral and the moonworlds, and a few public lanterns were all there was to light our way. Another half hour had the hastily assembled flamethrower tied firmly down in the tray of the cart, and concealed under a tarpaulin. The blacksmith threw in a couple of cavalry crossbows and a score of bolts "Just in case." We then set off to secure our night-vision equipment, with Halland driving and Lavenci and I sitting at the back of the tray, not quite touching. In spite of everything, I still wanted to be near her. It was hopeless affection, and beyond explanations, but it was a fact. Thunder rumbled out of the western sky with increasing frequency, and lightning flickered amid the clouds.

"It promises to be a very unpleasant night," I said uneasily.

"For Pelmore as well as us," answered Lavenci. "He should be married and about to bed his wife by now."

"At least he will be indoors," I said with a glance to the sky.

"So, here we are. A one-handed ex-sorceress, and an inspector of the Wayfarer Constables. Before us is both the might of the empire, and the invincible heat casting of the Lupanians. We are armed with two lightweight crossbows, a ponycart, and a flamethrower."

"And a talking cat."

"A talking cat?"

"Yes."

"You jest."

"Quite frequently, but not just now. Wallas really is a talking cat."

Lavenci put a hand over her eyes. "I'm sure it will make all the difference."

"Actually, it will. Wallas can see in the dark."

Wallas was in the tavern where I had originally left him, soaking up hospitality as only a cat is able. Leaving the pony, cart, and flamethrower with Halland, Lavenci and I entered and sat at a table. Wallas was lying on the serving board, and noticed us immediately. He got up, came padding over, and jumped onto our table.

"Meow?" he declared innocently.

"Speak Alberinese, Wallas," I said softly. "Kavelen Lavenci knows about you."

"Ah, the hoyden noble!" exclaimed Wallas quietly. "I heard about the, ah, heroic repair of your honor, ladyship. Have you formed a liaison of passionate gratitude with the inspector as yet?"

"Three sentences, and I despise him already," replied Lavenci, glaring at Wallas.

"Lavenci and I have formed an alliance," I added hastily. "We intend to attack the Lupanians in the third cylinder tonight—after beating off the duke and his marines, that is."

Wallas flopped to the table, yowling with laughter and waving his legs in the air.

"You two, alone, against a fleet of river galleys crammed with marines, not to mention the deadly Lupanians."

"Well, yes, you seem to have our measure."

"Ridiculous!" he laughed, sitting up again. "Why there's a storm almost upon us as well. You'll get soaked, and will not even be able to see in the gloom."

"Indeed, Miral and the moonworlds are obscured by the clouds. That is where you come in."

Wallas gave a start, then scrabbled frantically to turn and leap from the table, but my hand shot out and seized him by the scruff of the neck.

"Wallas, old tomcat, how are you doing?" I asked cheerily.

"Murder! Heresy! Treason! Rape!" yowled Wallas, immediately securing the attention of the tavern's entire company.

"Wayfarer Constabulary!" I declared, holding up my crest plate as Lavenci wrapped the flailing bundle of fur, claws, and fangs in her cloak. "This cat is under arrest for suspicion of being a sorcerer in disguise."

Fortunately for me, taverns are places where people tend to have been drinking for some time. Faced with an overweight, talking cat being placed under arrest, most assumed that they had been in the tavern rather too long, and had been drinking far too much.

"Oi, ain't he *your* cat?" called one of the serving maids who had been looking after Wallas.

"He killed my real cat, and took his place to spy upon me. This lady is a member of the Inquisition Constables. She saw through his disguise."

This appeared to explain everything to most of the drinkers, who smiled with relief and turned back to their drinks. The shocked serving maids remained wide-eyed with alarm, however, and I wondered just what they had been doing with Wallas that they might not have done had they known that he was somewhat more than a black cat with an eating disorder and a drinking problem. Wallas was not one to give up without a fight however.

"Militia! Militia! Summon the yowrf—"

I clamped a hand over Wallas's mouth. He responded by biting my finger, but it was a small price to pay for silencing him. With Wallas securely bundled up in the cloak and held tightly, Lavenci and I hurried out of the tavern. Halland was waiting outside with a sack, into which Wallas was tied, with only his head projecting.

We gave Halland a ride to his home. This turned out to be a tiny, single-room cottage.

"Small for a man of my station, is it not?" he laughed as he jumped down.

"I'd heard you have a wife and three children, sir," I replied. "It must be crowded in there."

"They live in the baron's castle. I see them every week or so."

"So, the romance has cooled a little?"

"Ours was an arranged marriage. She was the eleventh daughter of a very poor kavelar, and I was an exiled, disgraced lancer in the baron's cavalry. The baron . . . required the marriage. I was appointed as militia commander over five volunteer spearmen and two archers—who shared the same crossbow. In the nine years since then I have built the militia into what it is today. There's little incentive to linger at home, you see."

"So the children . . ." I began, then managed to stop myself.

"Three, and they all resemble the baron," said Halland without any attempt at guile. "That was why he required the marriage."

"Oh!" exclaimed Lavenci. "So, er, your wife must be, er, passably devastated by his death?"

"Devastated, no. Very angry, yes. Until this morning she was the baron's most favored courtesan. Now she is merely my wife—in theory. Actually my family left the castle in a carriage this morning, escorted by four lancers and on the road to Alberin—but enough of tasteless romantic farce. Good fortune with cylinder three, friends, and act with care."

"Perchance a stray crossbow bolt may strike the duke and solve all our problems."

"Perchance I did not hear that. On your way, Inspector."

Large but sparse drops of rain were falling as we passed through the main gates of the town. Soon we were driving through the fields, still slightly ahead of the storm. Wallas's task was more to keep us on the road than navigate, for although he made several determined attempts to misdirect us, the flashes of lightning were only a half minute or so apart, and were enough to indicate our location.

"Ladyship, I was filled with admiration by your mathematical study of the Lupanian heat weapon," I said quite suddenly.

As far as I could tell I was not even thinking, but suddenly I was hearing myself speak the words.

"Why, Inspector, thank you, that means a lot to me," Lavenci replied, without a trace of anything but sincerity in her voice.

"Ah, so you do like to be admired for your intellect?"

"Perhaps, I do not think upon it. But I certainly like to be regarded well by intelligent men, like you."

That taxed my talent for snappy replies. Again I was confronted with the depressing fact that I liked her, even though she was liable to do something horribly hurtful to me, and probably with the aid of a less intelligent man—if I let her near me again. It was all so unfair.

"What do you think the Lupanians have come here to do?" Lavenci asked presently.

"Were I a Lupanian, I would not come all this way to hide in a pit," I replied. "They must have things that pass for horses and armor. If they can move with that heat beam, we are in very serious trouble."

"But why are they here?" Lavenci insisted.

"Why does any ruler invade the lands of another?" I asked. "Why do tomcats piss in each other's territory?"

"I do no such thing!" cried Wallas, who was now more angry than afraid. "I use the privy like real people. Have to maintain cultural connections with my true species, you know."

"The duke set off for the third cylinder with his river galleys within two hours of sunset," I continued. "We shall arrive there later than he."

"And do what?" asked Lavenci.

"Wait at the cylinder until it opens, probably a little after dawn. Every mother's son of them will be watching the hatchway as it unscrews. Lady Lavenci, you must set off a brilliance casting right over it, and while they flounder about blinded, I shall step past them, flame the Lupanians before they can deploy their weapons, then get back on the cart with you and leave with all possible haste."

"I am not a powerful sorceress, I am more of a scholar," said Lavenci, cowering slightly. "Such a casting will leave me too weak to walk more than a few steps for many hours."

"If all goes well, you will not have to do much walking."

We passed through a village, and lightning briefly illuminated a sign declaring it to be Thissendel. We continued on into the darkness. Suddenly the storm front lashed across us, but Lavenci had borrowed two raincapes from Madame Norellie, so we remained passably dry. As we skirted the edge of the forest through a continuous wall of pelting rain, lightning burst across the sky every five or ten heartbeats. Wallas complained continually.

"I have averaged three hours sleep for the two nights past," I shouted back at him. "I suspect that this night will allow me no sleep at all."

"I could have been safe and asleep in Norellie's house," said Lavenci, "and you could probably have been safe and asleep in Mervielle's bed, Inspector. Did you realize she was helping Norellie just so that she could see you again?"

"Who is Mervielle?" asked Wallas.

"A rather pleasant wench," I replied.

"My type?"

"Were you not in feline circumstances, perhaps."

"That was uncalled for. So, you and Lady Lavenci are not, er . . ."

"Our relationship is quite professional," replied Lavenci tonelessly.

"Oh, you mean he has to pay first?" asked Wallas.

"How would you like a flight halfway across the River Alber?" I asked.

"With half a brick tied to your tail?" added Lavenci.

"I say, I say, hate to change the subject, but I see the glow of lanterns up ahead," said Wallas. "I believe that we may have reached the third cylinder, and that the duke has indeed arrived there first."

At that moment an extended blaze of lightning lit up the countryside with a purple glow. A thing burst out of the forest ahead of us, a nightmare that had no precedent in all of my life's experience. It was about the height of Gatrov's watchtower. Imagine a battle helmet ten feet high, connected by complex, jointed latticework to a second helmet below it, with three latticework legs supporting the second helmet. Every joint glowed with crackles of violet fire. The entire thing must have stood a hundred feet tall, and I caught sight of tentacles holding a glowing sphere that was a heat weapon.

"Friggin' enormous spider with tentacles and wearing a helmet, dead ahead!" shrieked Wallas. "Suggest evasion!"

"Would you like the bag with the crossbows?" asked Lavenci, whose experience with battles was so limited that she could not distinguish between vague threat and mind-numbingly overwhelming danger.

Another burst of lightning lit up the descent of the enormous latticework leg of a second tower not thirty feet in front of us and right in the middle of the road. My subconscious apparently told my reflexes that seizing a handful of Lavenci's clothing and dragging her from the cart with me as I leaped was the most sensible thing to do in the circumstances. She shrieked with the pain of my touch, and along with her came the sacks with Wallas and the crossbows. Our descent was cushioned by a deep puddle. I tried to gasp, swallowed water, surfaced, and heard the clatter of the cart and pony continuing along the road, apparently missing the tower's leg that had descended before us. A half-dozen heartbeats later the tower's controlling intelligence—which could apparently see in the dark—caught sight of our vehicle, decided that it was a threat, and raked it with the heat weapon. The hellfire oil for the flamethrower detonated in a quite impressive fireball.

"Shit me," declared Wallas from somewhere in the sodden darkness.

"Shit yourself," I replied, lying low.

"Actually, I have."

"Ladyship, are you all right?" I called above the hiss of rain.

"My right knee hurts, and my left hand hurts a lot more," reported Lavenci from nearby. "Inspector, you said nothing about huge, walking towers."

"This is the first I've seen of them," I responded.

"My fur is soaked, I'm up to my balls in water, and I think

I have a broken rib!" said Wallas. "Can I be released from this bloody bag?"

"No!" I hissed. "You'll take off like a scalded cat."

"We're lying in a puddle of water in freezing rain, and you talk about being scalded?"

"Draw the attention of those towers to yourself and you'll soon be more than scalded."

The pony was dead, having been sliced open and burst by the heat casting. I could see this by the light of the burning cart, which was still more or less harnessed to it. We were only a quarter mile or so from the third cylinder, and I did not need another lightning flash to see the fireballs roiling up into the air as the two tripod towers annihilated the duke's flamethrowers. The duke's river galleys and marines soon went the same way.

We took the opportunity to crawl out of the puddle and into the relative shelter of a small stand of trees at the edge of the forest. From here we saw that one tripod had straddled the pit containing the third cylinder, and was shining an intense green light down onto it while the other strode about warily, occasionally picking off a surviving river marine with a spat of heat.

"It seems to be reaching its tentacles down into the pit," said Lavenci.

"Perhaps it is helping the new arrivals get their hatch open faster," I suggested—correctly as it turned out. "The rain does not seem to affect them."

"How could they have brought such huge towers across with them?" asked Lavenci. "I doubt that they would have fitted in the cylinder."

I considered our position. The attack had failed before it had started because of the towers, but it was still possible to do some good by discovering where the towers had come from. I released Wallas from the sack.

"Lavenci, Wallas, there's a half-fallen tree over there. We can use it for shelter."

The tree's wide trunk kept most of the rain off, but the view was no better. Light, smoke, clanking, and ululations were all that we could see and hear from the Lupanians, and that told us very little.

"Can't see what's doing," I said, straining to peer through the gloom with my farsight.

"To crawl to the edge of the pit would be death," said Lavenci.

"But they might not notice a cat—" I began.

"*No!*" snapped Wallas. "Not under *any* circumstances."

"Then I'll do it," I decided.

"After all we have just seen and been through, you want to get closer?" responded Lavenci.

"He's a hero, they do things like that," said Wallas. "I prefer the way of cowardice, because it is obvious that a live coward makes a better bedmate than a dead hero—ow!"

The green light from the tower lit my way as I slipped among the trees. The edge of the forest came to within perhaps two hundred yards of the third cylinder, and it was here that I climbed a tree for a better view. The bark was wet and slippery in the rain, but it was better than approaching the pit over open ground. As I climbed, I noticed a stray crossbow bolt stuck in the trunk. The river marines had fought back, that was clear enough. My farsight gave about as good a view as might have been hoped for.

The first thing I noticed was that there was a ghostly casting in the shape of a tower's hood floating in the air not far from the cylinder. Below this was a puddle of molten soil, apparently melted by a heat casting from the cylinder. Other magical castings flickered about in the pit, all trailing long, glowing webs and filaments. After observing their work for some time, I realized that the filaments were of molten soil, and that they were being woven into a third tower. The Lupanians did not bring their towers through the void, they spun them from the soil of the world they were invading. I thought long and hard on this as I huddled beneath the tree in my rain cape. The glass of a bottle is very hard, yet brittle. Draw molten glass into a long fiber and it becomes quite flexible. Perhaps weaving glass fibers produced a material that was hard without being brittle.

I spent more than three hours in the tree, during which the Lupanians began to assemble yet another tower as the third one began to grow legs. I decided to climb down and return to Lavenci, partly because I was no longer learning anything new, and partly because I was almost too stiff with cold to move.

"They are assembling two more towers," I reported as I returned to the shelter of the leaning tree. "We should flee while they are busy, and while it is still dark."

"First sensible thing you have said all night," grumbled Wallas.

"How do they make the towers?" asked Lavenci.

"They are spun out of molten sand and soil, as far as I can make out. That green light is the glow from their fabrication castings."

"They must have passed by the second cylinder and seen what Halland's flamethrowers did there," said Lavenci. "No wonder they were a bit cross."

"More to the point, they will make sure that there is a tower or two standing guard over all the remaining cylinders as they open. We have lost surprise, our only advantage over them."

"But there are powerful beings on our world, too," said Lavenci. "Perhaps the glass dragons can be rallied."

"Then we had better start rallying them right away. The rain seems to be easing, so time to begin a very, very cautious, and furtive walk back to Gatrov."

Lavenci's knee was quite painful, but I could not carry her because of the glamour. I improvised a crutch from a sapling, however, and she was soon able to manage quite a reasonable pace. We got about a mile before we came upon an empty cowshed on the edge of the forest. It seemed to have been struck by a heat casting, because part of its roof had caught fire and fallen in. The walls were of stone, and were still more or less intact, however. It did not take much persuasion to convince me to stop there, because the walls were a windbreak and we could dry our clothes and warm ourselves with the embers.

"Why do you think they blasted a cowshed?" said Wallas as he selected a warm and sheltered spot for himself. "Even I have never felt threatened by a cow."

"It was a target, and they were of a mind to shoot. I have seen lancers ride down and slaughter the enemy's sheep for sport, then leave the bodies to rot."

"Oh! I don't suppose they slaughtered any cows, did they? You abducted me before dinner."

"Feel free to search, Wallas. My priority is to get warm and dry."

"On second thought . . ." said Wallas, yawning.

Wallas curled up on a fire-warmed stone and was soon asleep. Lavenci and I spent the best part of the night steaming parts of our clothing over the glowing embers of the roof beams, and by first light we were dry, dressed, and ready to travel. By then the storm clouds had cleared to reveal a crystal-clear sky.

"Gatrov is the only large town within a thirty-mile circle; so the towers will attack there soon," I said as we got ready to leave. "We must go there."

"You want to go where those things are sure to follow?" asked Wallas.

"Yes. The folk there need to be warned. We go to Gatrov."

"After all you've done to me, why should I?"

"Because you are a cat, and because my hand has just seized you by the neck, and because I am a person who has had a very, very bad night, and is feeling inclined to take it out on *anyone* who crosses me."

"All right, all right, just making sure I know where I stand."

"We can have the town warned and evacuated with time to spare," I explained. "It took two days for the Lupanians in the first cylinder to build their fighting towers, those in the second cylinder are dead, so we have a day and a half before the towers from the third cylinder are ready. My theory is that the two operational towers back there will stand guard until the next two are complete."

"It sounds plausible," said Lavenci.

As theories went, it was extremely plausible, yet like most plausible theories, it was wrong. The towers had opened the third cylinder only hours after it had landed, then had added their casting power to that of the Lupanians who had just arrived. This had speeded up the construction process considerably. The invaders certainly knew the value of pressing an advantage, and of never allowing an enemy to pause and take stock.

Chapter Ten

WHAT I SAW OF THE DESTRUCTION OF GATROV

It would have been an hour or so after dawn when Lavenci, Wallas, and I reached the village of Thissendel. Nearly everyone was still asleep, owing to some World Mother revel conducted the night before—as far as we could tell from the empty jars, discarded clothing, and fertility charms under a large pavilion on the village grccn. Only the more dedicated drinkers were awake. We made an attempt to warn them about Lupanians in hundred-foot-high walking towers of spun glass, armed with heat castings, and possessed of bad attitude, but our audience merely asked what wc had been drinking and whether there was any left for them. We left the village to its fate and hurried on.

"Those in Gatrov will pay us no more attention," Wallas pointed out.

"The head of the militia, Commander Halland, believes us," I replied. "Our warning will be voiced about, and those with the sense to flee will at least have a chance."

"Well, of all people, *we* ought to have the sense to flee, yet what are we doing?"

"Wallas, by noon you may rest assured that I shall be on a barge bound for Alberin or a haycart bound for deep in the forest. You are welcome to join me, as are you, ladyship. The Lupanians will not arrive for another twenty-four hours. I think— what's that?"

"The Lupanians?" gasped Wallas and Lavenci together.

Not far ahead of us, a figure strode out of the cover of some bushes and stood confronting us in the middle of the road. He held an ax at the ready.

"Drop your purses and weapons, then turn back to Thissendel," he ordered. "A dozen crossbows are trained on your hearts."

"Pelmore, that's bullshit and we know it as well as you do," I replied.

"You!" he gasped, then he recognized Lavenci and began backing away from us as we approached.

"Don't tell me, you are leaving Gatrov due to the humiliating circumstances of your wedding," I said as we advanced on him. "You thought to rob a few florins on the way."

"At least you can no longer rob by seduction," growled Lavenci.

Pelmore seemed to deduce that we did not mean to attack. He put the ax back in his belt and stopped.

"So, how did the wedding go?" I asked brightly. "Was your sweetheart surprised by your, er, shortcoming?"

"My sweetheart, the pure and unblemished country maiden!" exclaimed Pelmore. "Pah!"

"What do you mean?" I asked, although I already had a fair idea.

"The wedding was at dusk, every vendor's family from the market was there. All went well until . . . until my false true-love came abed with me. She, she, she . . ."

"She told you she had been led to believe by older and wiser women that something more substantial was to be expected?" I ventured.

"She laughed. Laughed! I tried to explain that it was normal, but she . . ."

"Was only seventy-five percent virginal, and thus knew better?" I asked.

"The vile betrayer."

"Fifty percent?"

"The dirty little baggage."

"Twenty-five percent?"

"The shameless slut!"

"Surely not zero?"

"She had a fit of the giggles at the sight of my . . . problem. It loosened her tongue, and she let slip shameful truths."

"So, she'd had experience with the dalliance equipment of another?" I asked, welcoming the brief diversion from matters of mass slaughter, heat weapons, giant fighting tripod towers, and how to incinerate homicidal Lupanian warriors before they managed to do that to oneself.

"Half a dozen others!" snapped Pelmore. "At least. She said that their, their attributes were all ten times more impressive. Even Horry Cutfast had a bigger one."

"Who is Horry Cutfast?" asked Wallas, who was sitting on my backpack and keeping watch behind us.

"A spindly tailor's apprentice, who can neither dance nor play a tune. My own true love, not a virgin! And with Cutfast. And five others! But never with me!"

"She kept you dangling above her well of delights as an incentive to marry her" was the opinion of Wallas. "A sensible lad would have moved on to easier conquests. The stubborn ones are never worth the effort."

Lavenci folded her arms very tightly and stared at the ground with a pained expression. The parallels with what had happened between her and myself were painfully close.

"She, I, er . . . that cat on your backpack!" gasped Pelmore.

"Yes?" I asked.

"It spoke."

"Well you'd not understand if I meowed," said Wallas smoothly. "Pray continue your story."

"But, but—"

"Like you, Wallas has a glamour upon him. In his case, however, it is a little more drastic. So, what happened at bedtime?"

"She went straight out to the revel and announced that she was not going to consummate anything with a man whose willy looked like half a walnut."

"What did you do?" I asked.

"I could not face the humiliation, so I dressed, snatched up her dowry purse, and scrambled out through the window."

"Why am I not surprised?" muttered Lavenci.

"But I found the dowry coins were copper rubbed with quicksilver to feign greater worth."

"Virtue is its own reward," I added. "A pity you have none."

"When oh when will this curse be lifted?" wailed Pelmore, raising his hands to the sky.

"Later this morning, when we reach Gatrov and call in at Norellie's house," said Lavenci.

"But she needs clearance from a field magistrate first," Pelmore pointed out.

"I passed my field-magistrate accreditation three months ago," I replied.

"What? Why did you not say so?" demanded Pelmore. "I could have postponed the wedding until tonight!"

"But I wanted you humiliated, Pelmore, just as you humiliated Lady Lavenci."

"Thank you, Inspector," said Lavenci, with a little curtsy to me.

"So, Pelmore, now the scales are in balance, so we can have Madame Norellie wipe the slate clean," I concluded. "You and Her Ladyship can go your separate ways. Come back to Gatrov with us."

"Why?"

"In case both of you have to be present for the glamour to be lifted."

"What I can't understand is why you had Norellie bind yourself to him in the first place," said Wallas as we set off for Gatrov again.

"I certainly did not!" cried Lavenci.

"Well I didn't!" retorted Pelmore.

"Four of those Lupanian fighting towers, right behind us!" yowled Wallas suddenly.

I whirled so fast that Wallas lost his grip on my backpack and fell off. Sure enough, four of the spun-glass nightmares were visible in the distance.

"That can't be!" I exclaimed. "They take two days to build."

"I count four," said Lavenci.

"What in all hells are they?" demanded Pelmore.

"The Lupanian version of mounted kavelars," I replied, "but instead of riding a horse and using a lance, they ride towers a hundred feet high and spit fire."

"I suggest we hide," said Wallas, jumping up onto my pack again as I raised my farsight.

"They are making for Thissendel," I said, feeling a deep and cold pit open up in my stomach. I unslung my cavalry crossbow and levered the cord over the bolt clip. I pointed it at Pelmore. "Ladyship, you can touch Pelmore, alone of all men. He must carry you."

"Death is preferable!" snapped Lavenci.

"That *is* the alternative. Pelmore, take Lavenci upon your back and run for Gatrov."

"No!" shouted Lavenci. "I limp or I die."

With that Pelmore began to run. Wallas streaked off too, and was quickly ahead of him. Lavenci limped along behind them.

"Go to the docks, jump into the water," I shouted. "Hide beneath the pier."

I was standing on a slight rise as I observed the towers stride toward the village, and although it was a mile behind us, I had quite a good view. Three of the towers moved to surround the place, while the fourth made straight for it. They made an odd, honking sound, like the call of a goose the size of a dragon. The heat beam itself was invisible, but the casting held by the tentacles belched green smoke when in use. I could not have taken more than five breaths before the entire village was blazing.

It was now that I saw something of their strategy for surrounding the village. The three outer towers began to pursue the fleeing villagers who had thus far survived, snatching them up with their tentacles and dropping them into baskets behind the lower cowl. The baskets had not been there the night before, I was sure of that. After no more than a minute, the baskets seemed full, and the remaining villagers were killed by merely being flung high into the air. Those who had fled somewhat farther were burned down.

At this point I thought to turn and see how far my charges had run. Pelmore had cut across a field, and was almost at the city gates, and Wallas was nowhere to be seen. Lavenci was making remarkably good progress, considering her injured leg. I also noted that Gatrov was hidden from the towers by the hill—except for the watchtower and castle.

Estimating that I would catch up with Lavenci as she reached the city gates, I began to run. I reached her no more than a hundred yards from the walls of the town. At this point someone in the watchtower must have noticed what was going on at the village, for they began to ring a bell. The bell tolled approximately nine times before one of the Lupanians noticed and thought to do something about it. The watchtower's crowning gallery was hit squarely by the heat weapon, and it disintegrated in a messy cloud of blazing fragments.

"The range of that thing is at least two miles," I gasped to Lavenci as we ran.

Now the heat weapons were trained on the castle, setting the thatch roofing and the soldiers on the battlements ablaze. We reached the town's gates, and were only admitted because I waved my Wayfarer crest plate at the guards and said that we had to warn the commander of militia about the Lupanians. They were closing the gates behind us as the Lupanians reached the hill, and a single blast of the heat weapon had both gates and guards reduced to ash and smoking fragments. Rooftops all around us began to explode into flames and billowing smoke as we ran for the river.

"The piers, hide under the piers!" I cried between gasps as I ran, but nobody heeded me.

The wreckage of the tower's gallery had fallen into the river, where it lay half-submerged like a vanquished warship. Ahead of us, Wallas and Pelmore were waiting at the edge of the wharf. Pelmore said something about not being able to swim, but I merely pushed him in the chest, then flung Wallas after him. I dropped my pack and the two crossbows on the edge of the wharf. The pier had been built of stone arches overlaid with timber, and the water was shallow enough for an adult to stand on the bottom. Wallas swam for Pelmore and clambered onto his shoulder. Moments later two more figures came running over. It was Riellen and Azorian.

"Sir!" she gasped. "The Lupanians can crawl really fast on their tentacles. They have reached the town."

"They have machines," I explained. "Jump for the water. Hide under the pier."

"I tried to hold a rally and organize a citizen's information network to spread word of the danger, but nobody would listen."

"Constable, get down there, guard the others."

I was aware of something crawling up my leg as I set off across Wharfway Plaza, and a voice piped out, "Constable Solonor reportin'!"

Without saying a word I snatched the gnome from my trouser leg and stuffed him into my coat pocket. I suppose my first thought was to get people off the cobblestone plaza and into the water before the tripod towers arrived, but none of the frantic folk there paid me any attention. Then I saw some militiamen pushing a large, heavy wagon out of the double doors of what I had taken to be a storehouse. Mounted on the tray was a ballista, which was basically a huge crossbow that fired clay pots of hellfire oil.

I cannot say why I abandoned any thought of telling people where to take refuge, and joined the crew of the ballista. I have only vague memories of what I shouted at them, but it was to the effect that their target was a hundred feet high and could shoot something hotter than hellfire farther than two miles. They were inclined to believe me, having just seen the town's watchtower cut down by something so far away that nobody knew where it was.

"Will you stay, sir?" barked the ballista captain as his men began to wind back a bowstring thicker than my arm. "Seeing as you know the enemy's size and speed."

"I've no training for ballistas," I cried back. "I'm only a Wayfarer."

"Can you stand with us and call the range, sir?" demanded the captain.

"That I can, sir."

"Then give height and range. What is your name?"

"Scryverin, Wayfarers, Inspector."

"Danzar, militia, Captain."

Of what came next I have only impressions, because so much was assailing my senses. There was a thunderous hooting and ululating, the screams of an entire town, bells and gongs sounding, and the rumble of buildings collapsing. We were on the wharf, facing out across the Alber River. Five barges were on the water, with those aboard frantically working the long sweep oars. Then we saw it, a tripod, already in the water, wading for the barges, a vast, glittering spider and octopus all in one, still taller than any building in Gatrov even though it was partly submerged.

"Stone me knackers!" cried someone behind me.

"What range?" shouted the captain, doggedly focused on

firing his machine and hitting the target. "Call the range, Inspector!"

I held out my arm, my thumb raised against the tripod tower.

"Four hundred yards, it looks to be half submerged," I estimated.

"What height?"

"Fifty feet above the water, at a guess."

As we watched, its tentacles raised the heat weapon casting and slashed at the closest barge. It flashed into flame, broke up, then sank within only a dozen or so heartbeats. Briskly and methodically, the tower dispatched the other barges the same way.

"Can't we help?" I shouted. "Can't we do anything?"

"Out of range," replied Captain Danzar. "Stand firm, call range."

"Three hundred yards, and looks to be fifty feet of it out of the water."

"Which of those pods at the top is the better target, Inspector Scryverin?"

"Either, I don't know."

"Marshal, track the top pod on the inspector's call," called the captain. "Inspector, continue to call the range."

"It's coming this way," I babbled.

"Call the range, sir!"

"Two hundred and seventy yards, sixty feet clear of the surface."

The tripod tower was advancing on the wharf from the river, methodically raking the buildings with its heat weapon as it waded. The fact that it was concentrating on a yard-by-yard annihilation of everything and everyone was what gave us our chance. Ours was only one of five ballistas installed on the wharf. The crews of two others must have rolled out their weapons for a shot as well, because I saw the smoky blur of a pot arcing across the sky to splash near the tripod's legs. The Lupanian machine's hood whipped about with astounding speed for something so big, and it slashed the wharf's south side with its heat weapon. Another pot flew, but this one went wild by at least thirty yards. The hood turned again, and raked another part of the wharf with fire.

"Two hundred and fifty yards, about seventy feet clear of the water," I estimated.

Range is in yards, elevation in feet, I clung to that fact of artillery convention while terror clawed at me and forge-hot death scythed buildings and people down.

"Two hundred yards, ninety feet clear—"

"Fire!" called the captain.

I have no recollection of the ballista firing, but I clearly remember the top hood of the tower swinging around to face us just as the hard, heavy ceramic pot of hellfire oil arrived. The smoking pot struck it full in the faceplate, bursting in a great gout of flames, and apparently smashing through the mirrorlike plate and splashing fire into the cabin within. The tripod tower kept walking, and for a moment I thought that we had hit nothing vital, then I realized that it was just striding along undirected, like a chicken relieved of its head. One of the legs struck part of the wreckage of the port's watchtower, then the tripod toppled and fell headlong. Its heat weapon struck the river, and the resulting explosion smothered us in steam and showered the wharf in hot water.

"Reload, at the double!" screamed Captain Danzar. "Stand by your posts! Wind and load! Wind and load!"

"There's three more," I called, backing away from the ballista and looking about frantically.

"Stand by your post, sir!" shouted Danzar. "Sight target and call range."

"Directly overhead!" I shrieked as a tripod tower's leg came down not two yards from where I stood.

I stumbled backward until I came up against the wall of the Bargeman's Barrel. Whatever was directing the fighting tripod was apparently unaware that the ballista was directly beneath it. It stood above us, sweeping the cobblestone wharf with its heat weapon. Buildings blazed up like handfuls of straw thrown on red hot coals, people burst like ripe tomatoes flung against a stone wall.

Then the nightmare really began. I saw Roval, Mervielle, and several other people come running out of a lane and dash for the edge of the wharf. I prayed to no gods in particular that the thing would not look down, but in the next heartbeat the girl who had tried to share my bed only the day before burst into a smoky cloud of black fragments as the heat beam struck her. At the edge of the wharf I saw Lavenci clamber over the edge. Riellen was behind her, trying to drag her back, but the albino turned and punched her in the face, sending her plunging back into the water.

"The leg, aim for the leg!" cried Captain Danzar, and through the smoke and rain of ashes I saw his crew aiming point blank at the tower's nearest latticework leg.

"Oi, Inspector, is it always this rough in the Wayfarers?" called a small voice from somewhere in my coat, then I saw the trigger marshal heave a lever back.

The pot of hellfire oil burst amid the latticework of the leg, ten feet below the hood. As far as I could tell, it did no damage whatever, although the oil burned fiercely. The shot did secure the Lupanian's attention, however, and the tentacles came around with the heat weapon.

"Danol, run!" called a female voice as I began to run for the edge of the wharf. "I'll give cover."

Lavenci was standing with one of my little cavalry crossbows between her boots, trying to draw the string back with her good hand. As I ran for her, the heat weapon's beam must have sliced through the tender wagon loaded with pots of hellfire oil. The explosion of the air-oil mixture swept me into Lavenci and over the edge of the wharf. My head collided with the stock of her crossbow, and I remember no more.

Chapter Eleven

DEAD GATROV

 I came to my senses quite some time later. It was nearly noon, and my head felt as if it had been split open. Captain Danzar was splashing water on my face, and Lavenci and Riellen were kneeling to either side of him and looking very anxious.

"Awake at last," said the captain. "Danol, can you speak?"

"Dreams . . ." I responded. "Nightmares."

"All real, I regret to say," said Lavenci in a very ragged voice.

"Kavelen Lavenci disobeyed your orders," said Riellen sullenly.

"I am not a Wayfarer, he has no authority over me," retorted Lavenci with a sideways glare at Riellen.

"Ladies!" snapped Danzar impatiently, and they fell silent. "Inspector, do you remember anything?"

"I remember much," I said as I tried to sit up. "I *want* to remember very little. Mervielle, I . . ."

Both Lavenci and Riellen winced at the mention of her name. That was enough.

"Died instantly," said Danzar firmly. "We gathered up what there was of her and dropped the bundle in the shallows, weighted with stones."

"She was only eighteen" was all that I could say.

Miraculously, I had no injury other than a large lump on the head, some shallow cuts, and several spectacular bruises.

"You have been senseless for three hours," said Danzar as he and Riellen helped me up. "I checked the town and castle. Every structure has been razed or burned out, and the few survivors have fled for the forest."

There was a dull, numb tone to Danzar's voice, and it was plain that he was coping by not thinking upon the full enormity of what had happened. I resolved to do the same.

"Well then, who has remained?" I asked.

"Those gathered here are Lady Lavenci, Constable Riellen, Constable Roval, Pelmore Haftbrace, a grass gnome, a cat that talks, a foreign student, Commander Halland, you, and me."

"Not Norellie Witchway?" I asked, with a sense of disappointment whose intensity surprised me.

"There is a very large crater where Madame Norellie's house once stood," said Lavenci.

"What manner of weapon caused that?" I asked.

"Certain adepts in sorcery can store etheric potential in amulets," Lavenci explained, her arms folded tightly and her expression grim. "They channel it into charmed things, control it, and hold it in reserve."

"Like those who become glass dragons?"

"In a fashion, yes, but those sorcerers who become glass dragons can actually weave the energies into vast bodies of force. When they are killed, well, the liberated energies could destroy a city the size of Alberin. Destroy some lesser amulet, such as Norellie had, and you get a lesser explosion. Nevertheless, it is not a good idea to be standing close by. The Lupanian who killed Norellie doubtless got quite a surprise."

"Was the Lupanian's leg damaged?" I asked hopefully.

"No. We saw three come to the wharf to carry off the fallen tower. Their legs seem to be very tough."

What Lavenci did not say was that her last chance to have the constancy glamour lifted had vanished when Norellie died.

"We put up a hell of a fight," said Captain Danzar. "One tower down. The faceplates are their weakness, but their magic deflects metal weapons."

"Lady Fortune must have been in an exceptionally good mood for our hellfire pot to find such a target," I commented.

Roval and Pelmore returned from checking the remains of the market, and reported that food was still to be found there. They also said that there were surprisingly few bodies, presumably because people had died while hiding in buildings that had been set alight. Commander Halland arrived to check on me. He had been returning from the first cylinder's empty pit when the tripods attacked Gatrov.

"We must get to Alberin and warn the regent," I said as Riellen helped me to sit up. "I suppose a boat or horses are out of the question?"

"No horses, and no boat, but there is a barge," said Halland. "It hit the pier yesterday and sank."

"Er, I was hoping for one that was still afloat."

"All of those were destroyed. This one was missed because it was below the surface, but it can be salvaged. Leave it to me."

I struggled to assemble logistics and numbers in my head. "There are only eight people, one gnome, and a cat available here. You would need a crane, a dozen horses, and fifty men to get the barge raised, dragged to the slipway, and beached for repairs."

"Oh no, we have a much cheaper method here," said Halland, as if the problem were too trivial for words.

Leaning heavily on Riellen I got to my feet, and as I looked over the edge of the wharf I realized that while raising the barge was not a trivial matter, it was within the abilities of six men and two women. The deck of the barge was just below the surface, and all that projected above it was what looked like a large bellows from a smithy's forge and a tube going down into the water. Halland explained that a dozen ox hides had already been placed within the barge by divers, each with a pipe leading to it from the bellows. Two men working the bellows for some hours could inflate the ox hides and get the barge floating low in the water.

"Normally it would only be to tow it to the slipway, where a team of horses would drag it clear of the river," explained Halland, "but were the bellows to be worked continually, there is no reason that the barge might not float for days, to drift down with the current as far as Alberin."

Roval took the first pumping shift with Halland, working the bellows for a full two hours while Wallas kept watch from the top of the highest pile of rubble nearby. The others foraged in the ruins of the market for food, and I was left to rest. The pumping was very slow work, but gradually the hides inflated and displaced the water within the sunken barge. What was left of the figurehead after the collision was visible by the time Azorian and Pelmore took over, and by late afternoon the deck was about six inches above the waterline.

"Give it another hour," said Halland. "We may get it nine inches clear of the water, but no more."

"But look at the bubbles," I said. "We must keep pumping to keep it from sinking."

"Would you prefer to swim to Alberin?"

"Point taken."

"Look, ah, I heard about the baron's castle," I said awkwardly. "So lucky—I mean, your wife and family escaping."

"It is no concern of mine. They were all the baron's own."

"But—"

"I was only Uncle Halland. Remember, the baron was, how shall we say it, a passionate man."

I shook my head.

"How could you live such a life?" I asked, abandoning seemly manners for a moment.

"Oh, there were compensations, like my appointment as militia commander. Then again, the baron's wife slept with me from time to time, out of sheer spite I suppose." He flung a stone to skip across the water. "Now all that is gone, and all of Gatrov. The loves, hates, politics, intrigues, alliances, prospects, scandals, betrayals, and secrets. The hopes for the future, the pride in the past, the annual incomes, the prospective inheritances, and the plans for inheritances. It is like the continent Torea, when that monster Warsovran unleashed his ether machine and melted the place down to the bedrock: nothing left but the memories of a few survivors."

*⋅ *⋅ *

When he had gone I sat down against a bollard and closed my eyes. I was almost immediately aware of a frantic scrambling sound, followed by a yowl. I opened my eyes to see Solonor and Wallas facing off against each other a few yards away. The grass gnome was armed with his tiny spear, and Wallas was fluffed up like an overweight featherdown cushion.

I asked something along the lines of "What the hell is going on?"

"That little wanker in the green tights stuck a knitting needle in my bottom," declared Wallas.

"That cat, it spoke Alberinese!" exclaimed Solonor.

"I speak over a dozen languages," said Wallas huffily.

"But most cats only speak Feline Yowl and Underfolk Standard."

"Constable Wallas, Constable Solonor, who started this?" I asked.

"That lard barrel in a fur rug is a Wayfarer?" gasped Solonor.

"You recruited a gnome?" asked Wallas, with scorn dripping copiously from the last word.

"And what's wrong with gnomes?" demanded Solonor.

"Nothing that a little salt and a few hours marinating in a nice, full bodied red wine would not cure," replied Wallas smoothly.

"Solonor, did you attack Wallas?" I asked.

"I wanted his scrotum as a backpack, but he were so fat that I couldn't work out which end were which when he were curled up and asleep."

"My scrotum as a backpack?" sneered Wallas. "How very lower-class."

"Lower-class!" exclaimed Solonor. "Constable Riellen

warned me about your kind, lackeys of the oligarkysomething establishment, she warned me, she did."

"Hold a moment, Solonor—did you say Wallas was asleep?" I exclaimed. "Wallas, you were meant to be on watch."

"It was only a catnap," muttered Wallas. "I am a cat, after all."

"Constable Wallas, Constable Solonor, I order both of you to leave each other alone," I concluded wearily but firmly. "Wallas, get back to your post. Solonor, stand with him, and stab him in the fundamental with that spear if he looks like nodding off again."

"But sir—" began Wallas.

"Wallas, believe me, this is the easy way. If *I* ever catch you asleep on sentry duty again, you will be taken to a place of diet, and there you will be hung by the tail until thin."

They left together, still muttering threats and insults. I closed my eyes again, and this time I did manage to get some actual sleep. I was awakened by the sound of feet crunching through charcoal and shattered stone. Lavenci sat down beside me and unwrapped a canvas parcel. In it were pastries, some slices of roast meat, cheeses, bread, and a jar of expensive wine.

"So, the foraging went well," I observed.

"Pelmore, Roval, and myself found that many stalls and carts in the market were smashed but not burned," Lavenci explained. "I've tried the wine, it's excellent."

I tasted the wine, which was red and a very nice vintage, then drank two mouthfuls.

"No more?" she asked.

"Best keep it for when things get worse," I suggested before returning my attention to the bread and roast.

"Things can get worse?" asked Lavenci. "Here, have my share. It's ladymeat, a pork fillet."

"Ladyship, I couldn't."

"I am a vegetarian, Inspector. Remember?"

* * *

It was during this somewhat informal and early dinner that Halland arrived and announced that the barge was sufficiently high in the water to be usable as transport. He ordered that we wait until it was actually twilight before we set off, just in case the fighting towers were still in the area. It was a relief to be leaving the nightmare ruins of the town, but for me it was possibly too much of a relief. Pain was building up behind both of my eyes, and nausea was clutching at my stomach. I tossed the remains of my dinner to those pumping at the bellows, rather than wasting it, then began to untie the mooring ropes.

With Pelmore and Captain Danzar pumping at the bellows, Halland at the tiller, and Roval, Lavenci, Azorian, and Riellen pushing on the twenty foot barge pole, the vessel began to move ponderously away from the remains of the pier. I remained ashore, casting off the ropes. The barge began to catch the current.

Suddenly the scene collapsed into flashes of swirling color before my eyes. My legs jellied, and I dropped to my knees, my hands over my face.

"Sir, what is the matter?" came Riellen's shout.

"I'm blind!" I cried back.

"Don't move, sir, I'm coming."

"No Riellen, you can't swim!"

The barge must have been close enough for her to jump for the pier, because I heard the thud of her feet as she landed. Then I heard Halland calling for her to catch the mooring rope. She grasped me by the arm and tried to drag me away.

"Get up, sir, come with me."

"Constable, I can't stand. Leave me! That's an order."

"Don't panic, sir. Just letting go of you to tie the rope about your waist."

The departing barge dragged both Riellen and me over the edge of the pier and into the water. When my head was above the surface again I heard Lavenci screaming at the uncomprehending Azorian to help her haul in the rope. After what seemed an eternity I felt myself bump against the side of the barge. Hands grasped at me. One of them must have belonged to Lavenci, because I heard her cry out with pain, then I was being laid out on the deck.

"I thought I gave you an order, Riellen," I wheezed between coughs.

"I disobeyed, sir. Shall I put myself on report?"

"Blinding headache," I mumbled, almost as an apology.

"The ordeals of the days past must have caught up with him," said Lavenci. "Healers call it delayed shock."

"Hit my head . . ." I mumbled.

Hands hastily fluttered about my head, and again Lavenci cried out in pain.

"There's a large lump," she gasped presently. "Danol? Danolarian!"

I was still conscious, but a great lethargy was weighing down all my limbs.

"You never can tell with blows to the head," said Halland. "Most likely he bleeds within his skull."

"What's to do?" asked Riellen.

"Complete rest . . ." suggested Lavenci, her voice fading and echoing as the maelstrom of colors before my eyes faded to blackness.

✷ ✷ ✷

I found myself standing before Madame Jilli the Ferrygirl. This time she was smiling, but it was a badly disguised smile of concern.

"This is not another migraine," I said before she could speak.

"No Danol, it is much worse."

"I know symptoms, I have done Basic Medicar Techniques for Inspectors. I have daemonglare poisoning, do I not?"

"So many people only pause to think once they are dead."

"So I really am dead?"

"No, but you are in a lot of trouble."

"Actually, I had noticed."

"You can still save yourself."

"How?"

"You will have to face up to things, things that are very cruel."

"Things with horns, pitchforks, and pointy tails?"

"Things much worse than that."

"Er, for how long?"

"It will not be eternity, but it will seem like it."

"Ah, so what are we doing?" I asked.

"You shall soon return to your body, and live. Someone is helping."

"But you said I was in a lot of trouble."

"Death is the escape. Life is the torture."

"So I shall live?"

"Yes."

"Oh," I sighed as I looked up at her, with sheer relief almost dissolving my body. "Do any of the souls ever tell you how pretty you are?"

"Why Danol, how sweet, thank you. Most souls are so wrapped up in thoughts of their fate that they never stop to consider how I feel. Go now, go. You are alive, and I have real clients to carry."

A figure shambled soundlessly out of the darkness.

"Why Captain Danzar, brave, brave Captain Danzar," sighed the Ferrygirl, enfolding the dead soul in her arms. "Such a humiliating way to die, after fighting so bravely against the Lupanians. What you need is a nice cuddle before you get into my boat."

✳ ✳ ✳

I waved as Madame Jilli pushed her boat away with Captain Danzar sitting near the bow, then I became aware of someone else beside me. I turned, and recognized Azorian.

"Something terrible has happened on the barge," I said to myself, not expecting the soul of the student to reply.

"There is nothing wrong on the barge," he replied, staring after the ferrygirl's boat. "I am not dead, and neither are you."

"But . . . we are here, on the shores of the afterlife."

"Captain Danzar is dead, you are close to death, and I am holding on to the string by which your life dangles over the chasm of eternity."

"So you are a healer?"

"I am a fabricator."

"I don't understand."

"On your world there is no word for what I do."

Suddenly I understood. Azorian was from Lupan. Trust my word upon it, you tend to be much calmer about things when you are at the edge of death. The astounding revelation merely had me surprised, rather than catatonic with shock.

"Can I assume that you are, er, different from the Lupanians with the heat weapons?" I asked, hoping that my question was sufficiently diplomatic.

"Yes. The glasswalkers are warriors, but I am a mere artisan. I was not meant to make the journey here."

"These glasswalkers, are they here to conquer our world?"

"Please, no more for now. You must return to your body, or even I will not be able to hold you."

He took me by the arm, and we began to walk away from the riverbank. The landscape faded into a uniform grey; then I was aware of hardness pressing against my back. My stomach burned, and not a muscle of my body would respond. I could hear the creak of the air pump, and the lapping of the water around the barge.

"I am making the damaged parts of you whole again," came Azorian's thought in my brain. "I have been working your lungs, and beating your hearts, too. In an hour you will awake. You should even be able to stand."

"Did the same thing happen to Captain Danzar?" I thought back.

"Yes. You were both poisoned. I could not save both of you, together. My apologies."

"Why me?"

"Because you have been kind to me, and I appreciate kindness."

I suddenly had a new appreciation of the merits of being kind. "I can hear things from . . . the world of the living, and I can feel the deck under my back."

"That is because you are alive again. To put it in your language, you are doing a type of darkwalking," Azorian explained. "Part of you is existing in the world of the ether, the life force."

"But I don't know how to darkwalk. Riellen does all the darkwalking in my squad."

"That is why it is so hard to bring you back. Now rest, rest."

✦ ✦ ✦

I lay listening to the sounds around me. There were occasional voices, sometimes Halland called orders, and once I heard Wallas meow. The creaking of the pump never ceased, neither did the lapping of water. At last I heard footsteps approaching.

"But the inspector and Azorian are here," said Riellen's voice.

"Here at the bow is as private as we may get," replied Lavenci. "Azorian cannot understand us, and the Inspector is beyond hearing."

"What is Azorian doing? He had been holding the inspector's head and chanting all night and all morning."

"I do not know, Constable."

"Why did you bring me up here?" asked Riellen.

"For privacy, Constable Riellen. So that we can say what we like."

"But sister, I always say what I like."

"I've noticed. Constable, the inspector is dying, yet I know so little about him. Can you speak of him to me?"

"I know nothing of his background, ladyship."

"Oh come now! You must have learned *something* of him after two or three years serving with him. What about little, personal things?"

"He has his weaknesses," said Riellen guardedly. "But they are nothing out of the ordinary."

"Constable, the man is dying! What harm will it do if I learn that he picks his nose or farts in the bathwater? I know he was in the Torean fleet that invaded Diomeda, but—well, he is just amazing. After just three years in this realm he already knows enough Alberinese to pass for a local as long as he speaks slowly. I put it to you that Danolarian was a young Torean navy officer, and a very bright one at that."

"There is no crime in that, ladyship."

"Or possibly a ship's sorcerer."

"He has practiced no sorcery since I have known him!" snapped Riellen.

"There are other Toreans in the ports of Acrema and Scalticar. They talk freely about their pasts, and some even boast about crimes committed in kingdoms that have been burned to ashes. Why is Danol so secretive?"

"Ladyship, he has always been a good, brave man, and a very just inspector. I have learned much from him. Why are you so intent on knowing his past?"

"Danol once rescued me from the Inquisition Constables. For a short time we courted each other, then he was sent back on the road. He says he wrote, but I received no letters. I traveled to Gatrov because I learned he was to be there—I have powerful friends who can find out such things. We had a—a misunderstanding about my grubby past, and silly games I played with him. I had to agree to, to leave him alone after one last dance."

"It did not look that way!" said Riellen sternly, "but then I know nothing of courtship."

"Well neither do I!" snapped Lavenci abruptly. "That was the basis of my fight with the inspector."

"What do you mean?"

"None of your business!"

"Those who choose bedmates unwisely often look for excuses, ladyship. It is common among the upper classes."

There was an icy silence that was probably shorter than it seemed.

"You mean Pelmore and myself," said Lavenci at last. "I have yet to work out how that happened. One moment I was dancing with Danolarian, alive with delight to be in his arms, the next I was a giddy girl of fifteen again, wandering through a huge revel in search of adventure, and determined to learn of the pleasures of dalliance with some exciting, wicked stranger. Pelmore stood out from the crowd as if light were shining from his face. My breath became short, my pulse raced, my body burned, my lips were engorged with blood. Then, in bed, at the very moment that . . . that things of the most intimate nature commenced between us, it all dissolved. I was lying beneath a stranger, and I had no idea how I got there. Leaving that mystery aside, however, Danolarian blundered in on Pelmore and me while we were undressing, quite by chance. Might he have gone away and cast the constancy glamour upon us, in a fit of jealous rage?"

"The inspector is not a sorcerer, you vile, unfeeling, upper class, counterrevolutionary bitch—with respect, ladyship."

"Perhaps not, yet the glamour that binds me to Pel-bore still stands!" retorted Lavenci.

"Pelmore is a fine but oppressed worker."

"Then *you* try kissing him."

"Pelmore himself may have commissioned the glamour," suggested Riellen, changing tack with uncharacteristic speed. "He might have thought to better himself by marrying you, a rich lady."

"Then why did he rob me and flee? I have thought through the logic of all this, constable. Perhaps Madame Norellie fancied the inspector, and sought to remove me as a contender for his affections."

"Madame Norellie?" gasped Riellen. "No!"

"She spoke of him with affection, she even gave him her drawers to carry into battle as her favor."

"The class traitor!" snapped Riellen. "Such an upper-class act."

"How emotional of you," said Lavenci smoothly. "So, the inspector is high in your esteem too, Constable Riellen? Has your revolutionary body been warming his on the cold nights in the mountains?"

There was a hiss of breath being drawn, then someone, probably Riellen, cleared her throat.

"My virginity is intact, and my friendship with the inspector is pure," declared Riellen. "I have served with him for three years, as both colleague and follower. He taught me all I know about fighting, law enforcement, discipline, and survival. He is not a true revolutionary brother, but he tolerates my orations and revolutionary studies. My only delight is to serve him. When he is of a mind for some amorous company, I find him a lamplight girl of good disposition and reasonable rates. I look after him when he is drunk, and I even cover his gambling debts from my savings. I am *always* there to tend his migraines, even when he raves and screams with the pain. He is my friend, the only real friend I have ever had. Can you say as much, ladyship?"

There was a rather awkward silence.

"No, I cannot say any of that," said Lavenci slowly, the way I now knew that she speaks when thinking very carefully. "I am no virgin, I have many friends, I know nothing of life on the road, but I can find my own amorous company. I also know when I am outclassed. In matters of virtue that is not hard to do. On the other hand, I do adore the inspector, and esteem him above all others. In spite of what I did to him, I know that he would never harm me, or desert me to danger, and that he loved me once. Nobody else, neither my friends nor my family, would have been so honorable as to drag my name out of the mud and wash it clean again, yet he did just that, back in Gatrov. If I thought it would bring Danolarian back I would journey down into the lowest circle of all hells and stay there in torment for all of eternity."

"Here is my dagger, give it a try," said Riellen.

"I knew that he loved me, yet I played a silly game and lost him," continued Lavenci, then I heard the thud of a dagger being flung into the deck. "You do not like me, Constable, and you certainly try to hurt me, yet remember that nobody has ever managed to hurt me as much as I have hurt myself because of the inspector. Good day to you."

Although my senses and control were by now improving from moment to moment, I made a special point of lying still. I heard Lavenci walk away down the deck of the barge, then Riellen grunting as she tried to extract her dagger from the decking. There was a snap and a muttered curse as the tip broke off, then Riellen walked away as well. I began to count. At one thousand I groaned and raised a hand.

"I can do no more for you," thought Azorian within my head.

"You have done more than enough," I replied silently.

Azorian released my head and started to shout some of his dozen or so words of Alberinese.

"Helpings! Inspector, helpings!"

On this cue I opened my eyes, rolled onto my side, and tried to push myself up.

"Danolarian!" called Lavenci.

"Sir!" gasped Riellen.

"Inspector!" said Halland.

"You're alive!" exclaimed Roval.

Everyone rushed forward to where I lay, and Lavenci even made the mistake of touching me. While she was rolling about on the deck, clutching her head, Halland began to brief me on what had been happening.

"Captain Danzar is dead, probably of what brought you low."

"What might that have been?" I croaked.

"We spoke with some lancers on the riverbank this morning. They said that the Lupanians also have a sort of smoke that kills, they saw it being used. It seems that you and Danzar caught a slight whiff of it on the Gatrov wharf."

"Ah, that makes sense."

"Azorian is some sort of medicar, he seems to have kept you alive while your body recovered from the poison. Lavenci can tolerate his touch, so she thinks he might be Dacostian."

"How does that follow?"

"Like Wallas, and like the grass gnome, she can stand his touch without feeling fire in her head. Dacostians, too, are a species apart from us."

I spent the next hour taking a little bread and water, and regaining the use of my legs. We were drifting with the current, but making reasonable time. Halland estimated that we would reach Mallow Landing by late afternoon. His intention was to requisition a dispatch boat there and row ahead to Alberin.

"With your permission, Inspector, I have volunteered to go with Commander Halland," said Roval.

"You have?" I replied, surprised that he was taking an interest in anything. "Yes, of course. I'll write you a ticket of transfer, but you will have to report to headquarters before you may enter another tavern alone."

"I shall be entering no more taverns, Inspector," he said as he saluted. "Thank you."

"Er, for what?"

"Patience, compassion, understanding. Nobody has ever given me those before."

There was very little I could say to that. I bowed, then con-

tinued my tour of inspection of the barge. On my way back to
the bow, I took Roval aside.

"Ugly work ahead," I whispered. "Are you up to it?"

"Aye, sir," he replied, looking a little puzzled. "What's to do?"

"Follow my instructions, quite precisely."

I had similar words to Halland and Riellen, then had Halland relieve Pelmore at the pump. After carefully positioning
Riellen and Roval, I collected a skin of drinking water and
two helmets, and finally seated myself at the bow again.
Riellen went first to Pelmore, then to Lavenci, telling them
that I wanted to speak with them. Roval and Riellen were behind them as they came forward and stopped before me.

"Pelmore, ladyship, kindly remove your purses and hand
them to me," I said calmly.

"What is this about?" began Pelmore as he took the purse
from his belt.

"I am taking an inventory of the money aboard the barge," I
said, trying to sound a little annoyed and distracted. "A complaint of theft has been made."

"Our world is to be annihilated, and you worry about a few
missing florins?" asked Lavenci.

"If they are not in your purse, you have nothing to worry
about, ladyship."

Pelmore laughed and tossed me his purse. Lavenci removed
her purse from her belt and dropped it into my hand. I untied
the drawstrings of both purses and tipped the coins onto the
palm of my hand. Both contained just florins and coppers, although some of Pelmore's coppers had been whitened with
quicksilver. I returned the coins to their respective purses.
Next, I inverted a helmet, poured some water from the skin
into it, then dropped Lavenci's purse in.

"Ladyship, drink, if you please," I said as I offered the helmet to her.

"I am not sure that I understand," she said as she accepted
the helmet.

"I recognized the symptoms of daemonglare poison when I
was fading from this world. Not many survive the encounter,
but I have read accounts by some of those rare survivors. My
symptoms were identical to theirs. Someone poisoned me,
and I have reduced the list of suspects to you two."

"But no berries were in my purse," said Lavenci, her eyes wider than usual with alarm.

"There was once a man who rubbed the juice of dae-monglare berries into his scarf, then dipped the scarf in his wife's wine. She died, but the wine stain gave him away. Even though there were no berries found on his person, the field magistrate soaked the scarf in wine and presented him with a goblet of it to drink. He confessed. You two foraged food from the market in Gatrov. One of you spiced it with something."

Before I could say more, Lavenci drank the contents of the helmet I had given her. She returned the helmet, and I tipped her a wink as I tossed the purse back to her.

"Pelmore?" I asked, offering him the other helmet, in which his purse now soaked in water.

"I gave meat to neither you nor the captain," he said firmly, stepping back. Roval pushed him forward again.

"But you gave *me* meat!" exclaimed Lavenci suddenly. "It was the ham fillet, the ladymeat."

"Well, yes, but you are alive, so clearly I am innocent."

"You have never shared a meal with me, Pel-borer, have you?" said Lavenci, her face blank but her tone sharp enough to perform amputations. "Not a meal, not a pastry during quiet afternoon at the market, and not a groundnut roll from either end."

"We shared a bed," said Pelmore huffily, "and we danced several times."

"Indeed, but you never saw me *eat*. You never learned that I am a vegetarian."

Pelmore gasped, and went very pale. Lavenci nodded.

"I gave your generous little morsel of ladymeat to Danolar-ian," concluded Lavenci.

"I ate some, then gave the rest to Danzar," I added.

There was a silence so pregnant that one might have been tempted to fetch a midwife. At last I grew impatient.

"Drink the water or confess to murder," I said to Pelmore.

"I, ah, may have passed tainted meat on to my truelove, quite by accident," said Pelmore.

"What truelove might that have been?" snapped Lavenci.

"Daemonglare berries are tough," I said quietly. "They must be squeezed very hard to get the colorless juice out. The most common method is to squeeze them between two coins. Now, drink the water."

"I'll not do it, you poisoned the water by sleight of hand—"

Roval's foot caught Pelmore behind the knee and he dropped to the deck in an instant. Roval, Riellen, and myself had him pinned before a moment had passed.

"Now, about that drink?" I said with a knee on Pelmore's chest, holding the helmet high.

"It was me, I confess, I confess!" he suddenly babbled. "I tainted the meat, but it was only because the bitch was threatening me! It was her or me, it was self-defense!"

Pelmore's confession was heard by all aboard the barge. Having tied his hands behind his back, I assembled everyone near the pump, where Halland could hear, then initiated a field trial.

"Interim field trial, case in session is the Regent of the Scalticarian Empire versus Pelmore Haftbrace, town of Gatrov, barony of Gatrovia. Charges determined to date: the attempted murder of a Wayfarer inspector, namely myself; the attempted murder of Kavelen Lavenci Si-Chella; and the actual murder of Captain Danzar of the Gatrov Militia."

"This farce will not be approved by any magistrate, you highway yokel," sneered Pelmore, then he hesitated, puffed up his chest, and took a deep breath. "I happen to be an agent of the Inquisition Constables."

"So?" said Lavenci. "I am the former lover of Laron Aliasar, presiding advisor to the regent of Alberin."

Suffice it to say that Pelmore lost control of his bladder at hearing that.

"With respect, ladyship, you were speaking out of order, and your comment must be left off the record," I said in what passed for a neutral tone.

"My apologies, Inspector."

"Daemonglare, each berry so poisonous that it can kill several dozen adults," I continued. "The symptoms are identical to those shown by me for the day past, and by Captain Danzar before his death. Pelmore, I put it to you that you collected the berries from an apothecary's stall, crushed them between two florins, and tainted a morsel of ladymeat ham that you then presented to Ladyship. You did not realize that she is a vegetarian, or that she would pass the meat on to someone else."

"You turd-hearted bastard!" muttered Lavenci.

"Pelmore Haftbrace, I find you guilty of murder, in intent and actuality, although by misadventure."

"That means you murdered the wrong person but are still guilty," said Lavenci.

"You have already been warned, ladyship," I said firmly. "I fine you one florin for contempt."

"Cheap at twice the price."

"In that case, I fine you two florins. Pelmore, your provisional sentence for the murder of Captain Danzar is death. The penalty for murdering or attempting to murder an inspector of the Wayfarers is also death, with an option of death by torture if the victim survives and petitions the ratifying magistrate. Mind your behavior, or I might decide to petition."

It was not long after the trial that we reached Mallow Landing. Halland hurried away to speak with some officials, then they all vanished into a nearby building. Presently they emerged, shouting orders to various people. Soon four men appeared carrying a long, streamlined boat over their heads. Another man followed with four long, spindly oars. It was one of the new Diomedan courier boats, which moved several times faster than other river traffic. It was launched, and Commander Halland and Constable Roval got in. They began to row, and the boat moved off so quickly that it seemed under an enchantment. Just then the barge settled beneath the surface of the water at the wharfside, leaving only the pump mechanism visible.

I had been to Mallow Landing two months earlier. It was a tiny place, and featured a customs house, a bawdyhouse, a tavern, a garrison of five militiamen, and a shrine to some god whose statue had been stolen. From the look of it, the place had been largely evacuated, except for the militiamen. A militia marshal unlocked the tavern for us. It was dark inside, and although someone struck a spark to a lamp, the flame was no more than a yellow dot in the gloom.

"We could sample the wines," Solonor's faint voice came echoing.

"Theft is a civil offense," Riellen pointed out.

"Then put me in the stocks," said Solonor.

"I've found glass tumblers," called Wallas from behind the servingboard. "Classy place."

"Bring them over," called Lavenci cheerily. "I'll leave payment."

"I'm a cat, remember? No hands?"

"Bleedin' big folk's measures," complained Solonor. "Anyone found a thimble?"

"No wine for me," said Riellen.

"Oi, my face won't fit into this glass!" yowled Wallas. "I need a saucer."

"Just tip it over and lap it up," said Solonor.

"Drink off the floor? Never! Hang your toast, I'll just sit here and wash my arse."

"Here's a saucer," I called.

"To Inspector Danolarian!" declared Lavenci. "He kept us alive and saw justice done."

"Inspector Danolarian!" chorused everyone else but Pelmore. Those who were drinking, drank. After toasts to Danzar and Halland, I beckoned Azorian over, took his hands, and pressed them to the sides of my head. The others must have assumed that I needed more healing after being poisoned, and paid us no heed.

"I wish to thank you," I thought.

"It is my role to fabricate," Azorian thought back. "It is my pleasure to help."

"Could you fabricate Kavelen Lavenci's hand to be whole again?"

"It would take many hours, but yes. She is badly injured."

"What payment do you want?" I asked in thought.

"My payment is being able to do good while my fellow Lupanians do evil. Bring the lady here, and remove her bandages. We shall start."

Azorian removed his hands from my head, and I found myself back in the taproom. The others were still sitting about, drinking wine in the gloom. I went over to Lavenci.

"Ladyship, Azorian can heal your hand as if you had never injured it," I explained. "Do you wish that?"

"I—er, I am not sure that I understand."

"He and I can walk in each other's minds, he has talents that are not of this world, if you take my meaning. I can mind-speak with him."

"He's a Lupanian?" she whispered, astounded.

I put a finger to my lips. "He can heal your hand completely. All I ask is that you tell nobody else where he is from."

"Danolarian, Danolarian, what am I to do with you?" she sighed softly. "You are so, so honorable. It was almost a relief to find that you had a few grubby little vices, just like mine."

"Ladyship?" I asked innocently.

"Don't pretend, I'm annoyed that you lied to me about being pure-hearted, but it does bring us closer together," she said brightly, not looking at all annoyed. "You are in my obligation for that."

"If what you heard is true, ladyship, then I shall certainly discharge that obligation. What have you in mind?"

"In seven years from the day of Pelmore's execution, I want my way with you in some pantry."

"Er, I, oh," I stammered. "So, er, what am I meant to have done?" I asked, hastily changing the subject.

"I'll tell you later. What is Azorian going to do with me?"

"Come along, he will explain."

I took her over to Azorian, and left them with her hands pressed together between his. Now I sat next to Pelmore.

"So, will you wait seven years to ride her?" he asked with an exaggerated leer. "She's not worth it, she lies out flat like a sack of feathers. Perhaps you know that already."

"No, I do not have the benefit of your experience," I said as I poured a little wine into a tumbler.

"My life for your dalliance, oh aye, but you will be disappointed."

I took a sip of wine. "Pelmore, you will die because you murdered a man. A very brave man, Captain Danzar, who commanded the ballista crew that brought down a Lupanian tripod tower. You will die because you brought me so close to death that I exchanged pleasantries with the ferrygirl herself. You will also die because you tried to kill a noblewoman. The fact that your death might actually benefit Kavelen Lavenci is entirely beside the point."

Reillen came over with a pitcher of wine. I held out my tumbler, and she refilled it. The sight of her set a thought batting away in my mind. It was actually not her strange talk about lamplight girls, gambling, and drinking to excess. That was probably just a minor lie to fend Lavenci off. No it was something else.

On a whim, I got up and walked over to the servingboard, reached over, and secured a large, thick book. Mallow Landing was so small that the tavern was the clearinghouse for mail. This was the mail register. I checked the entries for two months earlier, but did not find what I was looking for. On the other hand, perhaps I did. I closed the register and turned around—and for a moment the entire universe became a blaze of brilliant green light attending the mightiest concussion that I have ever felt, before or since. I seemed to float for a long time, and then my ears recovered. There was an almighty rumble and clatter as tiles, beams, and stonework came tumbling down around us. Dust was everywhere, as was an acrid, burning stench. The light of the lamp was gone, replaced by total blackness and the sound of occasional slides of rubble.

"Did the earth move for anyone else?" came Wallas's voice from somewhere nearby.

"It's the fifth cylinder," I croaked, very surprised to be still alive. "It must have landed right on top of the tavern. Can anyone else hear me? Call out."

"Constable Riellen! Reporting! Sir!"

"Constable Wallas, pleased to be alive, sir."

"Pelmore, and . . . I'm bruised and cut."

"Lavenci. I think I am all right."

"Azorian, *antil tellik m'tibri*," called Azorian, correctly deducing that this was a verbal head count.

"Constable Solonor, requestin' that you get this bleedin' cat's arse orf me back—sir!"

Silence followed for some moments.

"Anyone else?" I asked the darkness, but there was no response. "Wallas, what can you see with your cat's eyes?"

"Part of the roof seems to have stayed in one piece, and it is directly above us, sir."

"The fighting tripods will soon arrive to protect the cylinder as it opens," I explained urgently. "We have to be gone by then."

"Easier said than done, sir," replied Wallas. "I can see no openings big enough to admit a person."

"Gnomes is persons."

"Constable Solonor, shut up. Wallas, go exploring. See if you can find a way out with a short path, and one that we can dig wider quickly."

"I shall check, sir."

Whenever Wallas was seriously concerned about anything, he called me "sir." He had just called me "sir" three times in three replies, so things did not seem good at all. I felt in my pocket, and found a small sponge and two phials.

"I am going to make a light," I said between coughs from the dust.

The sponge began to glow green with some drops of the two philtres poured onto it and mixed. Riellen was a couple of yards away, lying on the floor. Nearby were our packs, and everything was covered in dust.

Chapter Twelve

WHAT WE SAW FROM THE RUINED TAVERN

Wallas had good news, bad news, disastrous news, and catastrophic news. There was a single, narrow path to the open air, which was good. However, it came out facing the pit formed by the fifth cylinder, which was bad. A Lupanian fighting tower had already arrived to stand guard, which was disastrous. The catastrophic news was that another of the towers was striding about annihilating what was left of the little port with its heat weapon. What saved us was the fact that the cylinder had splashed earth over the collapsing tavern, so that it did not resemble even the ruins of a building.

Leaving the others, I followed Wallas, widening the gaps in the wreckage until I could wriggle through. As we reached the open air, I saw that we were definitely on the edge of the pit gouged by the fifth cylinder. I could see smoke drifting about from the burning remains of Mallow Landing, while the green lights from a tripod tower played down on the fifth cylinder. Its tentacles were apparently helping those inside to unscrew the hatch.

"They must have got here within a dozen minutes," I whispered as we looked out over the pit. "They must have known where it would land."

"Then we are trapped, sir?" asked Wallas.

"Not for long. Two Lupanians seem to be in each cylinder. They will build two more fighting towers for them, then be gone by tomorrow evening to wait for the next cylinder."

As we were speaking, the access hatch of the cylinder came away. I saw a thing that looked rather like a large, wet leather sack waving a dozen or so tentacles emerge from the hatch and flop to the surface of the pit. Next came . . . what looked like a man. He seemed normal, even unexceptional, and was dressed in a dark blue coat that was trimmed with braid and had lots of gilt buttons.

"They—some of them are like us," gasped Wallas.

"From a distance," I added. "Wallas, I want you to tell nobody of this."

"But why, sir?"

"Because I know something you do not."

As we watched, the Lupanian took hold of a sort of harness on the tentacled creature and steered it back to the hatch. Two tentacles reached inside and drew out a body. This was carried some yards from the cylinder.

"Must have died on the trip through the void," I whispered.

"Which are the real Lupanians, sir?" asked Wallas.

"The thing with the tentacles seems only to be a beast of burden."

"It must be very strong, it handles great loads with ease."

"Call it a handling beast, then," I joked halfheartedly.

With no hesitation or ceremony the guard tower's Lupanian deployed its heat weapon on the dead Lupanian. Moments later nothing remained of the body but a molten puddle in the soil.

"Obviously sensitive about us knowing that we are passably similar to them," Wallas suggested. "Will they build a fighting tower for the survivor?"

"I expect so," I replied.

But the Lupanian did not begin building another tower. A short time later two more towers arrived. Their tentacles were linked together, and they walked together in a sort of lock-step motion. I recognized one of them as the damaged tower from the battle in Gatrov. The damaged tower and its companion bent their legs and lowered themselves into the pit. Now the Lupanian that had just arrived set to work with his tentacle machine, repairing the damage to the cowl of the tower I had helped to topple. This involved the cowl being split open like a sea shell, and I could see that there was a jumble of things inside that were totally beyond my experience. Nevertheless, I made an attempt to sketch the incomprehensible.

After perhaps an hour of chanting, incantations, arm waving, castings, and roiling energies, the tower was fully repaired. The handling beast was led back inside the cylinder, and seemed to screw the hatchway cover back from within. Meantime the other towers patrolled slowly, and from time to time there were screams and shrieks from somewhere out of my line of sight. The newly arrived Lupanian mounted the repaired tower and sealed the hood shut.

At a distance, the Lupanians looked very much like us, although a little thinner and taller. Lupan is a slightly smaller world than ours, so I would have expected them to be smaller. I have since learned that smaller worlds have less ground-force to pull objects downward, and this lesser force allows Lupanians to grow tall more readily.

Although they had no immediate use for the cylinder, they did not leave at once. Each fighting tower had a cylindrical cage at the back of its hood, and in this there was room for a half dozen adults. The cages were full, and at first I thought that those inside were prisoners of war. How very wrong can a person be? As we watched, one of the towers stepped behind a companion, lifted the lid of its cage with one tentacle, and reached in with another. This set the people in all the cages screaming and shrieking in terror, for they had apparently witnessed what was to happen at some earlier time. A struggling body was drawn out, and with my farsight I recognized Duke Lestor. He was still dressed in his mail and surcoat, and I could see the coat of arms on his chest. Two days ago he was a man of great authority and consequence, with the power of life and death over those brought before him. As an Alberinese noble he was still worth a huge ransom, but the Lupanians did not care for our sort of wealth.

The duke was held up before the hood of the fighting tower, with the tentacle wrapped around him several times to pin his arms. The faceplate of the tower now hinged downward, revealing the Lupanian who commanded it. He reached out, and took the duke's head between his hands. Whatever was happening, it must have been painful, for the duke screamed almost continually. It took a half-dozen minutes before the duke fell silent, and for most of the time I could see fluid dripping from his body. At first I assumed that he had lost control of his bladder, but I was wrong. His body was literally falling apart, the skin becoming like wet paper and the flesh turning to jelly. When the tentacle finally flung his body aside, it came apart in midair before hitting the ground. The next meal was selected, amid another riot of shrieking.

The Lupanians feasted on life force for over two hours, until their cages were empty. I managed to watch while another kavelar was drained, but when a girl was lifted from a cage I had to turn away and hide my face.

"They are vulnerable while feeding," I observed to Wallas. "From here you could kill one with a well-aimed crossbow."

"That would be suicide," he replied. "The others are always on guard."

"I suppose you are right," I muttered reluctantly, for I was certainly in a mood to kill.

The towers suddenly began hooting, then formed a line and strode off. Wallas and I merely lay still, too shocked and sickened to move. That was just as well, as a fighting tower came hurrying back, looking for any survivors that might have emerged from the ruins. Satisfied that all were indeed dead, it left again.

✳ ✳ ✳

I had the others crawl out to join us, and in the case of Pelmore the passage had to be widened farther before he could pass. Wallas was sent out into the pit first, in spite of his protests, but he was a cat and so far less likely to be noticed. I could see the smoke from a fire somewhere to the south, and Miral was low in the sky. I estimated that dawn was perhaps three hours away, but there was a moonworld high in the sky which added to Miral's light.

Very cautiously, we emerged from the ruins and looked down at the cylinder. There was a faint green shimmer about the hatchway.

"Some type of guard auton," said Lavenci at once.

Wallas returned, and reported that there were no other obvious traps or autons left to ensnare us.

"Riellen, keep everyone near the opening, and get them back inside if anything unusual approaches," I said, glancing about to get my bearings and wishing that I were about to crawl into bed for about twelve hours of sleep instead of crawling about in a ruined village.

Fires burned here and there, adding to the light from the sky. Apart from the stone piers, the wharfside area had ceased to exist. Looking down into the water, I tried to guess where our barge might have been moored. After scuttling along for several dozen yards, I finally caught sight of the bellows pump mechanism, still just above the surface. The barge had sunk again once Halland and the others had stopped pumping, and thus the Lupanians had missed its submerged bulk.

I crept down the stone steps and eased myself into the water, then waded along the sunken decking of the barge. With my hands on the lever of the bellows pump I waited for several minutes to make sure that everything was indeed silent and unmoving, then began to work the lever. The sound seemed as deafening as a trumpet fanfare beside one's ear, and every so often I stopped to listen for the *jingle-clink* of approaching Lupanian towers before continuing. After half an hour a strip of cloth that I had tied to the stock of the pump had risen perhaps a half inch clear of the water. The barge was indeed undamaged, and could be refloated! Miral was long down by the time I started back for the cylinder. A few hours of pumping would have the barge raised, and this time I was not going to allow a stop until we reached Alberin.

Dawn was lighting up the eastern horizon as I set off to return to the others. On the way back, I passed the twelve bodies left by the Lupanians' feeding. They were literally in pieces, their flesh like wet pastry, their bones crumbling. Duke Lestor's torso was held together only by his chain mail. They all looked as if they had been dead for weeks, yet they did not smell of decay. Something had been leached out of their bodies, something both physical and etheric. I could not bring myself to take samples, but like a good inspector I gathered impressions and scribbled notes with a char stick.

When I returned to the pit, the others were huddled together, and were staring and pointing.

"Has a Lupanian returned?" I hissed.

"No, but Azorian is down with the cylinder," replied Wallas.

"What?" I exclaimed in relief laced with exasperation. "Well why doesn't someone fetch him back?"

"None of us are feeling very brave, sir," Riellen replied.

I saw that Azorian had descended to the cylinder, and was standing at the rear hatchway with his hands held out. Without another word I scrambled down after him. The guard auton was sure to be able to kill any potential intruder trying to enter the cylinder, but before I reached him I saw the glow of the auton fade into nothingness. Azorian began chanting as I stood beside him, and to my astonishment, the hatchway began to unscrew again. As we stood watching, I took one of Azorian's hands and held it up. The fingertips were covered in tiny suckers. Beside us, the hatchway continued to unscrew. The hatchway came away from the hull, and was lowered to the soil by three tentacles from within. Azorian beckoned to me to enter with him as he clambered into the hatchway.

I approached the hatchway slowly, mindful of what I had seen when the first voidcraft's hatchway had opened. There was a screw thread about six inches deep around the circumference, while the hull's thickness would not have exceeded six inches. Somehow I had thought that it would have been thicker, given that it had flown between worlds and withstood great stresses. Suddenly the thought came to me that I was about to become the first of my world to enter a voidcraft, and with that I became almost eager. I heaved myself up and clambered through the hatchway.

The air inside was stuffy, and bordering on foul. I heard Azorian speak what might have been a minor spell, and lights came to life. I crawled along a narrow shaft between racks of cloth bags, then came out into an open space. Azorian was already farther along. He beckoned for me to join him, but I was too preoccupied with what was near the hatch to pay much attention to anything else. A handling beast was there. It reminded me of a terrestrial octopus, and looked to be about the weight of a small horse. A stirring amid the shadows beside it revealed that there were two of them. They regarded me steadily but without menace while Azorian rummaged beyond my field of vision.

Azorian now gave me a quick tour of the voidcraft's interior, miming the functions of various mechanisms. For me it was an unsettling experience, as I quickly realized that there was no floor; in fact, I had no sense of up and down at all. This left me feeling even more disorientated. At the rear were racks of porous bags. Each bag contained both crystals and a jar of some fluid. Pressing his hands to my head, Azorian explained that when the fluid and crystals were mixed they apparently generated breathable air. Every so often the voidfarers would bleed a little foul air into the nothingness beyond the hull, while new, breathable air was being generated by the crystals. Azorian also explained that the bags had cushioned him during the great stresses of the launching and landing.

We crawled forward along the curved hull until we came to a pair of seats held by flying buttresses. On a panel before each seat were glowing globes, levers, keys, amulets, and other things that I could not even begin to describe. Small, semitransparent autons stood above some of the amulets, their arms folded and their eyes following us. At the center of the forward seat's panel were four glass plates mounted in ornate frames. The plates were blank.

"Blood," said Azorian in Alberinese, pointing to a dried, green substance that was smeared over the rear seat. "Murderings."

The interior had all the magnificence of an emperor's cabin aboard a luxury galley. There were several racks of scrolls and charts, two chests of robes and boots, more chests of devices whose purpose I could only guess at, and a rack containing two shields painted with heraldic devices. Along with the last named was a pair of long levers with handles. The walls were painted with scenes from Lupanian history, depicting cities, temples, important-looking Lupanians, complex devices of gleam and glitter, and even a voidship. There was a battle scene on a tapestry attached to the hull with studs, and I recognized a pair of fighting tripods among the various war engines. Interestingly, they appeared to be wrestling with their tentacles rather than using heat weapons.

I climbed up along a buttress and into the front voidfarer's seat. What I had taken to be two lateral struts were not actually connected to the seat, but had sleeves and handles for the Lupanian's arms. They were made of a violet, translucent material that I did not recognize. Azorian clambered up beside me, and I gestured for him to put his hands to my temples.

"This is the steersman's seat," he explained within my thoughts. "The voidfarer sorcerer who sits here generates etheric wings that extend beyond the outer hull."

"But why?" I thought back. "There is no air for flying between moonworlds."

"Put two eggs in a wine jar, then drop it from a high tower. What happens?"

"A shattered wine jar and two broken eggs."

"The same would happen with a voidcraft, if it had no wings. Wings are of no use between worlds, but all four moonworlds are enshrouded in air. Thus wings are of great use for landing a voidcraft softly."

Azorian took his hands from my head, then reached out and worked a lever beside the active viewing plate in the panel before me. To my surprise the view on the panel moved, and I could see Lavenci in Miral's light.

"Magic!" I exclaimed.

"Mirrors," explained Azorian in Alberinese. "Toy."

I looked around for some moments, taking in the interior that was more like a work of jewelry than the inside of a craft that could fly between worlds. It seemed so advanced and exotic, yet whenever I stopped to marvel at a device, Azorian showed me that it was a clever but simple trick that even our own artisans or sorcerers could master. There was much to be learned here, but it was wasted on someone like me. I put Azorian's hands back to my head.

"This, er, voidship, it's magnificent," I thought, slowly and carefully. "Can you fly it? I would like to take it to my master in Alberin, he might learn from it."

"The voidship is like a crossbow bolt," thought Azorian in reply. "It needs a much larger machine to launch it."

"I see," I said, catching the analogy at once. "Pity, we might have learned a lot from it, and used that to fight back against the tripod towers."

"If you do not mind moving it at a slow pace, that can be done."

"Please explain?" I asked, both aloud and in thought, aware that the fate of our world might depend on what he was trying to tell me. "What do you mean?"

"You wish to move the voidship, is this so?"

"Yes."

"To where?"

"Down the river, to Alberin."

"It is light enough to float, and the handling beasts are strong enough to drag it to the river. Shall I command them to do it?"

"Yes, yes!" I exclaimed, immediately almost dizzy with hope. "Do it now. Please."

We climbed down from the steersman's seat, and Azorian unclamped the two shields and lever things with handles. Going down on one knee, he offered one of the levers to me on the palms of his hands.

"I, ah, don't have one of these," I responded, puzzled. "Thank you."

Yet again, Azorian placed his fingertips against my temples.

"They are the weapons of the murdered voidfarers," he explained within my mind. "You and I must use them, and avenge their honor."

"Weapons?" I said doubtfully.

"They are known as swords. I shall show you their use later."

Suddenly I laughed aloud, once I realized what they were meant to be.

"These will not work on this world," I thought.

"For what reason?"

"Azorian, every so often an apprentice blacksmith thinks to make a weapon that is all blade," I explained. "The trouble is that when swung through the air, the metal picks up raw etheric potential, and that burns the hand of the user as if lightning had struck it. It's a wonderful idea, but not practical."

"But these are glass blades," replied Azorian. "Millions of glass threads are dreamed together to form them. They pick up no ether from the air when they are swung."

"Glass? Is it strong?"

"Stronger than steel. Do you want one? They are from very reputable artisan houses."

"Yes . . . perhaps I do after all," suddenly realizing the value of what I had been given.

"Good. When we again have the leisure, I shall show you the basic way of the sword's usage. For now, we need to harness the handling beasts."

"So, er, you are definitely not one of the rogue sorcerers?" I asked, just to be sure.

"I am not a rogue," he responded firmly.

"I see. Then how came you to be in the first cylinder?"

"Later, the story is long. One last wonder to inspect."

He took his hand from my head and showed me two large, concave mirrors locked into frames near the front of the voidship. Both seemed to be carved into blocks of violet glass, and both blocks had handles cast into the edges.

"They are weapon crystals," said Azorian, touching my head again. "They are the core of the casting that generates the heat weapon."

Azorian was effective and efficient, and although I had no doubt that he really was a lowly artisan, I suspected that he might have been the winner of some Lupanian Artisan of the Year award. He coaxed the two handling beasts out of the hatchway, then had one of them screw the hatch back in place. Next he led me out over the vast expanse of hull, pointing out things that I had missed on the first cylinder. There was a sort of half-egg shape that I had just taken as a deformity, but was actually the outside part of one of the viewing devices. At the back was glass plate, behind it a mirror, and beneath the mirror a tube to the viewing plate. It was turned to face backward during the hottest part of the flight through our air, so that the glass plate would not be damaged. At several other points on the hull were recesses containing tie bars, so that chains could be attached to carry the voidship around in the pottery kiln as it was being built, and of course to load it into what Azorian described as the mountain-sized etheric crossbow on Lupan.

Using rope salvaged from the sunken barge, Azorian tethered the handling beasts to the voidship, then set them straining in the direction of the river. The voidship was very light for its size, and actually weighed no more than an empty barge. The handling beasts were about as strong as a team of a hundred oxen, however, and slowly the voidship came free of the soil and ruins. Within two hours it was clear of the pit it had gouged when it had landed. Another hour had it in the water, where it floated like an immense wine jar.

The pity was that the voidship made a very poor river vessel, because it rolled as soon as the weight of even a single person was put on top. Azorian suggested tying logs to either side as pontoons, but I had a better solution. The Lupanians had overlooked more than our sunken barge when they had arrived at the port. Also intact was a locker containing six carpentry axes. These could be used to fashion a pair of long sweep oars for the barge. With a handling beast working the oars, the barge could then be used to tow the voidcraft along the river, rather than just drift on the current as we had done when escaping Gatrov.

A handling beast was set to work pumping the bellows on the sunken barge, and we all stood watching in fascination.

"What took us a half day of pumping will take that thing a half hour at most," I said. "The sweep oars will take a lot longer to make."

"In a couple of days we can drift to Alberin, sir," said Riellen. "Why bother with oars?"

"We could be there by sunset today if we had barge sweep-oars," I pointed out. "There are tree trunks curing in that yard behind us. If I had six strong, steady, disciplined men the sweeps would be ready almost as soon as the barge was afloat again."

"There are people hiding in the forest, sir. I saw figures moving in the distance, watching when the handling beasts were dragging the voidship."

"Were there, indeed?" I said, stroking my beard. "I suppose anyone who can take orders and work in a team will do. Mili-tiamen, marines . . . Riellen, hurry over to the forest, try to find me half a dozen men in uniform."

"Sir!"

Riellen hurried away. I swept the countryside with my far-sight every so often, but all was still, and empty of Lupanian towers. To the south there were clouds of smoke rising into the still air, and I hoped that the Lupanians would be busy there for at least three or four hours more. They would eventually be back for the handling beasts in our cylinder, but from the air crystals that were activated, Azorian estimated that they had been left with air to last until sunset. If Fortune looked upon us with any sort of favor, the tripods would not return until then, when we would be long gone.

The handling beast worked tirelessly at the pump, with Azorian in the saddle and applying his fingers to what passed for its head. The sides of the barge came clear of the water, and within a quarter hour I knew that it would be floating well enough for us to set off. I turned back to the forest, hoping that Riellen would not be too long, and to my surprise I saw that she was already returning. There were six men with her, but . . . I lowered the farsight, blinked, wiped the objective lens on my tunic, then trained it on the approaching figures again. I then sat down on a pile of rubble, put my face in my hands, and tried very hard not to surrender to blind hysterics.

"Inspector, are you troubled?"

I lowered my hands. It was Lavenci, bending over and peering at me anxiously, with her hands on her knees. Her hair hung like twin waterfalls of milk to frame her face, and her eyes were like a pair of coals. She could come across as very endearing when she wished to.

"It's nothing of consequence," I sighed, standing up. "But thank you for your concern."

Riellen hurried up with her recruits, panting heavily but triumphant.

"Sir!" she barked, stopping before me to salute. "Six men in uniform, as ordered."

I folded my arms and surveyed the men from the forest, shaking my head.

"Constable Riellen, I do concede that these are men, there are six of them, and they are in uniform, but these are morris dancers."

Six men wearing white hats, tunics and trews, lots of bells and ribbons, and heavy black clogs immediately realized that they had failed some quite fundamental test. Their eager expressions fell so far and fast that I thought about trying to dredge up the energy to apologize to them.

"But Inspector, we want to help," said the man wearing the most bells and ribbons, and who was apparently the leader.

"Aye, and we learn routines fast, sir," said one who was even bigger and stronger-looking than Pelmore.

"And we work as a team," said another, who had a rebec poking out of his pack.

"And we have our own sticks," said the leader.

"Oh wonderful, I'm sure they'll be all we need against the Lupanian heat weapon," I responded.

"But Miss—er, Constable Riellen said that you were going to lead us against the oppressive, oligarchical oppressors from the Lupanian establishment," said the leader.

"I think she said we would oppose the oppressive, oligarchical Lupanian establishment lackeys," said the big man.

"Didn't she say—" began a man who was no bigger than Riellen.

"Enough!" I shouted. "I wanted *militiamen* with *basic war-*

fare carpentry skills, not light entertainment while we have breakfast—not that we have much food, of course."

"But Inspector, I'm a carpenter," said the big man.

"And so am I," said the tiny man.

"And I'm a wheelwright," said the man with the rebec.

"And the rest of us learn quickly and work as a team," said the leader. "We really want to do something against the, er, ollypressive . . ."

"Oppressive, oligarchical Lupanian establishment lackeys," said the big man helpfully.

The morris dancers got to work on fashioning the oars, and after that I experienced something very rare: no less than ten minutes of uninterrupted solitude. The person who brought it to an end was Azorian, who approached me holding his lever weapon, the sword.

"Learnings," he said, pulling it apart.

What he was left holding was a single blade about a yard long, with a handle on one end. I took out the weapon he had given to me, which was identical, to my eyes. The blade was an odd, translucent violet, and was sufficiently sharp to cut a hair dragged across it.

If made from metal, it would have been next to useless on our world. In principle it was the ultimate weapon for hand-to-hand fighting, but its virtues lasted only until the very first swing. Swing any long metal strip through the strong etheric field of our world, and energies soon built up and discharged like a little lightning bolt into one's hand. That was why we used only axes in personal combat, which were merely short blades mounted on long wooden poles. Azorian demonstrated several cuts, parries, and lunges in quick succession. Nothing happened to his hand. This strange, hardened glass definitely did not conduct energies.

Gingerly, I did some experimental cuts and parries myself. There was no blast of ether to sting my hand. For the next hour I was the sole student in the first tutorial in swordwork ever conducted on Verral.

The morris dancers had two rough but functional barge

sweep oars completed in about two hours. We mounted them amidships on the barge, in front of the second handling beast, then set off just as soon as everyone could be taken aboard. One handling beast worked the bellows pump with two of its tentacles, and the other rowed. The handling beast at the sweep oars was so very strong that it drove the barge and voidship through the water faster than the speed of a trotting horse on land.

"I can hardly believe the strength of those things," I marveled as I stood looking back at them from the bow. Azorian put this hands to my head again.

"The handling beasts are used to power the tripod towers," he explained. "They move the pistons, cranks and levers within the legs so that they can walk."

Yet another of the Lupanians' secrets had suddenly been uncovered before my eyes. At that time I had no idea what good it would do me, but like a diligent inspector in the Wayfarers, I added the fact to my journal. Whenever not working or mindspeaking with me, Azorian sat with Lavenci's hands pressed between his. By the time we were ready to set off again, her skin was healed, and the worst of the fractures in her hand were no longer noticeable. Best of all, she had some use of her fingers back again.

Chapter Thirteen

HOW WE SPOKE WITH THE LUPANIAN

During our first hours on the river Azorian and I spent over an hour in mindspeak, and he explained how the tripods worked. The handling beasts had eight tentacles. Two pairs of tentacles controlled each of the tripod's three legs, and the remaining two tentacles moved the hood with the Lupanian sorcerer in it. The tripod's tentacles were artificial, made of spun glass fibers, and were controlled by the Lupanian himself. The glasswalkers, as Azorian called them, also generated the immense etheric energies for the heat weapon.

The handling beasts seemed to have the intelligence of a horse or dog, and once the barge and voidship were at the middle of the river, Azorian was able to dismount and join us at the bow, leaving the beasts to work unguided. All of us were at the bow, except for the morris dancers. I had given one of the two crossbows to the dancers' captain, sent them to the stern, and told them to keep watch. Riellen scanned the horizon with a farsight for Lupanian fighting towers in search of their missing voidship, and I stood with the other crossbow over my shoulder to give the barge the appearance of being armed. After lunch Azorian held his hands up. I sat down, and allowed him to put his hands to my temples.

"Azorian, what is it like on Lupan?" I thought. "Do you have rivers there?"

"All is canals," he spoke in my mind. "They are old, very old. They were old when the ancients did their epic deeds. They are more narrow than this river. Very narrow, and very deep, so that there is less evaporation, and so less water lost."

"How did you get aboard the cylinder?"

"By chance. I was a fabricator of life castings with the Ethercast."

"Ethercast?"

"The etheric ballista that flung the Moonbird and nine other voidcraft to your world. It was built into an extinct volcano, and it went down three miles from the summit of the crater. I counted the steps every time I descended to the Moonbird, which is what you call Cylinder One. There were twelve thousand steps, in a tunnel through the side of the mountain. I remember my last trip ever so clearly. I emerged onto the narrow landing cut into the black, volcanic rock at the heart of Mount Dastvalas. I always paused to take breath, then looked up because it was such an overwhelmingly awesome sight. The shaft was narrow, but it continued up for nine thousand feet. The last third of it was a tower built over the cone of the crater.

"The Moonbird was fifty-five of your feet in length, but it

did not seem especially impressive at the bottom of the shaft. The hatchway was at the end of the tail, and was to be sealed with a screw plug for the flight between moonworlds. Everything was designed to pass through the hatchway, even if it had to be dismantled. I put my load of initiator crystals down, and allowed the guards to search me. There were no less than twelve searches between picking up my load on the slopes on the mountain and installing the crystals in the airbags aboard the Moonbird. The guards decided that there was no problem, and I was allowed into the voidcraft.

"I had the bundle across my shoulders as I climbed up into the hatchway. As one of the flight fabricators, I knew the interior as well as the voidfarers themselves, and perhaps better. The interior was very finely crafted, yet built for lightness and strength. The commander's couch was near the middle of the vessel, and most of the back space was filled with bags of airstone crystals. The heaviest of the equipment and supplies was stored at the front, so that the craft would be properly balanced when flying through air.

"I conjured what you called an auton between my hands, a spell, an engine of etheric energies. It was a tangle of bright blue threads of fire in the dim, phosphor-lit interior of the Moonbird. 'Release yourself and burn, on the fifteenth day from this very day, at this very hour,' I said slowly and clearly, then I placed it on the bag and watched the blue tangles sink into the fabric. They glowed faintly blue from within the airstone bag, and all around me was the glow of other airstone timer spells. Each spell would burst the jar of oil amid the crystals to release air into the master cabin of the Moonbird so that the crew of two could breathe. A master auton controlled a valve in hull, gradually releasing the cabin's air into . . . what? Whatever was outside. Nothingness, was the opinion of the greatest of our philosophers, so who am I to give an opinion? There was to be enough air for the commanding sorcerer and a cold sciences philosopher to survive for two weeks, plus air for a third week in reserve. The handling beasts were to be in a state of torpor on the flight, and would require little air.

"Suddenly a guard called out that the overmaster was to make an inspection. I replied that I still had to connect the bleed hoses. He told me to crawl between the racks of airstone bags and lie still until after the inspection was over. I lay still on the soft bags of crushed crystals. The overmaster! The overmaster should not have been there. Not as close to the launch as that, anyway. He had done other inspections, however, in fact he knew the craft well enough to be a voidfarer himself.

"We all knew that the overmaster liked precision and punctuality. The shaft, the tower, the Moonbird itself, they were all made with fantastic precision, and according to a schedule that had allowed no room for missed deadlines over ten whole years. I heard voices outside. One voice had such command that it could have ordered anyone in the empire to stand up to his earlobes in steaming hot pig manure for a week if he did not bow fast enough in the royal presence.

"I heard the overmaster crawl through the hatch, then begin to climb the rope ladder that led up the center of the Moonbird. From outside there was a sharp grunt, and then a guard cried out 'My lord, what—' before his voice was cut off too. Somebody else entered the hatch, someone who called out, 'Both guards dead.' I froze. I heard a third person clambering up the access ladder. 'Fortune be with you,' came the overmaster's voice. 'I shall arrive in the eighth vessel.' Someone laughed. 'We shall have the world all but conquered by then, sire.'

"The rogue voidfarers bid the overmaster farewell, then I heard the unmistakable whirr of the hatch being screwed shut by a handling beast outside the Moonbird. That meant they were preparing for the launch. I had to get out of the Moonbird and into a sealed shelter some hundreds of feet along a tunnel in the rock, yet I could not escape with the hatch being closed. There was the heavy *clunk-clack* of the three lug anchors being locked down to seal the hatch, and with that sound I knew I was trapped aboard.

"I lay still, my mind racing. The overmaster! He had ordered the guards killed, there was no doubt of it. Of the launch itself, well, words can never do justice to it. I rigged up straps to hold myself in place and lay in cushioned by the airstone crystal bags. I could feel water gently rocking the Moonbird. The vessel was light, and certainly light enough to float. I knew that the water was rising, floating the Moonbird into the base of a column of aetheric energies that extended fifty miles above the mountain and into the sky.

"I felt the shudder of the most massive concentration of etheric energies in all our world's history through six inches of ceramic wall. Etheric energies surged through the copper coils embedded in the Moonbird's structure, easing the vessel out of the water. More copper coils encountered more etheric energies. Within the space of three beats of a heart belonging to someone in a fairly agitated state, our craft was drawn out of the water and flung up the shaft at an acceleration in excess of twelve times the ground force on our world.

"A mighty weight pressed me down into the bags of airstone, and there was a terrible rumble and shuddering. Then I blacked out, and I remember no more until I awoke to no sound, shuddering, or weight at all.

"Of the flight through the void, there is little to say. I hung in my tethers for most of the time, floating, completely without weight. The crew slept at the same time, and it was then that I floated out of my hiding place to steal food and drink from the stores. I wrapped my wastes with care and packed them down among the airstone bags. As long as the air was not foul, I knew the crew would not check my refuge.

"I knew that the Moonbird was to encounter the third moonworld, yours, at the end of the journey. It was to fly down to the surface on etheric wings cast by the commander. The Moonbird would not land gently, but the shock was not expected to kill the crew. They would then unscrew the hatch, emerge, and begin their studies of your world. They were to urge your overmasters to build enormous mirrors, that could flash messages between our two worlds. It was to be the most grand, glorious scholarly exchange of learning in all of time.

"I overheard the rogue crewmen speaking, however, and what I heard shocked me. They were not on a mission to spread Lupanian knowledge and study Verral, they were setting out to conquer it. You see, the ether about Gigant, the lordworld, is strongest at your world's path around it. We of Lupan have lived our lives developing control over a much smaller background of ether. Now here, on Verral, we have vastly better powers of command over your ether.

"Lupan's orbit is in an area of lesser etheric energies, and thus we Lupanians have to be better at its control, storage, and focusing. You have always had more than you know what to do with, and have not had to bother. Our glasswalkers can gather together vast energies, then use them via the heat weapon casting. Our healers are also able to bleed off energies into patients to hold them back from the edge of death while transforming their bodies into the image of whatever is healthy. I did this for you, and I am doing this for the woman Lavenci—but that is another matter.

"The landing was worse than the launching. There was some etheric cushioning, and the craft was designed to lose speed by skimming through the soil for a distance, but it was rough. Once down, I remained in hiding. The crew were not expecting there to be anyone else aboard, so I watched and waited for a chance to escape. When I saw them preoccupied with that attack by your cavalry, I ran in the opposite direction. You know the rest."

☀ ☀ ☀

After we had finished speaking, I stood up stretched, then walked aft to where the morris men were sitting. I took their leader aside.

"I don't believe we have exchanged names," I said.

"Jael. Jael Jinger."

"I am Inspector Danolarian Scryverin."

"Oh! Surely not the Scryverin who played the sun down on Alpindrak?"

"Why yes," I replied, surprised yet again at how far the story of what I had done had traveled.

"Oh grand! Truly grand. Where are your pipes, then?"

"Wrapped in waxcloth, in my pack."

"Later, like before docking, might we try a tune? Got my flute here."

"I shall look forward to it."

"I'm the dancing master here. Like, we have two pairs to dance and one pair to play music, but my son's just joined as a dancer, so I'm taking a break to play music while he practices his steps." With that he elbowed me in the ribs. "The girls go for the dancers more than the musicians, you know."

I was only too aware of that, after a certain dance in Gatrov.

"Aye, but the musicians get free drinks," I managed.

"That's why I do both!" he chuckled, elbowing me again.

"Look, could you, well, handle the barge while I conduct some . . . difficult business. Discipline, and all that. A constable."

"Oh lordworld! Discipline of one of your own constables?"

"Yes. Watch the drama unfold, Jael, look upon it as a free show by a troupe of strolling players."

I walked the length of the barge, then sat down at the bow, wondering how to raise a particularly sensitive and delicate matter. *If I am wrong? Just say I might be wrong. There is scope for great damage here.* Azorian and Lavenci were sitting about ten feet away, their hands joined in his healing enchantment. Pelmore and Riellen were sitting opposite them. Wallas came sauntering down the deck of the barge, with Solonor marching beside him. The gnome had his tiny spear at his shoulder. Wallas hopped onto my lap. Solonor stood leaning on his spear.

"Wallas, do you recall me giving Riellen a letter to post at Mallow Landing, two months ago?" I asked in the softest of voices.

"Indeed sir. I remember saying at the time that it was the thickest letter I had ever seen."

"It was not entered in the postal register there. I checked, just before the fifth cylinder landed on top of the tavern."

Wallas thought about this for a while.

"Sir, I happened to be sitting behind Azorian yesterday, when Riellen and Lavenci came to the bow for some privacy. They had a very interesting talk about you. Nobody noticed me, but that's both the blessing and curse of being a cat."

"Indeed? What did they say?"

"Sir . . . permission to speak in a much louder voice, and ask you some leading questions?"

"Permission granted."

Wallas jumped off my lap, sprayed over the edge of the barge, stretched, then returned to my lap.

"So, back to Alberin again, city of expensive delights, exorbitantly priced wonders, and a quick and messy death for anyone with a large purse and a trusting nature," he said in a strident voice.

"Until the Lupanians arrive, anyway," I added as I leaned back against the bowlamp pole.

"I'm for those city gnomes and their taverns," said Solonor.

"Gnomes have taverns?" exclaimed Wallas.

"Aye, *and* establishments of pleasure," said Solonor earnestly. "Heard all about 'em from a cousin who used to hunt rats on the barges. Loose morals, they have."

"And what about you, Wallas?" I asked, scratching him behind the ears. "Still sticking to that nonsense that you never lay a paw upon female cats?"

"My spirit has pure morals and the most lofty of ideals, Inspector, but the flesh of lady cats is warm, soft, and covered in silky fur," Wallas conceded. "So what's your pleasure, sir? A pint, a pie, and a poke?"

"You have such a charming turn of phrase, Wallas."

"But what will your pleasure be, sir?"

"Not sure. I feel . . . oddly different. You know, I am relaxed now, yet I have no headache. I do believe that Azorian accidentally cured my predilection to headaches when he repaired the damage of the poison. It will be such a pleasant change to have a night off without the prospect of a headache once I began to relax. It's been so long, I've almost forgotten how to court a girl."

"Do what everyone else does. Hire one."

"Wallas, in three years, have you *ever* known me to do that?" I asked, speaking a little more slowly and clearly. I noticed Lavenci's head snap around.

"Well, no," Wallas replied. "Have you, Riellen?"

Riellen hunched over slightly, then shook her head almost imperceptibly. There was a sharp hiss of breath being sucked between Lavenci's teeth.

"Have you *ever* paid, sir?"

"Yes, once I did pay. It was Madame Jilli's in Palion. That was to celebrate surviving a rather nasty little battle, and I was alone in Palion for the first time. I hired a girl, took her out to dinner, walked her back to Madame Jilli's, kissed her goodnight, and returned to my hostelry."

Wallas gave me a particularly intense feline stare.

"Did you not forget to do something rather important and pleasant?"

"I was pretending to be welcomed back from battle by my adoring sweetheart, Wallas."

"For goodness' sake, Inspector!" exclaimed Wallas. "Are you trying to tell me that an adoring sweetheart would not have raised her skirts for you?"

"You don't understand chivalrous courtship and true romance, Wallas."

"From the sound of it, I'd not want to, either. Well, what about getting drunk for a change? I've never seen you do that, either."

"What? For three years past I've had enough problems with migraines without wanting hangovers as well. Nobody knows that as well as you and Riellen."

"No dalliance, no wine, no gambling," said Wallas, shaking his head. "I suppose you will be off to the library for your usual pastime, reading filthy poetry of the twenty-seventh century."

"*And* looking at the pictures, thank you Wallas. Allow me my few little vices."

"Any o' them pictures got gnomes doin' it?" asked Solonor hopefully.

"You should come with me, Constable Solonor, and see for yourself. You too, Wallas."

"Me sir?"

"Yes. You're an arsehole, Wallas, but you know how to be a friend."

"All part of being a cat, sir."

It was now that I tipped Wallas a wink, for Lavenci had turned away to disengage her hands from Azorian's. Slowly, steadily, like a very powerful and highly dangerous siege engine being wheeled into place, she stood up. She flexed her left hand. From where I was, it looked to be almost healed.

"Inspector, a word with you?" Lavenci said in a voice that was so acidic that it was a wonder her lips did not smoke and blister.

"Certainly, Ladyship, for a rare moment I have all the time in the world," I replied.

"I think that was an oxymoron, sir," said Wallas.

I casually took Wallas by the scruff of the neck, then held him out over the water.

"Wallas, do you know what I want you to do?" I asked.

"Yes, yes, shut up and let her ladyship speak," the cat replied patiently.

I put him back on the deck. Riellen was sitting hunched over, and seemed to have shrunk. Lavenci, by contrast seemed taller than a Lupanian tripod tower, and no less fearsome. She flexed her newly healed left hand, then stared directly at me.

"Riellen told me that she . . ." Lavenci paused. Riellen cringed a little more. "How can I put this delicately? That she procured the services of many lamplight women for the delight of a member of your squad."

"Really?" I asked. "They couldn't have been for Roval. Perhaps they were for Wallas?"

"What would *I* do with them?" asked Wallas, sitting down and licking a paw in rare embarrassment.

"Don't go fer ladies more than a few inches taller then meself," said Solonor.

"Well *I* certainly never saw them," I added. "Did you in fact say that, Constable Riellen?"

To her credit, Riellen managed to rally herself. She sat up straight and puffed out what there was of her chest.

"Her Ladyship must have misheard me," she declared.

"I did not!" barked Lavenci, stamping her foot.

"Well, who is to know, and what harm done?" I said soothingly. "Actually, speaking of doing harm, Pelmore, I do believe I have done you a little injustice," I called to the prisoner, who was still sitting near Riellen.

"How so?" he muttered sourly.

"I did not search everyone else for daemonglare berries yesterday. There might have been someone else trying to poison me. I have many enemies, after all. You might even get company for your hanging."

"Is that meant to cheer me?"

I took the ax from my belt and banged three times on the deck with the butt.

"I declare a field inquiry to be in session," I declared. "Usual rules of conduct apply. Now, everyone forward of the handling beasts turn out your pouches and bags."

All pouches and bags were produced and turned out. Nothing suspicious was found, of course.

"Your own pack remains strapped tight," Pelmore observed.

"Obnoxious though you are, you do have a point," I replied. "My pack should be searched, and Riellen's."

Riellen brought the packs over, then began to unbuckle a strap.

"No, Constable Riellen, I'll do the investigating, but thank you anyway. We'll start with my pack. What have we here? Half bag of trail biscuits, compass, code book, official orders, border papers, chip of Lupanian ceramic, farsight, spare florins, almanac, *Epic Love Poetry of the Eastern Draken-ridge Mountains, Erotic Alberinese Poetry of the Twenty-Seventh Century*—I'll leave that one out for you, Solonor, it's illustrated and I think it has gnomes in it. What else? Tinder-box, writing kit, seventh edition of *What Predator is That?*, package of dried fish for Wallas, *Field Medicar's Handbook*, field medicar's pack, field medicar's crest plate made out to Danolarian Scryverin, *Laws of Greater Alberin for Field Magistrates*, one half-empty waterskin, and a set of bagpipes in waxcloth. Better leave those out too, I've been asked for a tune later."

I repacked quickly, with the speed and efficiency of experience. Now it was the turn of Riellen to have a public viewing of her pack's contents on the deck.

"Two bags of trail biscuits, eleven books, waterskin, change of clothing, sewing kit, compass, writing kit, sheaf of pamphlets, almanac, combination tinderbox and medicar's kit but . . . no daemonglare berries."

"May I repack, sir?"

"Yes—but what is this book?" I asked, picking up a battered leatherbound volume. "The binding is in the Torean style."

"Oh, an obscure text on Torean representative government experiments at village level."

Until I had heard Riellen's lies while Azorian had been dragging me back from the edge of death, I would not have bothered to look more closely at the book. Now, however, I was not inclined to be trusting. I opened the book and glanced through the pages, which had a very odd texture, and were of quite thick parchment.

"Oi, this woman's got a gnome down her cleavage!" exclaimed Solonor, who had managed to heave open *Erotic Alberinese Poetry of the Twenty-Seventh Century* on the deck. "Headfirst, too."

"This is in a Torean scholarly language," I said casually, riffling through Riellen's book. "In fact it's Larmentalian." Over the top of the book I saw Riellen's eyes bulge. "My Larmentalian is a little creaky ... Looks like *A Gathering of Herbology, Hedgerow Castings, and* ... hmm, these words are a bit archaic. Looks like *Wyfe Knowings, Part the First*. Strange, too, that each page has a name instead of a number."

There was a moment of chilly silence in the hot summer air.

"How's he breathin'?" said Solonor, standing on my book of poetry and gazing down at the illustration.

"Perhaps he is being executed," suggested Wallas.

"Bleedin' hell, what a way to go. What's on the next page? Cor, look at that! He's lickin' her—"

"Constable Solonor! You too, Constable Wallas. Close that book and pay attention, this is meant to be an official hearing."

"Yes sir!" they chorused.

"Now Riellen, please explain about your book."

"It's not the book I thought it was, sir. I was keeping it until I could get it translated."

"But you do read scholarly Larmentalian, Constable?"

"Well, yes, but only slowly."

"Well now, perhaps I can help ... now here's a page that sets me a-worrying. Cocassien, the colorless, tasteless component of the caffin spice. Ah, and how clever! Each page is a packet, with a little sample of the substance within. Yes, there is a powder inside the package. I'd best avoid that one, it triggers excruciatingly severe migraines in people like me."

Lavenci glared intently at Riellen. Riellen had frozen in panic, and was not even blinking.

"What else is within this book?" I said, with a little more sarcasm in my tone. "Here is an interesting little brew ... mix ... boil while chanting when Miral is full ... tears of a virgin, standing naked ... administer two strands of hair from the couple ... may be kept in a phial for seven months and one day. No ... release, I think is the word, other than seven years from the death of one partner. To commence allurement glamour and so draw couple together, tie hairs together in a knot . . . burn knotted hairs to activate . . . *continuation beauty* . . . or does that translate as *constancy glamour?*"

"I liberated it from, er, a library," said Riellen in a soft, hollow monotone. "In Gatrov. I had thought to study it, and possibly find a way to lift the glamour on Revolutionary Sister Lavenci."

"It says here *Riellen Tallier, Clovesser Academy of Applied Sorceric Arts,* and the year is 3041," I pointed out, glancing inside the cover board.

"I, er . . ."

I paused to let Riellen complete her reply, but she was beyond replies by now.

"You could easily have secured hairs from Pelmore and Lavenci in the crush of the dance crowd." I continued, hardening my own tone quite suddenly. "A coin slipped to a serving maid, nothing easier. You wove glamours about Pelmore and Lavenci, an allurement glamour to draw them together, then a constancy glamour to bind them fast. *That* was why Lavenci was suddenly allured to that pig, and why he specifically chose her after winning the tourney dance. You did it because you thought she was paying court to me."

"Sir, no, no!" wailed Riellen with her hands held over her ears.

"Have you anything more specific to say to this hearing than no?" I asked.

Riellen fell silent, and did not look up. I heard the hiss of air as Lavenci took a deep breath, held it for a moment, decided not to speak words that would probably have etched glass, then exhaled again.

"You . . . you forced me into bed with Pelmore," Lavenci growled at Riellen. "You raped me."

"Second-remove rape carries the death penalty, even when by a woman," I said firmly. "Pelmore did not know, so it's probably not conspiracy. I'll have to check in the law book. Meantime, please do not interrupt proceedings, Lady Lavenci."

"Thank you, Inspector," Lavenci said in a level voice. "I am profoundly relieved to learn that I had no choice in the matter, and that *Revolutionaty Sister Riellen* caused my body to be violated by Pelmore Haftbrace."

Riellen's head jerked as if she had been given a slap to the face.

"Lady Lavenci, this is your first warning against speaking out of turn," I sighed. "One more such interruption will result in a fine of two florins. Now then, Constable Riellen, I put it to you that for three years you fed me with migraine-inducing powder whenever I was of a mood to celebrate any venture ended, *and* at any other time that I might pay court to some wench. Do you deny that?"

"No sir."

"Did you burn all my letters to Lady Lavenci instead of posting them?"

"Yes sir."

"Cor!" exclaimed Solonor, who had hoisted open the book of poetry again. "There's a lady gnome ridin' on this satyr's—"

"Solonor!" I shouted. "Get away from that bloody book or it goes into the river! Wallas, sit on him if he goes near it again. Now what in all hells was I up to in the transcript? Oh yes, *burned all my letters*."

"Constable Riellen, it takes a lot of talent to look worse than Pelmore, but you have done it," Lavenci muttered.

"Lady Lavenci, you are fined two more florins," I decreed, but she just smiled broadly.

"Sir, you have every right to hate me, it's true—" began Riellen.

"Hate you, no. Despise you, yes. You are no true revolutionary, Riellen, you have one set of standards for yourself and another for the rest of the world."

"I love you, sir!"

"What an upper-class notion," laughed Lavenci.

"Ladyship, you are fined a further two florins." I stood up. "Constable Riellen, put your hands together behind your back."

I bound Riellen's thin wrists, then returned to the bow. Before scribing up an account of proceedings from my dash-hand notes, I asked one last question.

"Ladyship, if you don't wish to testify against Constable Riellen, all references to your encounter with Pelmore will be struck from my proceedings. Do you wish to have Riellen executed for rape, and have the entire matter on public record, or will you grant her mercy and thus also preserve your honor?"

"What? Miss out on a chance to have Riellen knowing that

she lives only because I granted her the mercy that the little rapist did not show me? Of course I choose mercy, Inspector, by my very soul!"

"But I was raped too—" began Pelmore.

"You are under sentence of death, Pelmore," I interjected, "and should I petition the ratifying magistrate that will become death by torture. Would you like to know what death by torture involves?"

"Mercy," muttered Pelmore sullenly.

"I am going to sum up, then recommend sentence," I announced. "In my three years as a Wayfarer, I have never, *never* seen such a jumble of twisted emotions, petty hatreds, deceit, lies, vindictive bitchery, pious hypocrisy, and venal agendas. Pelmore Haftbrace of Gatrov, you are still charged with murder, and provisionally sentenced to death, but appear to be guilty of nothing further. Do you have anything to say?"

"Constable Riellen is right, the establishment protects its own," muttered Pelmore.

"Is that all? Splendid. Your original sentence is to be ratified when we reach Alberin."

I let everyone think about that for a few moments while I checked a fine point of law in *Laws of Greater Alberin for Field Magistrates*.

"Constable Riellen Tallier, you are charged with repeated assaults on your immediate superior in the Wayfarers— namely myself."

I checked my book of laws again. Everyone remained silent.

"*Knowingly causing harm to an immediate superior below the rank of marshal, fifty lashes recommended, should the superior press charges*. Multiply that by the number of migraines I have experienced, but allowing for my changes in rank, and it probably exceeds five thousand lashes. That is merely a recommendation, though. I sentence you to dishonorable discharge and lifetime exile, with the option of a flogging to be decided by the ratifying magistrate in Alberin. Constable Riellen, consider yourself suspended from duty, as of this moment. Do you have anything to say for the record?"

"Sir, I shall accept whatever sentence is ratified," Riellen replied shakily. "And if there is anything that I can do to make you forgive me, please say it."

"Forgiveness is not at issue here. Your professional integrity is. That is why you are no longer *Constable* Riellen. I declare these proceedings at an end."

Silence greeted these words. I banged the butt of my ax on the deck. The silence continued. I could see Lavenci's eyes displaying that ominous bulge that precedes an outburst of the most hysterical variety.

"I notice that you care nothing for *me* being trapped by a glamour for the next seven years," said Lavenci, glaring at Riellen. "Why is this? Are members of the nobility without rights in your brave new electrocracy—where all are supposed to be equal?"

"Ladyship, I apologize now," answered Riellen without raising her eyes. "I was too ashamed to speak to you—"

"Raise the glamour."

"I don't know how to."

"What?" shrieked Lavenci.

"Er, well, the counter-glamours were all in the second volume, which was not in the market stall in Clovesser where I found Volume One. All the other times, I . . . I just left the girls bound to their beaus."

"*All* the *other times*?" I exclaimed

"Forgive me!" squealed Riellen, squeezing her eyes shut and cringing.

"How many?"

"Five, sir."

"Five? I shall want names, dates, and locations."

"I shall set it all straight, indeed I shall."

"Words, words that cost nothing and mean less," said Lavenci with a sharp sneer. "So, precisely seven years from the hour that Pelmore hangs dead, I shall again have the freedom to caress any man that I *choose*. Congratulations, Riellen, you held me down and you had your way with me. I did not even get to *vote* on my fate."

At the word vote Riellen gasped as if stabbed, and tears spilled from her eyes. I put a hand over my own eyes for a moment.

"Now then, everyone except the prisoners will return to the task of reaching Alberin without being vaporized by the Lupanians," I ordered.

I heard the sound of Lavenci's boots on the deck. Suddenly there was a scuffle and a cry from Riellen, followed by splashing and bubbling. I lowered my hand from my eyes, to see Lavenci straddling Riellen and holding her head under the water with both hands. The barge rode so low in the water that this was not at all hard. I got up, walked over, and looked down at them.

"Inspector, would you be surprised to learn that I am fighting the temptation to cut Riellen's throat and push her overboard?" Lavenci asked.

"Not really."

"Supposing I were to declare myself defeated?"

"Well, Riellen would be in a little more trouble than she is currently."

Riellen wriggled frantically, but Lavenci just tightened her grip on my former constable's hair. Riellen blew some bubbles.

"Tell me, Riellen, who were all those lamplight girls for?" shouted Lavenci.

Riellen tried to buck Lavenci off, but the albino shifted her weight back a little and tightened the grip of her knees on Riellen's ribs.

"Maybe Riellen has somewhat more exotic amorous tendencies than we ever suspected," suggested Wallas from behind me.

"No, I think we are currently witnessing Riellen's first experience of being mounted by a woman," I replied.

We stood watching for a few moments more. Riellen was now convulsing occasionally rather than struggling.

"Er, might I point out that Riellen will soon drown?" asked Solonor.

"Ever had a migraine?" I asked.

"Ever had an allurement glamour?" asked Lavenci.

"Ever had over a hundred migraines?" I asked.

"Ever had a constancy glamour?" asked Lavenci.

"So, Riellen dies then?" asked Wallas, although with a tinge of real concern in his tone.

"Up to Ladyship," I replied.

"Give me one good reason why I should not continue to hold her face under the water for the length of time I spent under Pelmore?" demanded Lavenci.

"Admittedly I would not do it," I said slowly. "But it's the sort of thing that Riellen might do."

Lavenci immediately wrenched Riellen's head out of the water. With a remarkably well placed kneeling kick, Lavenci doubled Pelmore over, then heaved him onto Riellen and jammed his face against hers.

"You want my forgiveness, Riellen? Well your glamours once allured me into kissing *this*. Try kissing him now, if you can stand it."

"Look, er, perhaps we should leave you three alone to work out your differences," I suggested.

I cannot say whether Riellen did in fact kiss Pelmore, but after some moments she certainly vomited up a considerable amount of river water in his face. Now Lavenci heaved Pelmore upright, took a knife, sliced his tunic open, then seized him by the hair and jerked his head back.

"I am a biter when aroused," Lavenci declared. "I can provide a list of names of those who are qualified to testify as much. How many bite marks do you see on Pelmore's neck?"

Pelmore's neck was without blemish.

"For your information, Constable Riellen, bite marks last a lot longer than four and one-half days," I explained coldly.

"The allurement glamour lasts only until the very moment intimacy begins, Riellen!" shouted Lavenci for all to hear. "I can tell you that from direct experience. I got *no* pleasure from him, and here is your proof. I suddenly found myself lying beneath this *thing,* wondering what foul whim had put me there. *That's* what you did to me, you vile, hypocritical, little upper-middle-class bitch!"

That was actually as bad as it got. Lavenci released Pelmore, then pointedly washed her hands in the river. Finally she strode over to join us at the bow. Wallas rubbed against her leg as she sat hugging her knees.

"Here's one male who can touch you, ladyship," he suggested.

"Greatly appreciated, Wallas, but you're not my type," she replied, scratching his ears.

It was now that Riellen, her hands still bound behind her back and her hair still dripping, got to her knees, then struggled to her feet.

"Ladyship, I dedicate my life to your service," she announced softly in an oddly cold and level voice.

"I already have all the servants I need," said Lavenci. "Like *you,* I come from a *rich* family."

"Tell me what you want," insisted Riellen.

"What I want? I want the glamours lifted."

"There is only one glamour upon you now, ladyship."

"I meant *every* glamour you ever cast on *any* girl."

Riellen swallowed. "Agreed," she said, less confidently. "What else?"

"I want you to lose your accursed and hateful virginity within the week."

"Agreed," replied Riellen, hanging her head and blushing.

"To a *nobleman*."

"Agreed," managed Riellen, although with obvious difficulty. "What else?"

"Why should I be greedy? Inspector Danolarian, would you like Riellen's promise never to speak to you, write to you, or lay a hand upon you until the day she dies?"

"It would be a gift to treasure, ladyship."

"Then do it, Mistress Riellen," rasped Lavenci. "Not a word, not a touch, not ever again."

"Agreed," whispered Riellen.

"Mind, she will fail," said Lavenci. "Not a single glamour will ever be lifted, she will tie her legs together at the knees until the week is out, and she will certainly trail after you, Inspector. She has no backbone. Spite, malice, and bile are all that holds her up straight."

Chapter Fourteen

THE DEATHS OF THE SORCERERS

 Alberin came into view as the River Alber passed between the foothills of the Ridgeback Mountains and the Westcrag Ranges. All we could see at first was a heavy smudge of smoke on the horizon, then the palace towers became visible in the distance. By now we were only about five miles from the city walls. There were no forests or woodlands surrounding the city, only farmlands dotted with hamlets. People on the banks waved occasionally as we drifted past, and we could see groups of peasants at work taking in the early harvests. Horses plodded along the tow paths on both sides of the river, hauling barges upstream, but, rather ominously, we were on the only barge headed downstream. What really filled me with dread was the fact that nobody seemed at all alarmed.

Alberin is on a coastal plain, where the Alber River meets the Placidian Ocean. As we were approaching on that fifth day of the Lupanian invasion, the usual haze had been augmented by the smoke from a large and serious fire. My first thought was that the Lupanian fighting towers were there already, but once I got a clear view across the farmland with my farsight, I realized that only a single building was burning. It was somewhere near the palace, but not the palace itself. At that stage the sun was setting behind us, and the city was still miles away. By the time we were approaching the walls, darkness had long descended.

It was an hour after sunset when we docked at the customs landing by Riverside Gate. I was greeted by a customs guard, and taken to the assessor at a barred window in the Bureau of Coinage and Precious Metals. In the darkness it probably seemed that we had merely arrived on a pair of long, low barges.

"Wayfarer, eh?" the assessor drawled as he scribbled on his slate. "Missed some excitement this afternoon."

"You mean that fire?" I said, waving at the column of smoke that was still outlined by the pale, green light of Miral.

"Oh aye, the Great Cedar Hall. Gotta hand it to the regent, no flies on him. Be outa bed afore first light to be ahead of the regent."

"You mean he directed the city militia to contain the fire before it spread?" I asked.

"Nah, he *set* the hall afire. Now, what goods d'ye carry?"

"What? Hold a moment. Why did the regent burn the hall?"

"Because it were full of sorcerers."

"You mean he had them burned alive?"

"Aye, he lured 'em out of hiding from miles around with talk of endin' the Inquisition against sorcery so that an alliance could be formed ter fight this Lupanian invasion non-sense. Soon as they were in the hall and talkin', the guards locked the doors and *whoosh*! Lost a few of our own ministers and diplomats, mind, but the cause was noble. Alberin is now a sorcery-free city."

For a moment I reeled, both with fatigue and with the sheer stupidity of my ruler.

"But the Lupanians are *real*," I insisted. "They have terrible magical weapons."

"You seen 'em?" drawled the assessor with a total lack of interest.

"Yes! They took two minutes to level Gatrov and char everyone in it."

"Bollix. River pirates done it, wearin' costumes. Lupan's another moonworld. How'd they get here?"

"Come, I'll show you how," I said as I snatched the lantern from the guard.

Striding away down the stone wharf, I noted with satisfaction that both the assessor and the guard were following. I held the lamp up, illuminating the vast and very, very alien bulk of the voidship.

"In one of those!" I shouted, pointing.

I was not surprised that our arrival caused a sensation, but what did leave me gasping was the speed of the regent's political footwork. Having killed the three hundred most valuable people in the fight against the Lupanians and their magical might, he now arrested the only other people who knew how to fight back: us.

We managed to reach the shipyards near the mouth of the river and moor the barge and voidship before we were all arrested by Aquilin, the captain of the regent's personal guard. Wallas was, of course, overlooked for one quite obvious reason, and Solonor decided to stay within my pocket. We were marched up to Palace Hill, and down into the dungeons. This was not as bad as it sounds, however. Some monarch in the distant past had apparently decided that the chances of one day being sent down to his own dungeons were annoyingly good. Thus the walls, doors, and bars were solid, but the cells were well drained and ventilated, and neither damp nor smelly. We were all crowded into a single cell, however, where our names were taken, along with our papers, passes, seals, rings, and purses.

Taking both of Lavenci's hands and pressing them between his, Azorian continued his fabrication spell, as he called it. In the gloom of the cell, I could see just a hint of a corona around their hands, and I hoped that he could restore her hand as if it had never been smashed. Taking out my writing kit, I noted in my private journal that Lavenci could stand the touch of a male Lupanian, a male human cat, a male grass gnome, her constancy-glamour partner, and of course other women. I also speculated that Azorian might be using the same magical fabrication technique on Lavenci as was used to build the fighting towers. Had he done that with me as well? If so, what was his template?

Presently I heard a voice from a nearby cell.

"Inspector Danolarian, is that you?"

"Commander Halland, you're here too?"

"Indeed I am, sir, with Roval. Standard reaction of any ruler. When news arrives that you don't understand, arrest the bearer."

"So you were not believed?"

"Not entirely. Not at all, really."

Halland briefed me on the version of events that the regent was having voiced and posted throughout Alberin. I resisted the temptation to fall about laughing, then spent the next few hours thinking carefully about our situation. About midnight we were paid a visit by a palace official. He introduced himself as Wallengtor, the grand liaisory of the regent to the Guild of Town Criers and Brotherhood of Public Noticeboard Scribes.

"We have checked with the Wayfarers," he began. "Kavelen Lavenci, Constable Riellen, and yourself, Inspector, do appear to have legitimate identities and papers of passage. The rest of you have no official business in the capital, and that could go badly for you. Inspector, as the most senior servant of the regent in this group, what can you tell me of them?"

"Pelmore is my prisoner, and under provisional sentence of death," I said flatly. "Azorian is a Torean refugee, and has been assisting me. I enlisted the help of the morris dancers at Mallow Landing, when I had the opportunity to capture a Lupanian voidship."

"Ah yes, the long orange spindle," Wallengtor suddenly interjected. "It doesn't exist, you know."

"Beg to differ, sir. It is moored in the river, at Wharfside."

Wallengtor frowned unhappily, vaguely aware that one of those awkward situations had developed where decrees were not quite enough to bury the facts. It was the sort of situation where the enemy might batter down the gates, seize you, and stretch your neck across a chopping block, even though they had been decreed not to exist. Given the possibility that ignoring the facts could actually be worse than ignoring the regent, Wallengtor's resolve softened.

"The regent declared that the Lupanians do not exist, and that the invasion is really the Terrisians, wearing exotic costumes and using illegal magical weapons," he explained, now skirting a little closer to the truth. "The regent never makes a mistake, of course."

"Oh no, never," I agreed. "Who brought the news?"

"A certain Commander Halland of Gatrov. The regent heard his story, concluded that it was obviously a trick, had him imprisoned, and issued proclamations reassuring the populace that all was well."

"Oh the regent was perfectly correct, sir," I said with a broad and sympathetic smile.

"He is? But, but, what about the huge spindle floating in the river, and those two things with the tentacles, and, er . . ."

"May I be taken to an interrogation cell, sir?" I asked with a gesture to the door. "I have matters of a delicate nature to speak of."

The man mopped at his forehead with a lace kerchief.

"Of course, this is clearly a matter where discretion must be observed."

Lavenci rolled her eyes as we left, Pelmore laughed, and the morris men merely looked frightened. Riellen stared down at the flagstones. Once Wallengtor and I were alone in another cell, I lowered my voice and changed my tone.

"This is clearly a matter of saving face for the regent," I said softly.

"Oh indeed sir, I'm gratified that you grasp the political realities," responded Wallengtor, very much relieved to hear the sorts of weasel words that he understood.

"Why not say that the Terrisians are indeed invading, but that they have allied themselves with powerful sorcerers from Lupan, who have flown through the void to us in huge, orange spindles. Add that there is a conspiracy abroad to *conceal* the presence of the Lupanians—if you see what I mean."

"But the Terrisians are not really invading, are they?" asked Wallengtor.

"No."

"Then the west really is crawling with huge, three-legged sorcerers that breathe fire?" he concluded, now with a hint of terror in his tone.

"Yes, but the base of their power is sorcery and magic. With a few dozen good sorcerers we might have a chance to fight back."

"You are just saying that to annoy me, are you not?"

"Afraid not, lordship."

"But we—that is, the regent has just killed the last of our own sorcerers."

"So I heard."

Wallengtor paced silently within the little cell for some minutes. I sat back on the bunk and looked on sympathetically.

"Well, yes, the deaths of the sorcerers will indeed be a little hard to explain away if we launch a campaign to recruit any surviving sorcerers to the regent's service," he said as he continued pacing.

"As campaigns go, lordship, not a winner," I agreed.

"We also had it proclaimed that Baron Balbron died saving Gatrov."

"He was reduced to a small pile of ashes the day before Gatrov was annihilated."

"And that Duke Lestor repulsed the invasion."

"Duke Lestor's warriors were wiped out in somewhat less than a minute. The duke was eaten."

By now Wallengtor was so pale that he almost gleamed in the light of the single lantern.

"Oh dear, that will never do," he muttered, now wringing his hands as he paced. "The regent does so hate to be wrong."

"Then proclaim that the regent has discovered a Terrisian plot," I said as if the answer were so simple that it was boring. "Announce that lies are being spread that the Lupanians do not exist."

"Lies, yes, I like that."

"Say that the regent saw through the lies, and now he wants the truth announced to everyone."

"Oh I say, I like that even better."

"Now then about Pelmore, the clown who tried to poison me."

"Yes?"

"He was clearly trying to stop me reaching the regent with the news."

"Inspector, I like your style. But what about Commander Halland?"

"Oh just select some palace official that the regent doesn't like and blame him. Say it was he who had Halland arrested and issued the false proclamations."

Wallengtor had by now stopped and taken out a little writing kit. He scribbled on a reedpaper scroll for a while, kneeling beside the bunk.

"The burning of the sorcerers will take some explaining," he sighed as he wrote. "The regent was there in person, he ordered a trumpet fanfare, then lit the brushwood himself. A dozen artists were present, they sketched the scene, the regent has commissioned a huge painting for the palace reception lobby."

"Proclaim that they were Terrisian sorcerers, sent here to weaken Alberin from within."

"Young man, have you ever considered a career in diplomacy?" exclaimed Wallengtor, looking up from his scroll.

"Alas sir, my family is artisan class."

"Ah, pity. Now then, I must get all this down, and you must countersign it."

"It will be my pleasure."

"But, ah, the others?"

"I shall brief them, they will cooperate."

"Even the prisoners? Surely they will be vindictive enough to testify otherwise?"

"The constable will be no problem. As for Pelmore, gag

him until the execution. The man is under provisional sentence of death, after all."

"Ah, yes, of course, we can even have a special public execution. I'll brief your superiors." Wallengtor began to scribble a list of things to do at the bottom of his notes. "I'll have Halland and Roval released—oh, be a good chap and brief them on all this, will you?"

"Yes sir, and I shall brief the others, too."

"Have prisoners released," mumbled Wallengtor as he wrote.

"But not Pelmore and Riellen."

"Of course not . . . *Regent's declaration of thanks . . . five hundred florins each*—is that enough?"

"It will do nicely."

"Oh, silly me, we nearly forgot an official story. Something to make the duke and baron look as if they saved the day."

"Ah . . . *the baron died in a savage battle from which only two Lupanians survived,*" I suggested.

"But there were *only* two Lupanians in the first place."

"Nobody need know that. *One-third of the Lupanians lay dead after the attack in which Duke Lestor fell.*"

"But Halland killed them before the attack."

"But they were still dead after the attack."

"You really are in the wrong job, young man. Now then, we shall need heroes, so can you provide some suitable words? Nothing too heroic, mind."

"Well . . . *militiamen led by Commander Halland killed three Lupanians. A fourth Lupanian died when the voidship was captured by forces of the Wayfarer Constables.*"

"Splendid! Almost perfect!" cried Wallengtor with delight.

"Almost, lordship?"

"Constable Riellen. Her case is far too complex."

"You never said a truer word."

"She must either dance a jig in midair, or be a hero. The public will not understand, otherwise. Would you accept her being made a hero?"

"No, lordship."

"Even were she given a diplomatic posting to some distant place?"

"How distant?

"The penal colony on Estovel Island. It's surrounded by pack ice most of the year."

"I . . . could perhaps live with that, lordship."

Pelmore was gagged and taken away to the death cells. Wallengtor hurried off to confer with the regent. Halland and Roval were brought to our cell, where I explained what we would have to testify if we ever wanted to see the sky again. After perhaps half an hour Wallengtor returned with a very impressively scribed declaration. Unrolling it, he read it aloud to us, then set a writing kit down on the cell's bench. Halland read the freshly written words.

"There is nothing actually untrue in the words," said Halland, looking up from the scroll as Wallengtor offered him a goose quill. "It's just that the story told by these true words is a bloody lie!"

"It's these words or the dungeon," said Wallengtor firmly.

"And you're willing to sign, Inspector?" Halland asked me.

"The choice is either this dungeon, or five hundred florins, plus freedom, plus a pat on the back from the regent, not to mention being proclaimed a hero by the town crier. Add free ale from every tavern in the city, and don't forget nubile young women flinging themselves at you—"

"I'll sign," he sighed, accepting the quill and kneeling beside the bench.

Halland signed. I was next, then Lavenci added her signature to the scroll. Azorian signed in some very strange script, and the morris men followed in order of dancing talent. Solonor wrestled a signature out of the goosequill, then Riellen's hands were untied and she signed last of all. Wallengtor now called for the guards, the door was unlocked, and we were led out to the cell. I contrived to walk beside Lavenci as we climbed the stairs.

"I fear for Azorian's safety," I whispered. "Some idiot is sure to order his death if his identity is discovered."

"I agree. He could be hidden in mother's academy. I shall ask her."

Waiting for Roval, Riellen, Azorian, and me was a marshal

inspector from the Wayfarers. Waiting for Lavenci was her mother. The woman was tall, elegant, about fifty, and dressed rather like a Diomedan windrel dancer.

"Lavenci Si-Chella, just what have you been up to?" she asked in a vaguely amused tone. "Dirty, smelly, under arrest, and the guardhouse report said that you have some sort of glamour on you."

"Ladyship, it was my fault—" began Riellen, but I clamped a hand over her mouth.

"What sort of glamour is it?" the elder Si-Chella asked.

"A constancy glamour," said Lavenci.

"A constancy glamour, how exotic! You mean to say that you slept with some hedgerow sorcerer who bound you to himself? Well, that certainly beats most of my adventures. Come along home, you had best get into a bath, then some clean and scented robes before we investigate this constancy glamour."

Lavenci now took her mother by the arm and whispered to her. Madame Yvendel flicked a glance to Azorian.

"Of course you may call upon us later, Azorian," she said with a raised eyebrow and a knowing smile.

Lavenci and her mother left. For several dozen heartbeats nobody said anything.

"A tad more liberal than my mother," said Solonor from my pocket.

The marshal inspector from the Wayfarers now stepped forward.

"Inspector Danolarian, just what have you been up to?" he demanded, waving a finger in my face. "Dirty, smelly, under arrest, and the guardhouse report said that you have eating migraine powder and daemonglare berries."

"With respect sir, up yours," I replied, my hands on my hips.

The morris men gasped with horror, but the marshal just laughed and clapped me on the back.

"Let's away to Wayfarer headquarters, lad," he said. "There's no bath or scented robes, but we can probably manage tea, biscuits, a towel, and a horse trough. The dirctant is out of bed and waiting to congratulate you."

We walked to the palace gates, where the voidship was already on display.

"Ah, one more matter, Inspector," said Wallengtor. "Those Lupanians on the barge."

"Yes?"

"Nobody can get them to move from where you left them on the dock. A guardsman prodded one with a spear, but it caught him with a tentacle and threw him into the river. Arrows were fired at them, but they were somehow turned away in midair. Could you possibly help move them to somewhere better suited to public display?"

We set off for the docks, where a large crowd had gathered around the handling beasts. Azorian made the two creatures clamber into a cage on the back of a wagon, and this was driven off to the palace. The morris men, who had come along to watch, then made straight for the nearest tavern, which was the Lamplighter. By now it was past 1 A.M., but the tavern was still open, servicing the needs of the nearby crowd. The crowd followed the morris men into the taproom, and I had the feeling that the sun would be up before the landlord finally closed and barred the door.

Next, with Azorian in tow, I called past one of the secret doorways to Madame Yvendel's academy. An elderly porter met us at the door, and said that Lavenci was having a bath, and that Yvendel was attending her. I explained that Azorian was to be staying there for some days.

"Come along young man, nothing but your virtue is in danger under this roof," said the porter as Azorian entered.

At Wayfarer Headquarters I presented my report and journal to the Directant, who promised to have it read by morning, then went back to the bedchamber built beside his office. I had a cup of tea and a ginger nut biscuit, and fell asleep in a cell that was not currently in use. Riellen spent the night in a locked cell.

The following morning I awoke to discover that the regent had issued a new proclamation. Apparently Gatrov had been destroyed after all, but the Wayfarer Constables had joined with the town militia to avenge that atrocity against the innocent. Halland had even killed two Lupanians with his bare hands, while I had wrestled two others into submission and brought them to Alberin. The evidence was on display before the palace gates, in the form of the voidship and the two caged handling beasts. I was in the middle of breakfast when a carriage arrived from the palace, with a summons that I should attend the regent. I had a fairly good idea of what he wanted, so I retrieved my official journal from the directant.

When I arrived at the palace gates, there was quite a large crowd gathered around my trophies. The handling beasts sat quietly and unmoving while they were pelted with rotten fruit and insults by the onlookers. Wallengtor hurried up to me, explaining that the regent had wanted to see the interior of the voidship, but then discovered that nobody knew how to open it. I gave the officers some instructions on unscrewing the base, then stood waiting with Wallengtor.

"There will be a little ceremony after the regent has inspected the voidship," Wallengtor explained. "The others of your party are being gathered as we speak."

"The regent is very gracious," I replied automatically.

"Of course if you had been nobles there would have been a five-thousand-florin purse, a grand parade all the way along the Avenue of Conquerors, and the city would have had a half holiday to honor your triumphs."

"I'm grateful for what I get," I replied, not the slightest bit interested in fortune, and even less concerned with fame.

"That Pelmore, are you sure he's a felon? He has a magnificent, heroic body, and we could feature him in recruitment parades."

Suddenly Wallengtor had my full and undivided attention.

"He murdered Captain Danzar, a hero. He also tried to murder a noblewoman, and he came pretty close to killing *me*!" I snapped angrily, aware that I was not showing appropriate deference, but also aware that heroes could get away with that sort of thing.

"Look, I really fancy the idea of Pelmore as a hero," Wallengtor insisted. "I've even had five hundred florins allocated for his reward. You really are a very young field magistrate, and your judgment may have been, well, clouded by hot blood?"

"Hot blood?"

"The ratifying magistrate could be persuaded that you were jealous of Pelmore's interest in Kavelen Lavenci, and that the severity of your sentence was your way of punishing him. Then there is Riellen. Riellen preaches treason, for which the penalty is death," said Wallengtor coldly. "You appear to have double standards, Inspector."

"Not so. Riellen advocates new systems of government, not violent attacks on our ruler. The only offense she has ever committed in the strict sense of the word is disturbing the peace. That is for local authorities to enforce, not Wayfarers. I have a very, very sound knowledge of the law's letter, lordship, but I also temper my judgments with regard to its spirit. I excused Riellen's political nonsense because it was harmless. As soon as I discovered she had been guilty of assault, I came down on her like a cartload of gravel."

"You are not a good field magistrate. Your justice is selective."

"Oh I agree. Should I walk into a room and find you about to bisect the wife of the regent with an ax, I would arrest you, charge you, and even put the noose around your neck, were that required of me. If you merely had her bent her over the dressing table with her robes up around her ears, and should she be smiling, I would just back out and pull the door closed—and try very hard to forget what I had seen. I distinguish between law and justice, lordship. Take comfort from that, should you ever find yourself hauled up before me."

Our philosophical discussion on the application of the death penalty and legislation associated therewith was interrupted by the arrival of a blacksmith and an armor repair forge on a cart. Moments later a squad of royal guardsmen arrived with the regent. I was introduced to our monarch while the blacksmith attended the hatchway. Our ruler was of middling height and had the broad shoulders of a warrior, but had gone to some lengths to soften and expand his abdomen with good living. I put his age at around fifty. He looked as if he had grown a beard to hide wrinkles, then dyed it a little too stridently black.

"You seem young for a hero," he commented as I went down on one knee and bowed.

"Thank you, sire."

"But very brave."

"Thank you, sire."

"I suppose you spent the night drinking and wenching?"

"I presented my report to the directant, then slept at head-quarters, sire. I was very tired."

"So, hardworking, virtuous, *and* a hero as well."

While the regent amused himself tossing stones at the han-dling beasts, the blacksmith rigged up a lever mechanism for the hatch. The guards then used it to unscrew the hatchway. I entered first, and set the walls glowing as Azorian had done. After a dramatic pause, I called to the regent that it was safe to enter. He insisted that all others were to be kept at a distance while we were within.

It would be fair to say that he was disappointed with the in-terior. I explained how air was generated by the crystals in the porous bags, but when he heard that there was no heat weapon aboard, his interest flagged.

"I see no fantastic machineries or mighty weapons," he commented. "Just two seats, and many, many racks of pack-ages. Why there are not even windows. How did they see where they were going?"

I thought it wise not to point out the weapon crystals, both of which were still locked into their frames.

"There is a mechanism for allowing the crew to see out-side," I explained. "It involves mirrors."

"Mirrors? I see, just a cheap trick. But how can it fly be-tween worlds without wings? I saw no wings."

"There is no air between worlds, sire. It needs no wings, it just hurtles along like an arrow from a crossbow."

"But your report mentioned wings."

"They conjured etheric wings once in the air of our world, sire. They used these to glide down and land. The etheric wings were collapsed upon landing—"

"Yes, yes, no mystery here, then. Just the sorts of things our sorcerers could do if we still had sorcerers."

"In principle, sire, although the engineering and sorcery on Lupan is very advanced—"

"Well can you take me for a flight in this, er, voidship? Nothing fancy, just a hundred miles up, to look at my realm with the eye of a bird, ha, ha."

"With respect, sire, it was all that I could do to drag this thing onto a barge and bring it here on the river."

"Then command one of the prisoners to fly it. They obey your instructions to move, after all."

"Sire, I command them only with signs and gestures—"

"Well bring them in here and make a few gestures!"

"Sire, they could well abduct you to Lupan," I suggested, giving up on the effort of talking sense to him.

"Oh! Yes, ha, ha, good point, that, yes indeed. Well then, we must have them tortured, to reveal their secrets."

"We do not know their language, sire. We do not even know if they speak."

"But dammitall, how do they talk?" the regent demanded.

"I suspect that they share their thoughts directly, sire. A sufficiently senior sorcerer could—"

"Alberin is a little short of sorcerers of any rank just now. What about a Metrologan, or a Skeptical? Sort of cold-science sorcerers, legal sorcerers, without magic, so to speak, ha, ha."

"An excellent notion, sire. I did not think of that."

"Quite so. Well, what to do? Can't have the riffraff learning that there are no fantastic secrets and mechanisms in here, can we? I shall proclaim that the Metrologans have been charged with discovering the secrets of this, er—"

"Voidship, sire."

"Quite so. I shall order a couple of Metrologans to sit in here for a few hours every day. Give the guise of working on its secrets, but bring a pair of dice and flagon of wine to pass the time, ha, ha. Damn boring place, I'm bored already. Don't know how the crew endured two dozen days in here—wait a moment! Those two chairs, they are for human forms. Octopus arses would never fit in there—they do have arses, don't they?"

I had anticipated this. I gestured to the decking plates where the handling beasts had been tethered during the voyage.

"Those harnesses back there are for the crew, sire."

"Ah yes, but then why have chairs for humans?"

I was concealing the fact that the Lupanians were shaped like us so that nobody would ask difficult questions about Azorian. Given the level of paranoia and stupidity currently abroad in Alberin's corridors of power, the regent was just as likely to torture our only Lupanian ally merely for being an enemy national.

"On our world we eat pickled octopus and squid," I explained. "I can only conclude that on their world it is animals shaped like *us* which are slaughtered and eaten. These seats were clearly for, ah, fresh meat during the voyage."

"Oh I say, how barbaric! Well, I'm a busy man, and I've learned all there is to know here. I'll tell the guards to obey you and no other regarding access to the voidship. Get to the Metrologan Academy and round up a couple of scholars to spend the day in here. Under no circumstances are they to tell anyone that there is nothing to be learned."

With that, the regent left. He had not absorbed the fact that the walls glowed of their own accord, or realized that the crystalline control mechanisms were all at the seats designed for beings shaped like us. The images of fantastically alien art and artistry that decorated the interior had somehow performed a brain bypass upon entering the regent's eyes. If the truth be known, he reminded me a little of my father, and a little more of my mother.

✳ ✳ ✳

Outside the voidship again, I discovered that the crowds had been pushed farther back, and that the men of the regent's personal guard were arrayed before us in dress armor and uniforms. Commander Halland, Roval, Riellen, and the morris men were lined up in the summer sunlight, although the morris men looked a little worse for wear. Lavenci was there too, with her long hair pinned up and her mother standing behind her. I was ushered to the line.

The regent presented both Halland and myself with a medal featuring his profile and ten star points. I was promised a promotion to inspector marshal rank, while Halland was given an appointment as reserve commander in the Alberin militia. The morris dancers were each given a gold crown, also featuring the regent's profile, and commanded to perform before the voidship for the crowds every day, at noon. Pelmore was condemned by the regent, who reaffirmed that any attack on the Wayfarers was an attack on himself. Because the regent's Acclamation Advisory Council was not geared up to cope with female heroes, Riellen and Lavenci were merely given medals with four star points and the regent's profile, and the promise of a five hundred florin dowry should they ever marry.

"But not to each other, of course, ha ha," concluded the regent, and everyone other than Lavenci and Riellen laughed politely.

I wondered where the additional florins promised by Wallengtor had gone. Wallengtor avoided my gaze.

* * *

The regent took his leave of us, and those who had matters to attend dispersed.

"Now, about Pelmore," I began as Wallengtor approached me.

"Oh the man is a scoundrel and deserves to die," he said, with a dismissive little wave of his hand.

"That is a very quick change of heart, lordship."

"Well, the regent has just honored you and condemned Pelmore, and the regent never makes mistakes."

"I see. So what now?"

"Oh, wander about and look heroic, but try not to get blind drunk in public."

"I meant about the Lupanians?"

"Ah, what about them?"

"They are invading us. I would have thought that this means war."

"Oh, not necessarily. The regent will brief and dispatch some diplomats and a hundred kavelars this afternoon. I'm sure some compromise can be arranged. The Lupanians might be persuaded to betray the Terrisians and ally themselves with us. Well, must go. I have to scribe up news of all this for the criers and noticeboards."

Wallengtor bustled off. I went over to Halland, who had been standing within earshot.

"Can you believe the man?" Halland said softly. "Barely twelve hours ago you and he fabricated that story of the Terrisians and Lupanians being in alliance, and now he believes it is true."

"I am trying very hard not to think about it," I admitted.

"What will you do now?"

"Go to the Metrologan Academy and have a couple of academicians sent back to study the voidship. What are your plans?"

"Both the baroness and my wife are at the palace. I imagine

they will want to see me, now that I have been released from the dungeons and honored."

"You sound reluctant to go."

"Yesterday, before you arrived, they both put out rather strongly worded statements condemning me. Now it will be my fault that they put out the statements."

"Why not follow my principle? When faced with an unpleasant duty, try to postpone it."

Halland laughed. "Do you mean down to some tavern for a pint?"

"No, no, legitimate business. I have to relay the regent's orders to the elder of the Metrologans. Why not come along with me, then stay to give their people an extensive briefing."

"You, sir, know the ways of command."

I glanced in Riellen's direction. Something akin to nausea clutched at my stomach for a moment.

"Commander, kindly inform Riellen that she is to follow me to the Metrologans, then to Wayfarer Headquarters," I said coldly.

✳ ✳ ✳

Justiva, the Metrologan elder from Torea, met us at the academy and listened to my version of what the regent had ordered. She then summoned two students and dispatched them to the voidship. Seeing that the regent had not asked to see my journal, I now gave it to Justiva, for the Metrologan priests and academicians to study.

"Ah, good," she said, riffling through it. "This will make a nice comparison with the transcripts of our other witness, an old, er, colleague of mine."

"You have another witness?" I asked, surprised that anyone might have got to Alberin before us. "Can we meet him?"

The other witness was summoned, and it was Norellie Witchway, who strode into the room some moments later. Exclamations and astonished exchanges established that she had been so impressed by Lavenci's calculations regarding the Lupanian heat weapon that she had packed a few of her most valued possessions into a ponycart and left Gatrov at dawn the following morning, only two or three hours before the Lupanians had attacked. She had looked back and seen the flames, smoke, and tripod towers in the distance.

"This is wonderful!" said Halland eagerly as she finished. "We must compare observations."

"I did feel sad to think that you two died with the town," she confessed to Halland and me.

"Oh aye, and the commander certainly wept in the ruins of your house," I replied, playfully adding a little embroidery to the truth.

"You did, Commander?" exclaimed Norellie. "For me?"

There was one of those silences where everyone kept casting sidelong glances at each other, but not saying anything.

"Perhaps your eyes were watering from the smoke?" suggested Elder Justiva at last.

"Yes, yes, I'm sure that was it," agreed Halland.

"It was very smoky," I agreed.

"Were your eyes watering, Inspector?" asked Justiva.

"Now that you mention it, no."

"But my eyes are very sensitive," said Halland.

"Ah, that must have been it," said Justiva.

"There was a lot of smoke, I could see it from miles away," said Norellie.

"It was probably something to do with the fires," I said with a wink at Halland. "I'd best be moving on. You are, of course, staying here, Commander?"

"Er . . ."

"I agree, you can do most good here."

I took Norellie aside and made it quite clear that I wanted private words with her.

"Lavenci needs you to lift the constancy glamour," I said in an urgent whisper.

"I know, a lady named Madame Yvendel has already approached me about it," she replied. "I've tried, and I can't."

"But you said—"

"I know what I said! This time it did not work, none of my words of power could unlock it."

"But—"

"This glamour is like a padlock that has been designed to break after it has been used once. It cannot be unlocked."

"Would you be so kind as to quiz Riellen on this?" I asked. "I presume you know that she cast the glamour?"

"I was told as much by Lavenci, in great detail, and very loudly."

We went to where Riellen was waiting, and Norellie asked her some quite complex questions about her methods of casting glamours.

"I chanted in no keywords," explained Riellen guiltily. "I wanted Lady Lavenci locked away with Pelmore forever. Please tell the inspector—and Her Gracious Ladyship—that my sorrow exceeds—"

"Madame Norellie, kindly tell Riellen to follow me to Wayfarer Headquarters," I interjected. "I have learned all that I need to."

✳ ✳ ✳

Leaving Commander Halland to his fate, I continued on back to Wayfarer Headquarters with Riellen. We walked along the towpath beside the river, and with a move so casual that I almost missed it, she tossed a small, glittering thing about the size of her medal from the regent into the water. We exchanged no words whatsoever as we walked. It was early afternoon by the time we reached Wayfarer Headquarters, and the guard at the entrance said that I was to attend the directant at once. Leaving Riellen in the common room, I went to his office and was admitted without having to wait.

The directant was one of those nobles who liked his work, and did that work out of a real sense of civic duty. He shunned the fine robes of other courtiers, and wore his crests on common Wayfarer marshal clothing. He was even said to spend time in the training yard every week. On the other hand, he demanded obedience to the crown, and I was not showing many signs of it.

"I could not help but notice that your version of events is somewhat different from that on the public notice boards," he observed without bidding me to sit down.

"My report is as close to the truth as I could manage," I replied.

"Look, you did damn well, Inspector Danolarian, have no doubt of that. Sit down, man, sit down. Capturing the voidship and Lupanians, yet sparing time to rescue a noblewoman from some murdering peasant. Glorious, simply glorious."

"Thank you, sir."

"The trouble is Riellen."

"Never was a truer word spoken, sir."

"You describe her as, ah, and I quote: 'more flaky than a pastry shop after an earthquake.' You go on to describe how she has been poisoning you for three years."

"Rendering me ill with headaches due to romantic infatuation, sir, rather than trying to actually kill me or commit mutiny."

"Bad business, bad business indeed. Look, Inspector, I shall be honest. Not much of that to be seen these days, eh? The regent wants heroes, and because of you, we Wayfarers are heroes. I like that. This report on Riellen casts doubt about the level of professionalism in our ranks, however. If the citizenry of Greater Alberin see Riellen dishonored by us after being honored by the regent, well, the regent looks like a fool."

"My report does not have to become public, sir."

"*Yes it does.* The regent has ordered your official report made public. The trouble is that he has not read it. As it stands, the report would cause considerable embarrassment to the regent."

I rubbed my face in my hands for some moments, considering my position. It seemed to be time for compromise.

"I agree to rewrite my report, sir, but only on the condition that you accept a separate report on Constable Riellen's behavior regarding myself."

"But that would affect your relationship with her as her immediate superior."

"I shall not serve with her again, sir."

He leaned forward, looking concerned and putting a hand to his ear.

"I did not quite catch that, Inspector. I do hope it was a request and not a statement."

"It was a statement, sir."

He glared at me. I stared back calmly. The standoff lasted seventeen breaths, by my count. At last he sat back, folded his arms, and forced a smile.

"Oh of course, I can deny you nothing. You have been proclaimed a hero by the regent, and to discipline you would make him look like a fool."

"I'm sure that would make him awfully cross, sir."

"Indeed. But just how long do you think you will remain in such high esteem?"

"A week, sir?"

"Less, much less. An hour after the three hundred sorcerers were being honored in a public parade, they were being burned alive. The same crowds were cheering both times."

"If Pelmore Haftbrace can be hanged for murder, why should Riellen escape the penalty for her own crime?"

"Pelmore, yes. I was about to mention him as well. A very senior Inquisitor wants your report rewritten to exonerate him."

"What? The man is a murderer, cold-blooded and calculating. The gods alone know how many successful murders he has committed without being found out."

"You could say that he mistook you and Lady Lavenci for sorcerers."

"I *shall not*—sir."

"Inspector Danolarian, the inquisitor general is . . . let us just say that he has influence. Influence over people with influence over me."

"If you say so sir."

"A very powerful lady has made a personal appeal to him on Pelmore's behalf."

"The regent has already condemned him in public," I pointed out.

"He has?"

"The regent does not make mistakes," I said pointedly.

"Damn you," whispered the directant, then he raised his eyebrows and reached for a quill. "Very well, then, you win. Pelmore dies, Riellen goes . . . but so do you. Wayfarers must obey orders from above, because those above have an overview denied to minions like yourself."

"Riellen assaulted me for three years, she broke discipline. Now you ask me to break discipline and ignore the rules?"

"In matters of state, appearances are everything. In matters of the heart, appearances are everything."

He pulled at a bellrope. Moments later Riellen was shown in. She saluted me, but otherwise gave the directant her full attention. She showed no emotion.

"Constable Riellen, you must know what I have learned from Inspector Danolarian's report. You have acted disgracefully, shamefully. Like the inspector here, I have a great admiration for your sheer drive and spirit, but you have not only broken the law, you have done it too consistently to have your actions classified as a crime of passion. I count one hundred and fourteen offenses, totaling five thousand seven hundred lashes. You are not under sentence of death, but such a punishment will certainly kill you. Exile is another possibility. Inspector Danolarian, what would you do, if in my position?"

"Your judgment is sure to be better than mine, Directant," I replied. "You are in a position of higher authority, and thus have a better view of the overall picture."

The slightest flicker of a scowl crossed his face.

"Would that all of my Wayfarers had your sense of deference to authority, Inspector. Constable Riellen, hear my sentence. You will remain in Alberin for precisely four weeks, on light duties and playing the part of a modest hero. After that, you will be rewarded with a very unpleasant diplomatic posting overseas. This posting will last for as long as you remain alive. Dismissed."

"Sir!" said Riellen and I together.

"Not you, Inspector, stay behind—and close the door on your way out, Constable Riellen."

The directant stood up and gestured to his desk. I walked around and sat behind it, and he placed a field writing kit and service reedpaper before me.

"You will now rewrite the pages of your report as we agreed, and will not leave this room until the work is done."

"I shall also include the separate report on Constable Riellen."

"And I shall have it taken straight down to the kitchen and dropped into a fire. Why bother?"

"So that I shall have submitted it, sir."

"Suit yourself."

The work took several hours, by which time the afternoon

had very nearly become evening. At last I stood before the desk again. The directant resumed his seat.

"All in order, Inspector, very well done," he said smoothly. "Now then, when the report reaches me that Pelmore is dancing his last jig, I shall be writing out an authorization transferring you to the Inquisition, where you will have the rank of inspector marshal—except that they call it inquisitor marshal. Should you wish to modify your recollections of Pelmore's and Riellen's actions before the transfer, do get back to me. Consider yourself on leave until then."

"I do not find that acceptable, sir. I shall resign."

"If you resign, it will be from a commission ordered by the regent himself. That will be taken as a direct insult to the regent, and that will get you into a lot more trouble."

Chapter Fifteen

"THE BANKS OF THE ALBER"

 With my meeting with the Directant of Wayfarers at an end, I collected my pack from the porter, then walked out into what remained of the day's sunshine. Once I was on the towpath beside the river, I took off my medal and flung it into the water. I wondered if Halland's medal might be at the bottom of the river too, and about what Roval and Lavenci might have done with theirs.

I walked very slowly along the tow path. I had lost everything, that thought kept pounding through my mind. I had so little, yet even that was all gone. And for what? Justice? Well, yes. Pelmore was a killer and a danger to others, so he deserved to die. Riellen? That was personal, and carried with it a very strong sense of betrayal. The sun was down by the time I reached the Lamplighter, and I sat quietly in the taproom for a

time, drinking ale and listening to a pair of quite talented rebec players. One began playing an unfamiliar but haunting
tune. I could not recall ever hearing the tune before. My memory with music is not at all bad, yet the tune seemed neither
very old or very new. Suddenly a girl began to sing, and the
conversation in the taproom died away.

"As I wandered out, by the banks of the Alber,
I spied a brave Wayfarer, handsome and clever.
His arm bore a wound, there were none that were
    braver.
Let us drink a good health, to the Wayfarers bold.

His hair it was black, and his face it was comely.
He stood by himself, and his eyes they were lonely
His company was dead. None lived but he only.
Let us drink a good health, to the Wayfarers bold.

I bound up the wound that his arm it did carry,
Then I said unto him, and I never did tarry,
'Lie with me tonight, maybe some day we'll marry.'
Let us drink a good health, to the Wayfarers bold.

'If I dare for to love you,' says he, 'you may sorrow,
'I may die on my journeys, so grieving will follow,
'So I'll not take your heart, on the highway tomorrow.'
Let us drink a good health, to the Wayfarers bold.

'Oh I never shall marry, I'll lie alone burning,
'If suitors do come, all of them I'll be spurning,
'Unless once again, my brave love you're returning.'
Let us drink a good health, to the Wayfarers bold."

I got up and walked over to the girl while the company was
still clapping.
"What was the song, miss?" I asked. "It was quite lovely."
"Thank you, Inspector," she said with a little laugh of
embarrassment.
"Is it very old?"

"Oh no, sir," she replied, "a lady sung it here, maybe three, four weeks ago."

Three or four weeks. That was highly significant. Lavenci was still in Alberin then.

"Did you see her? What did she look like?"

"Eyes like coals, hair like snow. Very comely, she was. All admired her. She said that she wrote it for her lad, who was away with the Wayfarers. It's funny, you know. She's been here a lot over the months past. I asked if she was at the tavern to find some company until her lad returned, but she said no, she wanted to learn what us lassies talked about while courting. Wasn't that strange?"

"Perhaps not as strange as you might think," I said, more to myself than her. "Do you remember anything else about her?"

"She danced, I remember that. Funny thing was that she only danced with those lads who had a girl. Those as was alone had not a chance with her."

"Thank you, miss, thank you so much."

I returned to my table and thought about the song for a long time. Lavenci had esteemed me sufficiently to write it, the evidence for that was as clear as any examining magistrate could wish to see. She had been keeping her affections to herself, that was obvious as well. It was almost as if Lavenci were being faithful to me, pining for me, and learning to do the things that I liked. She also wanted to learn what girls talked about while courting. That left me really puzzled. Girls talked a load of rubbish, just like their lads. Perhaps she had been trying to change herself, perhaps she really was studying to become romantic. I had once changed myself deliberately. Had I slighted her for being what she was trying to escape from?

The wave of guilt that clutched at my stomach very nearly had my ale returned all over the table. There had been a moment like this, four years ago, when I had fought in the focus of a six-on-one training melee. I had killed two of my sparring masters, so wild had been the action, but I was a prince, and princes do not have to apologize for such things. Nevertheless, their deaths had wounded my soul.

A hand thudded onto my back, a full tankard was set down in front of me, and a voice asked:

"What's a famous man like you doing in a place like this?"

I looked up to see two other Wayfarers.

"Andry, Costiger!" I exclaimed, standing up at once. "Andry, how is your wife?"

"Baby girl, three weeks ago."

"And the boy?"

"He can walk, but he can't understand orders yet."

"Sounds ideal for the Wayfarers."

"Into everything, and raising hell."

"Oh ho, officer material, no less."

"Takes after 'is dad," laughed Costiger.

At this point we were joined by a man who looked familiar, yet who I could not quite place. His head was shaved, and he looked to be somewhere in his thirties. Suddenly I realized that it was Roval, looking the way he was when I had met him, three years earlier.

"Danolarian, I hear you played the sun down on Alpindrak," said Andry.

"That I did, lad," I said, still staring at Roval.

"I was in something of a mess when you saw me last," said my constable, responding to my stare.

The most senior surviving member of the Special Warrior Service was neatly dressed, shaven clean, and actually seemed alert and sharp.

"So, no girl as yet, Danol?" asked Andry.

"Well, I've seen what a couple of women did to you," I replied noncommittally.

"Oh no, no, no, that's what the *wrong* sorts of women will do to you," said Andry hastily. "Now, take my Merrial."

"Oh no, you'd punch me in the face!" I laughed, elbowing him in the ribs.

"She's a shipwright's daughter, but she's steady as the day is long, sharper than a fox with training in law, yet with more love in her than every other woman I've met put together. Speaking of women, how's Riellen? I hear she got a medal too."

"Yes, and a posting to somewhere far away, as an envoy," I replied.

"Bet it was Vindic," said Andry.

"I'd like to go to Vindic," said Costiger. "Lots of dancing girls."

"You could go as Riellen's bodyguard," Andry suggested.

"Don't want to go that much," replied Costiger.

"Three years on the road together, and you didn't kill her!" laughed Andry. "I lost ten florins when she got through one year of service with you, yet her neck remained unbroken."

"I'm a patient lad," I replied.

Andry, Costiger, and I had served as mercenaries in Sargol, then had deserted together to Alberin. Andry had decided to become a gentleman, and had worked his way up from common sailor to the lower nobility before deciding that one can be gentlemanly in whatever class one chooses to be part of. The huge and brawny Costiger still lacked direction, however, and relied on Andry, Essen, or myself whenever he had to make a decision.

Andry leaned over the table, glanced about, and raised an eyebrow.

"So what's the true story with these Lupanians?" he asked. "Did you really slaughter three score of them?"

"Pah, I helped to kill one. They're tougher than a glass dragon. Commander Halland from Gatrov got two, but that was by surprise. It won't happen again. They learn quickly, and never make the same mistake twice."

"Those two in the cage seem harmless."

"Don't you believe it."

"Roval said they feed on captives," said Andry.

"Aye, I've seen them doing it," I replied.

"They eats us?" gasped Costiger.

"That they do. Their sorcerer-kavelars move about in walking towers a hundred feet high, and their weapons are castings hotter than a glass dragon's breath. They can do this at one mile."

I showed then a sample of the glazed rock from the tower. They were impressed.

"So what's to do?" asked Andry. "I have a wife and family. Should I put them on the first ship out of here?"

"Yes!"

"But surely we can fight back!" insisted Andry. "You said three have been killed."

"Four. One died on the flight across the void from Lupan."

"Two per voidship, and ten voidships, that's one in five of their number gone already."

"I doubt that any more will die so easily," I assured him. "Remember, they learn fast."

"So do we," said Andry.

"Do we really? Remember Commander Halland of the Gatrov Town Militia, the man who killed two Lupanians? Has he been put in charge of the Alberinese army?"

"Er, no. But we heard that Duke Lestor died while defending Gatrov. We heard he destroyed a Lupanian siege tower with a single arrow, so they can't be so very powerful."

"Bollix. Duke Lestor was eaten. I saw it happen. Halland is the only real chance for Alberin."

"Halland, good man," said Roval, nodding but holding the expression on his face neutral. "I knew him in the SWS."

"Halland was in the Special Warrior Service?" I exclaimed.

"Yes, until he was brought low by a woman, demoted to kavelar, and sent to Gatrov. Could you come outside for a moment, lad? Special message."

Out in the street, Roval told me that the Palace Guard was combing the city for me. There was a briefing being held in the Metrologan temple, for the benefit of the regent's courtiers, nobles of the military, and senior Metrologans and Skepticals. Halland was to speak, and so was I. Being scholars of magic, but not sorcerers, the Metrologans had been spared by the Inquisition. Just as well, as it happened.

Roval and I passed the ruins of Cedar Hall on the way to the Metrologan temple. Ashes, bones, and partly melted bits of magical paraphernalia were being shoveled onto carts by torchlight, so that the daytime crowds did not see the scale of the deaths and get squeamish. An occasional burst of etheric energy crackled amid the debris. At the entrance to the temple we were met by a deaconess who took us to a tiered lecture hall that was packed with important-looking people, many of whom were awake. A young nobleman, Laron, the man I referred to as the master, was speaking.

"So in conclusion, a study of reports from travelers, bargemen, and even carrier birds shows that the Lupanians have destroyed eleven towns, these marked by the red crosses." He pointed to a large map hanging on the wall behind him. "They have also conquered seven cities and eighty towns without a fight. Their tactic is to go into an area and make an example of one town, thus frightening those round about into surrendering. Any questions?"

There was a vaguely restless muttering and stirring. A few hands went up.

"You say there are no more than twelve of them, so far," Duke Magnisseran of the Imperial Light Cavalry pointed out. "How can they control three dozen provinces?"

"They can speak our language, using some sort of magical casting, and they have been recruiting followers in droves. Remember, they say that they are the Gods of the Moonworlds, appearing in solid form."

"And people believe it?"

"Oh yes," said Halland earnestly. "The Lupanians are cruel, arbitrary, overwhelmingly powerful, and rather impressive to look at. They demand human sacrifices, too. People seem to like all that in a god."

"Then we are doomed," I whispered to Roval. "If our people will not fight, who will? The grass gnomes?"

He put a finger to his lips and pointed. Justiva, Elder of Metrologans, stood up to field the question.

"We Metrologans have influence with the glass dragons," she announced. "Messages have been sent, requesting help."

"And?" Lord Wallengtor asked.

"And we are now waiting. There are no more powerful beings in all the world than glass dragons. If anyone can save us, it will be them. They can command energies of a similar intensity to those of the Lupanians."

In the silence that followed, various knowing looks, winks, nods, frowns, and grins were exchanged.

"They had better flap over in a hurry, else it will be too late," joked some baron, who was wearing ermine-trimmed robes in spite of the heat.

"Nobody tells the glass dragons what to do," warned Justiva in turn. "They will want to know that we are worthy of their help."

"Worthy of their help?" I hissed to Roval, suddenly exasperated by all the profound musings of important and knowledgeable people. "And if we are not, what will they say? *Oi, that's a nasty hole in the humans' end of the ship, lucky it's not in ours.*"

"Try to moderate your tone a little if you want to be taken seriously," replied Roval softly as Laron took another question. "You are speaking next."

As Laron finished his next reply, Roval walked forward with both arms raised and stood before the podium.

"Lords, learned ladies and gentlemen, I am pleased to announce that the next speaker has arrived," he announced. "Wayfarer Inspector Danolarian Scryverin of the West Quadrant has survived four encounters with the Lupanians, and was on Captain Danzar's ballista team when they brought down a tower and killed its Lupanian glasswalker. Before he speaks, however, I wish to announce that a demand for Alberin's surrender arrived with an envoy from one of the conquered cities within the hour past. Lancington, I'm led to believe."

"That's barely fifty miles away," said Duke Magnisseran.

"Fifty-one, by a good road. The envoy's detached head was sent back by way of reply. In view of the successes of Commander Halland and his forces against the Lupanians, the regent feels that Alberin's warriors and heroes are more than adequate to meet any threat to the city."

Warriors and heroes? I thought as I closed my eyes and put a hand to my face. *Us?*

"I now call upon Inspector Danolarian to address the meeting on his encounters with the Lupanians."

I kept my address as brief as possible, but it still stretched out over another three-quarters of an hour. My account of the speed with which the baron and his force had been annihilated caused some skeptical mutterings, as did my impressions of the demise of Duke Lestor's river marines. I was dreading the questions at the end, but to my relief Halland was called up as soon as I was finished.

As Halland outlined his experiences fighting the Lupanians, I noticed that Norellie was in the audience, was paying particular attention, taking notes at what I considered to be all the appropriate places, and even giggling at his occasional jokes. Rather than try to meet the bored, vacant eyes of the nobles, or the piercing, attentive stares of the scholars, he gave her his attention.

As the questions were dying away, Justiva raised her hand

"The Metrologans and the armed forces of Alberin have been granted unlimited resources to lead the fight against the Lupanians," she said as she stood up, thrusting her breasts out to astonishing effect. "How do you think all that might best be used? Think carefully now, we need an honest answer, not words that you think we want to hear."

An honest answer, I thought. *Well ladyship, you asked for it, and he might give it.*

"With respect, Learned Elder, that is like being handed a bag of gold by the master of a sinking ship," Halland replied.

Silence greeted these words. Whether it was stunned silence or bored silence, I cannot tell. By now my impression was that few in the audience were taking the threat seriously.

"Well then, what would you advise the people of Alberin to do, were you in charge?" asked the elder.

"Pack their belongings and some food onto a fast horse and ride for the mountains, before the Lupanians set eyes on the severed head of their envoy."

These words brought laughter from everyone, as I had both feared and suspected they might. There were no more questions, so Duke Magnisseran concluded the proceedings for the night with words about the wisdom of the regent and the military preparedness of Alberin. Norellie went over to speak with Halland as he left the podium, and I walked over to join them.

"Inspector, the commander has been speaking of the Lupanians to me all afternoon," she said brightly as I arrived. "What a pity you were not there."

"My apologies, madame. Wayfarer business."

"We should like to examine your private journal," said Justiva as she joined us. "Do you have it easily to hand?"

"Indeed I do, Elder. It's here, in my pack."

"Oh splendid! Would you be willing to go through it with myself, Commander Halland, and some of our specialists in the cold and etheric sciences?"

"Indeed I would, Learned Elder, but I have little knowledge of scholarship."

"Splendid, that means you will have no preconceptions about what you saw. We may also have questions on points that you did not think to put on paper. When is convenient for you?"

"Any time is *convenient,* Learned Elder. Right away is *expedient,* however. The Lupanians move very, very fast, we cannot afford to delay our preparations by even a night."

"Well then, we shall be ready for you within a quarter hour," she responded. "Hall of Neophytes. Roval will take you there."

Justiva, Norellie, and the others wrote continually as I read from my journal, asked intelligent questions, and generally seemed to have grasped the full seriousness of the situation. This gratified me, but they were not the people who were in power, and could make no decisions of importance. Reading the journal again brought to life the horrors of the days past: the close-run escapes, the slaughter, the destruction, and the misery. I skipped the two field trials aboard the barge, but Justiva took charge of the journal when the other Metrologans set me sketching the tripods, the handling beasts, and the casting that was the heat weapon. For hours my mind was filled with images of glittering latticework legs striding across the fields of high summer, while Justiva and Halland read and reread my journal, and students plied me with questions as they built models of the towers and voidships out of wood, paper maché, and resin.

It was perhaps the fourth hour past midnight when Justiva left us to attend some other matters. By now a five-foot-high model of a fighting tripod stood at the center of the floor on three latticework legs, its rope tentacles hanging limp and the mirror plate of its hood staring blankly at us. The students were still working on a pottery-clay mockup of a handling beast.

"I don't like the way that thing is looking at me," Halland said as he munched on a bran and honey biscuit.

"It's only a model," laughed Norellie, taking him by the arm.

"From my perspective, it looks like the one wading in the Alber River, just before Captain Danzar's ballista brought it down," I said. "Any moment now I expect the heat weapon to come to bear on me . . . and then I'll be standing before the ferrygirl."

Norellie took a towel from the basket of biscuits and draped it over the cowl of the model.

"Better?" she asked brightly, putting a hand on her waist and rolling her hip in the commander's direction.

"Thank you, ladyship," we said together, both of us just a little astonished.

"Would that the originals were so easily overcome," added Halland.

"Well then, I must seek easier victories elsewhere," she tittered.

I realized that I was softly humming "The Drawstring of the Drawers," and stopped immediately. There is something curiously unsettling about women who are so very skilled at the allure of men as was Norellie. They become so very good at it, they develop some ill-defined yet very destabilizing talent to sweep aside common sense and inspire rashness. Now Justiva reentered the room.

"If you do not mind me saying so, Inspector, you look terrible," she observed as she sat down at the table again. She riffled through my journal. "You have lived through an extraordinary eight days."

"Only eight days?" I sighed as I rubbed my eyes. "It seems like eighty."

"And what has this to do with Riellen?" Norellie asked, holding up the fingers of her hand outstretched.

"Five? Perhaps the number of people gathered together that she needs to hold a rally?"

"No, it is more than the number of people I know who would not have wrung her scrawny little neck for what she did to you for three years. I am not among them."

"You are a woman after my own heart," agreed Halland.

"Why, Commander, what a flatterer you are," she said, batting her hand at him and raising an eyebrow. "We really must rest now, yet there is so much more to talk about. Perhaps you could sleep here in the temple compound for the night—oh, and you too, Inspector."

I do believe that she fancies the commander, I thought. *I wonder if he believes it?* I rubbed my eyes and stifled a yawn.

"Perhaps the commander could accept your most generous hospitality," I said, my head on ever so slight an angle, and my eyebrows raised a trifle. "I am staying with friends, however. They will worry if I do not return at all. What say I return for breakfast?"

"I'm sure I could also find—" began Halland with an embarrassed glance from me to Justiva.

"Oh no, no, no, Commander," insisted Norellie, taking him by the arm. "Come with me, this is one night when you will lie in comfort."

But probably get little sleep, I thought as I glanced to Justiva and raised my eyebrows again before I could help myself. She gave me the barest flicker of a wink in response, then nodded imperceptibly.

※ ※ ※

I was in fact sleeping at the Lamplighter, and had to rouse the landlord to be let in. After a mere four hours asleep I was up again, washed, dressed, and in search of breakfast. There was a small market on the riverside, and I went straight to Greasy Alfrodan's Gourmet Rolls, my favorite stall for breakfast. There, directly in front of the stall, were Lavenci and Riellen. They appeared to be in the middle of some icily polite exchange.

"Ah, Inspector, I was getting worried about you!" declared Lavenci as I walked over and went down on one knee to her.

"Er, how so, ladyship?"

"Well, you once said this is your favorite place to breakfast, so I have been waiting here since dawn in the hope of speaking with you."

Riellen twitched as if she had been prodded in the back with a very sharp dagger.

"I regret your discomfort," I said as I got up. "Pelmore's hanging at noon would have been an easier place to find me. The execution cannot proceed unless both sentencing and ratifying magistrates are present."

"I'll not be attending, that turd has wasted enough of my life already," Lavenci declared; then she turned on Riellen. "Leave us. My dear friend Danolarian and I must speak of matters that are not for the ears of virgins."

Severely discomforted, Riellen cowered, saluted, then hurried away.

"What did she want?" I asked as we watched her go. "More apologies?"

"The little rat has been doing some research. She came here to warn me against the temptation to suicide."

"Really?"

"Three of the couples who she afflicted with the constancy glamour were in Alberin, she has checked upon them One man drowned himself in the Alber. Another's partner vanished, so he was hanged for suspected murder. The third man sailed for Helion Island in search of the cure, but his ship was never heard of again. The two surviving women have become nuns in the Contemplative Order of Divine Etheric Transcendence."

"People in that order spend most of their time darkwalking. Many of them never return from it."

"They are the ones who have transcended, and both women may be trying to do just that. Danolarian, if an allurement glamour is rape, a constancy glamour is nothing short of murder. It warrants the death sentence, and I told Riellen as much."

"Reluctant as I am to admit it, Riellen did not know that until now."

"And if she had?"

"I would have recommended that she hang beside Pelmore. Well then, why are you here, ladyship?"

"I have eaten here every day that you have been away— except for when I traveled to Gatrov. Today I waited, though. I knew you would come here, and I had something important to tell you."

"In that case, may I buy you another breakfast?"

"Oh! You would? I mean yes, yes. More is the pity that it is not breakfast after a night lying naked in your arms."

I bought two groundnut rolls with parsley and fried onions, and we sat on a wall overlooking the river to eat. Lavenci took only two or three bites before glancing at me, clearing her throat, and taking a deep breath.

"Danolarian, I did not petition for Pelmore to be spared!" she said in a harsh, forced voice, before flinging her roll into the water and burying her face in her hands.

"Someone did," I responded quietly, taking little interest in my own roll.

"Mother dragged me off to see Elder Justiva of the Metrologans the morning after I had been freed. Justiva is from Helion, and she knew a little about the constancy glamour. At the temple we met Norellie, who had been wise enough to flee before the towers razed Gatrov. They both tried several spells and castings, but none worked. Both Justiva and Norellie agreed that the glamour can only be lifted if both partners are still alive."

"Lavenci—"

"No! Please, hear me out first. When mother and I were alone again, I told her everything. It took hours. She—she thinks Pelmore's sentence should be put off for some months. I told her that Pelmore murdered a fine and brave man, in cold blood, and for that he should hang. I'll take my seven years of celibacy and call it a lesson in the very expensive school of experience. However . . . Mother used her considerable influence to try to have Pelmore's sentence changed to a lifetime in some dungeon. I know that pressure was put on you, and that you resisted. The word is that your career in the Wayfarers is over, so take this."

She dropped a little scroll with legal and merchant bank seals into my hand.

"What is this?" I laughed wearily. "A recommendation for a job in a bank?"

"A bank note for eleven thousand florins, nearly all of my personal wealth."

"Eleven thousand florins?" I gasped. "I cannot accept this! It's more than my wages for twenty years!"

"Yes, don't spend it all at once."

I took a bite from my roll, then offered it to Lavenci. I had to drop it into her hand so that she would not feel my touch. A barge glided slowly by, drawn by a horse on the towpath. A ferryboat followed, bearing two merchants who were laughing and waving their hands.

"We used to sit here and quote poetry to each other," I said as a squad of militiamen marched along the tow path beneath past us.

"I slapped your hand away here," replied Lavenci in barely a whisper. "It will always be accursed in my memory."

Below us, the marshal in charge of the squad called for three cheers for the Alpindrak piper and his lady. I forced a smile onto my face and waved. Lavenci puffed her chest out and waved too.

"His lady," she sighed. "How I have longed to hear those words," she said once the squad was past. "Had it not been for that slap, it might be true today."

"Recently, well for just four days past, I have been wondering about that slap," I said, just a trifle timidly.

"As well you might."

"I should like to hear the story behind it."

"No, please, you would think badly of me," she replied breathlessly.

"So, it was as I thought," I said, looking as glum as I was able. "I did not think you that type."

"Type? What type?"

"Where I come from it is called the peon princess. Such a girl bestows her favors upon the lowborn, while spurning the advances of her peers and betters. She delights in the power to elevate the lowly and cast down the mighty. Strange, you do not seem cruel, yet only cruel ladies think to play such a game."

The spring of the trap was set, the hook was baited. Lavenci did not want to be thought of badly, yet I was fairly sure that she was even less anxious to be thought of as what I had described.

"I could tell you a story, but you may never wish to speak with me again," she declared with her hands steepled over her mouth and nose.

"But perhaps if I heard it we could then go our separate ways in peace," I suggested.

Lavenci thought about this for a time. I watched as a

charred plank drifted past on the water from inland. I had a fairly good idea how it would have been set on fire.

"Very well," she said, lowering her hands and rubbing them together. "Once upon a time there was a sickly girl with a beautiful, suave, alluring mother, and an older sister who had charm and wit sufficient for an entire troupe of comic players. The sickly girl was very intelligent, however and on her fifteenth birthday she graduated from her mother's academy, and was made the youngest sorcery academician in the history of Diomeda.

"It was then that she discovered a curious thing. If she found any youth in the academy comely, he would be too intimidated to refuse her advances. She made it her business to seduce students in unusual places where they might be chanced upon; she wanted to gain a reputation as a hoyden. Soon her suave mother and witty sister no longer thought of her as a shy virgin, and the girl found it exciting to discomfort her mother's staff and students, and to keep them guessing who might or might not be in her favor. Years passed, then she met a lovely boy, and in the most romantic of circumstances. She wanted to be his sweetheart, to be courted by him, but she knew nothing of the protocols of courtship used by people who were actually in love. Poor girl, *she simply did not know what to do*."

Lavenci paused to catch my glance, and let me see the pain in her own eyes.

"She must have managed something," I suggested, somewhat startled.

"Oh yes, she treated it as an elite scholar like herself would. For five frantic days she read romantic novels in every spare moment, then met with her beau each evening. She tried to apply all that was said in the novels about sweet, coy maidens being courted. The novels were very specific about what nice girls did when a boy's hands wandered up skirts or down blouses, and thus she slapped her sweetheart's hand when he touched her breast. Poor, sensitive boy, he was mortified, and she was too proud to apologize. The next day he was sent away to war. Months passed, and while he was away, her beau met another soldier who boasted of doing the most intimate things possible with a girl who he described closely, then named. It was, of course, the boy's sweetheart.

"When the boy returned to the city, well you can imagine what happened. She had read a lot more books, and she tried to tease him, to show off her sharp wits. He asked her why she would share gross familiarities with others, while despising him so much that she could not even bare a caress of his hand. Suddenly desperate and mortified, she flung all her games and façades aside and frantically offered him anything and everything that might please him. Alas, it was too late. He spurned her, and went his way. She was left inconsolable."

"What happened to her?" I asked,

"That part of the story has not happened yet. Would you like the rest of this roll? I am no longer inclined to eat."

Lavenci offered the remaining length of roll to me. I declined, feeling nauseous too.

"You had to make all those mistakes," I ventured, staring across the river. "For you, there was no other way." I turned back and caught her eye. "Now you are wiser."

"Am I really?" asked Lavenci, shaking her head.

"I think so. Anyway, did you ever stop to think that I might have problems too?"

"Really?"

"Really and truly."

"Then I should be allowed to hear your story, and make up my own mind," responded Lavenci, eager yet anxious, all at once.

Now it was my turn. Ever since Riellen's trial aboard the barge I had been steeling myself to reveal my past to Lavenci, yet I had not known how to. In a curious sort of way, putting it into a story made it easier.

"Once upon a time there was a prince, the son of an emperor. He was tall, clever, healthy, very well educated, and skilled with weapons. On his thirteenth birthday a princess from a client kingdom introduced him to the arts of dalliance, and thereafter he never spent a night alone, and all his bedmates were of royal bloodlines. Before he turned fourteen he had killed two training partners in fencing accidents, had earned a degree in cold sciences, and could speak many languages.

"It was now that the emperor assembled the largest war fleet the world had ever seen, to conquer some distant kingdom. The empress would not let the prince sail with the fleet, but he was bored with luxury and security. He disguised himself as a commoner and enlisted on one of the ships. He was tall and strong, and could pass for one five years older. It was a hard life. He had to do filthy, menial work, his hands grew blistered, he fought bullies, learned to splice ropes, ate coarse foods, received a flogging for some petty offense, but became popular with his shipmates.

"The prince grew to like the life, because he was being accepted for himself, and not his rank, wealth, and birthright. He had just been promoted to able seaman when word of a disaster reached the fleet as they lay anchored off a tiny island. A terror weapon, unleashed by the emperor, had destroyed the entire continent of Torea. The father of the prince had become the greatest murderer in the history of the world."

Lavenci gasped and dropped the remains of the groundnut roll to the towpath below us. A stray dog snatched up the morsel and ran off with a half-dozen other dogs pursuing it.

"You are Prince Darric, son of Emperor Melidian Warsovran of Damaria," she whispered, shrinking away from me along the wall.

"No, I am not," I said with a little chuckle. "Neither am I able seaman second-class Allidian Orence. Not since the fifteenth night of sixthmonth in 3140, anyway. That was when I found the body of Danol Scryverin in Diomeda, the night the city fell to my father's invasion fleet. He had destroyed a continent by accident, now he was carving out a new realm by yet more warfare. I was revolted. I was the son of the worst murderer in the history of our world. Thus I *became* the dead Danol Scryverin so that I might escape my birthright. I learned Alberinese and Diomedan . . . and you know the rest."

"Wensomer's half brother," whispered Lavenci, more to herself than me.

"Yes. Madame Yvendel had an affair with Father when they were both young students, at what was then your grandmother's academy in Diomeda. Wensomer is their love child. I met her when I was seven years old. She told me that she had a half sister, and that Rax Einsel, the court sorcerer, was the father."

"Father," said Lavenci dreamily. "I met him once, in Diomeda. Just once."

"Really?"

"We embraced, we spoke of many things for an hour, then he was gone. I think he knew he was about to die."

"I knew him well, I should tell you all I can remember of him. He taught me the basics of magical castings, cold sciences, and applied logic. He was a kind man, and very witty. It was he who helped me run away to sea. I suspect that he knew what was about to happen to Torea. His last words to me before I boarded the ship were 'You will like Diomeda, my truelove is there.'"

"His truelove?" exclaimed Lavenci. "He actually *loved* mother?"

"That's what he told me, but he named no names. Years later Wensomer became empress of the new Scalticarian Empire, and one day I saw her during a parade and recognized her. Father bequeathed to both of us a strong streak of leadership and affinity for power, but we both fought the temptation to use it. I deliberately remained a lowly Wayfarer, and Empress Wensomer conducted a dissolute and scandalous royal court so that people would treat her reign as a joke. On Alpindrak she told me that the girl I was courting was her half sister, and Rax Einsel's secret daughter."

"You also learned what a filthy, cruel, game-playing slut I—"

"Stop that!"

"But—"

"Stop and listen. I sleep with a princess who has been carried into my bedchamber on a gold litter by four eunuchs. You raise your skirts for a student on the academy roof, and laugh up at the stars as you make love. Why is one act noble, yet the other base?"

She thought about that for some time. An armed river galley glided past us, heading upstream, probably to fight the Lupanians.

"Let me, please, let me tell you this, Danolarian, listen. The night I slapped your hand, you—you looked so bewildered and hurt. I was so ashamed of myself that I didn't have the courage to kiss you goodnight. After you walked me home, I ran up to my room and threw up in my underwear drawer. Then I cried all night. The next day I got your note, and I thought that you had left on account of what I had done. No letters came—"

"Riellen burned them," I reminded her defensively.

"*Now* I know that. I researched your history, and that made me love you all the more. Yes, now I've said it. I loved you then, and I love you now . . . but you have seen me be such a monster. You could never love me in return, there is too much filth, too much hurt between us."

I considered this, wondering how to reach her, how to make her believe how I felt.

"I am not one for pantries," I said softly. "Neither do I like half-wit virgins. The girl I loved walked the streets of Alberin with me on the night of her rescue from the Inquisition Constables. She held my hand, she danced with me in the Lamplighter, we drank ale from the same tankard, she exchanged jokes with me in nine languages as I walked her home, then she kissed me goodnight. She pined for me while I was away, she was faithful to me whenever she went to a tavern dance, and she even wrote "The Banks of the Alber" for me. Do you happen to know where that girl went? I still love her."

"Danol . . ." began Lavenci, but sobs were already beginning to contort her face.

Lavenci burst into a flood of tears that lasted for quite some time. I extended a hand, and ran a finger down her hair, lightly, so she could not feel it. Even more carefully, I lifted some of her milky white tresses and pressed them to my lips.

"Clever, clever Danolarian," she said approvingly between sobs. "You can even cheat the constancy glamour."

"Poor girl, this must have been such a strain," I said. "Are you feeling all right?"

She shook her head and gave a rueful little smile.

"So strange, those were almost your very first words to me, when I crashed into you in that dark street, pursued by the Inquisition. 'Are you all right, miss?' That voice, those words. Danolarian, as soon as I heard you speak, I knew I was safe. Danolarian, I, I . . . might I dare to feel safe again?"

Her voice, full of fearful hope and desperate trust, melted me within. Suddenly I let out a theatrical sigh, slapped my knees, spun about on the wall, and dropped to the ground. I took an imaginary chalk and slate from my jacket and drew an imaginary tick.

"Things to do: Item one, straighten out difficulties with truelove. Done. Item two, lift glamour from truelove in seven years by hanging Pelmore today. As good as done. Item three, help defeat the Lupanians. Well . . . I think that will keep until tomorrow." I handed the imaginary chalk to Lavenci. "Have I missed anything?"

"You missed the hardest task of all," she said critically, wiping her eyes with her sleeve.

"What is that?"

"Item four, come home and meet my mother."

"I survived the Battle of Racewater Bridge, how much worse can she be? When should I present myself for inspection?"

"Tonight, at the tenth hour. Dinner will be included."

"I shall be there, one way or another."

"So will Wensomer."

"Wensomer? As in Empress? She is back in Alberin?"

"Yes. She thinks you are very cute, you know. Wensomer's half brother! I am really, really looking forward to tonight."

After a rather lengthy farewell to Lavenci, I went to the Metrologan temple. I was informed that Norellie was still in bed after a long and exhausting night. I then asked after Commander Halland. I was told that he was also asleep. I insisted that he be roused. I was told to wait. I noticed that the deacon did not hurry off in the direction of the men's dormitories. Wayfarer inspectors notice things like that.

Halland presently appeared, wearing a white bedchamber gown embroidered with pink hearts transfixed with red arrows.

"You are late for breakfast," I pointed out.

"Sorry," he mumbled. "Er, refectory's this way."

"So, problems sleeping?"

"No, not at all."

"In spite of the air being thick with perfume?" I asked, batting at the air between us.

"Very funny."

"And the flea that left a bite one inch across on your neck?" Halland gave a strangled gasp, raised the collar of the gown, and wrapped it closely about his neck. We reached the refectory, which was a little hall with tables and benches. We sat down, and were brought bread, cheese, and rainwater mixed with juice.

"You did sleep with her, based on evidence presented no denials will be accepted."

"Actually, no. Technically I didn't sleep with her."

"I think I understand."

"I was two years out of practice."

"I sympathize. Did you manage to discuss the Lupanians any further, or was the conversation more along the lines of 'Not yet,' 'My turn on top,' and 'Yes! Yes! Yes!' "

"Is this just gratuitous sarcasm for its own sake, or do you have a point to make?"

"Sir, friend, I have been promoted to the Inquisition, remember? After Pelmore hangs at noon, I shall be sworn in, and after that I shall vanish—voluntarily or otherwise, whichever comes first. If there is anything else we can say of the Lupanians, it must be now."

"The Lupanians," he said absently, rubbing at the love bite. "They are too powerful to confront, we both know that. They may be mortal, but their power is unimaginable and they never make the same mistake twice. Alberin is the largest city in northeast Scalticar, and they have learned from the conquered peoples that it is the capital of an empire that covers most of the continent. They will want Alberin conquered. Lavenci has calculated that their weapon can set reedpaper afire at five miles, and you of all people know that it melts stone at one mile. They will come here and raze Alberin to terrify the rest of Scalticar into submission. It is only a matter of time."

"But Justiva mentioned the glass dragons," I pointed out.

"Justiva has heard nothing back from them. They are aloof, arrogant beings. They will respond in their own time, but the Lupanians could be here as early as today."

"What will you do?"

"Work with the militia while the militia exists, then hide with the Metrologans. And you?"

"Serve the crown, while a head attached to a body is still wearing the aforesaid crown—oh, and hang Pelmore."

The next matter to attend was visiting the modest house where Captain Gilvray had lived with his wife Dolvienne. Lady Dolvienne was wearing the black of mourning, but admitted me graciously and had a servant prepare and serve tea. For a time we recalled old times in the Sargolan Empire, and of how my squad of reccons had been sent by Princess Senterri to hunt down and kill Dolvienne and Gilvray. We had instead deserted and fled with them to Alberin. Since then they had married and lived happily for three years. Gilvray had been about to be awarded letters as a medicar from the imperial guild when he had been murdered.

"Three years of happiness, it seems so little now that it is all we shall ever have," Dolvienne said sadly as we sat in the little vine-smothered courtyard at the back of the house.

"Some get a lot less than that, ladyship," I pointed out. "Some get nothing at all."

"Then if suchlike ever comes your way, do not hesitate, Danolarian. What you have now may be as good as you get, and *all* that you ever get."

A half hour later I was standing in Astigian Square, watching the shadow of the public sundial advance on the mark of noon. Pelmore arrived to face his sentence. He was in a cart, in chains, and stripped to his drawers. There was a blindfold over his eyes and a gag in his mouth. Someone had given him a very hard time in the dungeons, as he was covered in grime, dried blood, bruises, and cuts. Strange to say, his curly blond hair was clean.

The sundial was a dragon, carved in blackstone. Its head was bent, and the shadow of its single horn traced out the sun's position on grooves in the flagstones. Of more concern to Pelmore was the iron ring held in its teeth, however. From it hung a noose. There was little ceremony when a common felon was hung. The cart was drawn up beneath the dragon's head, and the noose was lowered, then tightened about Pelmore's neck. He struggled in the grip of two hooded guards, and tried to shout something in spite of the gag. A hooded driver sat patiently with one hand on the reins and the other on the brake lever. The crowd was chanting:

"Hurry, hurry,
"To Astig.
"Pelmore's soon
"To dance a jig."

The crowd fell silent as a crier strode up to the cart. I walked up to stand beside him, and we were then joined by the ratifying magistrate.

"Be it known to all and sundry that by decree of a magistrate of the Wayfarers, ratified by a sentencing magistrate of Alberin City, on evidence supplied in a properly constituted field trial, Pelmore Haftbrace, late of Gatrov, is guilty of the murder of Captain Danzar Borodan of the Gatrov Town Militia, the attempted murder of a noblewoman, and the attempted murder of a Wayfarer inspector. The penalties are death, death, and death, to be served concurrently. Inspector Scryverin, Magistrate Talliser, are you in agreement?"

"Aye," I responded.

"Yes," agreed Talliser.

"Executioner, you may carry out the sentence at your pleasure," concluded the crier.

"Gid-yup!" called the driver, releasing the brake and flicking the reins.

The horse ambled forward. Pelmore tumbled from the cart, accompanied by his captors, who had forgotten to release him. The guards tumbled to the flagstones, one of them clutching at Pelmore and partly dragging off his drawers as he fell. Pelmore kicked and jerked in midair. The crowd laughed, cheered, and applauded. The guard got up, gripped the body around the middle and swung. Pelmore's neck dislocated and stretched. The figure on the end of the rope ceased to struggle. The two guards and the driver bowed and the crowd applauded, even though it had been a rather sloppy execution.

✦ ✦ ✦

Something was nagging at my mind as I walked away. There was an incorrect detail, something out of place. I was an inspector, after all, and it was my vocation to inspect. Presently I noticed that another youth had fallen in beside me.

"Just the man I wanted to see," he said, and I turned to discover that I was walking beside Laron Aliasar, presiding advisor to the regent of Alberin, and master of the disbanded Secret Inquisition Constables—which had never really existed anyway.

I immediately stopped, dropped to one knee, and bowed. I did so with such speed that one of the guards escorting Laron nearly fell over me. Several people nearby correctly assumed that Laron was someone important and dropped to one knee as well. Laron hastily waved me up, then took me by the arm and hurried me on, after a word to his guards to stay out of earshot.

"Lordship, I must apologize—" I began automatically.

"Danolarian, give the lordship bit a rest. We have served in the same reccon squad, drunk in the same taprooms, danced with the same girls, and nearly drowned aboard the same ship. Fortune has made me a courtier and you an inspector, but there's an end of it. What did you think of Pelmore's dancing?"

"I dislike that type of dancing at the best of times, sir, but he murdered a brave and honorable man, so he deserved it. And you?"

"I just wanted to see him dead. Academician Lavenci is very dear to me."

"I know you were once her lover."

"Not for some months past," he said with a little laugh. "But we are still friends. She . . . relieved me of my innocence when we were at an academy in Diomeda. After a fashion."

"After a fashion, sir? Are not such matters somewhat unambiguous?"

"Don't ask. Well?"

"Well what?"

"You and Lavenci?"

"At this very minute in seven years' time we shall be in a particularly intense physical-contact situation. The rest of our plans are none of your business."

"So, you two are reconciled?"

"Yes, as of this morning."

"Good, excellent," he exclaimed, rubbing his hands together, as if he had just brokered a mercantile deal of great profit. "Well, I'd better have myself arrested now."

"Arrested? Why?"

"The regent wants someone to blame for something, you know how it is."

"Why don't you flee?"

"Because it is expected of me. And you?"

"I have an order to attend Wayfarer Headquarters."

"Ah, yes. You are to be rewarded by a promotion into the Inquisition. I hear things, I know. Because you refused to change your report to exonerate Pelmore, the directant of Wayfarers is handing you to the inquisitor general on a silver platter. You could flee, if you are unexpectedly brisk about it."

"That would mean leaving Lavenci again. I'll not do that."

Chapter Sixteen

DEATH OF A GLASS DRAGON

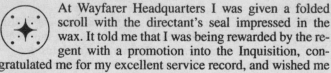 At Wayfarer Headquarters I was given a folded scroll with the directant's seal impressed in the wax. It told me that I was being rewarded by the regent with a promotion into the Inquisition, congratulated me for my excellent service record, and wished me well. This was followed by an instruction to report immediately to the Office of Inquisition in the regent's palace. I set off for the palace by the most direct route, stopping only to buy a curried egg roll at a street stall. A man in a dark grey cloak who had been walking quite briskly about a hundred paces behind me suddenly slumped against a wall and became a loafer. I set off again. By now my shadow had reversed his cloak to be brown, and stuck a feather in his hat. He hurried

after me, and I somehow felt that I knew him well. Exceedingly well.

I presented my papers at the palace gates. Why is it that on the occasions when you want some irregularity to be found, you are always waved straight through with a smile? The Alberin palace was actually an old castle. The inner wall and citadel had long been demolished for the present complex of halls, hostelries, stables, and such, but the outer wall had been left intact. True, it was now whitewashed and decorated with tasteful sculptures, but the wall was in excellent repair and the watchtowers were still manned. Over the two hundred years past there had been several occasions when all that had stood between the ruler and an angry mob had been the palace guard and the wall. That had been the one lesson from history that Alberin's monarchs were all happy to learn. Seven tall, thin towers rose above everything else, and were visible from all points of the city. They reminded everyone, every day, where their ruler was, and that he just might be looking down upon them.

There were other buildings in the palace grounds, such as the barracks of the palace guards, storehouses for times of siege, and chambers of various organizations. The last named were organizations that the regent liked to keep close to himself. The Royal Incarceration Services were among them, but so too was the Inquisition. For such a well-known and powerful organization, the Inquisition had an oddly unremarkable building: just three floors high, unadorned, with small windows—all barred—and at the main entrance only four guards, all in white surcoats and gleaming chain mail.

Once more I was admitted with no fuss whatsoever, and the hospitality clerk assigned me a lackey. The lackey took me straight up to the third floor, where he rapped smartly on a door marked INQUISITOR GENERAL. The door was opened by a man who was perhaps in his forties, of average height, but fairly rotund. He was introduced as the inquisitor general; then the lackey introduced me and I presented my papers. I noted that the doorframe was lined with green felt, and that there was more felt on the back of the door.

"You may have noticed that I have no administration clerk," said the inquisitor general as he sat down behind his table and gestured to a chair. "That is because I trust nobody, do everything of importance myself, and run a very tight ship. What does that tell you?"

He sat so still that he might well have been a skillfully carved and painted statue, had not his lips been moving. Here was a keen observer who was used to complete control, and who knew that he had the power of life and death over more people than anyone else except for the regent. The room was dingy, for the internal shutters of the windows were closed; however, the reflector behind the single burning oil lamp was turned to focus on me.

"You have more pieces of the mosaic than everyone else, sir," I replied.

"Very perceptive," he responded. "Why were you not so perceptive yesterday, in your interview with the directant?"

"He asked me to make a judgment with only the pieces to hand, sir."

"One of those pieces was my request regarding Pelmore Haftbrace. Why did you ignore it?"

"Had he *ordered* me to falsify my report, I would have noted that order in the report, then done so."

"Ah, a stickler for the rules," he said, his voice dropping in tone, yet becoming all the more menacing for that. "Well here is your first lesson in the Inquisition's rules. The rules are conceived, born, raised, twisted, slaughtered, and buried within these four walls, and between the ceiling above you and the floor that supports you. The Inquisition is all about hunting out, controlling, and eliminating sorcery in all of its shapes, forms, and disguises. To do that, we are above all laws except for that law commissioning the Inquisition in the first place. That law is above the regent, and even the former empress. It was passed by the first and only conference of all Scalticar's rulers, three years ago, the one that set up the empire. The Inquisition is above kingdoms, Inspector Danolarian Scryverin, and once I write your name into my central register as an Inquisition marshal, a breach of discipline will be a refusal to obey my word. Pelmore's death caused me to lose face with someone of considerable importance. Gaining control of you will buy back a little of what was lost."

He stood up, lit a candle from the oil lamp, and turned to a grillework screen behind him. Keys jingled; then he slid the screen aside.

"Before you get any thoughts of leaping up, vaulting my desk, and killing me with your bare hands while my back is turned, bear in mind that a dozen mechanisms are ready to slice you up very severely should you even so much as fart with too much force. Ah, here we are, the central register."

As I had approached the chair to sit down, I had noticed some repairs to what seemed to be damage from bladed weapons, so this was no surprise. He returned to his table, sat down, opened the register, and held his candle close.

"I need less administration than my brother nobles because I have but a single copy of the most vital records of the Inquisition." He reached under his table. There was a soft clunk. "You have probably inferred correctly that I have disarmed the blades focused on your seat, along with the trapdoor to dispose of your body for collection. Should you feel inclined to leap up and attack me, however, do reconsider. See these cuffs on the sleeves of my jacket? The tubes are not just decorative, they also contain spring-loaded needles. Were I to point my arm at you and make a fist, four dozen poisoned needles would fly your way. Any one could kill you ten times over, and in as many heartbeats. Now then, I have seen five different spellings of your name in various documents and registers, so could you tell me your preferred—"

There was a loud blast from outside, rather like that of a terra-cotta tile the size of a cottage roof being dropped onto a stone floor. Another such blast quickly followed, then another.

"Did you hear that?" snapped the inquisitor general, staring at me as if it might be my doing.

"I hear it, sir, but I don't know what it might be."

A deep, grinding rumble replaced the sharp, shattering blasts, intermingled with shrieks and screams; then came a concussion that shook the building no less than a moderately powerful earthquake. The inquisitor general ran to the room's only window, rattled keys, then flung the shutters back. I saw billowing dust and smoke.

"Come over here!" he cried as more of the sharp blasts echoed among the palace buildings. "Tell me what is happening."

The top had been removed from one of the seven towers of

the palace, sending hundreds of tons of stone blocks crashing down into the grounds and onto lower buildings. Another tower, the one known as Dragonperch for the three years past, had a brilliant light blazing out from a spot on its side, about thirty feet from the summit.

"The Lupanian heat weapon, sir," I said as I watched fragments of stone melting and exploding away under the intense heat.

"But those towers are built of stone!" he shouted, even though I was right beside him. "How can stone burn?"

"Sir, if you dig a rock from under the snow and drop it into a campfire, it will burst apart from uneven heating. This is the same principle, but magnified a million times."

"But the Lupanians don't exist, the regent said they were a trick to increase the war budget."

"If you say so, sir."

The top quarter of Dragonperch tower began to topple, but slowly, as if it were falling through water. The rubble came down on the barracks of the Palace Guard.

"The Lupanians that don't exist are attacking the palace, so that Alberin will be left leaderless," I said as we watched the dust billowing upward. "That is their standard tactic, even though it does not happen."

"This building is right beside Skylance Tower!" shrieked the inquisitor general, pointing upward through the window.

"There is no danger, sir, for none of this is happening."

"Run!" shouted the inquisitor general, taking me by the arm and dashing across the room.

Out in the corridor were guards, clerks, lackeys, and people wearing hoods, all jostling each other and making for a crush of bodies that marked the head of the stairs. Slamming the door behind us, the inquisitor general pushed me away and ran with the others. I dropped to the floor, then crawled back the way we had come. I had remembered that the inquisitor general's iron ring of keys was still in the lock to his window shutters. The door to his office was thus unlocked. Without standing, I checked that were no others behind me in the corridor, and that all those pushing and struggling at the stair head had their faces turned away. Depressing the latch, I slipped back into the office. The building shook with the concussion of another tower falling.

Before me was the open grille of the inquisitor general's racks of files and registers, and on his table was the central register of all inquisitors. *So much to do, so little time,* I thought, quite literally salivating at the sight of what was before me. Here was I, a former member of the Secret Inquisition Constables, a squad dedicated to saving sorcerers from the Inquisition, alone in the innermost sanctum of the Inquisition.

I dropped into a shadow and raised my cloak to cover the paler skin of my face as I heard the latch of the door clack. Had the inquisitor general glanced about as he entered, he would have seen me for certain, but because he looked straight to the window shutters where his keys still hung from the lock, I was out of sight by the time he had retrieved his keys and turned back. He dashed to his table, picked up his master register, and tossed it through his grillework door, then slammed the grille across and locked it. *Must be the first time in his life he's ever panicked,* I thought as I watched him. *Should have known that his self-discipline would soon drag him back to his senses, though.*

And then my almost-employer was through the office door again and his keys were rattling in the lock. *How long before Skylance Tower is struck down by the Lupanians?* I asked myself as I hurried over to the locked grille. With a heavy crowbar, a mallet, and a chisel, I might have got the grille open in ten minutes or so, but everything down to my writing kit had been taken when I had entered the building. My arm could fit between the bars, and the nearest rack was more than an arm's length away . . . but not the master register of all inquisitors! When it had been flung through the door, it had bounced off a rack and fallen within reach.

Kneeling down, I stretched out, grasped the register, and pulled it out. Without really thinking I ripped the cover boards off, opened it at the middle, then wrapped the pages around my stomach and tied the drawstring of my trousers tightly over it. I watched my hands take all the lamps down and splash oil about the place. How to get out? The door was locked, and looked solid—but the inquisitor general had said something about a trapdoor and my seat. I took down the single burning oil lamp, then looked behind his table. There were at least a dozen little levers, each marked by a symbol. I depressed them all, then tossed the cover boards of the master register onto my chair's seat. Half a dozen crossbow bolts flashed down out of the ceiling and thudded into the chair and cover boards; then the floor beneath the chair swung downward. I hurried around the table and looked down. There was a drop of about ten feet to the floor of the room below. I tossed the lamp that I held at the grillework, where it smashed, igniting the oil that I had splashed about. I eased myself through the trapdoor, hung by my hands for a moment, then dropped.

The room was empty. By the light of the fire above, I made my way to a door. It was not locked, and beyond it was some sort of guards' common room with stools and a table. Scattered on the table were cards and mugs, and beyond this was an open door. Obviously they had left in a hurry, and I too left in a hurry. There was a mighty crush at the stairs on this floor as well, and all the while I was wondering when the Lupanians would turn their heat weapon on Skylance Tower. By now there had been no fourth concussion from another tower falling, and it seemed to me that one was well overdue.

After what seemed like an eternity of pushing and struggling I emerged into the open, and saw that the tops of only three towers had been sliced away. The dust and smoke had not really settled by now, yet people were pointing to the sky and shouting about glass dragons. I thought I saw a winged shape pass overhead. It might have been a seagull flying low, or else something with wings hundreds of feet across flying a lot higher. The inquisitor general emerged from the building, screamed for someone to attend him, then caught sight of me and ran over.

"So, you weren't slow at running away, Scryverin!" he shouted angrily, and I realized that I had beaten him out of the building. "What's happening?"

"People pointing at the sky and shouting about dragons, sir!" I barked, saluting.

"There! I knew there were no Lupanians!" he replied, his terror now edged with anger. "The glass dragons destroyed those towers."

He ran off, shouting for his horse and cavalry guards. I was left alone amid the dust, smoke, and panic-stricken palace staff and guards. I saw the regent gallop through the gates escorted by quite a large squad of guardsmen. A number of people who did not manage to get out of the way sufficiently fast were trampled. Turning back to the Inquisition building, I noted with satisfaction that smoke was now pouring out of a window on the third floor. Nobody else seemed to notice or care.

Suddenly there was an intense blaze of light from somewhere beyond the palace, and it seemed to last a dozen or more heartbeats. There was a stunned silence at first, and then everyone began shouting and screaming. I looked to Skylance Tower, then to the Inquisition building, then to the shattered stumps of the three stricken towers. Only now did I remember that there would be prisoners in the cells of the Inquisition building, and even if Skylance Tower was not toppled onto it, I had set the building afire. I strongly suspected that nobody would bother either rescuing the Inquisition's prisoners or fighting the fire.

I reentered the building unopposed, and stopped before a directory board lettered in gold paint. INTERROGATION—ONE AT EAST suggested that the torture cells were on the first floor, east side. Suddenly a blast of sound like a clap of thunder going off in a tavern's privy literally shook me to the core of my body. My first thought was that Skylance Tower and fallen, but then I was still alive and the building was still standing around me, so I went on and tried not to think about danger.

Everything was open to me; it was as if only the inquisitor general had bothered to lock up after himself. I found a heavy mallet caked with what appeared to be dried blood, and discovered that one really hard, well-placed blow just above a cell's lock would smash the mounting and screws from the timber, opening the door. In the eleventh cell I found Laron.

"Are you all right, sir?" I called, moving on the next cell.

"Indeed, sir, I've only been here two hours, and they'd not got around to entertaining themselves at my expense."

Suddenly I realized which innocent senior advisor had been cast down by the regent at my recommendation. I decided to say nothing on the subject. In all, beside Laron, I released fourteen men and women, all sorcerers. The last two were respectively on the rack and strapped to the water-torture chair. These needed help to walk as we made our way out. The palace grounds were comparatively deserted by the time the sorcerers, Laron, and I gathered outside the Inquisition building and tried to decide what to do next.

A group of guardsmen in black surcoats with the regent's crest now came jogging out of the swirling dust and smoke, then stopped before the burning Inquisition building.

"There's a fire!" shouted a voice.

"Yes, I can see it's burning, but we still have to kill those prisoners as well," shouted someone else. "Only the top floor's burning, it's safe enough for now."

The dangerous thing about an inquisition against sorcerers is that much of the evidence collected has, well, sorceric properties. Take amulets, for example. Some crystals and gems can be used to store etheric energies that are normally built up in our bodies. Some Lupanian had found that out when he destroyed Norellie's cottage. Then again, most books of power are merely books containing powerful spells and arcane knowledge. A few, however, are books with actual etheric power stored within them. This is so that when a sorcerer is being burned at the stake and inquisitors are standing around clapping and tossing his books onto the fire to roast him with his own learning, the power stored within one of those lesser-known books of power will be released in an uncontrolled fashion by the flames. There appears to have been such a book in the inquisitor general's grille collection. A mighty blast suddenly belched flames from every window on the third floor, the roof was blown upward, and the walls of the building peeled outward. As the dust cleared it was apparent that the Inquisition building's height had been reduced to about five feet.

"Well *I* don't think it was safe enough," declared the grey-haired sorceress beside me, who then fainted into my arms.

It seemed like a good idea to take the liberated sorcerers to the Metrologan temple. I had decided this after stopping at a deserted armory and dressing my charges to look vaguely like guardsmen. At the temple I declared to the priestess, who was guarding the entrance with a pair of garter crossbows, that we had been sent by the regent to protect the temple from Lupanians. At this point Halland came out and recognized me, and we were hurried inside without further explanations.

The first thing that I demanded was to know the whereabouts of the privy. Admittedly it had been quite some time since I had had the opportunity to relieve myself, but more to the point I wanted to study the master register of the Inquisition in private before saying anything further to anybody.

Laron's name was not there. Neither was Halland's, Wallengtor's, Andry's, Justiva's, Norellie's, Roval's, Riellen's, or Lavenci's! Pelmore was noted to be their representative for the barony of Gatrovia, which was no surprise. Having established who could be trusted, I emerged, ready to call a meeting, but now Justiva appeared, took me by the arm, and directed me through the corridors to the infirmary. There I found Roval lying on one of the bunks. There was a bandage over one of his eyes, but otherwise he looked uninjured. Laron, Andry, and Halland were with him, along with Justiva and several of the sorcerers that I had just freed.

"Best to sit down, lad," said Halland as I entered. "Roval's in a lot of pain, and Justiva means to put him to sleep for some hours after he talks."

I sat on a bench as Justiva took over sponging Roval's face from Norellie.

"We're all here now, so best to begin," said Halland. "Roval was up in the temple's observatory tower with a farsight when the Lupanians appeared. The glass dragons were expected, and he was keeping watch. The Lupanians arrived first, however. Constable Roval, are you able to tell your story again?"

Roval opened his remaining eye, scanned all those present, then asked about those he did not know. When Justiva vouched for them, he spoke.

"I was looking out to sea when the first spire was struck," he began. "I turned away to see what magical thing was nearby, but I saw no dragon or etheric casting. There was nothing within the city. Using the farsight, I then began scanning beyond the city walls, and presently I saw two of the tripod towers. They were standing together on Rackridge Hill. Both were holding a sparkling light that gave off smoke of some sort."

Rackridge Hill is seven miles distance from the palace, and well beyond the city walls, I thought at once, wondering if we had been wrong about the limits to the heat weapon's range.

"I saw a tower attack Gatrov Castle from two miles distance," I pointed out. "The heat weapon set the roofs afire at that distance, but it seems only to melt or shatter stone at a mile or so."

"By combining their heat weapons, coordinating their aim very carefully, and focusing on a single spot, the Lupanians seem to be able to strike at a much greater range," explained Roval.

"Please, discussions later, let him finish," said Justiva.

"It was now that a glass dragon appeared, flying high over the city," continued Roval, sounding as if his strength was fading. "I would have missed it had not I lowered the farsight for a moment to rub my eyes. As I watched, the towers seemed to angle their heat weapons upward, but when focused in unison like that, they seem more slow, and unable to hit a moving target. Then, so suddenly that I did not notice it except as a blur and a lance of flame, another glass dragon swooped up from behind the hill and struck at one of the tripod towers with its flame breath.

"For a moment I tried to follow the second dragon; then I turned the glass back on the tripods. The northernmost of them was intact, but the one beside it trailed smoke from the hood. I lowered my farsight for a moment, to take in the entire scene. I saw the undamaged tripod's heat weapon sparkle and belch smoke repeatedly as it aimed at the dragon, which was circling around for another attack. Then there was a flash as the dragon was hit. It tumbled from the sky, and hit the ground on the crest of Rackridge Hill. The glass dragon that had been circling over Alberin now broke off and dived, heading out to sea, tumbling and weaving as it fled. I suspect that it was well out of range of the Lupanian anyway, for when I turned my farsight back to Rackridge Hill, the tower had turned away and was examining its ruined companion. Suddenly it turned and strode over to where the stricken glass dragon lay. I saw it approach the body, its heat weapon raised and ready; then it extended its two secondary tentacles again, took a step forward, and seized the dragon. The dragon suddenly revived, and they struggled for a moment. All I remember after that is intense brightness, a flash of the most pure and penetrating light imaginable.

"I remember rolling about in the rainwater gutters of the tower roof, clutching my right eye. Had I not had my left eye closed to use the farsight with my right, I suspect that I would have been blinded completely. After a time a great blast of sound rolled over me, but I cowered down, keeping my gaze down on the guttering, afraid of losing my remaining eye to another blaze of light. My first thought was that the Lupanian had suddenly turned its heat weapon on the academy's observatory tower, but I have since learned that it was not the case. Sometime later I was found, and helped down to the infirmary. That is all."

Justiva told one of her priestesses to give Roval a sedative, then she ushered the rest of us out into the corridor.

"We have had a stream of injured coming to the temple for treatment," she said as we stood milling about. "Some were hurt when the palace towers collapsed, but a few others happened to be on high buildings looking in the direction of Rackridge Hill. They were blinded, every one of them."

"So what happened?" asked Halland.

"Glass dragons are very dangerous in defeat as well as victory," said Justiva, her voice barely audible. Perhaps because she spoke so softly, everyone listened. "They accumulate etheric energies all through their long lives, but how they store them I cannot say. When one of them dies, another is always on hand. We used to think that they were merely looting the energies, but I think we have just learned that they are really preventing a massive, uncontrolled release. What Roval saw was a glass dragon's death, and its etheric energies bursting free in an instant. The energies were considerable, as all of Alberin will testify."

"So, one glass dragon for two tripods," said Halland.

"That is the truth," said Laron, "but not the perception. People all over the city saw a glass dragon fleeing the Lupanians. In all of history, nobody has ever seen a glass dragon fleeing. Some even say that the great blast was from the Lupanian, killing the other dragon. People are saying that it is still striding about beyond the walls, hidden by the smoke and dust of the explosion. As far as most are concerned, it was a great victory for the Lupanians."

"The regent and all his court have fled the city," said Halland. "They took the cream of the city's fighting men as their escort, and fled through Hill Gate for his summer palace in the Ridgeback Mountains. Everyone saw them leave."

"Still, the Lupanians have lost two more tripod towers," said Laron.

"They will be more careful now," said Halland. "They are very powerful, but few."

"Out of twenty, six are dead," replied Laron. "That is a rate of nearly one per day."

"Not so," said Halland. "They learn each time, and become harder to kill."

He was right. Each time it had been harder to kill them. It had taken a glass dragon to kill the last two, and glass dragons were the best that our world could send against them.

It was past midafternoon as we left the infirmary. With the Palace Guard, Royal Guard, and a fairly large part of the city militia gone, the role of maintaining order in Alberin had been largely vacated. The citizens of the capital did not react quite so rapidly to the threat from the Lupanians as their rulers, however. Unlike their rulers, they did not have access to the summer palace in the Ridgeback Mountains, so they had to do things like pack what was portable, find transport, organize protection, and fight off the more pushy of the looters—who were not waiting for the houses to be vacated. By early evening neighborhood security gangs were fighting looter gangs, while some of the better-armed guilds were also discouraging armed visitors in search of easy pickings. Some group appeared to have taken control of the palace grounds as well, because nobody who entered came out again. Unfortunately no pronouncements on what people ought to do came out either. I helped to fortify and barricade the Metrologan temple for about an hour, then set off for Wayfarer Headquarters.

Some citizens were leaving Alberin already, loading a few

horses with gold and provisions, and riding off with all possible haste. Others, with less portable wealth, were piling furniture, clothes, cooking gear, tools, and weapons onto carts, or were barricading themselves in their mansions, houses, cottages, and hovels. As an armed man carrying nothing of obvious value, I was considered to be a hard and unrewarding target, and thus was left alone.

I was somewhat surprised to find the Wayfarers' building still open for business. Because the Wayfarers were an organized force with fighting skills, many folk from surrounding streets were gathering nearby with their packs and carts, ready to flee once word arrived of somewhere safe to flee to. Wallas and Solonor met me at the door, and told me that the directant was one of the few senior officials who had not fled the city. Lacking orders from any central authority, he had decreed that the force was to maintain itself and discourage anarchy, but not take sides in any political conflict. I presented myself for duty, explaining that my transfer to the Inquisition was not entirely feasible because of the Inquisition having fled, and its building having exploded and collapsed. The directant's lackey told me to wait for orders, so I sat down in the common room to wait. Wallas jumped up onto my shoulder from behind.

"Oi, Inspector, what about a hand up?" squeaked a voice from the floor.

I picked Solonor up and placed him on the table. Wallas jumped over to sit beside him.

"Does the directant really think that the Lupanians give a toss about our politics?" I asked them.

"He wants someone to tell him what to do," said Wallas. "People want power, but those who get it suddenly realize that the florin now stops with them. They then decide that they are really much happier being mere marshals or lieutenants, and they go looking for a prince to give them orders."

A clerk arrived with two scrolls, one for me and one for Solonor. I opened mine and read it while Wallas and Solonor struggled to unroll the other.

"It appears that my transfer to the Inquisition has been canceled," I announced. "My status . . . inspector marshal, with five florins a week extra."

"I've been officially assigned to your squad to replace Riellen," declared Solonor, standing on the bottom of his scroll while Wallas held the top with his paws. "Same pay as Wallas. So, what are your orders then, guv?"

"Do you worship my body, adore my mind, and feel twisted with jealousy at the sight of me so much as speaking with a woman?"

Solonor blinked, then scratched his head.

"Er, no, no, and no, but I think you're a clever bastard who's good at stayin' alive and who's never lost nobody in his command to enemy action."

"In that case, you can indeed replace Riellen. Fall in."

Solonor walked along the scroll, allowing it to roll itself up; then he stood to attention beside Wallas, who was sitting up smartly with his front paws together.

"Now then, I am concerned for nonhuman Alberin," I explained. "The gnomes, the cats, all the nonmagical beings and animals. They need to be told about the danger from the Lupanians, how to prepare for it, and when to hide. Do you two think you could liaise with those nonhumans of the city who will not be included in the official decrees?"

"Cor, it's a big city, guv, an' I've got small legs," responded Solonor.

"You address the inspector as 'sir,' " said Wallas.

"Wallas, I carry you about the place on occasion without, shall we say, loss of face," I began.

"You want me to let Constable Solonor ride on my back," replied Wallas, anticipating what was in my mind.

"More than that. I want you to recruit hundreds of cats to carry hundreds of gnomes. I want you to organize a nonhuman militia and underground crier system."

"Cor, I reckon those young gnome hoydens would get the hots for a Grand Gnome Liaisory!" exclaimed Solonor.

"Directant of the Imperial Cats' Militia," said Wallas experimentally. "I like it."

"Is it worth carrying a gnome to earn it?" I asked.

"A title is a title, and it is three long years since I was a courtier, with a title. Did I ever tell you—"

"I require a simple yes or no!" I said testily.

"Yes."

"In that case, get to work. Explain the importance of staying out of sight, and having sealed refuges in case the Lupanians use poison smoke. Station a cat and gnome to wait at the Lamplighter, I shall go there whenever I have news to spread."

With Wallas and Solonor on their way, I spent some time patrolling the refugees waiting near headquarters. I gathered that people were afraid to flee out into the countryside with night approaching, and were waiting for the first light of the morning to leave the city. Most that I spoke to thought they would stay with the general group for protection, because gangs were setting upon the unprotected before they had even cleared the city walls. Nobody seemed to have a very clear idea of where they might go, but most thought that the Ridgeback Mountains offered the most opportunities to hide.

Soon after sunset I decided to return to the Metrologan temple and see what was to be done there. I walked through streets teeming with drunken, singing Alberinese, many dancing with no clothes at all in the heat of the summer night. As I walked, I took time to drag drunken revelers off the streets, chase occasional looters, and break up the odd fight, all the while fending off women proposing "One more before we all gets eaten, luv?" and advising those preparing to flee Alberin about what they really needed to survive on the open road. Some tavern owners were giving away their drink for free, and orgies of revelry were under way that were bigger than many armies. People drank, danced, sang, fornicated, vandalized, and looted whatever could be carried away. Not that they carried it very far, of course. Much costly furniture lay abandoned a street or two away from where it had been pillaged. Drunken looters staggered about flinging gold coins to the crowds, and the poor wandered into the looted houses of the rich and made merry with whatever remained therein.

Back at the Metrologan temple, I learned that Laron had ventured into the palace, and discovered that several dozen elderly, retired guardsmen had been offended by the idea of the palace being looted after they had put three or four decades of their lives into keeping it secure. Thus they had raided an armory and set themselves up to repel all comers. Being the most senior courtier left in the city, Laron appointed himself interim regent, swore the retired guardsmen back into active service, and began issuing orders. Justiva sent me straight on to the palace, and there I found Laron surrounded by people who wanted things back to normal and were willing to work for free. Essen, Andry, and Costiger were there as well.

"Andry, Costiger, go to Wayfarer Headquarters and tell the directant that he must use the Wayfarers to keep order among the people who are fleeing the city tomorrow morning," Laron ordered while two clerks scribed out an original declaration and a copy for the records. "Danol, not you. I'm worried about the voidship. I want it secured from damage. Essen, get a squad of guards together to protect Danol while he moves it."

"Sir—that is, lordship—"

"I don't care what the bloody protocol books say, call me sir!"

"Yes sir, but the voidship is fifty feet long and weighs seven tons. Anyway where are thieves going to take it?"

"A mob may attack it," Laron pointed out.

"Apart from some flaking when it flew through the air as a shooting star, the hull is harder than diamond," I replied.

"Be that as it may, Inspector, I do not want it left in the open. A mob attacked and killed the handling beasts not long ago."

"Killed?" I exclaimed. "But they are very strong, they can defend themselves."

"Not when straw and pitch is heaped on their cage and set afire. Someone knew their weakness, someone with masters who ride dream-fabricated glass-fiber towers a hundred feet tall. Someone who wanted no lessons learned from the handling beasts. Take a team of horses, have them haul the void-ship and its wagons into the palace grounds."

"Very well, sir."

"At first light you and all other Wayfarers are to help escort the citizens as they flee Alberin. I have issued a general order."

"Escort them, sir?"

"Yes. Defend them as they travel. Fend off outlaws, looters, and suchlike."

"And Lupanian tripod towers armed with invincible heat weapons?"

"Very funny. Danol, the citizens are beyond my control, but I still have a duty to serve them. I must help them get away, and give them a head start against the Lupanians. It will be the last service that an Alberinese ruler ever performs."

"Yes sir! But do you not plan to flee as well?"

"No," he said firmly. "When the refugees are clear of the city, you are welcome to return here if you wish. If you decide to flee, I shall understand. Now then, is there anything else?"

"One small matter, sir."

Taking Laron aside, I handed over the master register of the Inquisition, explaining what it was and how I had acquired it.

"It will give you a slight edge when deciding who may be trusted," I explained.

"You are a truly remarkable young man, Danol," said Laron softly, hugging the master register to himself.

It took the better part of an hour to move the voidship into the palace grounds. With the work done, I then went to the Metrologan temple to explain the new orders to Justiva. I found the place deluged with the injured from the vast, riotous orgy that Alberin had become. Justiva was coordinating all the other Metrologans when I found her, and was carrying a tray of bandages.

"I find it hard to believe that the Lupanians can do worse to us than we are doing to ourselves," she said after I explained the new arrangements with the voidship. "Alberin is like a battleground."

"The pillaging and riots should die down by the morning," I suggested. "Most folk are just waiting for the dawn so they can flee."

"Good, that should leave us free to finish moving the temple's library into the sewers, cellars, and other secret places of the city. We Metrologans are staying."

"I guessed as much. Laron has ordered the Wayfarers to escort the exodus. I can't think which of us will be in more danger."

"Our world is falling apart before our eyes, Inspector."

"I know. It will be a long day tomorrow."

"That it will. Will you sleep here tonight? You are welcome."

"Thank you, but no. Kavelen Lavenci has invited me home to meet Madame Yvendel."

A pained expression slowly spread over Justiva's face. She put her tray down on a bench, then pressed her hands against her temples as she slowly shook her head.

"The Lupanians are closing in to annihilate us, the city is in total chaos, civilization is about to fall on its face, we are all liable to wind on some alien menu before the week is out, yet you are going home with a girl who wants to introduce you to her mother?"

"Well, yes. We must keep our priorities in perspective."

Chapter Seventeen

DINNER WITH MOTHER

I set off for the Lamplighter to secure a drink and steady my nerves. The tavern was an island of order within a sea of anarchic revelry and mayhem, and I was welcomed, being a Wayfarer. Within the taproom people still paid for their ale, and were mannerly to each other. There was no reason for it, as money had ceased to have worth throughout the city, but good behavior, manners, and mutual respect were all that we had left, so we preserved them. The mood was particularly subdued, however, and the patrons were not of a mind for false gaiety. Many were wearing foraged armor and carrying weapons. We were all aware that not one in a hundred of us would escape death or slavery in the days to come. Not far away a girl stood with her arms around the neck of a youth armed with a cheap but sturdy ax. She was singing to him, and I caught a few words of a familiar song.

". . . I stepped up to him and I said without tarry,

" 'Lie with me tonight, maybe someday we'll marry' . . ."

Her voice broke on that line, and many of the drinkers present looked profoundly moved. I sat watching them for some moments, wiping my eyes. The largest and most muscular tabby cat that I have ever seen thudded onto my table. It was missing most of one ear, and clinging to its back was a gnome that looked as if it earned a living as a brush in the tavern's privy.

"Militia-gnome Wolwor and Militia-cat Rrowll, Wharfside Incontinent Underground Militia, reportin', sir!" said the gnome, shakily climbing down from the cat.

"I think you mean Wharfside Irregulars," I responded as I sat up with astonishment.

"Er, yeah. Got orders, guv—sir?"

"Orders, yes," I replied, gathering my thoughts. "Spread the word. Do not join the exodus of humans out of the city. Stay in Alberin, prepare refuges down low, in places that will not burn. Choose places that can be sealed off from poison smoke. Lay in food, stay off the streets, and avoid the looters."

The cat made a rumbling sort of noise.

"Er, yeah, thanks. Sir, some of us wants ter fight. How does we do that?"

"You can be of more use to the, ah, war effort by spying," I improvised. "That is why I want you in Alberin when the Lupanians take over. Spy on them, learn their secrets, steal their weapons. Understand?"

"Cor, 'ear that?" said the gnome, elbowing the cat. "Secret agent. Wimmin go fer secret agents."

The cat gave no sign of understanding. The gnome climbed back onto the cat and grasped two handfuls of fur, then spoke in some underlanguage. The cat sprang off the table and vanished. I got up to go as well. It was approaching the tenth hour.

Revelers were still on the streets as I left, drinking, smashing jars, dancing, and being sick. Three men recognized me as a Wayfarer constable and challenged me over some real or imagined incident of times past. I told them to stand aside. Predictably, they took offense. One charged me with his ax before the other two could bracket me. I drew my sword and blocked in high prime, as Azorian called it, rotated inverse, and cut for the side of his head. Before he had hit the ground I did a drop-lunge to skewer the man to my right, managing to stab him chest-center and pierce his transverse artery. Meantime the one to my left had chopped for my head but missed, because of my drop-lunge. He took two steps and swung high for a downward chop, but he was already impaled on my sword.

"Oooh, but ain't 'e a champion!" exclaimed a girl who was standing with her breasts free of her robes, holding a jar of wine high. "I'm the prize, lad, d'ye know it?"

I left her to the bodies and strode on. Screams, shouts, singing, the ringing of ax blades clashing, and the breaking of glass came to me from the darkness beyond the occasional burning building or furniture bonfire that I passed. I reached the neighborhood of Madame Yvendel's secret academy.

"Danolarian!"

I dodged and spun about at the voice, then Lavenci stepped out of the shadows.

"Ladyship, you should not be out here!" I exclaimed.

"The correct form of address is 'darling' or 'truelove,'" she replied, waving her hands impotently. "Danolarian, I must speak with you before you enter the academy."

"But it's dangerous out—"

"Shush and listen! Not an hour ago my half sister made a joke about you sleeping with her while I sleep with the Lupanian boy for the next seven years. Believe me, please, I shall *never, never* do that, my love. Please understand, I wanted you to hear it from me before some stupid misunderstanding sunders us again. I am *not* sleeping with him."

"I trust you, Lavenci. Why do you worry about a joke?"

"I do not want any possibility of you being hurt again. I— I have been seeing a lot of Azorian. After he completely healed my hand, and he revealed vast amounts about Lupan and his people's sorcery and cold sciences. Mother and I have sketched him in every detail, tested his strengths and castings, and even taken samples of his hair, blood, and the like. He . . . he also did something else with me—no, nothing like that. After he healed my hand he began to make me slightly Lupanian."

I blinked. "How—or should I say why?" I asked. "Please explain."

"Azorian, a Lupanian male, can touch me. He thought that if I had the inner form of a Lupanian, the constancy glamour would no longer affect me. He changed me inside, so that my life force is now Lupanian. Please, hold out your hand, I want the first man I touch to be you."

I extended my hand. Lavenci's pale fingers hovered so close that I could feel the heat from her skin. Her hand closed on mine—and sparkles of blue flashed behind her eyes as her body convulsed, racked by the constancy glamour. I had to let her pick herself up off the ground unaided.

"It is as I feared," she whispered, standing before me with her head bowed. "The glamour repels all male humans. Making my life force Lupanian did not help."

"Perhaps if he changed me, so that I was Lupanian?" I suggested.

"That may not be possible for a while, Danolarian. Azorian is very sick."

"Sick?" I exclaimed, instantly alarmed. "How?"

"I am not sure, but his fabrication spell is a very severe strain when working on live bodies. Building a tripod tower is child's play by comparison. Over four days he spent three hours out of every four refabricating either you or me, and apparently only one hour in four is considered dangerous."

"He is our only friend among the Lupanians. His loss would be a catastrophe."

"I know. After the attacks of this afternoon he worked more frantically than ever. He sat with me in the fabrication spell for six hours without a break, but then he just toppled and fell. He is asleep now, best to leave him resting. I'm sorry, this will cast a pall over the evening, but I still want you to eat with us."

We began to walk for the entrance to the academy.

"Have you heard about the Wayfarers?" I asked.

"Yes. You are to escort people out of the city tomorrow, before the Lupanians arrive. I shall have to stay here. Laron has plans for a squad of scholars to stay within the city, in hiding. We shall study the Lupanians when they take over, learning about their cold sciences and magic. The city is full of secret, hidden, forgotten places. Mother thinks we shall be safer here than out on the plain. She has spent much of her life not being noticed by the authorities, so she should know."

For a dozen or so heartbeats we stopped and stared into each other's eyes. There was so much to say, but I had contained myself for so long that I could not release my tongue to speak freely. I thought to skirt the subject, then edge inward.

"In seven years you will be free of the constancy glamour," I began.

"That is the theory," she replied, now frowning. "Will you really wait seven years for me?"

"I shall look upon it as a chance to prove my love for you."

"Your love, for me," she said dreamily, with a little smile. "I had despaired of ever hearing those words from you." She now looked up, but her face was full of concern and worry. "Danolarian, it may be more than seven years," she explained.

"But why?"

"Remember, a glamour cannot be lifted unless both partners are alive. Remember too that mother has influence. I suspect that she used that influence to have someone else hanged in Pelmore's place. She wanted him alive to continue her experiments to free me earlier."

"I did see him hang," I assured her.

"You saw *someone* hang. That man had a comfortable padding on his stomach, I questioned Laron about that. Pelmore's stomach resembled a washerboard, I of all people should know." It was now that Lavenci broke up, and began to sob. "So unfair! I know how Pelmore feels beneath his clothing, Danolarian, yet nothing of your body."

She led me into Madame Karracel's Exclusive and Intimate Services. Begun as a mere front for the Academy, it was now making an impressive profit. In the lounge, several alluringly dressed women smiled and waved, then we walked down a passageway. Part of a brick wall swung back at Lavenci's touch. Beyond it was complete blackness. With the door closed again, she conjured a soft glow in her palm then led me through a maze of corridors, passageways, courtyards, stairways, and doors. Finally we stepped out . . . into what was in-distinguishable from a room in Diomeda!

There were beaded, tasselated hangings everywhere, soft, deep rugs underfoot, incense burners, and piles of huge, heavily embroidered cushions encrusted with beads, mirrors, and polished semiprecious stones, and candles held by iron dragons in various poses, not all of them very dignified.

A sparkling curtain of beads was drawn aside, and Madame Yvendel, the tall, svelte, elegant woman of indeterminate but mature years, walked out to greet us. She was dressed in silks that would have been exotic even in Diomeda, and while there was a sprinkling of grey in her long, black hair, her legs could have belonged to a woman in her twenties. Her silk robes managed to show a great deal of those legs, of which she was obviously proud.

"Where *is* your guest?" she asked imperiously, after a glance at my Wayfarer's clothing. "And why have you brought your guard in here?"

"Mother, this is Danolarian Scryverin, Inspector, Wayfarers, West Quadrant."

"Charmed, ladyship," I managed, bowing.

"Danolarian!" she exclaimed. "My apologies for not recognizing you, the light is dim in here."

"No excuses, Mother," said Lavenci in triumph. "You forgot him, and there's an end to the matter."

"Forgot him? Ridiculous! I remember the night he rescued you and brought you home. You had two broken ribs from the Inquisition Constables. Silly girl, all you did was kiss him goodnight, and ask when he would be at the Lamplighter again. When your father rescued me from the dungeons of the summer palace at Narmari, why I had him into bed with the breath knocked out of him before his drawers had even hit the carpet."

"Mother! Really!"

"What?"

"Try to show more sensitivity when discussing my conception."

"Whatever."

Madame Yvendel circled us once, obviously appraising me. "So, will it be one more for breakfast?"

"Yes!" snapped Lavenci.

"Wait a moment, what about the constancy glamour?"

"We *can* share my bedchamber and we *can* share our nakedness, even though we may not touch," replied Lavenci, with a firm, dangerous edge on her voice. "Besides, Danolarian can kiss and caress my hair."

"Well, allow me to be of the same service as your hair," Yvendel said brightly as she stepped between us. "Lavenci, Danolarian, take my arms and I shall escort you into the dining room."

Madame Yvendel led us into another, similarly furnished, room, where a meal that was exotic and generous, rather than sumptuous, was set out on a low table. We lay down on cushions, Diomedan style, and began to eat various dips on flatbread. I passed tests in Diomedan etiquette, having lived a short time in Diomeda. There was a place set but vacant, probably for Wensomer, I surmised. Lavenci and Yvendel bickered continually. I felt like asking a few pointed questions about Pelmore, but refrained for the sake of good manners.

A gong sounded somewhere in the distance.

"Ah, Wensomer at last," said Yvendel.

We stood up as Wensomer entered. She was wrapped in what looked to be quite a heavy cloak, given the heat of the summer night. She swept it off and cast it aside, revealing some scraps of red meshwork and jewelry, a pair of sandals, and nothing much else. She also looked exceptionally fit, and had the best developed abdominal muscles I had ever seen on a woman.

"Look, it's the succubus costume I wore for my fourteenth birthday revel," she cried, holding her arms out. "It fits again."

"It may not if you breathe too deeply," observed Lavenci.

"Mother, we might have a problem, due to the arrival of—who is that?"

"Wensomer, may I present Danolarian," said Madame Yvendel.

"My sweetheart!" declared Lavenci firmly.

"Your sweetheart," said Wensomer, nodding knowingly. "Except for the constancy glamour—wait a moment. Alpindrak, the inspector from the Wayfarers who tracked me there, er, Scryverin, is it? The youth with the rather nebulous past? Lavenci's former sweetheart—except that you still are?"

"Your servant, ladyship," I said with a bow.

"Well, I really was hoping to meet you in better circumstances, and here you are. Does Lavenci need someone to occupy your talents while her constancy glamour is wearing off?"

"No I don't!" snapped Lavenci.

"Pity. Inspector, had the light not been so bad at Alpindrak Palace, I might not have flown out of your company so soon. Strange, you are not a spotty student, lecherous academician, homicidal peasant, or even a seven-hundred-year-old reformed vampyre. Lavenci usually likes them peculiar."

"You should talk!" called Lavenci. "You married a corpse five years dead to become empress."

"True, but I did not sleep with it. From what I heard of Pelmore—"

"You tried to seduce a man whose penis was a small dragon that hated women. Then you turned him into a cat!"

"*That* was an unfortunate accident."

My imagination seriously contemplated suicide after trying to conjure an image of a human-shaped Wallas getting into bed with Wensomer.

"What family does not have the occasional frank exchange of views?" asked Madame Yvendel, putting an arm around me and gesturing back to the table.

"Oh no, you must take a place beside me," said Wensomer, bracketing me from the other side and pressing a rather large breast in red netting against my chest. "I have done more work on your origins, and a certain reccon who served with you four years ago says that you had a strong Torean accent, and that you worked fanatically hard to change it."

"You're right, I am Torean," I admitted, and out of the corner of my eye I saw Lavenci wink, then nod discreetly.

"I knew it!" Wensomer exclaimed in triumph. "I am part Torean too. Mother once made one boast too many, and I worked it out. I think it is so romantic, being from a people of a dead continent. We Toreans must stand together, except when lying down, of course."

Lavenci put her hands on her hips and faced us squarely with a very stern look on her face.

"Sister dear, this is getting all very tiresome," she declared. "If you wish to seduce Danolarian and exercise his primary sexual characteristic until it screams for mercy, then go ahead, it is between you and him. I certainly will not be able to do the like with him for seven years, and I suppose I should not be selfish. One the other hand, I would strongly advise you to ask his birthname before you do anything rash."

"Birthname? Very well Danol, what is your birthname?"

I cleared my throat, then looked from Yvendel to Wensomer.

"Darric Gregoral Warsovran," I said in as steady a voice as I could manage.

As slowly as if they were moving through water, Yvendel and Wensomer disengaged from me and drew back, eyes wide and jaws hanging slack.

"Melidian's son," whispered Yvendel.

"My brother?" gasped Wensomer.

"Half brother, actually," I said as casually as I could.

"My brother!" said Wensomer excitedly. "I should have guessed. You showed so much skill, tracking me across all of Greater Alberin. Did I tell you I watched you play the sun down on Alpindrak? My brother. Do you do magic?"

"No."

"Pity. Look, do lie down at your place. Taboulan garnish? Holvis? Tarengan?"

The serving maid entered with a plate of savory chicken pieces.

"Mirriel, have you met my brother Danolarian?" called Wensomer.

"Charmed, sir."

"He fought in the Charge of Racewater Bridge, on the side of Princess Senterri."

"And he's my stepson," added Madame Yvendel.

"And he's my sweetheart!" Lavenci pointed out rather more loudly than was necessary.

The serving maid hurried away with some empty plates. Wensomer drained a goblet of wine. Not to be outdone, Lavenci did likewise. Madame Yvendel suddenly got up and left without a word.

"How could a spineless wonder like you charm the hearts of my brother?" said Wensomer.

"I find Lavenci enchanting," I began.

"She knows nothing of the real world, she's a social cripple," laughed Wensomer.

"*You* always had freedom to do anything!" snapped Lavenci. "I didn't."

"And everything that I did, *you* came along and did better!" retorted Wensomer, suddenly reddening. "Took me five weeks to solve the enchantment-stability equations of Lel Vestoller the Wise. You did them in half an hour."

"You should have left the ether values as variables and inverted the—"

"You use your intelligence to humiliate me!"

"Well, you're too lazy to use *your* intelligence. Besides, I never became empress."

"Well, you've lined up the Emperor of All Torea to be your bedmate!" Wensomer shouted back.

"Ladies, please," I begged, but nobody seemed to notice me.

"You were always the star of every revel and feast!" cried Lavenci. "The men always crowded about you."

"*You* seduced *my* Laron on the *roof* of the *academy* during his *graduation reception*! I was so humiliated."

"*You* made a point of seducing *every one* of my partners, *including Laron.*"

"You bettered every one of my academic triumphs, you always did in hours what took me months, you little bitch!"

"Little? I'm three inches taller than you!"

"My curves are better. What do you think, Danol?" I opened my mouth. "See? He agrees. He's my brother. He'll always be my brother. You are only his sweetheart. He may leave you."

"Ladies, ladies," I cried, but at this point Madame Yvendel returned.

"Danol, you may like to see this," she said, opening a large folder. "Here is your father's graduation scorecard for 3112, see, his marks were very high. Here's the love letters he wrote and left under my door, and this is a picture of the ship he fled home on when he heard I was pregnant."

"With me," said Wensomer.

"What else? A lock of his hair, our first condom—"

"Somewhat redundant by then," Lavenci pointed out.

"Here's the key that Rax Einsel duplicated and used to free me from the dungeon in the summer palace."

"Rax was *my* father," Lavenci reminded us. "He was a deadly shot with a crossbow."

"I called him Uncle Rax, he was a nice man," I said.

"Was he really?" asked Lavenci.

"I've always wanted a brother," said Wensomer, reaching unsteadily for another jug of wine and raising an eyebrow at Lavenci. "Have you met my brother?"

"Yes!" snapped Lavenci.

"Here's a sketch I did of Rax," said Yvendel. "Rather heroic, I think."

"I remember you!" Wensomer suddenly exclaimed, taking my hand. "My first voyage to Torea, I was disguised as an ambassador's daughter. It was in the summer palace at Narmari. You and I bored a hole in the back of the royal privy and we played "Whose Botty Is That" until the guards chanced upon us. We had to apologize before the entire court."

"I was very young," I said pressing a hand over my eyes for a moment.

"What a wonderful stepson," said Madame Yvendel, absently picking up the goblet that Wensomer had just filled and draining it. "I'm tired of being surrounded by women, spotty youths, and bloodless sorcery academics. You are a fine young man, I'll have a spare room made up."

"He sleeps in *my* room in *my* bed!" shouted Lavenci.

"You can't even touch him without being sick," retorted Yvendel.

"He can hold my hair," replied Lavenci. "Danolarian, I want to apologize for my family."

"Have you forgotten about mine?" I sighed, by now regretting that I had not just invited her down to the Lamplighter and taken my bagpipes.

"What was it like, growing up as Warsovran's son?" asked Wensomer.

"I was given everything," I replied, relieved to be on a neutral subject. "I learned languages, archery, riding, astronomy, medicraft, the ways of command, the skills of strategy—"

"I meant girls. I heard that you lost your virginity to a princess on your thirteenth birthday."

"I'd rather not—" I began, by now rather beyond despair.

"I was fifteen and a half for my first time," said Wensomer.

"And I was fifteen," retorted Lavenci.

"See what I mean!" cried Wensomer. "She always has to go one better—and she did it with my favorite guard, too."

"You treated him shamefully," began Lavenci.

"Here is a sketch I did of your father in 3111, during classes," said Madame Yvendel.

"Would you like to see my soft-toy collection?" asked Wensomer.

Wensomer led me away to her bedchamber. Her soft-toy collection consisted of several dozen pink, fluffy dragons with silly grins and large genitalia.

"Really, it means so much to me to have a brother," she confided, grasping my arm with both hands while swaying rather heavily. "I'm tired of living in Lavenci's shadow."

"Er, but, you were empress, and you were the most powerful sorceress in Scalticar."

"Pah, raw power, who gives a toss? Lavenci is monstrously intelligent, she betters me in everything that matters, and she does it so easily. Promise you'll not side with her against me?"

"I'm sure diplomacy will triumph," I promised.

We returned to the dining room. Dessert featured another acrimonious exchange about former lovers, magical theory, disastrous experiments, important people and exotic, dangerous beings the three women had killed, spectacular hangovers they had experienced, and people they wished they had not woken up beside the next morning. After that, the serious drinking began. I had the impression that Yvendal, Wensomer, and Lavenci loved each other dearly, yet they antagonized each other beyond comprehension. It was little wonder that Lavenci had not been able to confide in them for courtship advice.

Yvendel was quite probably the most erudite scholar I had ever met, and Wensomer was the most powerful surviving sorceress on the continent, but Lavenci was actually the most intelligent of the three by a very large margin. I must have dozed for a time, and when I awoke, there was brightness at the top of the lightwell in the ceiling. Wensomer and Lavenci were having a targetry competition at a carving on the wall, Wensomer with little fire castings, Lavenci using table knives. Yvendel was stretched out with a lute and singing something about false lovers in Larmentalian.

"Ladies, it is dawn and I must go," I announced as I got up.

"But you were going to sleep here!" exclaimed Lavenci, then she glared at Wensomer. "You kept all that banter going all night deliberately!" she exclaimed accusingly.

"I did not! I was getting to know my long-lost brother."

Wensomer and Lavenci got up a lot less steadily than I had, and Wensomer held up some of her sister's hair for me to kiss before giving me what I thought was a somewhat more than sisterly kiss on the lips.

"I'll stay with the exodus until I can do no more good, or until the Lupanians attack," I announced to Lavenci. "After that I shall return here."

"Within two days we shall no longer be in this place," said Madame Yvendel.

"Then how can I find you?" I asked.

"Will Wallas be staying?" asked Lavenci.

"Yes."

"Then I shall have him check the laneway beside the Lamplighter at dawn and dusk every day. Just be there then, he will find you and lead you to us."

By now Madame Yvendel was on her feet and meandering across in my direction.

"Danolarian, I'm sorry that . . . er, I destroyed your career with . . . Wayfarers," she managed as she stood swaying before me. "I've got gold, somewhere, for you. Make up, for you, that is."

"None required, ladyship," I said, genuinely uninterested. "The world is dying, careers and gold no longer matter."

"Young Darric, hard to believe. D'you not miss, er, palaces, lovers, wealth, power?"

"No. I fled from them, and I would never go back, even if they still existed. I do not want to become like my father."

"Neither do I!" agreed Wensomer, draping herself over me. "Took a lot of orgies to prove it, too."

Madame Yvendel clapped her hands smartly.

"Bid your goodbyes and be away, everyone, I must talk with the young inspector before he leaves."

"No!" snapped Lavenci. "*I* want to see Danolarian after you are done."

"Then I shall take him to your room. Now go."

Madame Yvendel seemed to pull herself together surprisingly quickly once we were alone. I surmised that she had been feigning drunkenness.

"Lavenci is a romantic girl, not wildly hedonistic like Wensomer," she said. "Please, never hurt her feelings. I ask that as her mother."

"Madame, I have already gone to great lengths to protect her."

"So I have noticed. People say I am rather too liberal, in fact many would say I am downright immoral, but I love my daughters. Lavenci's soul is vulnerable. She's like me, she tries to be in control all the time, so most of her lovers have been spotty, chinless tossers, nothing people who could never inspire love. She thought Laron was another of those when she seduced him, and she got a wonderful surprise when she learned how thrilling a bold, chivalrous, honorable lover could be. The trouble is that Laron . . . has problems. He has seen too much for too long. He's an old man's mind in a young man's body.

"Then she met you, and for those few days that you courted her I heard nothing else but Danolarian stories. She wanted her first night with you to involve perfumed sheets, a gown of Cathenir silk, soft lights, romantic music that she had composed for you and you alone, the feel of your body against hers for all of the night's hours, then awaking in your arms. She wanted to walk out into the streets of Alberin with you, proudly holding your hand. She has never done that with anyone else, take my word on it, and she says nobody has yet seen her totally naked. Her bedroom is still waiting for you, perfumes, gown, candles, lute, songs, and sheets not yet slept between by any other man."

"Madame, please. I am not sure I can take much more of this, it is very upsetting."

"Ah, my apology."

"I must go soon."

"Do so, and with Fortune's blessing."

"Er, but may I have one last question answered?"

"Ask."

"Did someone else hang in Pelmore's place?"

"Is this a trick question?"

"No."

"I have no idea," she said with a shrug. "The directant of Wayfarers told me that you would not relent, and that the execution would have to go ahead."

"Are you sure?"

"I would not lie to you, Danolarian, take me at my word. I may not be well behaved, but I am honorable. Come now, time for you to pay Lavenci a visit."

I was left at a door with a white fist clutching lightning bolts painted on a black background sprinkled with stars. I knocked, and little tendrils of enchantment swirled about my fist, presumably checking who I might be. The door opened of its own accord.

Lavenci was standing in a room jammed with hangings, trinkets, amulets, carvings, statues, and lanterns. The dark blue Diomedan carpet on the floor was so thick that it was like walking in grass, and incense that I recognized as a now rare Torean type was thick on the air. Lavenci lay down on a vast pile of cushions that might have been a bed. The door closed itself behind me.

"You wished to see me?" I asked, feeling somewhat intimidated.

Lavenci glided into an upright position, although she swayed slightly as she stood before me.

"I wish I could say you were the first to enter this bedchamber," she said as she removed a clasp pin from her neck. "Still, I can say that Laron was my only other guest here, and that I banished him from this place because of you."

"Lavenci—"

"Listen, please! No man has ever seen me completely naked, Danolarian, not even Laron. I always finished undressing beneath the bedcovers, or in total darkness. All I have to offer you is the sight of my nakedness, but even the constancy glamour cannot stop me doing that. Look upon me, Danolarian, and—"

Suddenly there was a scream from outside. Lavenci and I rushed out, and I drew my glass sword as we approached an open door at the end of the corridor. The little room was furnished with things that looked as if they did not quite fit in anywhere else, it was the sort of room set aside for guests.

Madame Yvendel was kneeling beside a bed, upon which Azorian was lying. Wensomer arrived behind us.

"He is quite cold," said Madame Yvendel in a distant, hollow voice. "He must have died early in the night."

Lavenci fainted into Wensomer's arms. With Azorian dead, my life force could not be altered to mimic that of a Lupanian. Lavenci and I were still barred from each other by the constancy glamour, with no chance of escaping it. Worst of all, with Azorian also died our world's only Lupanian ally.

Lavenci did not revive before I left, but at least this allowed me to kiss her lightly on the lips. The constancy glamour only worked on conscious people, and I wondered how many women had drugged themselves asleep so that they might share a bed with some lover.

"When she awakens, swear on your honor as my sister that you will tell Lavenci that you saw me kiss her," I said when Wensomer presented herself for her turn.

"Little brother, I swear."

"And within a minute of her waking up, not ten years hence."

"Damn. All right, I swear, I suppose."

"Swear definitely."

"All right, all right, I swear!"

Chapter Eighteen

EXODUS FROM ALBERIN

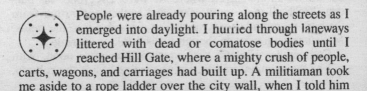 People were already pouring along the streets as I emerged into daylight. I hurried through laneways littered with dead or comatose bodies until I reached Hill Gate, where a mighty crush of people, carts, wagons, and carriages had built up. A militiaman took me aside to a rope ladder over the city wall, when I told him

that I was one of the Wayfarers charged with keeping order outside. While actually standing on the wall, I took a moment to survey the countryside. To the south and north of the city it is all flat, open coastal plains, but the foothills of the Ridgeback Mountains began only a mile from Hill Gate. Given the choice of flat, open country as far as the eye can see, and the shelter of nearby hills, forty-nine out of every fifty citizens were opting for the hills. In the streets and square behind Hill Gate was a solid, writhing mass of refugees, while outside was a ragged column of drab, dusty despair that extended as far as the turn at Tower Hill.

I descended the rope ladder on the other side of the city wall, then hurried away, parallel to the column of refugees. Because I was carrying nothing more than a pack with a waterskin and some dried meat, I moved quickly over the ploughed fields and through the ripening crops growing there. The fleeing citizens were not totally without order, but then there were only a hundred of us Wayfarers and militiamen to keep order among over a hundred thousand refugees. Thus what order there was might be described as minimal in the extreme. Fifty mounted militiamen had been sent on ahead to clear the road of outlaws, so the rest of us were left to try to keep order and minimize deaths in the torrent of desperate humanity that was pouring northwest for the hills.

I recognized Costiger about half a mile from the walls, and decided that here was as good a place as any to join the column. Andry was with him, and it soon became clear that we had no hope of keeping any sort of control, and that all that we could do was break up fights, and drag the fallen and injured clear of the road. The more aggressive of the refugees tried to attack us or order us about, and during the course of the morning I killed two and survived a dozen fights. The speed of the column was such that it covered about one mile every hour, but we Wayfarers stayed where we were. Everyone was burdened with all they could carry, and as they got farther from the city, more and more was being discarded into the fields. My water ran low, even though I was drinking sparingly.

Commander Halland arrived sometime after noon, with five of the mounted militia. He was riding beside the column, back toward the city, and was leading a prisoner whose arms were bound. Upon seeing Halland I called out and asked what conditions looked like ahead of us. He dismounted, removed his helmet, and ran his fingers through his hair.

"There are horsemen lurking about in the hills, watching," he said, keeping his voice down. "Some are outlaws, waiting for a chance to strike at the refugees and take some plunder. We've spent the morning riding down and killing the slowest of them. They were not the only ones watching, however."

He reached into a saddlebag and drew out a surcoat of blue that was stained with dust and blood, and bore several cuts. At the center of the chest was a large orange starburst of six rays with two tiny white stars to either side. There could be no more universal symbol of Lupan.

"You—you took this from, er, a man?" I whispered.

"Yes, but his horse, armor, weapons, clothes, all were from Juriar Province. There were three of them, keeping their distance. We gave chase without realizing who they were, just to drive them off. This rider's horse trod in a rabbit hole and went down, we would not have caught him otherwise. I had him bound, and had to gag him too. He was raving about the gods from Lupan who were here to conquer us, and cast down the defectives and degenerates from Empress Wensomer's rule."

"She reigned over the three most peaceful and prosperous years in Greater Alberin's history," I pointed out.

"Which was not to the taste of some folk, apparently. The Lupanians are recruiting humans, and there are some very willing recruits out and about."

"And you say they are watching the exodus?"

"Yes. I suspect that our people are marching straight out into the hands of the invaders and their minions."

I took off my helmet and flung it to the ground, then rubbed my face in my hands. By now several other militiamen and Wayfarers had gathered around to listen. Among them were Andry, Costiger, and Riellen.

"Well what are we to do?" I demanded of nobody in particular. "There are tens of thousands left in the city, all trying to get out onto this road and flee. We can't force them back, not even with ten times our numbers."

"I thought to deliver this character to the acting regent for questioning," said Halland, with a jerk of his thumb in the direction of the prisoner. "My plan is then to ride ahead and destroy a bridge. What do you think, Inspector?"

"Why bother, Commander?" I replied. "Every bloody carpenter and stonemason in the city is in that crowd, they would have it rebuilt faster than you had knocked it down."

"But on the road these people will be starving in very short order," said Andry. "Thousands will be dead by this time tomorrow from accidents, attacks from outlaws, and fights among each other. They must go back to Alberin."

"But in a few days the Lupanians will be back, and the city will be a death trap," I pointed out.

"Inspector Scryverin, with respect, you fought back in Gatrov, and brought down a tower," said Costiger. "They don't sound all that tough."

"Oh aye, but Gatrov was still destroyed, and more cylinders are arriving daily."

"So what do we do?" demanded Andry.

"Well I think the oppressed and suffering people have had enough!" cried Riellen.

"I agree, Constable," responded Halland, "but it's what to do about it that's got me floundering. Perhaps we should destroy the bridge at the Redstone Gorge, then station what cavalry and archers we have on the other side to stop the crowd rebuilding it."

"You would fire on *our* people?" asked Andry, aghast.

"It's for their own good!" retorted Halland.

"That makes us no better than the Lupanians and outlaws!" I shouted.

"Then you give the orders!" Halland shouted back, ripping the field command sash from his shoulder and flinging it at me.

"We should recruit a field militia from the crowd and use them to keep order," suggested Andry.

"While the crowd does what?" demanded Halland.

I sank to the ground as they argued, my head in my hands. We were beaten, there was nothing more certain than that. We had no strength, no plan, no advantage, and certainly no control. This was anarchy, on a road into the wilderness. Everyone was frightened, and all that they could do was run. We had been deserted by our rulers, and now we were fighting among ourselves. Sounds washed over me: the bells and gongs ringing out back in the city, the wailing of children, curses, cries, screams, the rumble of wagons, whips cracking, the tramp of boots, desperate shouts that "The Lupanians are coming!," and through it all, the forlorn, piercing cry:

"Brothers! Sisters! People of Alberin! Why are you fleeing? Are you going to let the alien imperialist tyrants take Alberin without a fight?"

I put a hand to my eyes, took a particularly deep breath, then stood up, straightened, and looked around. About a hundred feet away was a small, thin figure standing on an overturned cart, waving a lightweight fencing ax in the air. I bent over, snatched up Halland's command sash, and held it high.

"You give me command, I'll take command!" I shouted, and those around me immediately fell silent. "Halland, ride across the fields to Riverside Gate, take this traitor to the palace, then report back here. The rest of you, drag the fallen from the road, and keep the road clear of discarded goods. Our objective will be to keep people moving for the hills with the best speed they can manage."

"But—" began Andry.

"Silence! Our objective is to save whatever few we can. If the number is but one out of a thousand, then that is what we shall do. Halland, put your prisoner on a horse to make better haste, and leave your men here to help until you return. Well? You have your orders! Obey them!"

My father was suddenly alive again, and men were saluting smartly and hurrying to do what I had said. My heart sank. The hand was on my shoulder, and I dared not look down to check whether the foot was a cloven hoof. It was too late, I had done the one thing I swore I never would. I had taken charge. Only a miracle could save me now, and only an even greater miracle could save the world. I took Costiger by the arm.

"Constable, go get Riellen off that cart and give her my orders," I said, pointing to the tiny, gaunt, gesticulating figure. "We shall drag the fallen off the road, and we shall keep the others moving. *Nothing* else!"

"Yes sir."

I turned away from them and got to work. A heavily overloaded woman fell only yards from me, and a man begin to kick her and shout curses. I pushed my way over, spun him around, punched him in the face, then pushed him away. It took at least a minute to drag the woman through the press of the crowd, and as I pulled her clear I saw that the prisoner was being hoisted onto a horse and tied into the saddle. Andry staggered clear of the crowd with what looked like a trampled bundle of cloth over his shoulders. Again I became aware of the thin but strident voice.

"If you flee now, you only put off slavery!" Riellen was shouting to the weary and frightened procession of despair. "Slavery for yourselves, and slavery for your children. The children who look to you for protection, for shelter, for leadership!"

"Ya can't fight thunderbolts, lady!" called a mud-spattered man who had moved aside from the crush. He had four children with him, but no wife.

"The Lupanians may fight with thunderbolts, but we *can* fight back!" cried Riellen. "A snake cannot use a battle-ax, but a snake can still slay a warrior. Rats do not have crossbows, but it's hard to kill a rat with a crossbow. People of Alberin, the Lupanians are sweeping all before them because our stupid, unelected kings send armies to fight them. That is not the way! We must lay traps for them, harass them, give them no peace, slay their servants, and burn whatever they might capture. We will fight for Alberin, but we will burn Alberin if they take the city. The free voters of Alberin can *never* be beaten!"

By now I had pushed my way through the scatter of refugees who were using Riellen's oratory as an excuse to stop for a rest. I suddenly realized that among them was Costiger.

"I thought I told you to get her down and away," I said, taking him by the arm again and pointing at her.

"That you did, sir."

"Then why's she still up there and shouting shyte?"

"Well sir, what she's saying is sort of inspirin'."

"What? But you're a constable of the empire, and under orders!" I exclaimed. "My orders! There's bodies and injured to be dragged off the road."

"Due respect, sir," interjected Costiger, "but the empress is gone, the city's being abandoned, and command's away te dogs. You say run, so that one in a thousand lives. Riellen says fight."

I was caught off-guard by this. Empress Wensomer was long gone, the regent and his military commanders had fled, lower-rank officers were making decisions that were normally reserved for nobles, and I had assumed command well beyond my authority. I was following the only course possible, helping the few and fit to escape while flinging the many to the wolves. There was no other way, yet . . .

It was now that I noticed that most of those passing cast a glance in the direction of Riellen, even if they kept moving. Some had stopped. There were three dozen people crowded about the cart, and more were breaking away from those on the road all the time.

"We must stop the Lupanians *here,* or we shall *never* stop them!" Riellen was shouting. "Brother, sisters, stay and fight! We will pull down their proud fighting towers. Stand behind us! Stand up to the Lupanians! Stand and fight!"

Oddly enough, it was the Wayfarers and militiamen who were the first to sway in her direction. Halland joined us, along with three of his cavalry. Riellen was calling for people to fight, and they were fighters. Although she was a small, scrawny girl with spectacles—and a voice sharper than an assassin's dagger—she was also dressed in a Wayfarer's tunic and trousers.

"But what's to be gained by dying, miss?" called a marshal of the militia.

"We must give the Lupanians no targets, brother. No armies marching out to meet the mighty Lupanian fighting towers and their death fires. We must lie in hiding, and give them a hail of stones, arrows, and hellfire oil as they pass. We must cut down their turncoat followers. We must make the price of victory too high for the Lupanians. Who will stand with us?"

"We're with you, Miss Riellen!" called Costiger, waving a fist.

"But who'se yer commander, miss?" called a female voice.

"Aye, Miss Riellen," called another. "Who d'yer mean when yer say us?"

"The *people* are my commander," she replied, casting her eyes over the onlookers hurriedly. "But there, one of them is Commander Halland of Gatrov. He killed two Lupanians in their voidship. With him is Inspector Danolarian, who brought down a Lupanian death tower in the battle for Gatrov, and who stole a voidship and took two Lupanians prisoner. Even the Metrologans and Skepticals are with us! Their scholars are probing the voidship for the secrets of their magic and weapons."

That is definitely stretching the truth a little, I thought.

"You means all them great folk is with us here and now?" called an incredulous voice.

"Aye, that we are!" shouted Halland.

Suddenly everyone was cheering. Looking around, I saw that the line of refugees had broken, and was swelling around Riellen and the broken cart.

"Regent Corozan has fled the city and made a pact with the Lupanians' lackeys, but Revolutionary Brother Acting Regent Laron has stayed in Alberin to organize us!"

I blinked. I was fairly sure that Laron was unaware of his new title.

"The great Revolutionary Brother Roval, the last of the Special Warrior Service, will train those who stay. Acting Regent Laron will organize you! Revolutionary Commander Halland will lead you! Revolutionary Inspector Danolarian will fight alongside you. Brothers! Sisters! Don't let them face the enemy alone. Fight for your city! Alberin is *your* city. Cut down the Lupanians, smash their fighting machines, drown their heat weapons, and scatter their traitorous lackeys. Set up a voters' state with no king and no emperor!"

"But Laron worked for the empress, and for Regent Corozan," shouted someone from back in the crowd.

"Brother Laron was sent to the palace dungeons by the Regent Corozan for spreading revolutionary wisdom, and Brother Inspector Danolarian liberated him!" explained Riellen.

"That Brother Laron's a nice, sensible lad!" called a haggard, elderly-looking woman.

"Then vote for him, sister. I like Laron, too. I shall vote for him when we have elections for the presidian of Alberin. And when we have our presidian elected, let us all stand together, *all* of us! Soldiers, washerwomen, priests, lamplight women, initiates, artisans, street sweepers, carpenters, merchants, and clerks! All of us, stand and fight."

By now the crowd around her cart was blocking the road, and people who had already passed were hurrying back.

"Sorry sir, but I'm with her too," said Costiger; then he pushed away through the crowd to stand by the cart.

I was left alone with my thoughts. Riellen had actually stopped the exodus. Those in authority had fled. The people of Alberin had been fleeing too, but with no idea of where to go. Who was in charge? Nobody. Who was leading? In theory, nobody. In practice I had to admit that Riellen was the only real leader within at least a hundred miles . . . unless I took over, and that was a very bad idea.

"So what's to do, Inspector?" asked a voice beside me. It was Andry.

"I . . . I think her words are sound," I said, afraid to say otherwise.

"I'm with her, Inspector," said Andry.

"I am too," added Halland. "Come on lads, time to be seen."

We got up onto the cart and gathered around Riellen, a girl of the very most junior rank in the Wayfarers. She took the cue with flawless timing.

"Here now are Commander Halland and Inspector Danolarian, to tell you how we will crush the imperialist, oppressor exploiters from Lupan!" she cried, taking Halland by the wrist and holding his arm as high as she could. "Commander, speak to us now, if you please."

Halland stepped forward to a crashing, thunderous wave of applause and cheers.

"I am not a deserter or a mutineer, but our rulers have deserted us, so I am taking action to protect you all," Halland began. *That's it, pure treason, we're now candidates for the death penalty,* I thought. *All we need is a Wayfarer inspector to arrest us.* "Our nobles have deserted us! Our regent has deserted us! Miss Riellen has guts, she says stay and fight. Regent Laron is brave. He has stayed to defend the city! I say that Miss Riellen and Regent Laron need all the good soldiers they can get. I'm with them too. I'm going back to Alberin!"

Once again, everyone was cheering, but everyone was by now about ten thousand people.

"Tell them what to do, sir!" called Riellen to Halland above the noise. "Tell them to follow you back."

"But we don't have a flag, banner, or pennant!" he pointed out, suddenly alarmed by what he was being given charge of. Conducting a rally was one thing, but making an undisciplined crowd follow orders is another entirely. What we needed was something to get them all together, to give them unity. What we needed was a chant. I remembered a lazy, sunny afternoon on a barge floating down the River Alber. It had been only ten days earlier, I realized with astonishment, but it seemed like decades. Riellen and Wallas had been composing chants. I took a lungful of air, raised my fists to the sky, and cried:

"*Ri-el-len!*
"*Will lead us!*
"*We'll never be defeated!*"

As a chant, it was not particularly sophisticated, but sophisticated chants are never rousing chants. To the frightened, leaderless people of Alberin it said that some girl called Riellen was with them. Whoever Riellen was, she was planning to fight the Lupanians. That automatically put her ahead of all the others in authority. She also had military-looking men rallying around her, so she was clearly a fighting leader. A fighting leader. She was a leader who was actually going to lead and fight. That inspired confidence. The crowd took up my chant, and within moments it was deafening.

"Commander, sir, why are they chanting about me?" asked Riellen, shouting to Halland to make herself heard.

"Because you're their leader, and they want you to know they're behind you."

"Me sir? No, no, no, no, what I want them to do is to go back to Alberin, where we shall hold a rally and elect representatives of the voters to—"

"Riellen! Wake up to yourself and look around you. There's ten thousand people gathered about this wagon who are waiting for your lead, because you are the *only* person standing between them and the Lupanian conquest of Scalticar—and maybe the world!"

"But sir—"

"Miss Riellen, do you have any orders for us?"

"Orders?" asked Riellen, whose plans had clearly not yet moved below strategy and into tactics.

"Miss Riellen, I respectfully suggest that we lead our recruits back to Alberin, where we will plan the defense of the city," he said, gesturing back in the direction of the city. "Is that your order?"

"But there has been no vote."

Turning away from her, Halland held his hands high for silence. Silence came quickly.

"I proposed that Miss Riellen be declared elector of Greater Alberin until elections are held," he improvised. "Who says yes?"

A thunderous roar was the response. To me it sounded like nothing in particular, but it was the right noise in the right place, at the right time.

"Who says no?"

Silence greeted the three words. The first electocratic movement in the history of the known world had conducted its first election, and now it had an interim leader.

Riellen refused to ride a horse. She said that it was the sort of thing a noble would do, and citizens should ride only if they needed fast transport. Thus it was that she led the citizens who had rallied around her on the half-mile trek back to their city on the shoulders of Costiger and Halland, who were the two tallest among us. They were all chanting my words: that Riellen united them, and that they would never be defeated. As they marched, the exodus from the city faltered, stopped, then began joining in the return.

Chapter Nineteen

ALBERIN AGAINST THE LUPANIANS

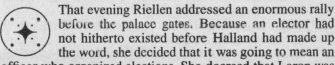 That evening Riellen addressed an enormous rally before the palace gates. Because an elector had not hitherto existed before Halland had made up the word, she decided that it was going to mean an officer who organized elections. She decreed that Laron was to continue as acting regent, and appointed Halland as commander of the Electocratic Militia of Alberin. In turn he ap-

pointed Roval as marshal general of Citizens' Militia Training. I was made one of several dozen marshal inspectors by Roval, which means that I was to decide which recruits could dispense with basic training, and which of them needed to be shown which end of a crossbow to point at the enemy.

"This is ludicrous," I muttered as Laron and I drank a beer in the former regent's private audience chamber. "Thanks to Riellen, nine tenths of Alberin's population is back in their homes, and countryfolk are arriving by the hour to join in the fight. Those under the regent's command are the bulk of the city's warriors, however, and they are safely in the summer palace, fifty miles away."

"Too true," said Laron.

"So, you have a city full of people awaiting your orders."

"Up yours, Inspector."

"What will you tell them?"

"You're trying to depress me. I condemn you to death, go away and kill yourself."

"Alberin still needs your orders."

"I'm open to suggestions."

"But you're the acting regent."

"I'm actually Revolutionary Acting Regent. Or is that Interim Brother Regent? I try not to listen when Riellen is talking."

"I'm only an inspector. That's a commoner, in case you have not heard."

"Commoners don't exist anymore. Only citizen voters."

"What are your orders, Citizen Voter Interim Regent Laron?"

"Perhaps Halland could lead."

"Halland's not an administrator," I pointed out. "*You* are needed to organize the city."

"Riellen is insisting on elections for presidian in three days."

"Are you going to, er, stand?"

"Riellen wants to see me about that once she finishes writing out a declaration of citizens' rights, and has had a meeting of the electoral advisors."

"What are they?"

"I'm not sure, but apparently I am one," Laron sighed with either resignation or hopelessness. "So are you."

"Sorry? The what?"

"The Revolutionary Interim Council Electoral Advisors of Greater Alberin on Lupanians. You are one of the few who has actually seen a Lupanian up close and lived to talk about it, so you qualify for membership."

The meeting of the electoral advisors took place in the former throne room. The throne had been taken out earlier, smashed up in the plaza before the palace, and the pieces consigned to a number of bonfires upon which supplies liberated from the royal siege stores were being roasted for the consumption of those whose food had been looted. We sat on stools at a very plain, square table, one to a side. At the first meeting there were only four of us: Riellen, Laron, Halland, and myself. Riellen commenced the meeting by drawing a line across each corner.

"Because I propose having eight people on this council, brothers, I propose that we cut the corners off the table so that we have eight equal sides," Riellen explained.

"Er, are not the legs under those corners?" asked Laron.

"Excellent point, brother, we must have the legs relocated as well. Now, I propose that we require a Citizens' Advisor. What others do we need?"

"Training Advisor," said Halland. "Oh, and Intelligence Advisor."

"Medicar Advisor," suggested Laron.

"I wish the meeting to consider a Sorcery and Cold Sciences Advisor," I said, meticulously avoiding a direct comment to Riellen, who I had still not forgiven for the previous three years.

"All of us should address the meeting if we are to be truly equal," Laron pointed out. "Citizen Danolarian has a good point."

"Excellent. Does the meeting accept this?" asked Riellen.

"Yes," we chorused.

"I nominate, er, the city crier for Citizens' Advisor," said Riellen.

"He is Citizen Wallengton, and I nominate Roval for Training," said Halland.

"Learned Justiva of the Metrologans for Medicar," said Laron.

"Academician Lavenci Si-Chella has better firsthand knowledge of the Lupanians than any other scholar," I pointed out.

"Has that been proposed to the meeting as a suggestion?" asked Riellen.

"Yes," I said firmly.

"Citizen Danolarian for Intelligence," said Halland.

"Declined!" I said flatly. "Acting Regent Laron can do better."

"Does the meeting accept those nominations?"

"Aye," declared the others, although Riellen hunched over a little as she spoke.

"Nay," declared my lone voice. "I have no place here, I propose that my place be left vacant for special advisors to be coopted as needed."

The next vote included the amendment, and was unanimous.

"Scribe citizens, are we speaking too fast?" Riellen asked those scribbling the minutes behind each of us.

"We're coping, Miss Riellen," said the youth behind Riellen.

"Excellent, now to business. I propose an election date three days from now. The people must see quick results from our reforms. Brother Laron, will you tell the meeting how the city is progressing with defense?"

"Well, folk have been ordered to gather every bow, crossbow, spear, and ax that can be found, whether it be in a cottage or the royal—er, former royal—armory. That gives people a notion that we are actually doing something. Every arrow and bolt must be gathered as well. Everyone who can make arrows and bolts must be recruited and put to work within the hour, and all militiamen—no, *everyone* who can use a bow or crossbow must report for drilling and instruction. That includes women, if they have ever used a bow in hunting."

"But the idea is not to take on the fighting towers directly!" protested Riellen.

"Quite so, elector, but the followers of the Lupanians form quite a sizable army, and they may need to be repelled," said Halland, anticipating Laron's thinking. "The fighting towers must be dealt with separately."

"May I point out to the meeting that the women and children of the city also wish to help?" asked Laron.

"They don't know how to fight," I pointed out.

"But how long would it take to teach a woman how to hit properly with a stick, and stab effectively with a kitchen knife?"

"Not long," I said. "I've arrested a lot of women who have done it to their husbands with no training at all."

"Brother Inspector Advisor Danolarian, the meeting requests that you see newly appointed Elector Advisor Roval about organizing a series of half-day seminars on hitting with sticks and throwing rocks," said Riellen, going to some effort to remain neutral. "When you are done, see Elector Advisor Wallengton about informing the citizens, and Elector Advisor Halland about appointing and briefing instructors."

And so the meeting progressed, rather like a very light wagon being drawn by a team of very strong horses that were galloping as hard as they could, while totally out of control. Some catapults from the merchant ships in Alberin's harbor were to be seized, operating teams gathered and trained, and dummy catapults assembled. Halland ordered every drop of pitch and oil in the city to be collected, along with rags and straw. Notices and declarations were sent out every quarter hour or so, but we remained. A carpenter arrived to modify the table. So did Wallengton, with a couple of dozen criers. Then came Roval, with one eye bandaged. Justiva arrived, and told me that I was needed outside the doors to the throne room. There I found dozens of people waiting for instructions from Riellen. Lavenci was there too. I beckoned her into the throne room, then across to a corner where we could whisper in private.

"She rules this city," hissed Lavenci, her black eyes huge with alarm. "She can have us killed anytime she wishes."

"You are thinking like a noble," I replied. "Riellen is the very opposite of a noble. *You* have been appointed to her council of advisors."

"Garbage! That was a trick to get me here for execution. They sent a carriage and a dozen guards. I only came here because I thought you were in danger."

"*I* had you appointed."

"I— what?"

"Lavenci, the carpenter seems to be finished with making an eight-sided table, and the meeting's next item will be a report on Lupanian cold sciences and magic."

"Oh, I must hear that."

"Actually, you're giving it."

At about 1 A.M. I finally escaped Riellen's meeting. Lavenci was condemned to stay there until all business was complete. That was liable to be when everyone was carried out, fast asleep. Being who I was, I was able to commandeer a cart, horse, and driver from the dozens that were lined up in the hope of being told to help in some way. I managed to sleep on the load of hay in the tray while I was being driven to the chambers of the public mortician. This was near Felons' Arch, above which was Pelmore's head on a pike. I had it brought down and held a lantern to it, but the birds had given it some attention by then, and there was nothing remaining of the face that was recognizable. Next I walked across the square to the public mortician's chambers.

Normally the headless bodies of executed felons were rowed out into the bay, where they were sunk with a bag of cobblestones tied to their ankles. That generally happened on the day of the execution, but public order had collapsed on that day. More to the point, the public mortician and most of his staff had fled. The sole remaining man on duty was Seetoll, who was pale, emaciated, and clothed in rags. If ever a man had grown to resemble the merchandise of his trade, Seetoll was that man. He normally took the night shift, because his appearance disturbed grieving relatives, who tended to call in during daylight. The sorts of people who came calling at night tended to be less squeamish.

"Pelmore, aye, never did get him off on his final voyage," he said when I asked about Alberin's last official public execution.

"Perhaps someone else took him?" I suggested.

"Not so, not so, I allus do the executed. Stendel's religious, and he says the bodies of the damned contain soul-polluting humors. Heavearn reckons they're more likely to 'ave ghosts, so he won't touch 'em." He indicated a body on a bench, covered with a brown blanket. Even with the blanket in place I could tell that the head was missing. "That's him. Most of him, anyhow."

I removed the blanket. The body was a day and a half dead, but the hot weather had him a little ripe already. The wrists were still bound behind his back. I took out my knife and slipped the blade beneath his drawers.

"Not gonna do nuffin weird, are ye?" Seetoll asked suspiciously.

I slashed the cloth and drawstring away. I was confronted with buttocks covered in blond hair.

"Aye, nattyral blond he were," said Seetoll.

"It certainly looks that way," I replied.

I had Seetoll carry the headless body to the mortician's boat, with instructions that it be disposed of in the usual fashion. I also tipped him twenty florins.

"Natural blond you were not," I whispered to the departing boat, "and neither were you really Pelmore."

I had been presented with a very good view of Pelmore's fundamental in Lavenci's room on the night that the first cylinder had fallen. The hair thereupon had been very dark, perhaps even black. Pelmore was not blond by birth, but neither did he bleach his hair below waist level. Some other prisoner had mistakenly been rendered blond all over. This being the case, whoever did it was not using Pelmore as a model. Thus Pelmore had escaped by then, and the hanging had been a cover-up.

A half hour later, the body of someone who had been hanged, then beheaded, was at the bottom of the harbor. I was on the way back to the palace, where I was quartered.

The following morning I was awakened in my palace room by Laron. The sun was on the horizon, and shining horizontally through my window. He closed the door after him and handed me a mug of hot caffin brew. I explained my allergy and handed it back to him. He began to drink it as I went behind the screen to wash and dress.

"News by carrier bird is that Dromdenburg fell to the Lupanians two days ago," Laron began. "Four towers and ten thousand human collaborators fronted up. One of the towers set the citadel afire with its heat weapon. The gates were flung open, and every pole in the city had a white flag run up without a single tripod tower stepping over the walls. The Lupanians sent in some human collaborators to accept the surrender, and these selected a thousand healthy adults as 'tribute.' The prisoners were herded off to the Lupanians, and apparently a large pile of crumbly bones and muck was later discovered by the man who sent the auton bird with the report. Bariosa fell to the Lupanians without a fight. The nobles and troops headed for the countryside, and the population followed them in quite a lot of haste. The Lupanians took over an empty city that was largely intact. Laffin tried to fight."

"Who would surrender to the Lupanians when they know what is going to happen?" I asked, coming back around the screen as I dried my hair.

"I said 'tried,' not 'fought.' Suffice it to say that four towers walked to within a quarter mile of the walls, grew castings in the shape of large, black globes, and tossed these over the walls with their tentacles. They burst as they landed, and generated a black smoke which killed everything that breathed it. The smoke became harmless dust after about a quarter hour, but by then nearly everyone in Laffin was dead. Our report came from a lookout who was keeping watch at the top of a temple spire. He later collected a sample of the dust as he fled, and our agent included it with his report."

"They definitely want the towns and cities intact, where possible," I said, stroking my beard.

"Yes, and those who fight for the Lupanians are treated better, by all accounts," said Laron, holding up a small glass phial.

"Looks like lampblack," I commented.

"It is lampblack. Lupanians magic somehow makes it poisonous for a quarter hour."

"Imagine what it could do in Alberin."

"Indeed. Before the war Alberin had a population of over a hundred thousand living within the main walls," Laron said, looking out of the window at the city. "Dromdenburg, Bariosa, and Laffin each have half that, or even less. The problem with this enemy is that sheer numbers are no advantage, however. Even if we had a million folk in Alberin, it would mean nothing against the heat weapon."

"But we also have a populace spoiling for a fight. The other cities did not."

"Laffin did. It also still had its army, kavelars, nobles, militia, and head of state," Laron pointed out, waving the report. "By my estimates, we still have ninety thousand people left, but no army. There are two battle galleys in the harbor, and their shipmasters have asked to meet whoever is running Alberin. Riellen is on her way to them now."

"Halve ninety thousand for the very old, very young, and the infirm, then halve what is left for the women, and you have just over twenty thousand souls who are even the right age and sex for fighting," I calculated. "Halve that again for those driving wagons, the carriers of weapons and supplies, the cooks, the messengers, and the medicars, and we would be lucky to have ten thousand."

"But women can drive wagons, cook, care for the wounded, and carry supplies for the fighters," said Laron. "Remember too, old veterans are already training the others. Even boys and girls are being drilled to run with bundles of arrows and bolts."

I rubbed at my wet hair again as I thought through all this.

"Very impressive, and were I attacking the city with a conventional army, I would be thinking twice about a direct assault. The trouble is that the heat weapon can start fires at two miles or more, and when several are focused together, they can be effective at over seven miles. The finest arbalast or ballista in Alberin could manage no more than a quarter mile. The Lupanians thus have around thirty times our range, and a far higher rate of fire. Add to this the smoke that kills, and . . . well, it's hopeless. I mean Riellen is very good at getting people running around, shouting slogans, and doing things for free, but all that enthusiasm will not be much good against heat weapons and poison smoke."

As Laron gazed out of the window at the rising sun, I picked up the phial of black dust and shook it. It resembled nothing more than ordinary lampblack

"What would you do, Inspector?" Laron finally asked.

I had a feeling that he would ask that question. I had been, covertly, arguing for surrender. Now I had to do it in the open, but I could not bring myself to do that.

"The Lupanians destroy and slaughter to teach us a lesson," I said slowly. "That means they want to avoid complete slaughter and absolute destruction. They want things intact, that is their only weakness."

"I know. I have a map with their conquests marked. There is a clear pattern. Except for Laffin, not a single city with more than twenty thousand souls behind the walls has been annihilated. Danol, there were only twenty of them sent over. They are not here to flush us out and kill us to make way for their people, they want to rule us. To rule, you need working cities and farms, administrators, artisans, constables, and even nobles. You need towns and cities. I agree with you. The invaders want to conquer as much as they can without total destruction and slaughter. That is indeed their weakness."

"But their *only* weakness—sir, with respect."

"Oh no, there are others, I have been talking with Commander Halland. The heat weapons shoot only in a straight line, but arrows travel in a curve. We can fire over a wall. They cannot. Then again, their fighting towers are made of spun-glass threads, we know that thanks to you, Azorian, and Lady Lavenci. It is a very strong material, but a direct hit from an arbalest bolt can breach it."

"An arbalest bolt has a metal tip. Remember, their magic turns metal aside. They are highly intelligent, they must have thought most of this through already."

"I wonder. Let us not confuse advanced magical learning and arts with intelligence, Inspector. My feeling is that these Lupanian warriors are their elite. In your experience, how intelligent are elite warriors?"

"Well, they generally have the wisdom to put their socks on before their boots, but Lupanian warriors may be different."

"I doubt it," said Laron. "But enough of that. Danolarian,

there is another matter that troubles me, a very personal matter."

"Yes?" I asked, puzzled. I had never had much to do with Laron at a personal level, even though we had known each other for three years. He looked uneasy, as if the subject were a sensitive one. I assumed that it involved Lavenci. I was wrong.

"Look here, about your Constable Riellen," he began.

"I no longer command her, sir," I interjected before he could say more.

"That is what disturbs me," he responded.

"Er . . . how so?"

"After the meeting ended, at about two A.M., she—she came to my bedchamber."

"No sense of personal space, that girl," I replied, not at all surprised.

"Then she took off all her clothes, and demanded that I, er, perform certain acts of a reproductive nature with her."

Now I was surprised. "Oh," I replied, but could think of nothing else to say.

"One very specific amorous act, in fact, and with no sheepgut security devices to be used."

"I see. And did you?"

"Yes, as a matter of fact. She said it was my patriotic duty. I asked *why me,* and she said that only someone good enough for Kavelen Lavenci was good enough for her."

"Goodness!"

"Well put. Lavenci and myself go back a long way."

"All the way, from what I've been told."

"It began late in 3140, in Diomeda. After that it was sort of on and off—"

"So to speak."

"Now look here, Danolarian, this is already hard enough for me!" snapped Laron, folding his arms tightly and staring down at the floor.

"Sorry sir, pray continue."

"Lavenci was a sheltered girl when younger, she needed a lot of medicar treatment for her eyes, on account of being an albino."

"The black dye for her eyes?"

"Yes. When her mother brought her to Alberin, well, we saw something of each other occasionally. Then she abandoned me for you."

"Sorry," I managed, although an attack of pride very nearly burst my chest.

"No matter. Now Riellen strides into my bedchamber while I am trying to take off my boots, and strips naked. She had the smallest breasts I have ever seen."

"May I ask what she was like?"

"You mean you don't know?"

"Don't be silly," I retorted, not a little offended at the suggestion.

"Well . . . probably somewhat virginal," ventured Laron.

"Probably?"

"Until now, my bedmates have tended to be rather, um, experienced, and generally older. Riellen did not seem to know what she was doing, and you have just confirmed that suspicion. She said if I did not cooperate, she would not lead Alberin against the Lupanians. Naturally I put Alberin's welfare before my personal misgivings, but, well, do you have any theories? I mean, she won't want to marry me or suchlike, will she?"

"She had a crush on me, and went to rather extreme lengths to keep other girls away," I explained. "It's all in my report. Mostly."

"No, Inspector, it is *not* all in your report, not even mostly. Everything that *you* know about is quite probably there, but there is sure to be more."

"If I learn more, you will be the first to know."

"Thank you."

He walked to the door, then turned back with his hand on the golden latch.

"Danolarian, you could have had my office on a silver platter. Why did you not want it?"

"Laron, do not ever ask me that question again."

✹ ✹ ✹

Having breakfasted, I set off across the plaza in front of the palace gates, and into the streets beyond. It is a very well known fact that idle people are more fearful than busy people, so Riellen had turned Alberin into something resembling an anthill with a honey pastry dropped upon it. Everywhere there were men, women, and children training, marching, drilling, carrying, and clearing away the wreckage of the vandalistic orgy of only two nights earlier. My duties involved those armed with just about anything that could fire something sharp in the direction of an enemy. A small number of the recruits in the new militia were women and girls, nearly all of whom could fire a light bow passably well. These were mostly noblewomen, or the wives and daughters of merchants. Some had also been taught to use light crossbows for social hunts in the countryside. The other odd thing was the sheer number of women doing pretty well everything else. They were driving wagons, carrying loads of arrows, distributing food, running nearly every stall that was still operating, dragging bodies out of laneways, and putting out the remaining fires. My overall impression was that women were running the city, and that it was no bad thing.

Down at the wharves, wagons with catapults mounted on their trays were driven past mock-up targets on wagons, with both driven at full gallop so that the crews could practice shooting at moving things the size of the cowls on the Lupanians' machines. This was going on at the wharves, so that if the bolts missed—and practically all of them did—they would fly harmlessly out into the harbor. Our siege engines would have only a single shot at a tripod tower before being annihilated, but a ballista had dropped a tower at Gatrov, so it seemed worth a try.

Hundreds of amateur and professional fletchers labored to make arrows and bolts, mostly in street workshops so that others could watch, and thus be trained en masse. I passed Essen and Andry drilling squads of pikemen for the inevitable attack, and noticed gnomes riding cats as part of my new messenger network.

All the while I collected names of people who knew how to shoot already, and sent the lists to the palace to join the archery brigades. Already Alberin had seven thousand rather promising archery recruits, and two hundred of them were women.

Everywhere there were posters. All had crude pictures of Lupanian tripod towers, and the messages were simple and to the point:

REGENT LARON SAYS WORK
COMMANDER HALLAND SAYS FIGHT
ELECTOR RIELLEN SAYS VOTE
COMMANDER HALLAND SAYS DEFEND YOUR CITY
REGENT LARON SAYS DOWN WITH LUPAN
ELECTOR RIELLEN SAYS EVERYONE IS EQUAL
REGENT LARON FOR PRESIDIAN
COMMANDER HALLAND FOR PRESIDIAN
DUKE FORNDAR FOR PRESIDIAN
ARCHPRIEST MARTISSEN FOR PRESIDIAN
INSPECTOR DANOLARIAN FOR PRESIDIAN

The last-named poster left me rather severely shaken. I ripped it from the wall, stuffed it under my belt, and resolved to shout at somebody about it as soon as was convenient.

Chapter Twenty

THE *MEGAZOID*

 Military training was hasty but intensive for the people of Alberin who were not already familiar with weapons. Everyone between the ages of twelve and eighty was given training in fighting with a length of wood in one hand and an eating knife in another. There were two basic moves: block with the piece of wood, then close and stab with the knife. Three standard ways of hitting with the piece of wood were also included, for those without knives. After five hours straight of block-and-stab practice in every street, square, plaza, courtyard, and market, the Wayfarers and militiamen had most of the city able to hit and stab with confidence, if not skill.

Another announcement was circulated at noon, and it detailed a short course on throwing rocks, by both hand and sling. Thus most of the city spent most of the afternoon twirling rocks held in folded lengths of cloth and slinging them at targets. Accuracy and range varied considerably, but at the end of the day I would say that out of every hundred rocks lobbed, five would hit a man-sized target at about a hundred feet. Those unable to throw competently were sent off for pike training—which meant learning to stand shoulder-to-shoulder across a street while pointing sharpened sticks eight feet long at a charging mob of maniacs.

In a sense I felt guilty because I was not training or being trained, but I kept telling myself that everyone's work was equally vital. The next meeting of the electoral advisors began at dusk, and featured eight brief and generally optimistic reports about progress in arming the city and discovering weaknesses in the enemy's weapons. Lavenci had particularly good news on the poison smoke. I was no longer required to attend the meetings, being important only as a symbol, but Lavenci kept me briefed.

"Azorian told me of the smoke weapon," she told me, holding up Laron's phial of lampblack. "A powerful casting spell is used to animate casks of lampblack into millions of little flying daemons. Each is the size of a pinhead, and they are charged with the desire to fly into the lungs of any living thing. There they cling to the wet inner tissue and explode as a small cloud of lampblack. This causes suffocation."

"Did he know of a counter?" I asked.

"Oh yes, it is very simple. Wet cloth worn over the mouth and nose, and wet gauze worn over the eyes. Moisture makes the lampblack autons explode, and thus spread the lampblack. Otherwise they lose their vitality after a quarter hour and explode anyway, leaving a black smear. If they hit water, they dissolve at once. I wrote out some instructions on using wet cloths to breathe through, then Laron sent out criers with posters telling people to have pails of water and wet cloths within reach at all times."

A squad of kavelars from the former regent was intercepted at the gates bearing proclamations that the city had already surrendered to the Lupanians. Apparently the summer palace had been approached by a tripod tower, and the regent surrendered at once. A baron was with the squad, and he had been appointed governor of the city. They were set upon by the militiamen guarding the gates, stripped of their weapons and armor, and flung into the palace dungeons for interrogation. The baron had said that an attack would come the next day if they were not allowed to report back by morning, using an auton bird.

"Tomorrow is too soon for them to move their human army to Alberin," I said when Lavenci had finished. "A forced march all day would get them to the city gates, but they would be exhausted."

"The baron said five hundred cavalry are camped about two hours' ride away, in the foothills."

"No, that is not enough to do more than enforce a surrender. It is the Lupanian tripods that will attack tomorrow. Will we be ready?"

"Riellen says so."

"From what I have seen, we'd need another five days to have the recruits steady enough to hold a line. Three days if we worked them exceptionally hard."

"Commander Halland says if we can destroy or damage one tripod tower, the others always break off to carry it away," said Lavenci hopefully.

"But come back very cross," I pointed out.

One good aspect of having friends in high places is that one has a great deal of freedom as long as one does not cost them money. Lavenci was busy with reports on the Lupanians, so instead of collapsing in the direction of my bed at once, I took a trip to the palace dungeons. These now contained just a baron and six kavelars. It was not these prisoners who interested me, however. There was a register of prisoners going back several months, and I was given access to this. Within the register was an entry for Pelmore, detailing when he had been admitted, the cell that had contained him, and who had handed him over for execution. There was a signature therewith, and all seemed in order. There were sixteen other entries active on that day, and a line had been drawn beneath these before the names of the baron and his kavelars appeared.

"Any idea what all these mean?" I asked the new keeper, tapping the page. "These entries that are not signed off?"

"Well sir, when I came down here with the Democratic Liberation Forces of the Free Alberinese Incarceration People's Militia, we found, er, this many bodies, all shot through with crossbow bolts. They was palace issue, so I'd reckon that the Oppressive Former Regent Lackey of the Expansionist and Imperialist Lupanian Invaders sent a squad o' c-bows down here to make sure none o' his enemies got liberated by those left in the city after he fled, like. Course—"

"I understand!" I said sharply, before he could draw breath and continue. "How many prisoners died?"

"I counted the bodies, just a minute and I'll tell ye."

He began to count off on his fingers. Having used up all fingers of both hands, he removed a boot, pulled off a sock, and counted out five toes.

"That many, sir," he said confidently.

"Are you very, very sure?"

"Oh aye, sir, 'cause I didn't have to take off me left boot, but I counted out all me toes."

Fifteen, I thought. Yet there were sixteen entries above the line that were not signed off. One prisoner was not accounted for. Perhaps Pelmore had not been the man executed. Perhaps Pelmore was still alive. Perhaps someone had set him free, or at least held him somewhere else. They had then taken out a physically similar prisoner, tied his hands behind his back, and bleached his hair, eyebrows, pubic hair, and even the hair on his arse. I checked the names. Ariosten, that was a Sargolan name. Many Sargolans had curly black hair, which would bleach well into curly blond hair.

Next I checked a dozen or so taverns for Ariosten, questioning the vintners and serving maids. At last one girl did remember him. There had been a fight over a lamplight girl, and in that very taproom. He had been arrested and hauled away to the magistrate. When it came to sentencing, there had been some problem about whether he should be hanged or beheaded, according to the girl. That was on account of his nationality.

"Big fella, he was," she said. "See this beam? When he stood 'neath it, his hair touched the underside."

The right height, I thought in triumph. Pelmore was also about that height. I returned to the dungeons. All of the guards who had formerly staffed the dungeons had either fled with the regent, died when the Inquisition building had collapsed, or were lying very low in the city. Thus I had nobody to question, but I do not give up so easily.

"Who maintained the persuasion equipment in here?" I asked the new keeper.

"Contract smithy."

Within the hour I was interrogating a blacksmith who was very anxious for his work in the torture chambers to be treated with discretion, and was thus exceedingly cooperative.

"Oh aye, I was working in there on the day," he said reluctantly.

"And did you see this man?" I asked, holding up a sketch I had made of Pelmore.

"Oh aye, nice piccy."

"What happened to him?"

"Why, you tortured him, sir."

"What? Me?" I exclaimed.

"Aye sir, and the tall, thin fella with you."

"So . . . what did I do?"

"You signed him out for special treatment. You said that the regent had granted you the right to give the felon a bit of a going-over, like, on account of him trying to poison you and all. Very considerate, that Regent Corozan—well, except for him being a counterrevolutionary, oppressive, oligarchical imperialist bloodsucker who—"

"What else?"

"Er, well, the guard in charge said I had to go with you, on account of a registered artisan having to be present to ensure proper operation of the persuasion equipment at all times. I went along, but when we reached the chamber door, you gave me a sign-off note for the rest of the day, and I went home. Got the note here."

The note was in *my* handwriting! Early on the morning of

Pelmore's supposed execution, two people had come down to the dungeons, removed him for torturing, then vanished with him. The executioner had then arrived, discovered that Pelmore had escaped, and told the regent. The regent had ordered someone to be made up like Pelmore, gagged and blindfolded, then executed. The glass dragons had then been defeated by the Lupanians, and the regent had decided to flee. He had sent guards down to execute those in the dungeons, presumably because some were his political enemies. The trail seemed to go cold at this point . . . but not quite.

Pelmore's rescuers were obviously not in league with the former regent. Thus they had probably not fled with him and his army, and thus were probably still in the city. Pelmore looked like Pelmore, and one of the others looked like me. They would be in hiding . . . yet one of them looked like me! Thus he would be confident about being seen as me, when out and about.

I returned to my quarters in the palace an hour before midnight, to find Lavenci curled up and asleep therein. I did not have the heart to wake her, so after scavenging a pillow and some bedding from nearby rooms, I curled up on the floor beside the bed and I slept as if I were dead. At dawn we were woken by one of the newly formed runner squad, and told that three Lupanian tripod towers were visible several miles away, advancing on the city.

The full story of the first Battle of Alberin is too well known to need another recounting from me. Wensomer and Yvendel had an overall view, as they had put auton castings on pigeons caught in one of the city squares, and spent the battle looking down at the city through the birds' eyes while reporting what they saw to Laron and Halland. My own story is as good an overview as anyone else got, however, as I was stationed on the tower of the Metrologan temple. My role was to observe and make notes in case the pigeons died. I had a farsight with me. I also had Wallas.

"Explain to me again why I am up here with you in one of the most exposed parts of the city, when I could be hiding in some exceedingly secure, deep, and comfortable cellar," Wallas asked, only his head projecting from my pack.

"Backup chronicler," I replied.

"Lower-Class Revolutionary Brother Inspector Danol, any attack that kills you will kill me, too."

"I didn't mean that."

"Then what?"

"You will see what is directly behind me."

"Use a human."

"You're a human."

"I'm a cat!"

"You're a human cat."

"But why have chronicles?"

"Because the Lupanians will annihilate Riellen's Electrocratic Militia. When that happens, the Metrologans will retreat into hiding and study them. These observations will help with the studies."

"Was that not the original plan?"

"Yes, but thanks to Riellen, instead of the citizens fleeing into the mountains to die of hunger, exposure, and a bad case of outlaw attack, the Alberinese have come back here to die of Lupanian occupation."

"But, but, what about all the arms and training?"

"Riellen's idea. Worse than useless against Lupanian tripod towers."

"So what is the plan of defense?"

"If there is one, nobody has told me— There! The tripod towers are moving again!"

Four Lupanian fighting towers were on the floodplain. The first three had been standing still for a time, apparently waiting for the fourth to join them, but now they were together, striding confidently for Alberin's walls. There was no Alberinese army standing ready before the city, or even on the walls. One tower raised its heat weapon and fired it, angling the beam over the walls. The roof of a large mansion in the exclusive south sector burst into flames. There was no retaliation from within the city, in fact no reaction whatever. Apparently deciding that the city was cowering in terror, the fighting towers strode onward. Not far from the walls they began hurling the black globes of poison smoke, and these burst and spread amid Alberin's streets and buildings. The tripod towers paused at South Gate. One tower blasted the massive wooden gates and crown arches to ashes; then the four of them strode single-file into the narrow streets of the city. Once within the walls, they separated.

It was now that Halland unleashed his first surprise. A bell began to ring, touching off more bells and gongs, and the ringing spread right across the city. As the ringing spread, thick, black smoke began to rise into the air.

"Poison smoke, all over!" yowled Wallas. "Where's my wet rag mask?"

"That's just our own fires, Wallas, they must be trying to spoil the enemy's view."

The smoke certainly spoiled the Lupanians' vantage from the hoods of their towers. My view was spoiled too, but then I was not trying to seize the city.

From this point onward, I can confidently say that the battle was an absolute and unmitigated shambles, yet because it was slightly less of a disaster for Alberin, Riellen was able to claim victory. Through my farsight, I could see a tower in the southwest of the city. It was cut off from its companions by a wall of smoke from around Bargeyards and the River Alber. I saw it stop, use its heat weapon on something ahead of it, then advance. Suddenly it stopped again, its tentacles hanging limp. Some smoke issued from its upper cowl, then dispersed.

"I think a tripod tower has just been hit by something," I observed for the benefit of Wallas.

"Is it annoyed?" asked Wallas.

"See for yourself, and report if it moves."

I looked away, trying for a moment to scratch my head through my helmet.

We later learned that the defense measures of the city left a lot to be desired. Squads armed with slings and pots containing a mixture of hellfire oil and pitch were roaming the city, looking for tripods to attack. At least a dozen buildings that were under construction and surrounded by scaffolding were mistaken for towers in the smoke, attacked, and set afire. The smoke itself came from thousands of pyres of pitch, rags, straw, and green wood, all distributed through the city, to be lit when the cascade of bell ringing began. Some squads attacked each other in the confusion, and one group actually set one of our own siege engines afire and killed the crew.

A tripod was striding over the houses in Bargeyards, advancing to where another tripod was standing. They ululated to each other as if arguing over who had started the fires; then the smoke of the burning city shrouded them from my view. I later learned that a squad of slingfires, as the sling militiamen with jars of burning hellfire oil were called, now chanced upon a tower's foot somewhere in the smoke swirling through Bargeyards. They began to whirl and hurl their jars of burning gunk skyward. At least five of the jars actually struck the top hood and spilled flames over the surface. One of those hit the faceplate.

The first I knew of it was two towers carrying a third, whose hood was smeared with burning oil, and which was trailing a lot of black smoke. For some reason they ignored the river, which was practically beside them, and made for the harbor.

"Oi, I see that tower in the south," called Wallas. "It's not moving at all."

"Keep watching, it may be a trick," I replied.

"Anything dangerous coming from harborside?"

"Just watch for dangers from the south."

The tripod towers waded into the water, continued out until their legs were about two-thirds submerged, then gently dipped the hood of the stricken tower beneath the surface. This extinguished the flames, and the rather badly blackened tripod tower was put back on its feet in the water while the other two towers ululated in vain to contact the fourth. The damaged tower now turned its blackened hood in the direction of Bargeyards and fired its heat weapon, in spite of the fact that the area was already burning.

When fighting an enemy that is not technologically advanced, but is nevertheless armed with ponderous but powerful weapons, it is an exceedingly bad idea to stand still for very long. Out on the harbor were two battle galleys, the *Megazoid* and the *Gigazoid,* and on their foredecks each had a ballista mounted. When word that the towers were advancing on the city reached the waterfront, every vessel bigger than a rowboat was ordered out to sea, but because the shipping channel through the reefs and shoals was narrow, a crush soon developed. Between the floundering deepwater traders and smaller vessels were the two battle galleys. Seeing the enemy in the water, the two insanely brave galleymasters decided that they were legitimate targets, and thus eligible for attack.

The truly remarkable thing is that the two galleys got relatively close before any of the Lupanians noticed. Finally a tower waved its farsight arm, as the towers do periodically, noticed the approaching galleys . . . and had a moment of uncertainty. The *Megazoid* was on my left, and the *Gigazoid* on my right, approaching the towers in a pincer movement. The tower took a couple of steps, to put itself to seaward of its damaged companion, then cast a black globe at the *Gigazoid.* The globe hit the raised boarding ramp at the bow, bounced off, and landed in the water where it bubbled fiercely. Lavenci said later that the Lupanian in the tower probably just wanted to kill the crewmen, leaving the galley intact for examination. Whatever the case, the *Megazoid* came on at ramming speed.

The tower now raised its heat weapon and fired a single, short burst at the *Megazoid.* It must have passed through the battle galley like a red-hot crossbow bolt hitting a silk battle pennant, but the beam of heat hit the vessel dead center—and thus missed the rowers, who were sitting to either side. It did, however, also strike the ballista that was on the deck behind the raised boarding ramp, setting its store of hellfire oil pots ablaze. Within moments the upper deck of the *Megazoid* was an inferno.

Now the tower turned to the *Gigazoid,* just as it dropped its landing ramp to expose its own hellfire-oil ballista. As it happened, the ballista crew had been winners of the Port of Alberin Siege Engine Challenge in the medium division for the past three years running, and could hit a ten-foot gate at two hundred yards. The hood of the fighting tower just happened to be about ten feet across. The ballista fired just as the heat weapon's ray hit the *Gigazoid.* A fifty-pound pot of hellfire oil flew true, and hit the tower squarely in the faceplate. It did not shatter, however. The Lupanians were apparently now using thicker glass. The tower began ululating for help, and the other two towers turned. By now the *Gigazoid* was burning fiercely and rowers were jumping for their lives, but the momentum of the sleek galley was driving it forward. The undamaged tower fired into the burning mass of the *Gigazoid*, but this only cut down some of its superstructure and did not diminish its speed. The battle galley collided with the tower, toppling it onto its own burning deck; then the burning mess continued on into the damaged tower.

The surviving tower now turned to its companions, striding after the burning, sinking mass of warship and towers, grasping for the hoods to rescue its companions. New towers could be built, but Lupanians and handling beasts could not be replaced. To this day I can scarcely believe what I saw next. It was the inferno that the *Megazoid* had become, with burning hellfire oil streaming out of its scuppers and flames and smoke trailing out over the water. Apparently the flames on the upper deck had not yet reached the rowers below, so that although even the oars were on fire, the galley came on. Back on the quarterdeck men were frantically beating at the flames with leather flails, trying to protect the two or three men at the steersman's pole. With no more than twenty yards between them, the tower noticed the *Megazoid*, raised the heat weapon, and fired. The beam literally sliced the battle galley down the middle, but the tower had not reckoned with the momentum of the much heavier *Megazoid*. The wreckage ploughed on and struck the tower, entangling itself in the latticework legs, then dragging it down below the surface as it sank. As I watched, the *Gigazoid* sank too, taking the other two towers with it.

"I say, anything I ought to know about, Inspector?" called the anxious voice of Wallas. "On this side it's still Alberin one, Lupan zero."

"Alberin three, Lupan two in the harbor," I reported.

"Very funny. What's really happening?"

With that I shook off the backpack and held it up for Wallas to see. The occasional thrashing tentacle breaking the surface was all that was visible.

"We beat them, Constable Wallas!" I shouted, tossing Wallas and the pack high into the air and catching it again. I immediately regretted this display of enthusiasm, as urine began to drip from the bottom of the pack.

It was just then that the thing passed overhead. It was a vast, silvery shape, like a bird's wings but with no bird between them. My impression was that it was not as big as a glass dragon, and while the dragons flew in silence, this thing gave off a continuous roar like a huge waterfall. It flew low over the south of the city, circling the stricken tower, then broke off and began climbing as it headed inland. The lettering on the wings was the same as that on the tripod towers.

That was all that I saw of the fighting. I later learned that the cavalrymen who had been brought along by the Lupanians had been watching from just beyond South Gate. They decided to ride in and take possession of the burning city, having quite reasonably assumed that the tripod towers had subdued Alberin. The first warning that they had of any potential problems was the Alberin Electrocratic Free Cavalry pouring out into the square behind the gate, a little behind a shower of arrows from the Alberin Voters' Archery Militia. While the Free Cavalry numbered only a thousand or so armored lancers, mostly retirees in their sixties and seventies riding cart horses, several thousand of the Alberin Voters' Defense Infantry Militia were behind them. All were in a particularly aggressive and confident frame of mind, after having learned from the signal gongs that the citizens had destroyed all four Lupanian fighting towers. About a dozen of the enemy cavalry managed to escape back through the shattered gate and flee after a short but bloody battle, but Laron was not at all worried.

"They will spread the word of our victory," he said as I presented a written report of my observations from the tower. "The Lupanians will be more cautious next time."

"Every win we have is due to Lupanian inexperience," I pointed out. "That was the first time they encountered battle galleys. Next time they will burn them to the waterline before they are within a mile's distance."

"But they have lost ten of their number. That is half of all those sent here."

"Oh aye. Two when Halland fried them in their voidship, one on the voyage here, two to an exploding dragon, four to bare-arsed carelessness, and only one in face-to-face combat. There are ten left, and I can see them being absolutely ruthless from now on."

"What would you do, were you a Lupanian?"

"Use the heat weapon against our forts and ships from a distance of a mile, blanket the city with poison smoke, then send in human warriors to take over. Never have a tower set foot in Alberin again."

✦ ✦ ✦

The fate of the tower in the city's south owed more to chance and farce than planning and ingenuity. It had stopped to burn an array of camouflaged dummy ballistas amid the smoke from burning hellfire oil and straw. Thus the street below it was shrouded in swirling smoke as it then took a step forward, but as its foot came down, a cart drawn by four horses and carrying a mobile ballista collided with the lattice work leg as the crew, which had just shot at it and missed, tried to get away in the confusion and smoke—but set off in the wrong direction. The Lupanian had looked down, and apparently been hit in the faceplate by a bolt from another ballista.

The Metrologans and Skepticals now had a practically undamaged tripod tower to study.

✦ ✦ ✦

Had the Lupanians attacked again that night or the following morning, Alberin would have been theirs for the taking. All that they knew, however, was that four of their tripod towers and most of their slave cavalry had been swallowed by the city. Clearly they needed to know how we had done it before they went on to tackle other cities, and thus we were given a respite by the cautious Lupanians. We all knew they would be back, however.

Once the fires had been extinguished, the dead and wounded attended to, the prisoners led off, and the reports compiled, we found that barely nine hundred Alberinese had died. Most of these had been on the *Megazoid* and the *Gigazoid,* or had not worn wet masks for the poison smoke, so that the city had come out of the conflict relatively unscathed. I expected Alberin to collectively celebrate with an orgy of excess that would exceed even that of the night following the regent's desertion, but most people were just relieved and exhausted, and were content to merely go to bed. After submitting my report, seeing Lavenci, then helping with the fires, I too spent a few hours asleep.

I was roused around the fourth hour past midnight by Wallengton, and driven in his carriage to where the stricken tower was standing. I arrived to find the area barricaded off and under guard. Laron was there with several Metrologans and Skepticals, and a makeshift ladder had been rigged up for access to the Lupanian war machine.

"We are spreading the story that a ballista crew shot the thing in the faceplate," said Laron as we stood looking at the torchlit monster.

"Story?" I asked. "I see the remains of a ballista over there."

"The true story is a little more complex, Danol. Their bolt missed, flew about three hundred yards, passed through a window of Honest Hassel's Exotic Diomedan Imports, and killed a pile of expensive carpets. The tower then stepped on the ballista and its crew. Still, a victory is a victory."

"But hardly a glorious victory. Who knows?"

"In effect, nobody but you, Lavenci, Yvendel, Halland, and I. Only Lavenci and I have been within the tower's hood."

"So what really happened?"

"I don't know! There is a hole in the faceplate, a hole in the Lupanian and his seat, and another hole in the back of the cowl. There is melting around the edges of the holes, and I suspect that a stray shot from the heat weapon of one of the other tripod towers was responsible. It's a wonder that it does not happen more often."

I stood with my hands on my hips, looking up at the tower.

"So, shall I be named as the sole survivor of the ballista crew and credited with a second tower killed in the name of civic morale?" I asked, not entirely sure if my sarcasm was about to become reality.

"Seriously, have you ever thought of going into politics?" replied Laron.

"You're serious, aren't you."

"Yes. You've killed one already, so killing this one also is believable. Lavenci is inside the upper cowl, learning what she can. The handling beast in the lower hood is alive and well, by the way."

"Can the tower be made functional?" I asked immediately.

"That was my very first question to Lavenci when we arrived. Apparently that is like asking a blacksmith's apprentice if he can bash a vanquished kavelar's armor back into shape, dress up in it, then defeat ten veteran kavelars."

"Does that translate as no in Alberinese?"

"A very definite no, even were the tower undamaged—and it most certainly *is* damaged. On the other hand, we now have a tower to study. Why not climb up, look heroic for the onlookers over there, and enter the hood?"

I gave the distant drinkers a wave as I paused beside the hood's hatchway, was cheered enthusiastically, then I entered. Lavenci had a lantern with her, so it was well lit. The Lupanian was most definitely dead. Lavenci was lamenting that various important things that she did not understand had been damaged, and most of these involved controlling the tower. I could understand none of it. The inside of the tower looked like the interior of a vast box of jewelry as far as I was concerned, being all glittering, faceted studs and lights, glass levers, and plates with moving lettering that ran across from the left and vanished to the right. There were no steering poles, speaking tubes, or reins to the handling beast, or anything else that I could have understood. I had thought that there would at least be a farsight with some sort of mirror system, but there was nothing of that nature. Neither was there a crossbowlike stock and trigger for the heat weapon. I prodded at the walls, which were all cushioning and colored studs.

"So, it is not all glass," I said to myself, then took the glass-weave sword from the dead Lupanian.

I looked out through the faceplate, across the city. It was the view of a titan, a god. Had the Lupanians merely wanted us annihilated, we would not have stood a chance, yet they seemed to want to conquer and rule. I mentioned this to Lavenci.

"I too, am puzzled by their behavior," she said, standing back. "On their world it is common for the big cities to be isolated during invasions, or so Azorian said. They are then starved out, and the city is taken intact."

"That is also what we do here, on Verral," I replied, nodding. "But the Lupanians have vastly more power than us, so perhaps they are impatient."

"I have a different theory," said Lavenci. "Not many on Lupan knew that this was an invasion. It was to be an expedition of scholars, traders, and the like. The invasion might have been a conspiracy between an emperor and some others who wanted to rule an entire world. Most of Lupan might be on our side."

"That is of little use. Lupan is a very long way from here."

"Indeed, but the great ethric ballista that shot the voidship to our world is still intact. The invading Lupanians only have perhaps a year before more voidships can be fashioned by their sorcerers from pools of molten glass and special pottery clay. If the rogues have not conquered our world by then, we might ally ourselves with the new arrivals. All we have to do is hold out."

"Are you sure?"

"Is a blacksmith's apprentice sure what a king will do with the ax he is sharpening and polishing?"

"Not in my experience."

"Well I have no such experience, but what *is* evident to me is that the Lupanians are in haste."

"A hasty enemy makes mistakes of judgment," I said hopefully. "Aye, perhaps all we must do is hold out for long enough."

"True," said Lavenci, "but it is the desperate yet powerful enemy that I fear."

At dawn the access hatch of the lower cowl was opened, and the handling beast was lowered into a wheeled cage by an improvised crane. The cowl was rotated with ropes so that it faced west. The tentacles hung slack, still holding the concave mirror that was the core of the casting that powered the heat weapon. All in all, it was the very symbol of Alberin's triumph over the Lupanians. Very slowly Alberin awoke and began to lick its wounds. No more towers appeared on the horizon, and both repairs and military training resumed.

I was highly skeptical about the idea of calling an election in the middle of a war. Riellen was adamant, however, and would take no advice from anyone. The campaign had been in full swing from the day after Riellen had been pronounced elector, and there were nearly eleven dozen candidates. These had sent their supporters into the taverns to buy drinks for all, plastered broadsheets on all public noticeboards, and held rallies to promise what they would do if elected presidian.

The Avenue of Conquerors, the only long, straight, wide road in Alberin, was the venue for the election. All candidates were instructed to gather with their supporters at noon, each at a designated place along the avenue. On the stroke of noon, a count was made by Elector Riellen's clerks, while officers strode along the city walls, noting the votes of the militiamen still on duty. Seven out of every ten Alberinese voted, although families tended to vote as one. I had doubts about letting children as young as five vote, but then I was not Elector Riellen. At least she disallowed the proposal to allow dogs and horses to vote with their masters. At noon I arrived at my designated place on the avenue, to find quite a sizable crowd waiting for me.

"Most stupid idea that I ever heard of," I muttered as I stood with Wallas in my pack and Solonor in my pocket.

"Then why did you stand, sir?" asked Solonor.

"Laron's idea," I replied. "He said that if I had only a small crowd, I should concede defeat, then tell them to add their votes to his."

"How big is your crowd?"

"Some two thousand, but I'm still going to concede."

I was led up onto the balcony of a commandeered house by one of Riellen's elector clerks, then left to my own devices. A carpet of faces stared up at me as I raised my hands for silence.

"Citizens of Greater Alberin, I have been nominated for presidian because I helped destroy one, er, two, Lupanian towers," I began, "but you should not vote for me because of that. Candidate Laron is running the city, and he can organize people like me to destroy many more towers. Under Laron's guidance, four more towers have been destroyed. I am just a fighter, like the rest of you. Laron is who should be leading us against the Lupanians. He has proved he can beat them. Follow me, add your numbers to Laron's voters."

After some more words along those lines, I got my supporters chanting:

"*Who do we vote for?*
"*La-ron!*
"*When do we vote?*
"*Now!*"

I had been put at the westernmost end of the Avenue of Conquerors, so that my two thousand chanting voters passed pretty well every other candidate's group as I led them to join Laron's supporters. Folk from my crowd broke away and explained to other voters that I had added my people to Laron's. By the time I had reached Laron's rally site, my group had doubled in size. Interestingly, Halland then did exactly the same. In retrospect, I think that it was a fairly clever strategy, and that Laron had planned it out well in advance. Nominate some of one's closest supporters to stand, then suggest that they might concede—but lead their supporters to his rally point. Thus Laron not only was able to address his own supporters, he also managed to use us to address yet more folk on his behalf. It was a simple enough scheme to organize, but it needed to be done well in advance. None of the other candidates had thought of it, or of any scheme other than distributing free beer, threatening divine retribution upon nonsupporters, or claiming that it was their birthright to rule. An hour later we had our first result. Three of the candidates had over ten thousand votes each, and Riellen had decreed that everyone with over ten thousand votes should be in a second runoff.

I stood right across the avenue, on the outskirts of the crowd, to listen to the final speeches. Solonor was sitting on my right shoulder, Wallas was draped over my left.

"You realize, of course, that because I am a cat I did not get a vote," said Wallas.

"When a cat stands for presidian, I'm sure all that will change," I assured him.

"What about the gnomes?" asked Solonor.

"Run for gnome presidian, and exclude all the human competition," I suggested.

Duke Forndar was one of the nobles who had decided to flee by ship, so that he could take a lot more of his wealth with him than was otherwise possible. Thus it was that he had not exited the city as hastily as his peers, and so had been there to sense an opportunity to grasp power. His basic platform was that he was a ruler by birth, that he had a lot of money, and that Laron was a felon who had been released from legal custody without the consent of the former regent.

"Failed a very important intelligence test," commented Wallas, and I nodded in agreement.

"How so?" asked Solonor.

"What former regent fled Alberin, leaving the citizens to the mercy of the Lupanians?" I replied.

"Oh."

The Archpriest Martissen was head of the World Mother Templearians, and his position was that if he was not elected, then the World Mother would not stand with Alberin against the invaders from another world. The Templearians were the biggest religion in Alberin, and thus Martissen was confident of winning. He also pointed out that Laron was conducting an affair with Elector Riellen herself, and had affiliations with no organized religion at all.

"Ooh, that Laron's gone now," said Solonor.

"Why?" asked Wallas.

"Well, like, the man's been caught with his drawers down."

"In Alberin, the most scandal-loving city in the known world?" I laughed.

"The priest's failed an important intelligence test too," added Wallas.

Laron began to speak, but it was now that Elder Justiva found me. She drew me out of the crowd and away into one of the side streets that led to the Metrologan temple and academy.

"We have a problem," she said. "A messenger has just arrived from the south."

"So, it's bad news?" I asked.

"Catastrophic," she replied. "The messenger is something of a disaster as well."

I was told to leave Wallas and Solonor in the infirmary of the temple, then was taken upstairs. In a large and open loft within the temple I found Lavenci with . . . well, at first she did not seem much like a woman. Etheric energies crackled and sparkled across her skin, and glowed from her eyes and mouth. Tendrils of violet fire writhed and danced through her hair, and an aura of incompletely controlled energies had rendered her arms into blurred, unfocused things that extended some yards behind and above her. She stood before us, clothed only in energies, scanning our faces.

"This . . . not him," she declared in a voice that reminded me of waxpaper being crumpled.

"Inspector Danolarian Scryverin, Wayfarers, West Quadrant, at your service," I declared, dropping to one knee and bowing.

"You . . . young reccon . . . in my escort . . . years ago. Sweet boy . . . educated . . . dashing . . . honorable. But where is . . . Andry Tennoner?"

"None of us know," said Justiva.

"Then . . . I want Roval."

"Elector Advisor Roval, Intelligence?" I asked.

"My Roval," replied the cracking whisper.

"Roval is in charge of the welfare of candidates at the elections. He is still busy."

"Too late, then . . . you three . . . write."

We seated ourselves, and Justiva sent for writing kits and lap boards.

"This is Terikel, the previous Elder of the Metrologans," whispered Justiva as we waited. "Three years ago she entered the earliest stage of becoming a glass dragon. She glides on the winds with huge, etheric wings, and she never quite sleeps."

"Are they not meant to be very dangerous," I whispered. "I

mean, mortals in the earliest stages of becoming glass dragons are not entirely sane."

"Yes indeed."

"And, er, was she not the reason Roval took to the drink?"

"Yes. It was over another man."

"Four other men, as I heard it. The late prince of Alberin, a shipmaster, my former commanding officer, and Andry Tennoner."

"Enough!" hissed Justiva.

The writing kits were brought in by a deacon, who was then sent away. The neophyte dragon Terikel began to speak, and we wrote.

The glass dragons had been profoundly disturbed by the destruction of one of their kind by the Lupanians, and had retreated to their mountains lairs or taken to the upper atmosphere to ride the air currents in tranquility. Immortal beings get very sensitive about anything that might kill them, or so it seems. Terikel was a very young dragon, however, who did not yet have the caution born of centuries of life, and thus she had more boldness where danger was concerned. She had been drifting on the air currents five miles above the Lupanians, learning what she could about those just south of Gatrov.

Half of the Lupanian tripod towers were concentrated in this area, which was where the borders of Fralland, Zaldacia, Terrisia, and Greater Alberin came together. It was also close to Vosburgh, the capital of Zaldacia, which was built on the shores of Lake Askal. To give them credit, the rulers of Fralland, Zaldacia, and Terrisia recognized the threat quickly, and decided to unite their forces. Eight days after Gatrov had been destroyed, a combined army of over a hundred thousand kavelars, militiamen, cavalry, lake galleys, reccons, and irregulars had gathered in and around Vosburgh to confront the tripod towers that were slowly advancing in that direction.

What they had not realized was that the Lupanians could fly. A thing, smaller yet faster than a glass dragon, had been high above Alberin when we had destroyed the towers sent to conquer us. It was the thing I had seen. From what Terikel had said, this then flew four hundred miles south to Zaldacia in barely two hours, for she had seen it descending to where the three towers were preparing to move on Vosburgh. One presumes that a very thorough report was delivered.

When the three tripod towers finally advanced on Vosburgh the following morning, they were spaced about a mile apart, and with their flying engine circling above to warn of glass-dragon attack. Well-camouflaged ballistas were in their path, but the towers blasted all cover to ashes before they were within a half mile's distance. The westernmost of the towers waded along the shallows of Lake Askal, and it was this one that the dozen galleys of the lake fleet attacked. These were dash galleys, small, swift warships armed with ballistas. Each and all were cut in half and sunk at a distance of one mile.

Vosburgh fared no better. No longer interested in preserving our cities for their own use, the Lupanians merely slashed the rooftops of the lakeside city with the beams of their heat weapons. This caused a storm of fire confined within the city, and from what Terikel said, the place was ashes by nightfall. At least five thousand cavalry charged the towers, sacrificing themselves while militiamen with slings and hellfire jars tried to sneak up on them. Nothing got to within a quarter mile of a Lupanian.

"Towers . . . now gathering," concluded Terikel laboriously. "Walking north. Will be here, three days."

"This is very serious," I said to Justiva once Terikel had finished. "The Lupanians learn from their mistakes. Not a ballista or galley will ever get to within a half mile of their towers again, and that was how we got them every other time. Unless we can ambush them or somehow get close, we have no hope. Perchance they thought we would not be quite so dangerous as we have proved to be, but now they know it, and they will never again fight from less than a half-mile distance."

"Three days to prepare," said Justiva.

"From yesterday," crackled Terikel.

At that moment I heard a clattering of boots on the stairs to the loft, and Roval's voice calling out to us.

"Laron won," he called before he reached the door. "Now all he has to do is do the impossible, yet again."

Roval stopped a few steps into the loft, staring past us to the neophyte glass dragon.

"You," he said in a tone of voice that in my experience generally precedes attempted or actual homicide.

"Roval . . . my love," crackled the voice from a mouth that glowed greenish blue from within.

"You *were* my love," said Roval coldly, backing away a pace, and with a hand on his ax. "I was never yours. Yours were whoever was to hand when you felt inclined."

"Needed their help," replied Terikel, "against Dragonwall. Bought support . . . with myself."

"And who was the one man that you never approached?" demanded Roval. "I would have helped. We of the Special Warrior Service are very good at helping."

"No, could not . . . not for what was needed."

"Well, if told I could have sealed my hearts tight while you used your body to get your way. If you had explained it, I could have trusted you. No, you wanted to hurt me. You *feed* on hurt and betrayal."

Even a neophyte glass dragon is not a thing to make weak and futile pleas. Instead it stood in silence for some moments, then began to advance on Roval. Justiva took me by the arm and dragged me aside, and Lavenci needed no encouragement to move clear as well.

"Twisted, flawed, warped, I am, bent by an Elder from Torea, now ash in the wind," she whispered her voice like leaves blown on an autumn breeze. "Now, yours forever, and you are mine."

"Not with four other bodies in the bed between us!" declared Roval defiantly.

"Killing them, cauterizing the memories. Only way, to heal."

Standing only a foot or so from where Roval stood with his arms folded, Terikel reached out and caressed the back of his hand. Smoke sizzled up from his skin where the hot claws touched it. He flinched, but did not back away or cry out.

"Wanted that I touch . . . other than you . . . only one living man has known my touch. Soon, just you . . . it is my pledge."

Terikel began to back away now, gazing at Roval all the while. When she reached the loading doors of the loft there was a brilliant flash of light like a dazzle casting, and when I had blinked the dancing glows out of my eyes, she was gone.

"She, er, she delivered a report," I said nervously, holding up my scribbled sheet of reedpaper.

"Then you had best deliver it to Presidian Laron," Roval said with a polite but icy smile, before bowing, turning on his heel, and striding for the stairs.

✳ ✳ ✳

Laron's first act as presidian of Greater Alberin was to rename the electoral advisors as the Greater Alberin War Council. He liked using the word "war" rather than "defense" because it suggested that we were actually going after the Lupanians. It was to this council that I presented the young glass dragon's report.

"In short, the entire force of Lupanians is on the way here," Laron concluded when I had finished.

"Yes sir. And their policy appears to be to annihilate anything displaying resistance, or even looking suspicious, before they get within a half mile of it. They can fly, too, and at a speed many times greater than even a glass dragon can achieve."

"Many *times* more?"

"Five times, was Lady Terikel's estimate."

"But that would be approaching three hundred miles per hour."

"Yes. They can now fly anywhere on our world, and very fast at that. They can reach newly arrived, benevolent sorcerers from Lupan as soon as their voidships land. They will kill them as they emerge from their voidships."

Riellen's original octagonal table had been sanded, put on a larger base frame with eight legs, stained walnut brown, edged with gold leaf, and lacquered by the time this meeting began. It was not that Laron was fond of luxury so much as that the people around both him and Riellen wanted to do things for them. Riellen now had the title charter advisor, while the other six experts were just called citizen councillors. Laron unrolled another report and tapped it with a finger.

"A trend has been found in the use of the tripods," he announced. "From the script on the sides of the tripod towers I have noticed that the most recent arrivals are sent into battle first. Could it be that the Lupanians who have been here longest are becoming sick, and unable to fight?"

"Why should that happen to them?" asked Roval.

"Because it happens to us. Sailors from very distant continents sometimes die of maladies that would have locals merely feeling queasy. Azorian is dead, and he was in the first cylinder."

"But one tower from the first cylinder is still active," said Lavenci.

"That is a good point, Lady Lavenci," said Laron. "Do you have anything to report?"

"Azorian's castings were similar to our own magic, but he had a vastly greater ability to gather and control etheric energies. His powers here were a hundred thousand times greater than mine."

"That is a very precise figure," said Laron, leaning forward and clasping his hands.

"I improvised a measurement device, a type of balance beam that we both tried to push downward by minute castings."

"I see. And how much stronger than Azorian are the Lupanian glasswalker warriors? A thousand times? Ten thousand?"

Lavenci pressed her fingertips against her temples.

"Look, at these levels of etheric power it's meaningless to talk about amounts," she said.

"Sorry?"

"It seems that there is a limit to the amount of etheric energy around us. Everyone knows that—on Lupan, anyway. The etheric background is much weaker on Lupan, so the Lupanians are much better at drawing together power than we here, who have lived in plenty all our lives. Think of it this way: the difference between a very strong blacksmith's apprentice and a very strong warrior is not some small measure of strength, it is five or ten years of training with weapons."

"Can you expand upon why they are so much more powerful than us?" asked Laron.

"Don't you see? Look, even I could devise a casting to generate a heat weapon. It could cut a worm in half at one mile. Take me to a place where I am a hundred thousand times more powerful and I could use that same casting to cut a battle galley in half at the same distance—as Lupanians are doing here. The sorcerers on Lupan worked out that they could be like gods here. Some group of nobles found the idea very attractive."

"I see, I see. Does this give us any advantage, I wonder?"

"None that I can think of," replied Lavenci.

"We'll then, back to trickery," sighed Laron. "Do you know what the tripod towers use for distress signals?"

"I cannot say. I could study the controls in the captured tower."

"Then do so. If we can use the distress call to make the others think the, er, glasswalker is merely trapped, and not dead, we might lure them back into Alberin and again fight them at close range. What do you think?"

"It would be an act of desperation, but has anything that we have done been any more than desperation?" asked Lavenci.

After the meeting I visited some people who knew people who were good at finding out about people. They told me that they had learned nothing about Pelmore. I went to Madame Yvendel's to see Lavenci, but was told that she and Wensomer were examining the captured tower for clues to Lupanian magic, and were expected to be there all night. I returned to the palace, and there I fell flat on my back in the direction of a bed. During the night the Lupanian flying engine passed low over the city and dropped several castings of poisonous smoke. I did not awake until later, when all the bells and gongs of the city began ringing the alarm. Some said the flying engine had shone a great light down on Alberin, then dropped something into the harbor that sank three ships at anchor. After that we were left in peace.

Chapter Twenty-One

TEMPORIANS

I awoke a little before dawn to discover Wallas curled up on my chest. I sat up. Wallas tumbled off.

"Constable Wallas reporting for duty, Inspector," said Wallas, before sitting back, extending a hind leg into the air, and licking it.

"Anything to report, apart from yourself, for duty?" I said as I stood up and poured some water into a washbasin.

"Such ingratitude! I was up most of the night on your behalf."

"Cats are nocturnal, Wallas. Well?"

"Well what?"

"Well, have you learned anything?"

"No."

"Damn! Well, Wallas, it's dawn and you're on a bed. I have novice warriors to select to be slaughtered."

"Sir, I've been thinking."

"Good. Do it more often."

"*Who* are you chasing?"

"Pelmore, of course. And his rescuers."

"Who are they, sir?"

"Agents of the regent—ex-regent, that is."

"Pelmore was not among those who rode out of the city with the ex-regent. Thousands of people watched them ride past, including me. Before I was made a cat, I was a courtier, and courtiers like to watch what other courtiers are doing."

"But refugees left as well, Wallas. Oh I know that most came back with Riellen, but anyone wishing to flee the city would merely have stayed outside."

"Nobody knew that an electocracy would happen, inspector. Not you, not Pelmore, not me, and probably not even Riellen. I doubt that Pelmore tried to leave."

"The Inquisition may have rescued him. He was one of theirs. I've seen proof."

"They would have kept him in the Inquisition building. We all know what happened to that."

"Yes, in fact I was very nearly still inside when it collapsed."

"Let us play spot the conspiracy, sir. You could secretly love Riellen, yet be furious with her for three years of headaches. Do you love Riellen? Are you afraid to let Lavenci get too close because of that?"

"Riellen is sleeping with Laron, Wallas. Most of the city knows it. I am indeed relieved that Laron is teaching her the sweaty and exhausting delights of dalliance. My sole reservation is that I may owe Laron more strong drinks than I could ever afford on my wages."

"Riellen might be hiding Pelmore, still trying to keep you and Lavenci apart."

"Pelmore vanished before Riellen came to power, Wallas."

"Good point, inspector. Riellen is out, then, but what about you? You were a hero back then, when Pelmore vanished. You had enough influence to get admitted to the dungeons, perhaps even the influence to get someone out."

"Wallas, you are beginning to annoy me intensely, and I have people to train. Good morning to you."

"Where would *you* hide Pelmore—" began Wallas, but I slammed the door on his voice and hurried away.

* * *

I was assigned half a decile of archers. The forty-seven men and three women were not bowmen with massive arms, but a mixed bag of people, half of whom who knew how to aim a crossbow. The rest were strong enough to load a crossbow, so that a pair could operate a single weapon. They had been trained for three days, and could shoot off three bolts per minute. Accuracy was not an issue, because an army of the Lupanians' supporters would be very hard to miss. The reason that I was put in front of fifty crossbow archers was that I had faced the Lupanians several times and survived.

We were drawn up on the wharves, ready to fire out across the harbor. I had taken them through several volleys, and they were all smiles and confidence. Suddenly a shower of missiles erupted from the other side of the harbor wall, some of which trailed black smoke; then strangely dressed figures armed with pikes swarmed up onto the wharf, howling for blood. The archers fell back at once, some even dropping their weapons.

"Stand!" I shouted. "Fifth Alberin Presidian's Militia, stand ready!"

Some backed away a little more slowly, but none stood. I turned and faced the attackers, holding up both hands.

"That's enough, lads, well done!" I shouted, and the street urchins wearing sacks over their heads stopped at once. I turned back to the archers, who were by now looking very sheepish.

"*Never, never* break and run until the officer tells you to retreat!" I shouted, with a passable show of fury. "He's your leader. If you don't want to obey him, leave now."

I waited. Nobody left.

"This morning you ran from fish heads, rotten fruit, and burning rags on sticks," I continued. "In a day or two it will be arrows from the Lupanians' human recruits, each a yard long, that can skewer your body and leave you dead. Those shooting them want you to break and run. You want to scatter them with your crossbow bolts. Who will win? The side that holds firm. Now get back here and let's try again."

"Please, but what if it's Lupanians in towers a hundred feet high, each armed with a heat weapon that can slice a war galley in half at one mile?" asked a recruit who was wearing a blacksmith's leather apron.

"In that case turn, run, and try to keep up with your officer."

The rest of the day was spent getting the children and idlers to charge the archers and loaders time and again, throwing things and screaming abuse. By the time we broke for the day it was three in the afternoon, and my voice was ragged. The archers were by now standing firm and shooting, even when showers of fruit and fish heads were descending. They did not even break when attacked by children wielding pails of water, although they were surprised and annoyed.

* * *

I made my way to the Lamplighter, secured a tankard of ale, sat down, and thought of nothing whatsoever for a time. Then Wallas appeared and jumped up onto my lap.

"I have news," he announced.

"The Lupanians are attacking?" I asked, without enthusiasm.

"Someone was watching you training those poor fools to stand and die."

"Someone of more interest to me that the other two or three hundred onlookers?"

"Yes."

"Who?"

"You."

"Wallas, piss off."

"Listen! Just listen. Listening?"

"Yes."

"Think upon it. Someone who looks very like you. Someone who could have impersonated you and liberated Pelmore."

All of a sudden, what Wallas was saying started to make sense.

"Go on."

"When he left, I followed him to a storehouse in Wharfside. Chandler's Lane, Wall Tower Building."

"The bluestone place that's meant to be a thousand years old?"

"The very one."

Ten centuries ago Alberin had been a fraction of its present size, and the old city wall ran directly north from the river, starting at Wharfside. There were seven guard towers, and although the five southernmost towers had been dismantled to make way for other structures, the two towers in Wharfside were still intact and being used as storehouses. They were squat and ugly, yet were also large, solid and well built, meaning that they endured the centuries with little need of maintenance. They had outlasted some palaces.

For a time I thought about what to do. At the very least I wanted a long and truthful talk with Pelmore, followed by the completion of his sentence. Given what was on the way to the city, I was fairly sure that unless I had that talk very soon, it would not take place at all.

Andry, Costiger, and Essen entered the taproom as I sat contemplating my options, and suddenly my mind was made up.

"Wallas, I owe you a whole pail full of dried fish," I conceded.

"So, you believe me?"

"I think I shall investigate."

"Pelmore is in the loft room in the northwestern corner."

"What? Truly?" I exclaimed, fighting a temptation to wring his neck for not telling me immediately.

"Being a cat, I was able to climb down from the roof and look through the window. Oh, and one more thing. There appears to be a Lupanian device in the room with him."

A Lupanian device. Suddenly involvement with Azorian became a possibility. Anger suffused my body, as if I had swallowed some sharp, hot drink. Just what was it about Pelmore? Was anyone safe from his allure, or whatever it was that people saw in him? I was, clearly enough, but how did he enchant Azorian, Lavenci, Riellen, the inquisitor general . . . and perhaps Wallas? Was Wallas working for him as well? I was dangerously far down the road to paranoia, and desperately in need of answers. My three Wayfarer friends came over with tankards. I allowed them to have a quiet drink first.

"How was training?" I asked Andry.

"Need two weeks to be sure they'd not run," he conceded.

"Same with mine," Essen.

"Gentlemen, how would you feel about joining me in a raid?" I asked.

The Wall Tower Building had massive, iron-bound doors of oak, and its windows were wide enough to aim a bow through, but not much more. Even Wallas would have found them a squeeze. Banging on the door and calling out "Militia inspection!" roused someone on the other side, and presently there was the rattle of a bar being raised. The scrawny little keeper looked rather like a handful of twigs stuffed into a sheepgut condom. I pushed past him and looked around.

"Wayfarer Constables, this is a raid!" I said quietly, a finger to my lips.

"But you said—" began the keeper.

"I lied. Go to your room, lock the door, and stay there."

The center of the tower was open all the way to the roof, but there were three floors of rooms built around the sides and lined with balconies. Block-and-tackle landings on each balcony allowed goods to be raised and lowered, and those goods seemed to be of the low-volume and moderate-expense variety, such as fine cloths, spices, and imported pottery. We climbed the stairs slowly and quietly, our weapons at the ready. On the third floor I cocked the small cavalry crossbow that I had borrowed from Andry.

"The room is the one at the northwest corner," I said as we crept along the wooden balcony. "Costi, you shoulder the door open, hit the floor, and roll aside. I'll come next, Andry will be my backup. Essen, stay at the door, make sure that nobody comes in behind us."

For the last few yards no words were spoken, but then we Wayfarers are trained to work as teams, in silence. I pointed to Costiger, then the door, and finally patted my shoulder. Costiger's considerable weight smashed into the door, bursting it open. As he dropped to the floor I was right behind him.

"Wayfarer Constables!" I shouted. "Throw down your weapons and raise your hands!"

I had a fleeting impression of three people, some bedding and boxes, and a large, glittering thing that seemed more like a piece of jewelry the size of a ponycart than a Lupanian machine. The sight of it gave me a moment of panic, and I fired my cavalry crossbow at a part of the mechanism that looked important. A moment later I saw, well, myself raise something about the size of a small tinderbox. There was a sound like a wet cork being drawn across glass, and the universe was suddenly all brilliant white light.

There was no pain in my head as I came to my senses, but the room was spinning and blurry as I opened my eyes. When I managed to focus on what was before me, I saw that Andry, Costiger, and Essen were lying on the floor. Pelmore was sitting in a corner, bound and gagged, and a woman dressed as a militiaman was carefully removing my crossbow bolt from the mechanism of crystal and precious metals. Sitting on a box and pointing the tiny but quite devastating weapon in my general direction . . . was me.

"Ah, good, I remember waking up about now," I said to me. "Do behave yourself, Danolarian. I know you do, of course, because I remember it, but one never knows with this time business."

"Causality," muttered the woman repairing the strange machine.

"Who are you, and why are you rescuing Pelmore?" I asked.

" 'Rescuing' is such a strong word," said my image.

"Moving to more appropriate confinement," said the woman.

"Just as soon as we're in Bucadria I am going to remove his head," the image of myself said emphatically.

"Well I think we should perform a small but humane operation and sell him in the Wharfside slave market," said the woman. "We don't have the death penalty where I come from."

"I'm betting castration is not in the register of penalties either," said my other self.

"True, but abduction is also against the law, and we did just that a few days ago. Death is so final, and anyway, is it not more cruel to have Pelmore condemned to watch others doing it for the rest of his life, while all he can do is stand guard, and serve tea and cakes?"

"Er, who are you?" I tried again.

"This is Lariella, I believe you already know Pelmore, and of course, I am you."

"My friends," I said, uninterested in word games. "Are they dead?"

"They each got a direct hit from this stuncast, and will be asleep for another quarter hour. You have been revived deliberately."

"Will someone tell me what is going on?" I demanded.

"Your crossbow bolt nicked the mercury regulator for the temporal-displacement amplifier!" Lariella suddenly exclaimed.

"Er, what does that mean?" I asked.

"I thought you said that the bolt did no real damage," Lariella said, ignoring me.

"I remember the machine working after the shot," retorted my other self.

"Well at least two pounds of mercury have leaked out and run down between the floorboards. I suppose I can seal the tube with beeswax and bleed some mercury off from the quantum bypass reserve."

Whatever needed to be done did not take long. My other self kept the weapon trained on me as she worked.

"Lariella is descended from Riellen," he said as she worked. "Twenty-eight generations, is it not, Lari?"

"That's right, we have kept the family tradition of doing this alive for over a thousand years."

"I would still like to know what is going on," I insisted.

"I don't tell you, but you catch on," said my other self.

"Time to go," said Lariella, standing up and turning to face us with her hands on her hips.

"Go?" I asked. "Where?"

"Actually, it's when," said the other me.

I suddenly realized that Lariella was the fittest, strongest-looking, and healthiest woman that I had ever seen, and she was pretty close to the tallest as well. She hunkered down again and fished something about the size and shape of a pack of cards out of a box.

"My recording of Lavenci first singing 'The Banks of the Alber,'" she said with something approaching triumph as she clipped it to her belt. "It's just so romantic, I just can't wait to play it for my friend Darriencel. She's descended from you and Lavenci."

Now I was at a really serious loss for words. My other self handed the weapon to her then walked over to the rather worried-looking Pelmore and untied his feet.

"On your feet, Pelmore, we are about to terminate your existence," declared my other self.

The words were not chosen wisely, for in spite of having his hands tied behind his back, Pelmore struggled and kicked as he was forced across the room. He even managed a couple of kicks at the glittering machine, which he probably assumed was some type of torture device. His struggles ceased when

Lariella picked Costiger's ax from the floor and belted their prisoner over the head with the handle.

"Now look what you've done!" said the other myself. "He's out of it, I'll have to carry him."

"Where?" I asked again.

"We're going to sell him in the Wharfside slave market."

"White eunuchs were worth a lot in Wharfside," added Lariellen.

She began to strip off her clothing, revealing some type of purple, skintight garment that covered her from neck to wrists and to ankles. Her midriff had a set of abdominal muscles that put mine to shame, yet her figure was still very pleasing. Pelmore was soon tied over a bar behind the tandem saddle arrangement within the machine.

"At last, after a thousand years, Riellen's mistake will be put right," said the woman. "When my daughter is born next month, she will not have the burden of a thousand-year-old obligation to follow."

"You're eight months pregnant?" I exclaimed in disbelief.

"No, my husband is. Now then, just one more mistake to correct."

With that my other self and Lariellen lifted Andry from the floor and began to tie him behind Pelmore.

"Leave him, he's done nothing," I pleaded. My other self shook his head.

"Remember Wallas's gossip? I am afraid Andry lay one night with Learned Terikel, who is now a young glass dragon. She is no longer entirely human, and she is atoning for her infidelities to Roval by killing all her other surviving bedmates. Gilvray and that musician were two of them, the rest died from unrelated causes. Andry is the only other one, so he is in danger of having his heart ripped out. We shall take him into the past, and in a few moments he will be centuries dead. I have arranged money and protection for his wife and family. They have to stay here."

"Causality," said Lariellen again. "It's too hard to explain."

"Terikel . . . will never believe," I said, trying to get up.

"She will when I tell her," said yet another voice, from somewhere behind me. "Thank you for taking Andry to safety. My loyalty lives, even though love has died."

My other self and Lariellen climbed into the time engine and seated themselves.

"Ready, Danol?" asked the woman from the very distant future.

"When you will, ladyship. Goodbye, Lady Velander, goodbye, young self. Oh, and Danolarian, take my—and your—advice, and try to be a bit romantic with Lavenci tonight. Tomorrow you will both be too tired, because—"

His voice was cut off before I could hear any more. Parts of the thing began to spin, the entire structure blurred, along with its passengers, and then it became so indistinct that I could see right through it to the wall behind. It faded to almost nothing, then vanished with a soft *whoosh* like the slamming of a door. I heard footsteps behind me as someone walked away. Lady Velander, I had said. I knew her to be another young glass dragon.

I managed to force my limbs to work, and crawled over to where the machine had stood. A small puddle of mercury was draining between the floorboards. Pelmore's kicks must have damaged Lariellen's repairs, yet the thing had worked so I thought no more of it as I watched the last evidence of its existence drain away.

The others were still unconscious as I searched the room. I found nothing out of the ordinary, except for a strange book that had been printed with quite incredible refinement. There were pictures of people doing heroic things against Lupanian tripod towers, and the writing was somehow familiar yet not so. I put it in a bag just as a meow sounded outside.

"Come in, Wallas, it's safe," I called.

"What happened?" he asked, surveying the unconscious Wayfarers.

"Some weapon that stuns. You were right, Pelmore was here, but his captors have fled with him. They took Andry as well."

"Where? The window is too narrow, and nobody came out through the door."

"I watched as they became invisible."

"Really?"

Chapter Twenty-Two

"EVENING'S ALL FOR COURTING"

 Once Essen and Costiger were awake and on their feet again, we returned to the Lamplighter. For a time we discussed what we had seen in the Wall Tower Building, but could reach no new conclusions.

"Bucadria," said Essen. "You heard one of them say Bucadria?"

"That was the place," I responded.

"Alberin was called Bucadria about two thousand years ago. It was a colony of the Vindician Empire, and a big market for slaves and gold."

"Two thousand years ago," I said, shaking my head. "Perhaps I heard the name wrongly."

Right at that moment we heard the sound of drums outside and the jingle of armor and weapons. An excited buzz of voices sounded throughout the taproom, and people started to hurry out. Moments later, we were all listening to another voice, a small voice but one which had the penetration of a razor-sharp dagger.

"Brothers, sisters, I'm here to tell you that win or lose tomorrow, we can *never* be defeated!" cried Riellen in the street outside. "Alberin has elected a leader! Presidian Laron is the first leader in all the history of the world to be elected. Aye, and the great and powerful people do not like it. We elected a leader from among ourselves, and now we follow him! Win or lose on the battlefield tomorrow, we have shown the way."

At this there was much cheering and clapping, and it took a long time to die away.

"Tomorrow, citizens of Alberin, I shall be on the walls, fighting alongside you. Presidian Laron will be there too, and if we are killed, it does not matter, because *any* of you could replace us! While any one of us is alive, the spirit of Free Alberin is alive. They cannot kill us all."

Actually, they can and probably will, I thought as I slipped from the tavern and skirted the crowd in the street outside. Almost of their own accord, my feet began taking me in the direction of Madame Yvendel's establishment.

I was admitted to Madame Yvendel's academy by one of the students. This time Lavenci and her sister and mother were there together, and were having dinner when I was shown in. Lavenci and Wensomer were dressed in nondescript skirts, and resembled the wives of artisans. They both had their hair bound up in scarves, were somewhat grubby, and looked as if they had not been getting much sleep for several days. Madame Yvendel, on the other hand, was dressed as if she were running some sort of finishing school for courtesans in Diomeda. Very little furniture was left in the room, only some cushions and the table.

Lavenci waved off the servant who tried to attend me, and insisted on sharing some of her bowl of savory rice, ground nuts, and cheese with me. I took the bowl from her, and as I ate with a porcelain spoon she explained that she had found a way to activate some of the spells and castings in the captured tripod. It enabled her to listen in on conversations between the Lupanians.

"I do not understand," I admitted. "They communicate by hooting and ululating. Do you mean you can now understand their cries?"

"No, it is something more subtle. Some sort of cry that we cannot hear, but which can be made audible by some device or spell in the tower's cowl."

"So you can understand what they are saying?"

"No, but I can hear them talking."

"Which is of no use whatsoever," Wensomer pointed out.

I ate in silence for awhile. Madame Yvendel announced that she had by now packed most of the academy down into the sewers and cellars beneath street level. Wensomer and Lavenci both complained that their bedchambers had been packed and moved while they had been away with the captured tripod.

"We shall all be sleeping on cushions on the floor tonight," said Lavenci as I handed her bowl back.

"Am I welcome to stay?" I asked.

"Oh Danolarian, you are very, very welcome, but compared to the palace this is such rough living."

"As long as I can lie in your arms, even this place is a palace," I replied, feeling sure that I could have been more poetic if I had tried, but not feeling up to trying.

Lavenci gave a little sniff. "Side by side, not in my arms until seven years after Pelmore dies of old age," she said ruefully. "Until then I can but offer you my hair to touch, but nothing else. Sometimes, sometimes . . . it would be almost worth being doubled over with pain, just to feel the touch of your fingertips."

"Ah, Lavenci, you will never make an inspector in the Wayfarers," I sighed, pouring out a little wine for myself.

"Oh, and why not?"

"You fail to notice little details sometimes."

"Like what?"

"Like being brushed by my fingertips when you handed me the bowl."

"What?" she laughed, as if I had told a joke that she did not quite understand. "I was careful not to touch you."

"Not careful enough," I replied, bending the truth a little for the sake of dramatic effect.

"But I would have been convulsed with pain by the constancy glamour if . . ." Suddenly Lavenci caught the meaning of what I was saying, and the reason that I was smiling. "Danolarian, you did it!" she shrieked.

In a shower of crockery, wine, food, and cushions Lavenci was upon me, wrapping her arms about me and smothering my face with kisses.

"What did I say?" said Madame Yvendel. "Of course *Rax Einsel*'s pupil would find an engineering solution for a magical problem."

"Of course only *my brother* could have raised the glamour," said Wensomer. "Is any wine unspilled?"

Lavenci raised her face from mine, and I hastily took a number of deep breaths.

"You packed the entire bloody academy away!" she shouted at her mother. "All the bedding, perfumes, soaps, clothes, all the special things for my first night with Danolarian!"

"If you can give me about six hours I am sure I can find—"

"No! By then it will be dawn, and, and, and . . . Damnation! After all this waiting I am *not* having my beloved left with memories of embracing me scruffy, smelly, and on a floor! Wait a moment . . . Madame Karracel's is still open for business."

"The bawdyhouse?" I asked.

My recollections of the next hour or so are somewhat sketchy. Being marched into Madame Karracel's establishment via the concealed passageway. Madame Yvendel confronting Madame Karracel with a bag of gold coins. The male patrons being ejected in various stages of dress and undress, each with a handful of florins. Being stripped naked and bathed in perfumed, soapy water by Wensomer in a room whose door bore the sign CHAYMBYE OF BUBBLE FANTASYES. Having my hair dried by some sort of minor heat casting spoken by Wensomer. Being shown into a huge bedchamber smothered in hangings and carpets, with blue lanterns burning and star-shaped mirrors shining down from the ceiling. Seeing Lavenci standing there in a chamber gown of white silk, then watching her unfasten the gown and let it fall to the floor. Watching her unfasten and discard various other items of negligible white clothing, then step clear of the pile and do a pirouette with her arms extended.

"The Lupanians have killed us all, and I have gone to paradise" was the only response that I could manage.

"Your turn," she purred.

The red chamber gown was all that I was wearing, and it was the work of a moment to discard it and do my own pirouette. Lavenci shrieked in shock.

"Danolarian, your back!"

"Oh, er, that was a flogging on the voyage from Torea. Fifty lashes, for insubordination."

"And your leg!"

"Battle of Racewater Bridge, it was a lance."

"Your arm?"

"That was the invasion of Diomeda, another lance."

"No, no, the other arm!" said Lavenci, putting her hands over her head.

"A knife fight in Gatrov—actually you were there."

"That burn!" she said, advancing on me.

"Oh, now that time I really did think I was going to die. We were in the Sargolan town of Clovesser, defending Princess Senterri against a glass dragon and mmmff."

Lavenci wrapped her arms around me and again smothered my lips with kisses. For a long time we stood there, perfectly at peace in spite of the terrible doom hanging over both ourselves and the city. Presently Lavenci gestured in the direction of the bed.

"This is enchanting, but lying down will be better still," she whispered to me.

There is something profoundly pleasant and exciting about the commencement of lovemaking with a new partner for the very first time. Every sensation is exquisite, and every memory stays with you. For a long time we said nothing at all. The heat of the summer night was perhaps all that marred the experience a trifle. The pain from Lavenci's teeth in my neck did not seem to matter at all.

"Am I as good as the princesses?" Lavenci asked not long after a bell was rung for midnight.

"They just wanted to please, but you love," I replied. "Every move, every purr is saturated with love. I must look a bit of a mess, though."

"You are a hero and scholar, all in one. You are strong, bold, tender, and loving. I have never felt that before."

"Not even from Laron?"

"Laron is not strong, and he made love, rather than loved. Pelmore was a shell of muscle over emptiness, nothing more. When I think that we could have had all this three months ago, I—I just feel so ill."

"Lavenci, Lavenci, it happened the way it did, and we are in each other's arms now. Before us is the rest of the night, and after that . . . an exciting day."

"Doomsday."

"No, no. Tomorrow night we shall be back in your bed, and doing much the same as we are doing now."

"Pretty words, and oh so easy."

"Not just words. How do you think I broke the glamour?"

"I have not stopped to think of that, I must admit."

"I met myself."

"Pardon?"

"Myself, from some months or years hence. He—I—had a time engine. I plucked Pelmore out of this existence without killing him. Because he did not die, the glamour was violated, and it collapsed. Pelmore is now in the distant past."

I thought it wise not to mention the lady who had arrived with the time engine.

"So, you told yourself that, er, both of us survive what tomorrow brings?" she said, struggling to comprehend what even I did not entirely grasp.

"Yes, but nothing more."

"Nothing more. Well, that will have to do then, will it not?"

For all the delights of our hours together, they lasted only until the third hour past midnight. Madame Yvendel tapped at the door and called that both Lavenci and I were being summoned by Laron. Lupanian towers had been seen moving beyond the city walls.

Chapter Twenty-Three

ALBERIN ALONE

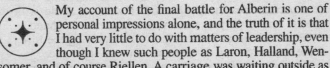

My account of the final battle for Alberin is one of personal impressions alone, and the truth of it is that I had very little to do with matters of leadership, even though I knew such people as Laron, Halland, Wensomer, and of course Riellen. A carriage was waiting outside as we emerged from Madame Karracel's establishment, and we were driven straight to the palace. There all the squad leaders were being given written orders by Laron himself. My orders had my squad guarding the approaches to the Skeptical temple, not far from the city walls. Once everyone had read their own orders, Laron revealed what Lavenci and I already knew to an audience of several dozen commanders and other senior officers. There were tripod towers beyond the walls. They could be seen in Miral's green light, striding about but keeping their distance.

"There are seven of them so far," said Laron. "My assessment is that they they are waiting for all the towers to arrive, then they will attack together. We have caused them too much trouble, and they now wish to annihilate us. They will stride to the most effective range for their heat weapons, then burn the city to slag and ashes. Are there any comments?"

Halland raised his hand. "Presidian, they could already raze the city with the seven towers they have, yet they do not."

"My thought is that they want to take no chances, and that they want to crush us with their full strength. Alberin has destroyed four of their number, and Alberin is the center of the empire."

Baron Hanzlin of the New Palace Guard waved for attention.

"With due respect to our brave militiamen and sailors, the destruction of the towers was sheer, bare-arsed luck. What can we hope to achieve this time?"

"We know that we were merely lucky, but the Lupanians do not. If we can lure a few of them into the city we may be lucky again. Kavelen Lavenci, do you think that you could activate the distress cry of our captured tower?"

"I know enough of their magic to do that, yes," said Lavenci after a moment's thought.

"Then go there, take a carriage, be ready to do it. I shall have teams of men there with ropes to rotate the hood and make the tentacles sway."

Lavenci gave me the most forlorn yet compelling of looks, then hurried away without another word. A noble with the crest of one of the provinces was next to raise his hand.

"Presidian, what is the point of encouraging the towers to come closer? Surely they are bad enough at distance?"

"If a tower steps within the city walls, it will be within range of our ballistas. If we can take down another two of them, it will have their numbers down to a third of what they sent here through the void."

"It is an act of absolute desperation," commented Baron Hanzlin.

"So? We *are* absolutely desperate. No more questions? Inspector Scryverin?"

"Permission to make my squad part of the guard on the captive tripod, Presidian?" I asked.

"Permission denied. You are dismissed, go to your posts and prepare to carry out your orders—not you, Inspector Scryverin. Stay behind, if you please."

Once we were alone, Laron dropped his hard and formal tone.

"The militiamen and recruits guarding the tripod are all more experienced than those in your own squad," he said, his arms folded tightly and his eyes gleaming in the lamplight as they challenged mine.

"I wish to stand in Lavenci's defense, and die with her if it comes to that," I replied simply.

"And I have to defend the city. Alberin has accepted all comers who have sought refuge here. Many of those are supporters of the Lupanians, and I suspect that they have orders to storm the tripod and protect the Lupanian they think is there. They may also attack the Skeptical temple. I cannot spare troops to defend everything, and you are all that I can spare to protect those in the temple against assassins."

"Sir!" I said, saluting.

"Hate me if you wish, Danolarian, but follow your orders. Now find your squad, position it, and be quick about it. My feeling is that whether it is night or day, the Lupanians will attack once they are all together."

By first light I could see that nine towers were standing ready. The Skeptical temple was located within arrowshot of the walls, and the roof gave a good view of the Lupanian towers gathering to the west. I could also see the captive tower above the buildings of the city, being rotated back and forth by militiamen with ropes. I thought of Lavenci within the hood, pretending to be a Lupanian. In a sense it was the safest place in the city, because once the distress call was started, the invaders would not fire on what they thought was one of their own kind. I had made a hurried assessment of the temple, and then ordered barricades for all four entrances. I then stationed all my archers on the roofs and walls. The rest of us, Essen's men, would meet any attackers on the ground.

With everything done and everyone in place, I looked out over the flood plain with my farsight. There were the nine tripod towers visible—and they were slowly advancing from the direction of the Westcrag Ranges. I knew their walk only too well by now, the loping gait, swaying tentacles holding the heat weapons, and ever-vigilant upper cowls. They were about five miles away, moving at about the speed of a cantering horse, which was a lot slower than their maximum.

"From what I know of their size, I put them at five miles from the walls," I said to Essen.

"They will do that distance in a quarter hour," he estimated, making quite a good assessment of their speed.

"They will bring their heat weapons to bear long before they reach the walls," I replied. "Individually at one mile, or combined from much farther. If they are of a mind to roast the city from such distances, we might as well give up now. If Kavelen Lavenci can convince them that she is a Lupanian, well, who knows?"

The ruse was simple. Lure one or more towers into Alberin to rescue their captive comrade, then attack them from cover, at close range. That was always the trick. I scanned the city, then returned my attention to the towers. At that range, I could not distinguish one tower from another, but they were arrayed in a straight line.

The first I knew of the battle commencing was the third and fourth tower from the left raising their heat weapons, and green smoke trailing up into the air. They played the beams of heat along the crenellations atop the city walls. I knew that the tiny sparkles of brightness were men and women being turned to ash in an instant—and suddenly the upper cowl of one of the towers burst apart.

"The tower, *our* tower!" shouted Essen. "It's a-firing on the Lupanians!"

I saw the captive tower with its tentacles held high by ropes and poles. Thick green smoke was pouring from a dark object between the tentacles. Lavenci! She had somehow got the heat weapon working. Even while that thought was in my mind the upper cowl of the captive tripod burst apart as a heat beam from the Lupanians slashed across it. I cannot remember whether I cried out or not, but Essen later said that I shouted Lavenci's name. Then the incredible happened, because the ropes and spars holding the tentacles up were still intact, and the heat casting continued to belch green smoke. It must have fired, I could not tell because the heat beam itself is as invisible as any other heat, and the distance was too great to see other effects. Another Lupanian on the floodplain fell, this time chopped messily apart by a downward slice of the beam. A third tripod's heat casting belched green smoke, then the remains of the captive tower burst apart from a direct hit from the Lupanian's weapon. Suddenly I noticed that all along behind the city wall, more than half a dozen tall buildings were emitting green smoke. *Decoys,* I remember thinking.

"She took two, Danol!" Essen seemed to be shouting from a long way away. "She fooled 'em, she was in the lower cowl, and she took two before they got her!"

Out on the floodplain just one of the seven surviving Lupanian towers had green smoke trailing from its heat weapon. It raked two buildings—and then its upper cowl exploded as well! One of the men turned back to speak to me, then cried out and pointed back over my head. Green smoke was pouring from the temple's observatory dome. *The observatory!* I suddenly realized. A telescope on a precision mounting. A telescope that could be used for aiming. Lavenci and her heat weapon had not been in the captured tower, but right above us, she was powering Alberin's only heat weapon, one formed around a mirror crystal taken from the fifth voidship. Lavenci could power the casting because Azorian had fabricated her etheric aura to be a Lupanian. Although he did not know the magical arts of fire castings, Lavenci had apparently been able to work them out for herself.

I looked back to the plain. The remaining six towers were standing still, their tentacles holding their heat weapons high, but none of those heat weapons trailed green smoke. One of the towers now tossed a globe of the poison smoke, but it did not travel even a third of the distance to the walls before hitting the ground and dispersing harmlessly across the country-side on a light wind. A moment later the upper cowl of the tower burst apart like a melon struck with a brick, and the structure beneath it toppled. The other towers now turned and began to flee. The entire city cheered. Someone who was less emotionally involved than myself declared that at this point the third battle for Alberin had been in progress no longer than a single minute.

That was not the end of the fighting, however. Although the smoke from the brief but deadly battle was thickening and beginning to spoil the view from where we stood, the observatory's heat weapon managed to hit the leg of one of the fleeing towers. It toppled, then cartwheeled messily as it crashed to the ground. My last clear view of events on the floodplain included our city's makeshift cavalry pouring out of South Gate's ruins and converging on the floundering, fallen tower. I later learned that it fought back with its tentacles, and at least a score of men were killed or injured in the hour of fighting before the cowl was hacked open, the Lupanian relieved of his head, and the handling beast sliced into bloody strips of meat.

That was not the last of the fighting within the city, either. A thousand enemy infantrymen had infiltrated the city among the refugees, then reformed into a single, fearsome brigade. These had initially tried to retake the captive tower, but once they realized that the observatory on the temple was the location of our single heat weapon, they had run a half mile through the city streets and smashed into Essen's minimally trained militia. The archers on the roof dropped some, but those of us on the ground had to face the rest. I descended to the street and ordered the ladder pulled up behind me. The enemy warriors were wearied from dashing a half mile with their weapons and armor, while Essen's people were fresh, but we were outnumbered. We were on the temple steps with our backs to the outer wall, however, so the enemy's superior numbers were far less of an advantage.

We held the infiltrators back from the temple doors for a full quarter hour, and had we not been there they would surely have burst into the temple and killed everyone inside. All along the wall, more infiltrators were attacking other buildings, decoy buildings that were undefended.

Lavenci's heat weapon was no help, because it was mounted on a telescope in the observatory. Thus it could not be lowered far enough to fire into the city. Gradually other militia squads arrived at the outer edges of the brigade of infiltrators, and very quickly their advantage was balanced with ours, then tipped in our favor. Not three out of every ten axmen in Essen's squad were alive by the time the fighting ended. Had I not been using the glass sword that Azorian had given me, I probably would not have survived.

Again my memories were clouded by exhaustion, pain, and trauma, but I do remember Laron kneeling beside me as I sat with my back to the blood-spattered temple doors.

"Lavenci is in the observatory," he whispered.

I looked up at him and managed to move my lips. "I knew you would let me fight for her," I managed.

By noon those who had fought in the most conspicuous of the actions were being paraded down the Avenue of the Conquerors. There were cavalrymen, the remains of Essen's squad, the sorcerers from the Metrologan temple, and other ranks of brave people who had fought in skirmishes that I had not witnessed. All the while the crowds chanted:

"Riellen

"Unites us.

"We'll never be defeated!"

I saw none of this, and only heard the chanting and cheers like the distant, rolling rumble of surf after a storm. Lavenci and I were lying in each other's arms on the observatory floor, both utterly spent. Above us, pointed out over the plain, was an astronomical telescope with a mirror crystal attached to it by hastily cut brass plates and rods. Essen was looking out through the telescope portal, his arms folded on the railing.

"Reckon you're right, ladyship, those other Lupanian buggers lost their talent for casting the heat weapon," he said without turning. "You say it's from feeding on the life force of folk from our world?"

"Yes, it changed them, it made them as you are," said Lavenci. "Azorian and I worked it out before he died."

✳ ✳ ✳

Laron gave a speech at the conclusion of the parade. He explained that the captive tower and other decoy buildings merely contained canisters of hellfire oil mixed with copper salts to produce green smoke. It had been a decoy from the very beginning, designed to distract attention from the Metrologan temple, where Alberin's surviving sorcerers cast a spell that would destroy the Lupanians with their own heat castings. The sorcerers were the heroes who saved the city, or at least that was the official story.

The truth was almost as unlikely. The decoys had been a trick to determine which of the glasswalkers in the tripod towers were the three most recently arrived, and so still able to cast the heat weapon. Once they opened fire, Lavenci then picked them off. The Lupanians were in fact closer to defeat than anyone other than Lavenci had realized. Continual gorging on the life force of those from our world had made their etheric selves resemble the folk of our world, Verral. It was only after the arrival of the seventh cylinder that they realized why their glasswalkers were beginning to lose their talent for generating the heat weapon.

Thus the sorcerers and sorceresses were the heroes of the day, and were honored by cheering crowds for all of the afternoon and evening. Lavenci and I took no part in it. Down in the Skeptical temple Wensomer lay in a trance, her eyes linked to those of a pigeon flying high over the city, and enmeshed by an auton. She reported on the fates of the remaining Lupanian tripod towers, and we did not leave our post until the sun was down and the city was plunging into another victory revel. We walked to the river, then took a ferry down to Wharfside.

"So unfair, little brother, they should be honoring the way you defended the temple," said Wensomer, trailing a hand in the water while Essen and I rowed.

"What about little half sister destroying the towers?" mumbled Lavenci.

"That too."

"I would prefer like a nice ale," said Essen. "Think I'll have one at the Lamplighter. Be a bit quiet, though, with Andry gone, Costi escorting Riellen, and you with ladyship, Danol."

"I'd prefer a bed behind a door bearing the words 'Do Not Disturb,' " I admitted.

"I'll write them on mine," said Lavenci.

We arrived at the academy to find that it had been largely unpacked from the cellars, and that Madame Yvendel had a welcoming revel well and truly in progress for us.

"Oh, my dear Essen!" exclaimed the rather rowdily drunk Madame Yvendel as we entered. "I have heard so much about you."

"Ah, er, ladyship, charmed, but, er—" managed Essen, trying to back through the door that I had already closed.

"Don't even think about leaving! I heard you were once Danolarian's commander, I want to hear all about the heroic things that the two of you did."

"While staring at the ceiling," muttered Lavenci to me. "Should we offer to help?"

"If he's not a big boy by sixty-four, he never will be," I replied.

We allowed ourselves to be honored by the students and academicians of the secret academy for an hour or so. By that stage Wensomer had passed out on a pile of cushions, with Wallas asleep on her stomach and Solonor asleep in her cleavage. Madame Yvendel was sitting on Essen's lap, stroking his beard, and whispering in his ear. He had a hand on her leg, so the interest did not seem to be entirely one-sided.

Lavenci's bedchamber had also been fully unpacked and restored, and by the ninth hour we were lying in each other's arms. I was learning secrets that even Laron did not know, for she believed that secrets not shared were the best kept secrets. With the Lupanians defeated they no longer mattered, of course.

"Azorian was actually a medicar," said Lavenci, her head pillowed on my shoulder, and an arm draped across my chest. "Medicars were thought best qualified to set up the systems that supported life on board the voidships. He could not speak war castings, however, and could only do a tiny heat casting."

"But you could, only on a very small scale," I deduced sleepily. "That worm analogy."

"Yes. He did not just heal my hand, Danolarian, he changed me inside to become a Lupanian. He then poured his unpolluted life force into my soul until he fell dead, but it meant that Verral now had one sorceress with the same command of etheric energies as the Lupanians. There were two mirror assemblies for the heat weapon in the voidcraft, it was only a matter of speaking the casting to activate one of them."

Lavenci explained that she had hit the captive tower in the faceplate with one of her experimental trials in the second attack on Alberin. On a later night she had sliced the Lupanian flying machine out of the sky, sending its two halves crashing into the ships at anchor.

"It was powered by the Lupanian inside speaking a heat casting that turned a reserve of water into steam at very high pressure," she explained.

"So its heat weapon was its propulsion?" I asked.

"Yes, it could drop poison smoke and spy, but nothing else. Mine was a lucky shot, but Fortune must owe me a great deal of luck, so why not? I have already told Laron that I shall never use the heat weapon against the people of our own world, and that matter is not negotiable. He will get Riellen to announce that the mirror assemblies for the heat weapons have all been smashed, because the voting citizens must fight their own battles, and not depend of magic from another world to protect them."

"A good principle, in any case."

"One question?"

"Ask."

"Would I make a good Wayfarer Constable?"

"Without doubt. Why?"

"To enlist, to be with you, to learn of the world, to learn common sense."

"I shall petition the directant," I replied, impressed.

Soon after that we were both asleep. It was the following afternoon before we awoke again.

There was no clean end to the war. A glass dragon destroyed one of the fleeing towers, burning through the cowls and pouring flames onto the Lupanian kavelar and handling beast. One Lupanian glasswalker simply abandoned his tower not far from the Alber River and vanished. Lupanian clothing and the naked body of a peasant were found nearby, so we presumed that he went into hiding. The last of the towers fell into a ravine above a meltwater river. It was found empty, and while many thought the Lupanian had drowned while climbing out, no body was ever found.

Some people found the prospect of two Lupanians roaming free to be very worrying, but there was little that the alien sorcerers could do. Their incredible powers depended on Lupanian etheric auras being freshly arrived on Verral. Research by the Metrologans showed that there was nothing a Lupanian could do that we could not, it was just that they could do it on a truly vast scale on our world—but only for a short time. Worse, they were mere ethersmiths, not sorcerers who understood the subtle nature of magical processes. One can imagine their desperation and bewilderment when their ability to use the heat weapon and fabrication castings failed. Nevertheless, they had very nearly conquered Greater Alberin, and the rest of the continent was already sufficiently impressed by their initial displays of power to surrender. What sort of empire might they have established? When the three wrecked towers were raised from Alberin's harbor, two of the drowned Lupanians were found to be female. Had they planned to establish a dynasty?

The handling beasts that survived the war are still alive. Today you can see them wallowing in the mud pit at Alberin's Zoological Gardens, and using their tentacles to catch fruit thrown by children. Laron ordered that all towers and fragments of towers were to be salvaged and brought to Alberin. You will all be familiar with the complete and relatively undamaged tripod tower that stands just inside the wall beside

West Gate, but the rest have mostly been dismantled and stored away in various places. The upper and handling cowls from one are on display in the throne room of the former palace, now known as the People's Educative Museum. For me it is quite unsettling to see children playing with the jewell-like controls of the tower that once stood terrible and triumphant above the ruins of Gatrov, but that is the lot of all veterans. By the middle of the year the worst of the damage to Alberin had been repaired, including the towers of what was now the Elected Presidian's Palace. The place where the Inquisition building had once stood was merely cleared and replaced with cobblestones, and a monument to all sorcerers.

Some days after the battle, Laron addressed a huge noontime rally. After congratulating all of Alberin's citizens for their defense of the city against the greatest odds that any army had ever faced, he announced that all known heat weapons had been smashed. This was not so much because he believed that using Lupanian weapons against our own world's folk was morally suspect, but because Lavenci thought so and had told him as much. She was the only person on our world who could cast a heat weapon over one of the mirror devices, so her opinion carried considerable weight. The drawback of this policy was that Alberin's enemies became quite heartened, and began planning an attack. Defeating the plague of electrocracy while it was still in its earliest phase was a very popular cause with the neighboring monarchies.

It was a month later that the former regent arrived with all his original forces, plus several thousand extra warriors, courtesy of the Fralland king and various other neighbors. He had been emboldened by Laron's declaration that Alberin now had only conventional weapons. His problem was that a very intensive campaign of training can turn a strong but amiable shopkeeper into a strong and dangerous warrior, and that month saw the citizens of Alberin put through some exceedingly intensive training. To concatenate a long and passably nasty story into its happy ending, the regent's army of restoration was defeated and scattered, and the regent himself captured.

As a Wayfarer inspector, I spent weeks accepting the surrender of men from the regent's shattered army, who had fled and hidden after we broke their advance. Most were from Alberin, after all, and just happened to have been on the wrong side. I directed them to what was being called the Enlightenment Encampment, where Riellen was giving lectures on Alberin's new political system. Those from the other towns and cities were sent back eventually, but Riellen first wanted them educated and enthusiastic with regard to voting and representative government. The wives of those prisoners who lived in Alberin combed the camps for them, and one by one dragged them off home, no doubt for some very harsh words and no prospect of dinner. The last I heard, the by now former regent was in what was called the University of the Dungeons, studying a course in electocracy, and not due for release until he had passed several exams with first-class honors.

The critical discovery of the war had been Lavenci's. By a combination of logic, mathematics, and reductive analysis, she had worked out that no Lupanian who had been on our world more than seven days used a heat weapon. This seemed odd, because Azorian had been here longer, yet was still able to do a clumsy, microscopic version of the heat weapon casting until the day of his death. After a great deal of thought, she had realized that the Lupanian warriors had gorged themselves on the etheric essence of our people, but Azorian had not murdered anyone and ripped their etheric essence away. All but the last few Lupanians to arrive had been absorbing the essence of prisoners without realizing that the more they fed on us, the more like us they became. After seven days, they could no longer conjure the heat-weapon casting. By the time the eighth cylinder landed, they had realized something was wrong, and by the last attack on Alberin they were using their four operational glasswalkers very, very carefully. Even with so few heat weapons left, however, the Lupanians could have subdued and ruled entire continents, so it was a close-run thing. Every time I think of that space of six heartbeats when Lavenci changed the world, I silently offer a prayer of thanks to no god in particular.

Chapter Twenty-Four

WRECKAGE

By Fivemonth Halland had been made the first governor of the Province of New Gatrovia. The former baroness was now his administrative advisor and had publically declared herself to be his mistress, while his wife was pregnant with a child that she publicly and loudly declared was his. The ever-sympathetic Presidian Laron had arranged for him to make quarterly trips back to Alberin, however, where Norellie just happened to be employed as an academician of her strange witch-magics with Madame Yvendel. While far from an ideal existence, Halland felt that all in all, life had improved.

The general feeling right across Greater Alberin was also that life had improved. The general feeling among its neighbors was that their own people wanted to be next. Riellen finished writing her charter, and Laron had it proclaimed at a huge rally on a bright autumn day in Fivemonth. It was staged in the square before the palace now renamed Electors' Plaza, and the fifty thousand gathered there were absolutely silent as Riellen suddenly announced that this was to be her last speech in Alberin.

"Free voters of Alberin, I am here to congratulate you!" she declared, holding her hands high in triumph. "You have established rule by elected servants of yourselves, you have vanquished the imperialist Lupanian invaders, you have repulsed the reactionary and oppressive regent, and you have driven off the invading monarchist armies. You will never be defeated!"

At this there was cheering that lasted at least a minute. I was watching anonymously from within the crowd, and was a little distracted at that moment—having just seized a hand that was fumbling for my purse and snapped one of its fingers.

"Free voters of Alberin, it is now time for me to leave you!" Riellen declared next, and this time there were cries of genuine horror and dismay that lasted a lot longer than the earlier cheering. "I must not stay in Alberin. If I do, you will think that elected rule will only work if *I* am there. You must learn to rule *yourselves,* through the presidians that you vote for, and all their advisors."

There was more cheering. By now several bystanders around me had seized the cutpurse, but were merely restraining him until the end of Riellen's speech. Now came the part that stunned me. It stunned the other fifty thousand who were listening as well, but I was rather more its focus than anyone else.

"You are beginning to worship me, and this must not be allowed to happen," pleaded Riellen. "I am no better than anyone else. I was once in love, but my young man did not love me. In my foolishness, I poisoned him, to make him seem sickly and unattractive to other girls. For this crime I was caught, tried, and sentenced to exile. Free voters of Alberin, I am not above the law, so I must now go into exile, forever. Make sure that no future ruler of Alberin ever uses official power for personal gain. Arrest those rulers who violate your laws, punish them, and elect new servants of the voters to replace them. Free voters of Alberin, all together now, after me:

"The voters

"United

"Can never be defeated!"

The crowd took up her chant like a rolling peal of thunder, and after one last gesture of triumph, Riellen stepped back and vanished from sight. She must have had a disguise, an escape route, transport, and papers all ready, because that was the last time she was ever seen in Greater Alberin.

That was not the only resignation in that week. Lavenci resigned from her mother's academy and joined the Wayfarers. I, on the other hand, was merely a senior inspector with the Wayfarer Constables. Although I was offered an important post in the palace, and promised support if I wished to stand for election as a presidial advisor, I merely requested to be left as an inspector. With *my* family background, I do not trust myself with power. Roval resigned his senior post as well, and returned to the Wayfarers. He did not explain why, but I suspect that his motives were similar to mine.

Thus it was that eight months after the Lupanian invasion began I found myself in the village of Walltoun in the Alterrian Mountains. This was part of the kingdom of Hadraly, and I was on a mission to collect three refugee sorcerers and escort them into exile in Greater Alberin. With me was my new squad of constables: Wallas, Roval, Solonor, and Lavenci. We had just completed a trip to the summit of Alpindrak, where Lavenci had played the sun down with her parlor pipes, Wallas had actually watched the sunset this time, and Solonor became the first gnome to make the trip.

It was around noon on a clear, still day in late spring as we sat at the open-air tables of one of the town's taverns, with Wallas lapping a saucer of wine, and Roval reading one of my illustrated books of erotic poetry with Solonor. Lavenci was holding hands with me when a serving maid stopped with a tray of drinks and curtsied before us.

"Your pardon, miss, but are you the lass who played the sun down on Alpindrak?" she asked, her eyes wide with admiration.

"Why yes, some weeks ago."

"Er, ah, well the landlord and his missus, and his daughter—like, that's me—we thought you and yours might like free drinks for, like, being here."

We were given our drinks, then Lavenci unpacked her parlor pipes and played a few tunes while some of the patrons danced. I reflected that my life was approaching perfection. I was traveling the roads with my beautiful and adoring truelove, my past was still secret, there was peace in that part of Scalticar, and we were doing some good for the persecuted sorcerers of other kingdoms. I thought back to a dream that I had experienced in Gatrov, a dream in which I had met Romance. Truly I was in her favor, and all through following her advice.

Lavenci had grown tougher and wiser during her six months on the road since joining the Wayfarers, and was learning all the time. She often said that she had never been happier, and I must confess that it was much the same for me. Perhaps in years to come we might return to the academy in Alberin, or even settle in some smaller town and establish our own academy. For now, however, life was as we wanted it.

A bell began to peal out the hour of noon. Wallas walked across the table, sniffed at my mug of ale with disdain, then winked in that unnerving fashion that only cats can manage.

"The three sorcerers will be at the public postings board by now," he said.

"I know. They will be dressed as mendicant monks, and soliciting to travel with a larger group for safety."

"They have our description, so *they* will approach *us*."

"Why are you so anxious to be off, Wallas?"

"I want to tell Wensomer that I tasted Senderialvin Royal. In three days we can be at the border of Greater Alberin, and in another five—"

"All right, all right, and the sorcerers will probably get anxious if we do not appear soon." I leaned over to Lavenci, who was playing "The Meltwater Hornpipe." "Best to end with this one, darling, then it's drink up and leave."

I went across to Roval and Solonor with Wallas, put the gnome on the cat, and retrieved my book.

"This is the happiest I have ever seen you," I remarked to Roval as I put the book in my pack. "Still, I keep wondering why you gave up a chance to be directant of the Greater Alberin People's Militia for life as a Wayfarer Constable."

"It was you, sir."

"Me?" I laughed. "Please explain."

"You showed me how to forgive the unforgivable, and even heal the hurt. I thought I could learn a bit more from you about outlook before moving on."

"Well, thank you, Roval, I am flattered. May I ask how goes it with you and the, ah, glass dragon?"

"Terikel? She has returned to the winds, and is happy. She made me the only living man who has slept with her, and from her way of thought, that heals the past."

"Does it in truth?"

"No. Brave and fine men who knew nothing of me when they met her died because relieving my indulgent grief became her obsession. Now Dolvienne has lost Gilvray, and Merrial and her children have lost Andry, yet I am still alone. The gifts of dragons are of value only to dragons, Inspector. It was your example that restored me to myself."

This had me not a little surprised. People of Roval's stature should have little to learn from the likes of myself, and I could not remember ever setting a good example for anyone.

"So you really are happy, Roval?"

"Yes sir. I am free of her, and she is free of both her dae-mons and myself. Three wasted years are a high price to pay for a good and pleasant life, but at least I have my life back now."

What makes a good and pleasant life? I wondered as I left Roval to pack up. Did we fight the Lupanians for it, and win? Did we fight for it when we defended our electocracy? Wall-toun was part of a monarch's realm, yet if I had to stay here with Lavenci for the rest of our lives, we would not be complaining unduly.

Lavenci ended her tune and began to pack away her pipes. Mountain ponies clopped past pulling laden carts, a blacksmith's hammer was ringing out in the distance, and at the nearby market I could hear a man calling out that something was selling for "Four a copper!" The dancers were now crowded around the serving board, and other villagers were beginning to arrive for their lunchtime pie and pint. Under electocracy it might be merely an improvement, but under Lupanian rule it could not have been pleasant. If we were ever even contented, it would have been the contentment of sheep being cared for while fattened for slaughter. We would have been things, not people. Even now it was hard to believe that we were safe. I half expected a mighty Lupanian fighting tower to suddenly come striding out between the two nearby mountains where the road to greater Alberin led, with the relentless *jingle-clink* of its leg joints, its heat weapon held high, and its terrible cry of—

"Brothers! Sisters! You all know why we're here!"

For a moment we all froze, then we glanced to each other in

near-panic while the distant speaker at the edge of the market-place paused to draw breath. I stood up for a better view. Riellen was standing on a cart, and waving a sheaf of pamphlets high in the air. She was about eight months pregnant.

"She looks like a broom handle with a melon tied to it," said the astonished Wallas.

Standing beside the cart I could see Costiger. Riellen continued, to an ever-swelling crowd.

"We are here to learn and spread the truth about the glorious revolution in Greater Alberin, where the oppressive, cruel, greedy, and unelected regent was brought low by the people. Not a king, not an emperor, not a duke, but the people. The people elected a presidian. The people elected the person who was best suited to rule. That man led the people to crush the might of the expansionist, genocidal, imperialist, warmongering Lupanian sorcerer-kavelars, then defeated an army sent by your reactionary, unelected and oppressive monarch to restore the former regent. But did Presidian Laron then send an army to invade your fair and beautiful kingdom? No! You, the people of Hadraly must overthrow your own rulers, you must vote for your own presidian. Down with the king of Hadraly!"

"What's votin', then?" called a carter from near where we now stood, hurriedly gathering our belongings together.

"That is a very good question, brother," replied Riellen. "The way of voting is explained in these pamphlets. Take them to those of you who can read, share them around, discuss them with each other. Start small. Vote for a committee to manage the marketplace, because running a marketplace is like running a kingdom."

"Are you that daft bird Riellen that all the travelers from Alberin speak of?" called someone from farther away.

"Yes I am, brother, but I am not important. Only my message is important."

"I vote Miss Riellen to be market presidian," called the wench who had been serving us, and there were half a dozen or so shouts of approval from the still bemused crowd.

"Please, no, I have not come to lead you. I am just a teacher. Sister Serving Maid, Brother Costermonger, it is people like *you* who should be standing for election—"

"Village militia!" cried someone.

"Save Miss Riellen!" cried several others.

By now we were packed and hurrying away from the tavern. Two monks were standing near the postings board as we arrived, both with their hands cupped to their ears to hear what Riellen was saying.

"You two, you are here in search of a larger party to travel to the border of Greater Alberin, right? We are that larger party. Now where is the third monk?"

My question was answered as the third monk came running over waving a brownish sheet of reedpaper and shouting, "Brothers, she touched my hand as she gave me a pamphlet!"

"Put that damnable thing in your sleeve, shoulder your packroll, and come with us!" I snapped irritably.

Wallas leaped up onto my pack with Solonor, and I hurriedly glanced around to ensure that nobody was watching us. Over by the market, a reasonably large riot was developing, and I could see Costiger helping Riellen down off the cart.

"I hate to say this, but should not we be helping?" asked Lavenci.

"The king of Hadraly is doomed, nothing we can do will save him from Riellen," I muttered as I seized Lavenci by the arm and pointed to the road back to Greater Alberin.

"But, but she's alone and pregnant, and she will be arrested," protested Lavenci, in spite of her hatred for my former constable.

"Lavenci, in order to break your constancy glamour I had contact with the future. I had help from . . . look, I can't explain, but I do know some of what is to come."

"But Riellen and her child—"

"Will be safe! A thousand years from now the *entire bloody world* will be voting for its leaders, thanks to Riellen. There will be statues to her everywhere. I know that her child survives. I've met one of its descendants from *twenty-seven generations* in the future. Now we must go! Come on!"

"Brother Inspector, it says here that even groups as small as three or four can profit from an elected—" began one of the refugee sorcerers, reading from the pamphlet as he trailed after us.

"*This* group is an *absolute monarchy,* and *I* am the absolute monarch!" I declared with exasperation. "Now put that away and shut up or I'll charge you with treason."

We hurried out of the no longer tranquil mountain village, leaving Riellen, her followers, and whoever was unfortunate enough to represent the establishment to battle it out. I had not told Lavenci the entire truth, and I probably never would. Riellen was not just a brilliant and charismatic orator, she was a passably good student of sorcery as well. She had known that breaking the constancy glamour by Pelmore's execution would leave Lavenci bound to him for seven years, but plucking Pelmore out of existence would not kill him yet would still break the glamour. Lavenci would be free to touch me from the moment that Pelmore vanished.

I could just imagine Riellen educating her child, telling it over and over what she had done, and how someone must invent a time engine to go back in time and abduct Pelmore so that Lavenci and I could be together and happy—allowing for causality, whatever that was. Generations had passed, each with the message being handed on, until a thousand years in the future one of her descendants had advanced the cold sciences far enough to build some unthinkably complex mechanism and become a timefarer.

Lariella had recruited some future me to be her guide. By the look of that self, I was not much older, so it would probably be in months rather than years. She had then taken us back to a time when Lupanian tripods strode the land. We had abducted Pelmore, then taken him . . . where? To the past or the future? Did he live out his days as a eunuch in some ancient Vindician harem, tortured by the sight of pleasures and delights that he could never again experience? Perhaps I carried out the death sentence that I was obliged by law and duty to do, and left his body lying in the streets of an Alberin two thousand years in the past.

We reached the mountain pass after half an hour at a rather forced pace, and there we paused to look back. Something was on fire back at the village.

"Looks to be that Riellen's supporters are already numerous enough to put up a good fight," I speculated.

"Looks to be that they might even win," said Lavenci, putting an arm around my waist and pressing against me.

"Brother Inspector," said one of the sorcerers, "we three have just formed the Free Sorcerers Liberation Voting Consensus of Hadraly, and have been discussing matters as we walked."

"I was afraid of that."

"We have decided that Brother Daclari and I should stay to support Miss Riellen against the oppressive monarchist establishment's lackeys in Walltoun, while Brother Aclarasor will journey on with you to become our envoy in Alberin. The vote was unanimous on all issues."

"Vote? There's only three of you!"

"Yes, but—"

"Never mind, do what you will."

And so we journeyed back to Greater Alberin, aware that a force far stronger than an entire army of Lupanian fighting tripods was spreading out over the continent of Scalticar. That night, as I lay in my little tent with Lavenci asleep in my arms, I realized that I would soon see the entire drama of the Lupanian invasion again when I traveled back in time. It would be like reading a book whose ending I already knew. It would be exciting and fascinating, yet there would be no danger at all. If only I had realized how wrong it is possible to be.